D0058994

Real Vampires Have Curves

GERRY BARTLETT

BERKLEY SENSATION, NEW YORK

THE BERKLEY PUBLISHING GROUP
Published by the Penguin Group
Penguin Group (USA) Inc.
375 Hudson Street, New York, New York 10014, USA
Penguin Group (Canada), 90 Eglinton Avenue East, Suite 700, Toronto, Ontario M4P 2Y3, Canada
(a division of Pearson Penguin Canada Inc.)
Penguin Books Ltd., 80 Strand, London WC2R 0RL, England
Penguin Group Ireland, 25 St. Stephen's Green, Dublin 2, Ireland (a division of Penguin Books Ltd.)
Penguin Group (Australia), 250 Camberwell Road, Camberwell, Victoria 3124, Australia
(a division of Pearson Australia Group Pty. Ltd.)
Penguin Books India Pvt. Ltd., 11 Community Centre, Panchsheel Park, New Delhi—110 017, India
Penguin Group (NZ), 67 Apollo Drive, Rosedale, North Shore 0632, New Zealand
(a division of Pearson New Zealand Ltd.)
Penguin Books (South Africa) (Pty.) Ltd., 24 Sturdee Avenue, Rosebank, Johannesburg 2196,
South Africa

Penguin Books Ltd., Registered Offices: 80 Strand, London WC2R 0RL, England

This is a work of fiction. Names, characters, places, and incidents either are the product of the author's imagination or are used fictitiously, and any resemblance to actual persons, living or dead, business establishments, events, or locales is entirely coincidental. The publisher does not have any control over and does not assume any responsibility for author or third-party websites or their content.

REAL VAMPIRES HAVE CURVES

A Berkley Sensation Book / published by arrangement with the author

PRINTING HISTORY
Berkley trade edition / March 2007
Berkley Sensation mass-market edition / February 2008

Copyright © 2007 by Gerry Bartlett.
Excerpt from *Real Vampires Live Large* copyright © 2007 by Gerry Bartlett.
Cover illustration by Chris Long.
Cover design by George Long.
Interior text design by Kristin del Rosario.

ISBN: 978-0-425-22096-2

BERKLEY® SENSATION
Berkley Sensation Books are published by The Berkley Publishing Group,
a division of Penguin Group (USA) Inc.,
375 Hudson Street, New York, New York 10014.
BERKLEY SENSATION and the "B" design are trademarks of Penguin Group (USA) Inc.

PRINTED IN THE UNITED STATES OF AMERICA

10   9   8   7   6   5   4   3   2   1

This book is dedicated to the memory of my husband,
John Bartlett,
a man who appreciated
an independent woman with curves.
You were my first hero.
Love, Gerry

One

Vampires are everywhere. Lose the all-vampires-are-rich-and-powerful stereotypes. Think Mike, the night clerk at the mini-mart. Brittany, the barmaid who brings your appletini at last call. Even the night stocker at your local superstore.

And, don't freak out now, but Mike could have looked deep into your eyes and willed you to follow him to the back room. There, he could have taken you down a pint before he sent you on your way with your cigs and six pack, and you *wouldn't have a clue.*

Cool, really. Forget those telltale fang marks. We can make them disappear along with your memory. No harm, no foul. Only the most depraved vamps would suck you dry and leave you for dead. Most of us have figured out that we live longer if we're discreet.

Yes, that's right, *we, us.* I'm Gloriana Eloisa St. Clair. Glory to my friends. Did you think all vamps were pale, thin and brooding? If only. The thin part anyway. But whatever shape or size we are when we're turned vampire, that's how we are *forever.*

Just my crappy luck that I was bloating the day I got the big V. I have curves, okay? At least that's my positive spin on things. I do what I can with what I've got. To look at me you'd think "healthy" twentysomething with a great sense of style, thank you very much. I'm blond, blue-eyed and tanned with the best spray on money can buy.

So how did I end up an older-than-dirt vampire? Long story short—a man, of course. Tall, dark and deliciously sexy. His name was and is Angus Jeremiah Campbell the third. After a little squabble with his father he changed his name to Jeremy Blade. His choice, not mine. When our paths cross, I call him "Jerry." He hates that. We've been on-again, off-again for centuries, currently off.

We met in London. Jerry was checking out the action and I was an actress at the Globe, back in the days when most female parts were played by men, and how sad is that? Anyway, I'd disgraced my family and married an actor. When he was killed in a really ugly accident with a slop jar, I'd have starved if the company hadn't let me take on some small parts. And I was good, a real actress, not one of those sluts who *called* themselves actresses. Billy Shakespeare loved me.

Then Jerry came backstage one night and the rest is history. I fell hard. Lust with a capital *L*. And, trust me, you haven't experienced the big *O* until you've gotten it on with a man's teeth in your neck. Jerry is irresistible when he wants to be. I begged him to make me vampire so we could be together forever.

If I'd only known . . . Turns out the man lasted forever, the love, not so long.

At least we never married. First, he didn't want to be "tied down," then a hundred or so years later, when he decided to do me a big favor and make it legal, I'd snapped to the fact that we were talking about literally *forever* together. No way. With a sixteenth-century man? You get the picture.

And imagine the same in-laws for *centuries*. Trust me, the Campbells weren't exactly thrilled when their eldest brought home an English actress. Two strikes right there. And we were living in sin. They didn't know whether to be relieved that Jerry and I hadn't tied the knot or horrified. I eventually brought them around, but by then I'd had enough of the Scottish Highlands and their crumbling castle. The place is in the middle of *nowhere.*

I'm social. I need people, bright lights, action. So I became an even better actress, blending in, moving on every decade or so when my twentysomething looks raised some eyebrows. That's the hard part, you know. Drifting. There's a vamp network for things like IDs, so that's no problem. No, it's being rootless that gets to me.

This time I stayed longer than I should have. Even Botox and cosmetic surgery couldn't explain to my mortal friends why gravity or crow's feet hadn't caught up with me.

Yeah, I like to hang with mortals. But I have lots of vampire friends too. I've run across quite a few over the years. I can smell them and vice versa. Oh, nothing nasty, like failed deodorant. A mortal can't smell us at all, but we've got heightened senses, especially when it comes to our own kind.

Sound creepy? Get over it. Vamps can be fun, real party animals. You may be wondering how someone born in 1580 can sound so *now.* I'm an actress, remember? And addicted to HBO. I still watch *Sex and the City* reruns. The shoes! Anyway, I'm a chameleon. I can listen to people talking and within minutes I'm *one* of them.

Right now, I'm on the move again. I've done Vegas and was lucky enough to get a gig dancing in a revue in a small club off The Strip. Clever costuming disguised my "problem areas," but my cups runneth over if you know what I mean so I was a hit. Now the club is going to be knocked down to make way for one of those megacasinos so I decided it was time to move on.

I'm going east this time. Austin. Yes, in Texas. I've heard it's a happening place. I've got vamp friends there, plus I've checked it out on the Net. There are the usual freaks. Vampire wannabes with dead-white skin, black lipstick and a total lack of fashion sense. But there's also a nice group of fellow vamps, including Frederick von Repsdorf. He's one of those fun vamps I told you about. He and his boyfriend live in a neat old house near the University of Texas. He e-mailed me pictures.

Okay, okay, I admit it. I heard Blade had been through there recently. What can I say? His folks are safely tucked away in the Highlands, and Blade without the baggage still floats my boat. I'm going to check it out. Austin, that is. Hills, cowboys, dot-com millionaires. Why not?

And there are opportunities for entrepreneurs. I'm not rich like a lot of vamps, including my ex. I've always had to work for a living because I'd never take a dime from Blade—then I'd be obligated. So I work. I made good money in Vegas but discovered I had a weakness for all-night poker games.

Yeah, I could have put the vamp whammy on the other players and read their minds, but I don't cheat. So I played fair, and found out I suck at poker. Enough said. A twelve-step program later and I've given up games of chance. Another reason Austin sounds good. No legalized gambling. The closest casino is a state away.

It's close to midnight when I hug my best gal pals, shed a few tears, then take off in my 1997 Suburban pulling a twelve-foot U-Haul. I know a cute little convertible would better suit my image, but I'm a collector. Seriously. I have a lot of stuff that I drag with me wherever I go.

I'm just crossing the Nevada/Arizona border and singing "Don't Cry for Me, Argentina"—love those Broadway show tunes—when my cell phone rings. Caller ID unknown. I answer it anyway.

"Frederick tells me you're moving to Texas."

Blade. Who else would assume I knew who he was and dispense with pleasantries, even though I haven't seen him for four years, three months . . . Oh, God, I was *not* counting.

"Keeping tabs on me, Jerry?" I could almost hear him grinding his teeth. I flashed back to the way he would stroke those bicuspids across my body . . . He wasn't saying anything. I sighed. "Yes, I'm on the road as we speak. Why?"

"Gloriana, you never write. You never call."

I stared at the phone as if it had sprouted fangs. Jeremy Blade being flip?

"Who are you and what have you done with my—" I couldn't finish the thought. Our relationship was too complicated.

"Your lover? Husband?"

"Definitely not husband." Leave it to Blade to propose when I'd had it up to here with family togetherness in the Highlands. There had been some talk of a handfast, but I deny we ever did it. But about that family. Would you believe Blade has four brothers and two sisters? His folks didn't become vampire until after all the kids were born. Then Mag and Angus let their adult children decide their own future.

No one knows how Mom and Pop Campbell decided when to pose the big question. Trust me, none of the Campbell kids were retaining water on *their* V-day: the day each one got to choose—vampire and immortality, or the pitiful life span they could have expected way back then. Just my luck that's a no-brainer for the Campbell clan. You try living happily ever after with nine vampires.

"What *am* I then?"

"I call you 'my ex.' That about says it."

"You're breaking my heart, babe."

Babe? I couldn't believe my ears and, trust me, a vamp's hearing is supercharged. Supercharged enough to glom on to the hint of a Scottish burr that had melted my resistance all those centuries ago. Nope. I was immune now.

"I can't break what doesn't exist, Jerry. Why are you calling me 'babe'?"

"I decided you were right about a few things."

That did it. I pulled off the highway and stopped the car on the shoulder. No traffic at three in the morning. And no wonder. This stretch of road wasn't exactly the scenic route. Rocks, scraggly bushes and sand. Period.

"*I* was right?"

"About fitting in. I've had a few skirmishes with some hunters recently."

I felt sick. Skirmishes in Bladespeak meant he'd come within inches of being staked. We all feared vampire hunters. Living forever can be depressing, but I sure didn't want to go out with a stake through my heart.

"God, Blade. What happened? Are you all right?"

"I'm fine. A new man you might say."

"Good. Because the old one . . ." I didn't have the heart to ream him out like I usually did. A world without Blade. I bitch and moan, but our always interesting love-hate relationship was one of the things that kept me going.

"The old one has missed you."

Now that tore it. "*Missed* me? Please. I know for a fact that you were in Vegas less than a year ago and didn't even bother to see my show."

"You know how I feel about that show. I hope to hell you're not planning to continue exposing yourself in Texas."

I felt instantly better. I'd told Blade my show was topless. It drove him insane. "I was a dancer, Jerry. Showing a little skin earned me a nice living."

"You don't have to work at all. I'm responsible for what you are—"

"Who, not what. And I begged you to do it, so *I* am responsible for my condition. No one else." God, we'd had this discussion at least a thousand times. Blade was nothing if not hardheaded. And with a memory like an immortal elephant. Once, almost three hundred years ago, I'd yelled at him that he'd ruined my life, robbed me of having children, blah, blah, blah.

It was a meltdown, brought on by too much Campbell togetherness. I'd gotten over it almost immediately, but Blade seemed haunted by it. I admit the children thing was a low blow. I don't know which would be worse. To see your kids grow old and die. Or turn them vampire so they can live forever and ever and . . . See? I thought about it. And I've come to terms with it. Jerry hasn't. Damn him, I would not feel *anything* for him. I took a steadying breath.

"Tell me about the hunters."

"A bad group. Led by a man named Brent Westwood. He's a billionaire big-game hunter who has decided vampires are the biggest game of all." Blade's voice was hard. "He takes trophies, Gloriana. He wears a necklace made of . . ." I heard him take a breath. A shaky breath. "Fangs."

I thought I was going to be sick. "And they call *us* evil?" I swallowed hard.

"There's more." Blade cleared his throat. "Be careful, Gloriana. He got MacTavish."

"Mac! No!" I leaned my head against the steering wheel. Mac had been Blade's best friend and I'd loved him like a brother. I felt tears slip down my cheeks. Yeah, vamps can cry and Mac was definitely worth a little dehydration. Mac had been light where Blade was dark, in temperament as well as looks. Funny and loyal to the core. I pressed a hand against my mouth until I could speak again.

"Mara?" Mac's wife. Beautiful. More like Blade than Mac had been, a bit on the broody side.

"She's a survivor. Sad, hurt, filled with lust for revenge. She's staying with me. Westwood got away and got a good look at both of us. I'm sure we're on the top of his list now."

I breathed through a nausea that I hadn't felt in decades. Blade's teeth dangling around a mortal fiend's neck. Not possible. Blade was too strong, too powerful. But then Mac had been just as strong.

"So you were there. You couldn't erase Westwood's memory?" Stupid question. We have to *touch* a mortal to do that. "Or zap him with your mind control thing?" No one could do a mind-meld like Blade.

"I tried. He wears some kind of protective glasses."

"How did he get Mac? An ambush?" I shut up. If I knew Blade, he was already blaming himself for Mac's death. He had a sense of responsibility a mile wide. Now he'd taken on Mac's widow.

"You could call it that. He knew us well before we sensed the danger. And, God damn him, I couldn't get close to Westwood. He's developed new technology. The glasses and some kind of scanner, a vampire detector."

I hadn't heard Blade this upset since he'd broken things off with his family. And don't ask me to go into that now, it's a long story.

I was shaking and feeling sick again. A vamp detector. This was really, really bad news. I pride myself on my ability to blend in with mortals.

"Are you telling me I could be outed by some kind of ray gun?"

"Mara and I saw his device. It looks like a cell phone, Gloriana. There's no way to know if he's scanning or not until he comes at you. And he's harmless-looking. Average height, build. Check him out on the Internet and print out his picture. Show it to every vampire you know." Blade spoke to someone in the room with him. Mara?

"I will. As soon as I get to Freddy's."

"Good. But, like I said, you still might not recognize him. He's not roaming around in camouflage and a Mossy Oak cap. He wears those tinted glasses, but they're ordinary too." He was silent for a moment while my mind whirled.

"Damn it, Gloriana, I need you here, where I can protect you."

I let that demand go for the moment. "How . . . how did he get Mac?" Garlic and crosses didn't take us out like in some of those legends mortals groove on. But the stake thing was all too true. "I can't see Mac standing still for anyone."

"He didn't. I told you Westwood is a hunter. He's got a bow and arrows made of some exotic wood. Obviously he's a crack shot. An inch or two off and we'd have dragged Mac out of there with us." More conversation with someone else.

"Mara said those arrows smelled funny. She thinks they're olive wood. Use that smell as a warning."

"How did you get away?" Vampire hunting as sport. What next? Vamps stuffed and mounted? Oh, God.

"When it was obvious Mac was lost to us, Mara and I got the hell out of there."

"I'm sorry. I loved Mac too. Poor Mara." I wiped at my eyes.

"Yes, it's hard. I'll say it again. Be careful, Gloriana." Blade sounded tired. Was he feeding? Centuries of caring for someone couldn't just be turned off. Even though I'd certainly tried.

"You weren't wounded, were you?"

"Slightly. I healed."

Slightly. Which could be anything from a nick on the arm to a gut shot. No wonder he sounded tired. Vamps heal when they sleep but it takes a lot out of them.

"Where are you?" Of course Mara was with him and how sick to be jealous of a grieving widow. She was Blade's friend. His *beautiful* friend. With the kind of flaming red hair and green eyes that any Scotsman would kill for. Certainly the Campbells loved her. And she was thin, of course. Next to her I'm an overblown English rose.

"Lake Charles. In Louisiana. I have a casino here. It's just across the Texas border. Forget Austin. You *will* join us. I can protect you here. I've got state-of-the-art security and guards around the clock. Now that we know about Westwood, he won't be able to get near us in the casino."

A casino. Why not just stake me now? I'd never told Blade about my little gambling problem and wasn't about to now. Being under Blade's protection . . . I'd never felt safer than when I was with him.

But he hadn't asked. He'd issued an order. And I quit following his orders over a century ago. Because I also tended to revert to a Glory I didn't particularly like with Blade. Dependent, giving up my power . . . Can you tell I read self-help books?

Damn it. Technofreak vamp hunters. No wonder I felt chilled to the bone and more than a little tempted to get to Lake Charles as fast as my aging Suburban could carry me. I sucked it up.

"I'll be with Freddy. He's as strong as you are, maybe stronger." A dig, but baiting Blade beat the full-out crying jag I felt like going for.

"Is Valdez with you?"

I glanced at my dog who was checking out the countryside.

"Of course."

"Keep him close until you get here. You are *not* going to Frederick. I will expect you—"

I hung up on him. Just like that. I turned off the phone before flinging it onto the seat.

"The big boss givin' ya grief, angel face?" Valdez. Obviously not your ordinary companion animal.

"He's not my big boss and I'm giving *him* grief." I grabbed a tissue from the console and blew my nose. "But I know he's *your* big boss. In your next report, tell him to kiss my—"

"Tell him yourself, sweet cheeks. Right now I gotta go."

When Blade and I parted ways, we'd argued until he wore me down and I'd agreed to let him provide protection for me. I'd expected bodyguards. Instead he'd sent dogs. Not ordinary pups, but creatures with special abilities. This was Valdez number one hundred and twenty-five. They had all been willing to give their lives to keep me safe. And they had. These dogs were usually mortal and it broke my heart each time I lost one.

I have no idea how he did it—vamp magic, I guess—but Blade had made each Valdez more powerful, more . . . interesting. Besides being able to create a circle of safety around me, the last dozen or so had been able to communicate. Not out loud, but in my head and inside any head within range. Impossible to tune out. And impossible to explain in a crowd. That's why we had strict rules about when and where Valdez can speak.

It amuses Blade to surprise me. The last one had sounded just like the Chihuahua in the fast food commercial. This one is a thug, Travolta in *Get Shorty*. What ever happened to the strong silent type?

"You gonna ignore me or what? I don't wanna hear no whinin' when I lift my leg on your CD player."

"All right. All right." I jerked open the door and hopped out. "Hurry. We're miles from nowhere."

"Don't I know it. Seems okay though." He sniffed his way to a bush and took care of his business. *"Next gas stop, I want a bag of Cheetos and some Twinkies."*

Typical. "I should get you a can of Alpo. That other stuff's bad for you." Can you believe this dog? I think he eats those things to torment me. I haven't had a bite, of food, that is, since 1604 and while I always liked my meals back then, I would have killed for something that smelled like a Cheeto.

"I ain't no ordinary dog. I'm a Labradoodle special and I got needs. You have any idea what they put in canned dog food?"

"Cheetos and Twinkies aren't—"

"So stop for a Big Mac and fries. And you owe me. So far I've listened to Evita*, Phantom of the Opera and* Oklahoma*. And,"* he gave me a long suffering look, *"you ain't no Chiquita Rivera if you know what I mean."*

"Chita Rivera. Chiquita is the banana." I know my pop culture. It's a survival skill. And, yeah, I knew what he meant. I can dance, and act, but sing? A girl can't do everything perfectly.

"Chill out, fur face. I could go back to 'We Are the Champions.'" My fave. And one I knew Valdez was really sick of. I'd heard him howl through it more than once to drown it and me out.

"I thought you were in a hurry." Valdez settled into his seat with a sigh. If he wasn't being so aggravating I'd bury my fingers in his soft fur and scratch his ears. Don't get me wrong. I love dogs. They're great company. Normal dogs anyway. But no way was I letting him eat fries in my car again. Talk about torture. And the delicious smell lingered for *days*.

"I *am* in a hurry." And I was seriously creeped out and seeing a wild-eyed hunter behind every scraggly bush. I put the car in gear.

"Then get the lead out, Blondie. You got three hours till daylight. And we're not stayin' in no cheap motel with a hard mattress. I've checked it out. Next big town's got several nice places that take dogs."

Like I'd let my dog pick a motel. Though he probably *had* checked it out. I've given up trying to figure out what this Valdez can do. He's part canine, part computer and all weird. And he reports to Blade so he's a damned spy. How? Some kind of mind-meld, I guess. But this Valdez and I have bonded enough that I know he won't rat me out about certain things. Like the gambling problem or the night I stayed out too late and almost got fried in the morning sun. That one cost me a case of Cocoa Puffs.

Pain in the butt or not though, I feel safe when I have Valdez sacked out on the foot of my bed. I heard a snort and glanced over at him. Did I mention he can read my mind? How irritating is that?

"What?"

He gave me a look and, yeah, I did feel that circle of safety wrap around me like a warm blanket.

"I've got your back, kid. Isn't that worth a Twinkie stop?"

I had to laugh. That voice in my head, big brown eyes and a wagging tail. "Whatever, fur face." We passed a sign. "Twenty-two miles to Twinkieville."

Safe or not, I kept checking my rearview mirror. Hunters are like rabid beasts. There's no reasoning with them. They're convinced vampires are all demons from hell who play Jack the Ripper all night and sleep in coffins all day. How wrong can they be? I prefer a pillow top mattress, Egyptian cotton sheets and Valdez curled up on the foot of the bed.

I sighed and glanced at my faithful companion who kept staring alertly out the window. Blade had never liked a dog in the bedroom. Valdez or Blade? Unfortunately, right now Valdez was the only contender in the sleep-with-Glory contest.

Two

"*Incoming. Pull over.*"

"You're kidding. Now?" I'd hung up on Blade. Of course he wouldn't just calmly accept that. Oh, no. He'd want a face to face. And it had taken him only, what, one hour and a Twinkie stop to fly to my side. Yep, fly. Did I mention he can shape-shift?

The black bird swooped in front of the car just as I was slowing down. I knew better than to ignore him and keep driving. Blade was relentless when he was on a quest. And his current quest was to make me do his bidding. My stomach knotted. I was *not* wimping out. I had *plans.*

I stopped the car and turned off the engine as bird became man. Okay, it's always kind of cool to watch. I *could* shape-shift, but I *can't,* if you know what I mean. A personality defect. Something about the whole now you're a bird or bat or, God forbid, even a dog, now you're a person thing freaks me out. Loss of control maybe. Or just plain fear. What if I forget how to do it and get stuck?

I glanced at Valdez. The idiot was grinning and wagging his tail as Blade popped open the driver's side door even though, of course, I'd locked it.

No one can do the vamp whammy like Blade. Before I could get a grip, I was out of the car and wrapping my arms around him. No. No. No. I shoved him away and pressed my hands over my eyes.

"Look at me, Gloriana." Blade's deep voice rumbled into my mind.

"No. Go away." Hah. How was that for willpower? If only I couldn't smell him, his totally male vampire come-and-get-me smell. I opened my eyes.

He was on his knees, rubbing Valdez's head and talking to him in a low voice. I didn't bother to tune in. Instead, I enjoyed the view. Leave it to Blade to show up in full Clan Campbell regalia, including broadsword. But he'd always had the legs for a kilt. Don't ask me how he can be a bird one minute and a fully clothed man the next. Much less how he can travel at warp speed. Just call it more vamp magic. A magic that still pulled me right to him.

"What's with the kilt? Surely you don't run a casino like that. Not exactly blending here, Jerry."

He stood and faced me while Valdez trotted off into the bushes. Blade's dark hair was a little wild and it was all I could do not to reach out to brush it into place.

"Customers love it. Think it's an act. Nothing like trying to win money from a tight-fisted Scot." He moved closer, his dark eyes roaming over me. I pulled down my "Elvis lives" T-shirt and wished I'd had a chance to throw on some lipstick.

"Why are you being so stubborn?"

"It's not stubborn. I just want to live my own life. Not yours." To hell with lipstick. I lifted my chin. "You can turn into anything you want. Maybe a gorilla. Then you can thump your chest and drag me back to your tree. But the minute you turn your back, King Kong, I'm outta there."

"You try my patience, lass. You're in danger."

"So what's new? I'm, no, *we're* always in danger. Hunters come and go, this one will go too."

"Westwood's different." Blade turned as Valdez loped toward the car. One nod and the dog took off again.

"Leave all this"—he swept a disdainful look over my packed Suburban and U-Haul—"shit and come with me."

"This shit is *my* shit." I hit him in the middle of his broad chest. Not that it did any good. I'm strong, but Blade's a rock. "Will you ever *get* me? I like my stuff around me. And I need my independence. If I'm going to live forever—" I shuddered. I'd stopped being grateful for *that* little gift a long time ago. "Then it has to be my way. Not yours."

"What's so wrong with letting me take care of ye, lass?" He put his hands on my shoulders. Oh, yeah. He thought the Scottish thing would melt me. There was a thaw going on, but this was too important to let my always interested libido take over.

"Everything."

He tried to pull me to him. I dug in my heels. He could have forced me. I knew it and so did he. Instead, he dropped his hands and stepped back.

"I am no' your enemy, Gloriana."

"Yes, you are," I whispered. Damn me for feeling ashamed when his frown hardened. I knew it hurt him when I asserted myself. It was a rejection. Again.

"Will you promise to call me if you need me?"

No soothing Scottish tones now. I felt his withdrawal as surely as if he'd morphed into bird mode and flown out of there.

I couldn't help myself. I moved close to him, slipped my arms around his lean waist and rested my head on his chest. I filled my lungs with his scent and felt his breath against my hair. He slid his arms around me and just held me. So many years together, so much history. In my own warped way, I love him, okay? I just don't *like* him very much. Not when he's doing his "me Scottish Highlander, you little woman" thing.

"That's that then?"

"That's that." I stepped back and watched as he whirled, a blur of motion, until a raven with blue black wings shrieked his displeasure then flew up and out into the night sky.

"You ever gonna cut the guy a break?" Valdez pushed his head under my hand and I rubbed his silky ears.

"If I went with him, you'd be out of a job."

"I could live with that." He yawned and jumped into the car. *"Ain't nothin' wrong with a dog's life. Eat, sleep, chase a few cats. Sounds good to me. I figure you'd still slip me a few Cheetos."*

I looked up at the clear night sky filled with a thousand stars and a sliver of moon. Somewhere a dark bird flew so fast only another immortal could see it. Was I insane for rejecting Blade again? I got in and started the car. Probably.

Austin. Finally. I'd taken quite a few road trips in my time, but this one had to qualify as the trip from hell. Love my old Suburban, but, especially when you're driving at night, you need reliable transportation and decent gas mileage. As soon as I start making some serious money, I'm trading this sucker in.

Lost a fan belt in Arizona. Overheated in the middle of the desert outside of Roswell. And the worst, the absolute worst, was the blowout in west Texas. You ever try to change a tire with a U-Haul and a lifetime (very, very long lifetime) worth of junk piled on top of the spare? I've got the vamp strength thing going on but it was an hour before sun up. Thank God for friendly truckers.

Enough griping. I like the look of Austin. Pretty capitol building. Hills. The city's bigger than I thought it would be, and even at three a.m. there's some traffic on the freeway. I find Freddy's house without much hassle. You've got to love numbered streets.

Freddy flung open the door of his two story brick bunga-
low as soon as I pulled up in front. "Glory! You made it."

"No thanks to this clunker." I let Valdez out and watched
him mark Freddy's bushes before he bothered to check out
Freddy. "It's good to finally get here."

"Still traveling with a beast, I see." Freddy bent down
and eyed Valdez. They had a quiet man to man conversation
that ended when Freddy got up to give me a hug. "You look
wonderful."

"So do you." Vampires do change over the years, you
know. Not age, exactly. But fashions, hair, cosmetic stuff can
make a difference. Freddy knew how to blend in and in this
college town he'd decided to go with a graduate student
look. He wore his jeans with a T-shirt that advertised of all
things a Willie Nelson Fourth of July picnic. I had to smile.

"A picnic?"

"It's a local tradition. Doesn't really get going till the sun
goes down. Next summer you'll have to go with me. Great
music." Freddy was tall, lean and could have been the love
of my life if he hadn't decided to come out of the closet a
few decades ago. Just as well. He was more like Blade than
either of them would ever admit. Strong, hard headed and
macho, despite the sexual preference.

I sensed more vamps inside just before a familiar throaty
voice bellowed a greeting.

"Gloriana, darling, give us a hug."

Us. Us as in Freddy's mother, the Countess Cecelia Haps-
burg von Repsdorf. The countess had become vampire after
she discovered her only son had turned. No way was she letting him live forever without her "guidance."

"CiCi." I was enveloped in a cloud of the exotic perfume
the countess favored, her special blend and really quite wonderful. I sniffed and held onto her for a moment, my cheek
against her soft cheek.

My own mother was a very distant memory and not a
pleasant one. She'd turned her back on me and consigned me

to hell just because I'd loved an actor. Not that she'd ever approved of anything I did anyway. I can't even imagine how she would have reacted if she'd ever found out I was vampire.

CiCi was the mother I wish I'd had, warm and loving instead of cold and judgmental. Okay, maybe a little judgmental. She held me away from her and looked me over.

"You look like hell, darling. What have you done to your skin? Is that a tan?" She was clearly horrified. "Own what you are, Gloriana. You should be pale, ethereal. I must give you a makeover immediately."

"Mother, let the woman sit down first, will you?" Freddy had his hand on Valdez's collar. "And say hello to her latest companion. Valdez, I assume?" He looked the question at me.

"Of course." I was relieved to see my dog wagging his tail. You never knew how animals would take to CiCi. With her strange perfume and booming voice, she'd sent more than one of my pups running for cover. Of course none of them sensed any danger to *me* in CiCi, just to themselves apparently. This one seemed to have developed an instant crush on her and was actually speechless.

"My, he's a big one, isn't he?" She leaned down to pat his head and give him a searching look. "Good. You need a protector since you are too stubborn to settle down with Jeremiah."

Jeremiah, Jeremy, Blade. This was CiCi as usual. "Jerry and I do fine on our own. Leave it alone, CiCi." I turned to Freddy. "Where's Derek?"

"Out." Freddy lost his smile and gestured toward the curb. "Shall I bring in your bags? At least what you need for overnight?"

"Sure, thanks. Just the tote on the backseat. We can worry about the rest later." I watched Freddy stride down the brick sidewalk.

"He's miserable, Gloriana." CiCi actually managed a whisper. "Derek is out hunting. He will not give it up."

"They *are* still together though."

"Oh, yes. Except for this little disagreement, they are quite devoted." CiCi led the way into a cozy living room. It was full of the kind of antiques I love and I exclaimed over them to CiCi's delight.

"Yes, I do love beautiful things. Frederick tells me you plan to open an antique shop. A good idea. Who else would know so much?"

I ran my hand over the front of the beautiful tiger maple buffet loaded with porcelain figurines. "I never had anything this fine back in the day, but maybe you can help me." CiCi looked startled. "Oh, not to work, of course. But to give me your opinion from time to time."

"Why yes. I would love that. And perhaps then I might consign a few things." She gestured around the tastefully jam-packed room. "Frederick says I have too much."

"Not as much as I do. Trying to cram it all into the car and trailer wore me out. And gave me the idea to do this shop thing. I'm actually ready to let go of some of it." I turned as the door slammed and Valdez growled. Freddy with my bag and another man, Derek. Think Hugh Jackman in *The Boy From Oz*. Yum. I recognized him from e-mail pictures.

Another myth exploded. You *can* photograph a vampire, but the mirror thing, yeah, that's true and a real pain in the butt for someone like me who wants to look good. I'd had to use the vamp whammy to get one of the other dancers to do my stage make-up. She's the one who'd talked me into the tan. Now I was rethinking it.

CiCi was nothing if not fashionable. Her black hair was pulled back to show off her flawless, *pale* skin and high cheekbones. Her sapphire pants suit perfectly matched her eyes and hugged her petite figure. I'm only five five, but when CiCi glided around the room, I felt huge and awkward.

Freddy and Derek were having a whispered conversation which of course I could hear every word of because of my more than excellent hearing. Derek had hunted near the university dorms and Freddy was furious.

"You did wipe his memory, didn't you?"

Derek flung Freddy's hand off his arm. "I'm not a fool. Leave it alone. It meant nothing. Now introduce me to your friend Gloriana."

I smiled and stretched out my hand. "Glory to my friends. It's a pleasure to meet you." Oh, God, Derek carried the scent of fresh blood. How long had it been since I'd allowed myself to sink my teeth into a sweet young neck? I inhaled then felt my fangs swelling against my gums and had to take a steadying breath.

"You see what you do to us?" Freddy's fists were clenched. "Glory's an inch away from going hunting because you come home smelling like O positive."

"I'm okay, Freddy. Really." Or I would be as soon as I downed a Bloody Merry. That's right, Merry, not Mary. My Merry's a canned synthetic blood, not a tomato juice cocktail. Another vamp invented it in the fifties, the nineteen fifties, that is. You get it at Merrymealsdotcom these days. Mortals think it's just an energy drink and depressed housewives claim to love it. It does pump you up, but not like the real thing.

Derek stood mere inches away. I inhaled again. Oh, I had to get away from that delicious aroma before I raced out of the house to search for the nearest warm body.

"Sorry, Glory." Derek gave Freddy a look that said go to hell. "But hunting is what we do. Why deny yourself? I can show you around if you like. The students here are wonderful. Young and healthy if you avoid the druggies and certain frat houses. We can check out Guadalupe Street or around the library."

"Enough, Derek." CiCi sat on an emerald green velvet art deco couch. Valdez settled at her feet and gazed up at her adoringly. Traitor. He looked over at me and thumped his tail against the Oriental rug. Shameless traitor.

"Gloriana just got here. Can't we have a civilized conversation? She doesn't really need to feed, do you, Gloriana?"

"No, I'm fine." Or would be once I got into my stuff and popped open the bright green can. Did you expect red? Too obvious.

"Ah, here's Sheba." CiCi looked down at Valdez. "You'll not bother the cat, sir. Or your stay here will be a short one."

Valdez sprang to his feet. I could feel his horror as a beautiful gray cat with bright blue eyes strolled into the room. She looked my way, obviously dismissed me as uninteresting, then headed straight to Valdez.

"CiCi, maybe I'd better book a hotel room." If fur flew I had no doubt we'd all be attending a kitty funeral.

CiCi placed a hand on Valdez's head. "You will *not* hurt my Sheba."

I had a feeling there was more than a bit of whammy going on. As for the cat, she sidled up to Valdez and rubbed her head against his chest. He practically vibrated with the urge to swallow her in one gulp. To my relief, Sheba moved on to jump into CiCi's lap. I sent Valdez a mental message to chill, but it wasn't necessary. He lay down at CiCi's feet.

"Now sit, all of you. Gloriana, tell us your plans."

I perched on the edge of a striped silk chair, as far away from Derek as I could get. I saw a tattoo on his muscular forearm, fairly modern looking spider webs. So he wasn't centuries old. No wonder he hunted so enthusiastically. Everyone was staring at me. Oh, yes. My plans.

"Vintage Vamp's Emporium. What do you think of the name?"

CiCi smiled. "Quite clever, my dear."

"You want everyone to *know* you're vampire?" Derek still stood, obviously wired from his night out. Feeding did that to you. Energized you. I did *not* miss the real deal.

"A vamp in the 1920s was a siren. A hottie to your generation." Freddy was clearly still pissed with his partner. He looked at me and forced a smile. "You should have seen Glory back then. Right, Mother? No one could Charleston like Gloriana St. Clair."

"Oh, I get it." Derek moved closer to Freddy and put his hand on his shoulder. He scored because at least Freddy didn't shrug it off. "Cool name. A vamp who's a vamp."

"That's the idea." I rolled my shoulders. "Sorry, folks, but would I be rude if I went to bed now? I've been driving all night."

"Oh, we are thoughtless!" CiCi glanced at the gilt and marble clock ticking on the mantle. "Less than an hour till the sun comes up. Of course you're tired. Frederick, show Gloriana to her room and help her settle in."

"Thank you for having me, CiCi. I hope to be more entertaining tomorrow night." CiCi just smiled and waved me out of the room. Valdez was hot on my heels. I could already see that I was crowding them in this house. With CiCi's large collection of furniture and knickknacks and three people already living here, there wasn't much space for me and my dog. I would have to make other arrangements as soon as possible.

Freddy picked up my bag again and gestured toward the stairs. "I've got it all fixed up for you. No trouble at all. You *will* stay with us. It's too dangerous for you to be on your own."

"Don't read my mind, it's not polite." I huffed up the stairs in his wake. "I'd rather not waste my energy blocking you."

"As if you could." He stopped in front of an open door. It was a charming bedroom with a four poster bed done up with a pretty vintage quilt. Heavy curtains had been drawn across the two windows.

"Okay, so I suck at some kinds of mental telepathy. I have other talents."

Freddy patted my hand. "Of course you do. Actress, dancer and soon to be shop owner. I think I've found the perfect location. We can go see it tomorrow night." He turned as Valdez trotted into the room. "Good, your protector is here. Promise you'll keep him with you whenever I'm not around."

"You sound like my ex. Blade said he'd talked to you."

Freddy got a grim look. "Yes. He told me about Mac-Tavish. This Westwood isn't the only hunter out there, either. Two vampires were killed in Houston the same day Westwood attacked Blade in Lake Charles."

I shuddered. I knew my geography. Houston was only about three hours away from here by car. "But not in Austin?"

"No, not here. But we're safer in groups, Glory. You can't just depend on a damned dog to keep you safe."

"Back off, vampire. Blondie's safe with me." My damned dog had sniffed out the room, then jumped on the bed to settle on the foot.

"Ah, now you speak." I walked over and tugged his ear. "Good job downstairs, with Sheba."

"Yeah, I don't know what came over me." He looked around the room. *"But if that cat tries to sleep with us, all bets are off."*

Freddy laughed. "Don't let Mother hear you say that. This is your *guard* dog?"

"Yes, he is. He really took care of me on the road. I even had to pay extra at one motel because Valdez scared the life out of a cleaning lady who tried to come in during the day."

"Damn straight. No one gets to Glory when she's sleeping."

I smiled and patted Valdez's head. "Of course I did sleep through what was apparently a 'vicious attack' according to the desk clerk. I had to take his word that the woman ran screaming across the courtyard and almost fell into the pool. I never heard a thing." Yes, we really do sleep like the dead and thank God for Valdez.

"You just made my point, Glory." Freddy ignored Valdez's "woof." "The mutt's probably mortal. Westwood wouldn't hesitate to shut up a barking dog."

"Not before I took a chunk outta him, ass—"

"Valdez!" I hugged Freddy again. "Don't worry. I'm staying. At least for a while. Thank you." I looked up at him. "Don't be so hard on Derek. We've been where he is. It takes centuries to develop the kind of self-control it takes to give up hunting. He's obviously not as old as we are."

"No, he's not. But he can be careless, Glory. He could endanger all of us."

I couldn't argue with him when he was probably right. Freddy ran a hand through his thick black hair. CiCi couldn't complain about her son's looks. He was pale, with bright blue eyes that could mesmerize you if you let yourself look into them too long. He was handsome, sexy and I'd have invited him into my bed in a heartbeat if I thought he'd be interested. He reached out to stroke my cheek.

"Nice to know, sweetheart."

"Damn it, quit reading my mind." I would have flushed if I wasn't about a quart low. I pulled a can of Bloody Merry out of my bag and popped it open. The older I get, the less often I have to feed. But smelling Derek . . . I took a swig, then sighed. "It's not the same, you know."

"Don't I just." Freddy grabbed my can and took a deep swallow, then handed it back. "You run out, just ask. Mother's got about fifty cases stockpiled. 'In case of emergency.' She still doesn't trust the Internet."

"Who does?" I sat on the bed and watched Freddy pace. It didn't take a mind reader to know he was still upset with Derek.

"Maybe you should hunt *with* him. Then you can control the situation." I sipped again. I could feel my strength returning.

"He'd love that, but been there, done that. You know?"

"Yeah, I know." It was so much easier to pretend you were normal when you didn't hunt. Sorry, but the thrill of being vampire can wear off, at least it did for me. Like, oh, two hundred years ago. About the time Blade and I split the first go round, actually.

Freddy was nodding. Of course he'd been reading my mind. I called him a name in there and he grinned.

"Sorry. Bad habit. Forget hunting. Now about this shop of yours." He quit smiling. "Maybe I shouldn't help you with it. Mother's right. Go back to Blade. He still wants you and can well afford to support you."

"Not up for discussion, Frederick. Go to bed, make up with Derek and leave me to my canned"—I wrinkled my nose—"elixir."

"Stubborn wench." He kissed my cheek then walked to the door. "It *is* good to see you again. Rest well. I'll see you in the evening. Your bathroom's next door."

"Rest well yourself, Freddy, and thank you for having me here. You're a good friend."

I sat on the bed and took another drink. They made a Bloody Merry lite but I'd learned the hard way that no matter what I did to lose weight, I woke up the same old same old. The down side to our healing sleep.

"Friend? That guy's nuts. Turnin' down a fine lookin' woman like you." Valdez bumped my hand with his nose and I buried my fingers in his fur.

"He called you a damned dog."

"Which I am. Scratch my ears. Yeah, just like that."

I sat there with Valdez close to me. He was warm, alive. As morning approached I felt more and more dead despite the rejuvenating effects of the Bloody Merry. I finished the drink and rummaged in my bag for a cotton nightgown. I was into comfort these days and looked about as sexy as a tree stump once I was ready for bed.

I found the bathroom and washed my face, studying my arms in the harsh light. CiCi was right, I looked stupid. I'd shower when I got up and use one of the loofas next to the tub/shower combo to start ridding myself of my loathsome tan. I *felt* pale, I should look pale.

What had happened to my high spirits? My optimism? I staggered into the bedroom and turned off the light. The room was black, just the way I liked it. I don't usually dream when I sleep, but I have to admit that knowing Freddy and his lover were down the hall in each other's arms got me all nostalgic.

Okay, okay, jealous. I needed a new lover, someone who would worship me and do whatever I wanted. Not someone like Blade, who knew just how to make me—God, yes— come apart in bed, but treated me like a lowly woman the rest of the time we were together. The next affair I had, I would be in control. And I was in Texas. It should be a cowboy. That thought was enough to make me smile as I sank into oblivion.

Three

"Wake up, Glory. It's dark outside."

"Go 'way," I muttered as I blinked and met green eyes that were disgustingly alert. I stretched and nudged Valdez with my foot. "I thought you were protecting me. Bite her."

"She's cute." Valdez actually rolled over and moaned when my intruder rubbed his tummy. *"Harmless."*

"You want to bet on that, *signor?*" Florence da Vinci smiled and showed an impressive set of fangs.

I reached over to snap on the lamp next to the bed. "You don't want to mess with Flo, Valdez."

"No kidding." Valdez sat up and eyed Flo who actually licked her lips. *"Yeah, I get your point. Hah. Hah."* He jumped off the bed and trotted to the door. *"I'm goin'. Someone downstairs will let me out."*

"Sure, beat it, you wimp." I sat up and held out my arms. "You look wonderful, Flo. Freddy didn't tell me you were in Austin."

"Not just in Austin. Here, in the attic. It's pretty cool. We're one big happy family now." Flo hugged me, then stepped back to look me over. She shook her head. "CiCi told me you painted yourself orange. What were you thinking?"

"I wasn't, apparently." I threw back the covers and got out of bed.

"You sleep in *that*?" Flo drew back in horror. "You don't let the handsome Jeremy see you so ugly, do you? Where's your sexy negligee?"

"Jeremy's not here and I don't *care* if he sees me ugly." Florence is an Italian Angelina Jolie look-alike who certainly knows her way around sexy. If anyone can put the vamp in vampire, it's Flo. No one knows her real name. I first met her when she'd simply shown up in Scotland one day.

"I didn't just 'show up,' *cara*. Magdalena invited me when we met in Roma. And if I want to take the name of my favorite city and that of my dear Leonardo, that is my business, no?"

"No. I mean yes! Your business, nobody else's." Living with a bunch of vamps who could and would read my mind when they felt like it was going to be a royal pain.

"Sorry, *cara*. I'll leave you in your sexless sack while I go dancing." Flo flounced to the door. I had to admire that flounce considering she was tottering on four-inch red stilettos that matched her short skirt and halter top. She was any guy's walking wet dream. No wonder Leonardo had painted her over and over again. According to her anyway.

"Wait!" I hurried after her, my gown billowing around me. "Dancing?"

She turned and hugged me again. "Hah! Got you. I'll try not to read your mind. It's not nice of me, I know. But you should learn to block us." Her eyes twinkled. "I sure don't let anyone read *my* mind."

When she was right, she was right. Maybe I'd been so busy blending and hanging with mortals, that I'd become lazy when it came to using my vamp powers. And hanging with mortals had a downside. You see them get sick, die even.

And while some vamps can turn a mortal without blinking an eye—hey, look what Blade did to me—I just *can't.*

Forever is forever, you know? Mortals don't have a clue what that really means. I was on a headlong slide into depression and realized Flo was giving me a sympathetic look. Of course, she'd gotten all that "Woe is me" crap.

"What's this about dancing?"

"We're making Freddy and Derek take us out, to show you a little of Austin's night life."

"You don't have to ask me twice. Twenty minutes. Okay?"

Flo looked me over. "Take thirty, *cara.* You *do* have something sexier in that bag of yours, don't you? Frederick brought in your suitcase. The big black one."

I was mentally unpacking. Jeans, T-shirts. Was there anything in there that didn't make me look fat?

"You are *not* fat." Before I could do more than squeak, Flo grabbed my gown, whisked it off over my head and dropped it on the floor. "I'll quit reading your mind tomorrow. If I don't forget." She took me by the shoulders and turned me around. "You have curves, Glory. Leonardo would have painted you nude, reclining on a velvet couch." She tapped her chin. "Oh, no, that wasn't Leo, that was my darling Pietro Rubens. I *do* love artists."

"Hello, I'm standing here naked while you're strolling down memory lane."

Flo laughed and tossed me my gown. "Be proud of your body, *cara.* You have the shape of a real woman. I myself have posed many, many times. The Mona Lisa. Pah! How can Leo be famous for that when he did so many lovely pictures of *me*? I am even sitting next to you know who in his painting of The Last Supper."

"You know anything about a secret code?" I couldn't help it. I read best sellers.

"Forget codes. *I* should be hanging in the Louvre. That Lisa. A peasant." Flo spit into her palm and shot what must be the Italian bird. "And that secret smile? I happen to know it was because *she* was really a *he*!"

I just gaped.

"Hurry and get dressed. Look sexy." Flo gave me a finger wave and headed down the hall.

I put it in gear, eager to get out and see more of my new hometown. Florence never failed to surprise me. Some vamps swear she's not exactly the brightest bulb in the lamp, but I don't believe it. She's clever enough to get vamps all over the world to take turns providing a home for her. Not just because she's ancient, but because everyone loves her *and* her stories.

Tonight's chapter had been a doozy. She's always sworn that Leonardo da Vinci had been vampire and her lover. Can you believe that? Even though Freddy's heard old Leo swung the other way. Flo also claims a monk assassin staked dear Leonardo because of his blasphemies in painting The Last Supper. Too bad Flo never bothered to learn to read or write. She has a best seller in her for sure.

An hour later we were on Sixth Street in downtown Austin checking out the club scene. It was crowded on a Saturday night. We'd left Valdez fighting off Sheba. As Freddy had said, safety in numbers.

I'd dressed in black, slimming of course, with a lacy top that showed some cleavage, always a crowd pleaser. Flo had actually approved after she'd thrown a black and red floral shawl over my shoulders. But now she'd disappeared, merrily following a fellow vamp into a jazz club.

"Don't worry about her, she'll be fine. In fact, she'll probably have to take care of Trevor. You think you've got a sense of smell. Flo can smell emotions. Fear, hate, love. Any hunters out there and she'll be the first to detect them."

"Good to know." Hard to see why she'd hang out with a loser like Trevor Danforth though. I'd met him a few moments before. I don't know what emotion Flo had detected from him, but I couldn't forget the smell of fresh blood that had hung around him. Obviously he'd been feeding, and so early in the evening. "Why would she have to take care of Trevor?"

"He's an alcoholic, Glory." Derek was on one side of me, Freddy on the other. Other women looked at me with envy. If they only knew my two handsome men dressed in yummy butt-hugging denim had eyes only for each other. Bummer.

"How can a vampire be an alcoholic?" We'd stopped in front of a club with country music booming out of the open door. "All of the ones I've met say they can't drink alcohol without getting sick. I only tried it once and thought I was going to die." You think mortals get hangovers? Try a six day death wish.

"He only feeds when the clubs are closing, or he sees a drunk leaving a club early. That must be what happened tonight." Derek shook his head. "The higher the blood alcohol level, the better for old Trev."

"You're kidding." I wracked my brain. Had I ever fed from a drunk? "Maybe you'd get a buzz, but I'd still worry about a hangover." "Cotton-Eyed Joe" started inside.

"Trev doesn't worry about hangovers when he's getting a double whammy. A vicarious high." Derek noticed my toe tapping to the beat of the music. "Forget Trevor. We promised you dancing. How's this?"

"Perfect. I'm *so* ready for a cowboy." I pulled them both inside. "Both of you will dance with me, not with each other. In here I think that would get you beat up. But we'll have a signal. If a good looking cowboy asks me to dance and I want to, I'll say 'Beat it, boys.'"

"That's a signal?" Freddy laughed and shouldered us through the crowd. "Obviously you're not into subtle."

"Nope." I scanned the room as we found a table near the dance floor. Fortunately the few waitresses seemed overwhelmed and no one asked for a drink order. I can drink things other than Bloody Merrys as long as they aren't alcoholic, but I wasn't here to drink. The bass was vibrating through my body and I was looking for Mr. Right Now.

Derek pulled me up and onto the dance floor and we twirled into a two step. The man could certainly dance. After a few minutes, the lights dimmed and the song slowed to a sexy ballad. Tim McGraw. What a waste.

I led Derek toward our table. Freddy had been joined by a cowboy. They stood with their backs to us. Nice broad back on Mr. Cowboy. Snug well-worn jeans, black Stetson and boots. He was tall, built and just what I'd been looking for.

"Dance, Cowboy?" I asked, putting my hand on his arm. Then he turned around, covering my hand with his. Blade. Damn it to hell.

"Dance? Sure, babe."

He pulled me onto the dance floor and into his arms. Chest to chest, thigh to thigh. Blade held me tight, his cheek against my hair and I didn't bother to pretend it didn't feel good. We moved to the music and, with my eyes closed, I could relax and lean into him. Solid. Strong.

"You look good." The words drifted into my mind just as Blade leaned down to press his lips to my neck. Right over the old jugular. Naturally that's a vamp hot spot and I felt his mouth on me clear down to my toes. My nipples sprang to attention and my body screamed "Come and get me."

No. No. No. I leaned back and looked up. He hadn't missed the Glory hallelujah reaction. He was grinning and looking so much like a real cowboy that my heart squeezed. Time for a distraction. I wasn't ready to climb back on *this* horse just yet.

"What's with the cowboy look?"

"I'm blending. What do you think?" He rubbed my back.

"I think you couldn't blend if your life depended on it." Oh, great. His life *did* depend on it. Mouth to brain—be nice.

"Maybe you could give me lessons. On how to blend." He looked around. "I thought I was doing all right." For once he didn't sound completely sure of himself. And didn't that fire me up even more?

"You are. Really. And I love the hat." My inner slut slipped my hand inside his back pocket. I've always loved his nice firm butt. "So why are you *here* blending? I thought you were in Lake Charles with Mara and your state-of-the-art security."

"I wanted to check on you. I left Mara there."

Glory one, Mara zip. As if this was a contest. I basked in Blade's concern for a moment. Whoa. "Check on me? Like I'm not capable of looking out for myself?"

"Here we go again." Blade tightened his hand on my waist. "For once, lass, can we no' just enjoy the moment?"

He'd brought out the big guns. He knows I'm a sucker for the Scottish accent. And I actually was a little blown away. I never dreamed he'd seek me out again so soon after I'd turned him down in the desert.

"Enjoy the moment. Fine. But we need to talk, Jerry."

"Jeremiah, lass. Och, but I've missed your fire."

"Hmmm." What could I say? Fire? Right now I was a four alarm. Blame it on my long dry spell, but if we'd been alone I might have shown Jerry some fire works. We'd always clicked in bed and he wasn't even put off by my thunder thighs.

How do I know? When we're making love, Jerry lets me into his thoughts. Talk about erotic. In their heads, men get pretty graphic, but they *love* the female body. When they're getting lucky, they're grateful and very appreciative. You might say "blinded by passion." Cool, huh?

I knew he was reading me. He slid his hand down to my butt and pulled me closer. And we danced. Even got two slow ones before the pace picked up and the lights brightened. Jerry led me back to the table where Derek and Freddy were talking.

"Let's go outside." Blade issued his order then guided, no, pushed me toward the door with his hand on my back. Naturally Derek and Freddy followed.

"Jeez, who died and put you in charge?" What had I just said? I had to get a grip on my big mouth. Blade's face hardened and he just looked at me. And let me see his grief for Mac. Dark, bottomless, the loss of the brother of his heart. And all his fault. If he'd only—

"Stop it!" I grabbed his hand and held on. "You are *not* responsible for Mac's death. Westwood is."

"I should have sensed the danger sooner. Mac and Mara were there visiting *me*." Blade squeezed my hand. "I'll not lose you, too, dearling."

Derek and Freddy were watching us. Freddy, for sure, was picking up on my chaotic thoughts, though no one could read Blade unless he let them in.

"Come home with me, Gloriana. I'll keep you safe or die trying."

I shuddered at that promise. I didn't doubt he meant every word.

"No freaking way." I grabbed his arm. "You mean well. I get that. Look at me, Jerry." His dark eyes met mine. "Read my mind, my heart. Whatever." I saw his jaw tighten.

"I have plans, Jerry. A life that doesn't include cowering inside a damned casino while you throw yourself in front of me to catch arrows in your chest." The world swirled around me for a moment and I wobbled on my high heels. Blade caught me, holding me tight against his side. I took a breath and pushed away from him, relieved that I was steady again.

"Believe me. I can take care of myself. And, if I do need help, I have friends here."

"She's right, Blade. We're perfectly capable of protecting her and she's opening a store here." Derek. Who'd obviously not been around Blade enough to realize he didn't exactly welcome interference.

"I'm sure you *think* you can protect her, Derek"—Blade swept him with a dismissive look—"when you're not trolling for students, that is." He locked eyes with Freddy. "Frederick, I'll talk to you later. Gloriana and I need to be alone."

Freddy, the coward, the deserter, the first-class chump, merely nodded. "You have a place to stay?"

"Aye."

And Freddy took off, dragging Derek with him. Just like that.

"What if I don't *want* to be alone with you?"

Blade leaned down and kissed my lips, slowly, thoroughly, sliding just the tip of a fang across them until I was damp and dizzy.

"Come along, sweetheart. I need you."

Hmmm. And didn't I need him? For comfort. Old time's sake. Satisfaction guaranteed. I could go on and on. Could you blame me if I followed him meekly to a silver Mercedes convertible parked at the curb?

"Nice car." Good. Despite a lust-fogged brain, I could at least speak again.

"I thought you'd like it. It's yours."

"Mine?" I determinedly squelched the urge to happy dance. The price of independence—do not accept expensive gifts even though he'd obviously read my mind and bought my dream car.

"Valdez told me how that piece of crap you drive endangered you on your trip." He tossed me the keys. "Drive."

Damned furry snitch. And now Jerry was trying to hook me with a little drive. But I'm not stupid. I got in and started the engine. Oh, but it purred. "Keep me," it whispered as I shifted into drive.

"Where to?" I pretended nonchalance as I pulled away from the curb. The cool night air lifted my hair and I felt like a princess in her coach-and-four. I waved to the peasants crowding the sidewalks as we breezed down Sixth Street as fast as the traffic allowed.

Blade gave me directions until we wove our way up to the top of Castle Hill and stopped in front of . . . yes, a castle. Talk about your stereotypes. The Gothic monstrosity perched on the summit with its stone turrets and massive wood door shouted, "Vampires live here. Keep out."

"You've got to be kidding. Who lives here?"

"A friend with a sense of humor. He puts on a great Halloween party. Maybe we'll come back for it."

"You're ruining the mood for me, Jerry, by assuming I'll do your bidding." I might as well speak my mind since he could read every thought anyway.

"Sorry." He leaned over and kissed me again, a long, lingering, tongue tangling symphony of a kiss that had me humming along.

Again. I'm not stupid. I was not going to keep the car. Or go to Lake Charles. But I *was* going to satisfy this itch that Blade, for centuries, had known how to scratch just so. I followed him inside. Up a stone staircase that could have come straight from Castle Campbell except that this marble gleamed and, of all things, a bat chandelier hung above the landing.

"Bats?" I laughed as Blade tugged me into a bedroom and slammed the door. "What? No coffin?"

"That's in Damian's bedchamber."

I fell onto the exquisitely soft, red-velvet coverlet. Blade grinned down at me. Oh I loved the way he looked when he wasn't angsting over all his responsibilities. This Blade was fun, playful as he fell on top of me. I ripped open the snaps on his shirt and ran my hands over his smooth chest and down his flat stomach. Always the same, always perfect. I could feel his need pressing against his jeans.

"Ride 'em, cowboy," I whispered as I slid down his zipper.

"Not yet, lass." He pushed his hand under my skirt.

"What the hell are you wearing?" He pulled up the fabric to look.

"Control panties. Not exactly a girdle, but——" He pressed a kiss on the heavy duty spandex just "there" and I wished the thing to hell and gone. It had been a struggle to get it on tonight, but it flattened my stomach and kept my butt from jiggling. How on earth was Blade going to work it off?

"Not to worry. And I like it when your butt jiggles." A knife gleamed in his hand. Did I mention why he'd picked Blade as his surname? Knives, swords, daggers have always been his weapons of choice and he's damned good with them. Years later someone created a comic book character with the same name—a vampire hunter. Talk about irony.

Forget irony. Jerry slipped the tip of his stiletto under the elastic above my navel. I gasped, then forgot to breathe as he slowly cut the spandex. It parted like butter until, yes, hello, he was right where he'd kissed me just moments ago.

My poor strangled tummy thanked him. But the cool steel of that knife so perilously close to my most private parts . . . Call me freaky, but I shivered with a perverse need to have him keep going. He looked up, his heated gaze leaving no doubt that he'd go as far as I wanted him to.

Did I stop him? Are you kidding? I opened my thighs and held my breath. And he kept going, the cold steel skimming across me, lower, lower until I grabbed his hair and made him look at me.

"You wouldn't."

"Wouldn't I? Anything for your pleasure, lass." But he tossed the knife aside and bent his head to trace me with his tongue and—hoo, boy—his fangs. Oh, God, but he had a way with his fangs. Heat, need and the satisfaction that I'd always felt only with Jeremiah Campbell sliced through me, sharp as that knife he'd used moments ago. I wanted him naked. And deep inside me.

Of course he heard my "Do me, baby" thoughts. His clothes vanished along with mine before he pulled me on top of him and drew my lips to his neck. I pressed my fangs into his tender skin and warm blood flooded my mouth just as hot satisfaction flooded my thighs. I couldn't think, but Jeremiah could, his voice whispering inside my head.

"Yes. Taste me, Gloriana. Come with me. You are beautiful. Mine. Mine."

He moved under me, hard and fast, his hands on my ass, urging me to keep pace. No problem. But I was coming apart, bit by bit. I shivered and called his name in my mind since I couldn't bear to release him and his delicious taste. Finally I licked his neck and threw back my head, wild as he reached between us to touch me.

"God, Jeremiah!" I leaned forward until he sucked one of my nipples into his warm mouth, the pressure making me clench around him. Oh, yes. He rolled us until he was on top. I opened my eyes and saw him there, so strong, the muscles in his arms taut as he held himself above me. But he was pale. He'd let me feed from him and he'd been hurt just days ago.

"Jeremiah." I pulled his head to my neck, shuddering with pleasure as he took me. If I live to be a thousand, I'm sure I'll never feel a pleasure greater than Jeremiah Campbell, hard inside me, drawing on my life force. I felt an answering pull deep inside. Powerful, seemingly insatiable. No wonder I held on to him with both hands. He took me and I took him until I was wracked with pleasure, dying and yet being reborn, again and again. Finally, I shattered. Complete. His.

Four

"I am not yours." Okay, so maybe I was a little late with that declaration.

"Of course not. You are your own woman. Damnably independent. *I* get *that*." He lay against the pillows and watched me as I crawled out of bed and attempted to pull together my outfit.

Damnably independent. Yep. But I couldn't get too excited about making that point when my knees were still weak and I couldn't look at him or I'd be right back in that bed for another round.

Get dressed. Right. Forget the panties. They went in the trash and I was glad to see those modern day iron maidens go. At some point he'd cut my bra apart too and that bugged me. Black lace double *D* bras aren't cheap.

I was surprisingly at ease prancing around naked in front of Jerry. Hey, he'd seen me in the buff more times than either of us could count and if my figure flaws hadn't sent him away screaming before, they sure wouldn't now.

"You're beautiful, Gloriana. I wish you'd realize that."

I pulled on my blouse, but left it gaping open as I faced him. Yeah, he did look like he was enjoying the view. I picked up my skirt and twirled it around my finger.

"I realize that you want me to obey you. Drive that sex-mobile to Lake Charles with you and lock myself inside your casino. But it's not going to happen." There. Could I make it any clearer?

He sat up and snatched the skirt out of my hand. "You are the most difficult woman I've ever known."

"Hmm. I'll take that as a compliment."

"Then mayhap ye'll come back to bed, lass." He grinned when I let my blouse slip off my shoulders and fall to the floor.

"Mayhap." I sauntered toward him, well aware of how my breasts quivered and my nipples said, "Taste me." He definitely wanted me again and, boy, was that a power trip. "I've always had a weakness for lusty Scots."

"First turn around and walk away. I want to see this butt jiggling you're so fashed about."

"Make me." I put my hands on my hips. He was beside me in a flash. Some vamps can do that, move at warp speed. Another vamp trick I'd never learned. He walked around me, then dropped to his knees.

"Aye, I'll make ye, lass. Make ye scream for me." He kneaded my buttocks.

"Will not." I gasped as he slid a finger inside me.

"Such a fine generous arse ye've got here. Soft." He stroked me with his tongue. "Tasty."

Generous indeed! But Jerry truly didn't care. He pressed his thumb between my thighs until I had to bite my lip.

"Did I hear ye moan then, lass?"

"No! I won't scream for you either, Jerry." I turned and pushed my fingers through his hair, soft with just a bit of curl in the dark strands. Strands that would never gray above a chiseled face that would never sag or wrinkle.

"Will ye no'?" He leaned against me and kissed my belly. "And if *I* scream for *you*?" He looked up, his eyes gleaming. "Will that please ye?"

"It might." I pulled him to his feet and wrapped my arms around him, more pleased than I liked to admit. I'd never been to Louisiana. Maybe . . . No, he was obviously doing a vamp whammy on me. But I pressed my cheek to his cool bare chest anyway.

Uh-oh. We're supposed to be warm, though I figure we're well below a mortal's normal temp. His heart thumped in the slow steady way all vamps did near dawn. About half speed.

"Take care of yourself, Jerry. You're still healing. You should have stayed home."

"I couldno'. You are my heart, lass. Come home with me."

I believed him. That he truly cared for me. But something in me insisted I had to make my own way. I couldn't belong to anyone. Even someone as seductive and as damnably delicious as Jeremy Blade. Sometimes I hate myself, you know? But logic, which I was struggling to get a grip on, told me this sudden urge to keep me close had a lot to do with Jerry's losing Mac.

Hey, when a vamp actually dies, it shakes us up. And makes a vampire want to do something life affirming, like, pardon my bluntness, maybe screw your brains out.

I dragged Jerry back to bed and made love to him, pushing him back when he tried to take charge. No. This was my farewell party for two. I kissed a path down his chest to his stomach, smiling as his muscles clenched. Lusty indeed. I licked the moisture from the tip of his shaft then took him into my mouth. I cupped his balls, squeezing lightly until he moaned and slid his fingers into my hair.

"Witch. How can ye send me away from ye?"

Obviously I was way too busy to answer him. Besides, I was close to caving. Nope. Not caving. There was more to life than sex. Wasn't there?

By the time I finally sat up to guide him inside me, I knew Jerry wasn't about to deny me anything. So I told him, in my thoughts, that we just wouldn't work. He was who he was and he wasn't going to change. And I was who *I* was and I wasn't changing either. He needed a clinging female and I needed a man who appreciated my free spirit and independence.

But issues aside, we did have chemistry. And he knew all my hot spots, from my tingling toes to the small of my back and everywhere in between. I held him to my breasts and fought the tender feelings that made me want to do his bidding in all things.

"Ach, lass, I canna fight ye. Do as ye will." His voice inside my head probably meant I'd won this skirmish.

Do as I will? I kissed Jerry, our tongues tangling, his fangs dragging across my swollen lips until I pulled back. My mouth wandered over his battle-scarred terrain, every nook and cranny so achingly familiar. I licked away the salt from his sweat-slicked body and watched him shudder. Oh, yes, I knew what drove him over the edge. When I finally sat astride my conquest, I felt bloody amazing. Vamp power. Got to love it. But I couldn't stop thinking. This had to end. If only—

He jerked me to him and kissed away my thoughts until there was only taste, touch and the need to push toward satisfaction. I sat up and tossed my hair back. I rode him until we both collapsed, gasping, too replete to do more than lie in each other's arms, breathing in the sharp, sweet essence we had created between us.

Jerry whispered inside my head all the sweet things a man won't actually say to a woman. That he needed me, that I pleased him as no other woman could, that . . . wait a minute. Other woman? The hell with it. I'd had other men too, it was inevitable when we'd been apart so long. And I sure wasn't going to let a little, okay, a lot of jealousy spoil some of the best sex of my lifetime. So I whispered back, assuring him that he would always have a special place in my heart and, call me a slut, in my bed.

We lay for a long time, just holding each other, until the vamp awareness that dawn wasn't that far away made me move off of him. I kissed his lips, firm now with the displeasure he didn't bother to hide. Yep, I was disobeying my lord and master yet again. I hated that and the fact that he never seemed to learn how to handle me. Jerry was anything but a slow learner in all other aspects of his life. But with me . . .

I sniffled a little as I got dressed, but Jerry didn't try to stop me or offer false words of comfort. I'd insisted on this parting. So I could just deal with it. We were both quiet and I, for one, was sad that separation seemed to be our destiny.

We were heading down the stairs when the front door opened. Vampire. I glanced at Blade who still looked grim. He hates rejection. Not that I'd rejected *him,* just his plans for how I should live my life.

"Blade! Is this your Gloriana?" A smiling man strode up to us. A smiling, happy vampire. Handsome as the devil too, dressed in a black silk shirt open to the waist and slim black pants.

I glanced at Blade. He nodded, not bothering to smile. "Gloriana, this is Damian Sabatini. The owner of this castle."

Damian took my hand and pulled it to his lips. He actually brushed it with a fang and I shivered. Whoa. In the vampire world this was considered a major pass. Did Damian have a death wish? But Blade was stone-faced. Of course he hadn't missed the intimacy *or* my reaction to it. Did I expect him to morph into a snarling jealous beast? He wouldn't. Not after I'd just declared my independence. Again.

I smiled at Damian. "Please, call me Glory. I *love* your house."

"Thank you. You must come back for my Halloween costume party."

"Sounds like fun." Blade wasn't saying anything. Pouting? Seething? I couldn't complain. I'd made my choice. So it had left my stomach in knots and a hole in my heart. I'd learn to live with it.

"Are you sure you won't keep the car?"

Ah, Jerry the vampire speaks. In a cold, clipped voice that masked what I sensed was his hurt. Yes, I do know him well after four centuries. Well enough to know that this too, would pass. I couldn't imagine he'd ever walk away from me completely. That responsibility gene of his.

"I love it, but no, thank you." I touched Jerry's arm. Solid and as unresisting as his will.

"And you won't come with me."

"I can't. I have plans here."

"Very well." Blade exchanged a look with Damian. "You'll take her back to Frederick's?"

"Of course." Damian actually bowed and clicked his heels. But the effect was ruined by the twinkle in his eyes. Green eyes if you can believe it. Startling with his dark hair.

Wait a minute. Forget Damian. Blade brushed my cheek with his thumb. "Good-bye, Gloriana."

"You're leaving?" I'd been dismissed, that was clear from the look on Blade's face. "What is this? My way or the highway?"

Blade dropped his hand. "Your choice, not mine. Take care, lass."

"But it's late." On cue, a clock somewhere in the house chimed four. "It'll be daylight—"

"I'll manage. Thank you, Damian. I'll be in touch."

I thought for a moment that Blade was going to just walk out the door. I really think he planned to. But he looked hard at Damian then grabbed me and kissed me. Not a "See you around, babe" kiss, but a "You're mine and I'll be back to claim you" kiss. Wow. I leaned into him, nipped his lower lip and kissed *him*. A "Right back at you, Jerry" kiss. And

"See if Mara can top this" kiss. He wasn't the only one who could stake a claim. Yep, we're both twisted.

"You sure you want to leave, Blade?" Damian sounded amused and that was definitely a mood killer for Jerry. He jerked back, gave me a long look, then turned on his heel and left.

"You can still go with him." Damian must have seen my woebegone look.

"No." Damian had a gleam in his eyes. Of course, he'd smelled sex on Blade and me. And he could probably tell from various jiggles that I'd lost my underwear somewhere. Did he think I was a slut? I smiled. Let him. He was reading my mind so I sent him a little message. His eyes widened then he laughed.

"I'll be careful, Glory. Shall we go?"

"Why not?" I stepped outside and saw red taillights disappearing down the hill. I refused to give in to the urge to cry or throw something. Instead, I checked out the long, low and very vintage black Cadillac convertible at the curb.

"Cool car."

"Thanks." Damian opened the passenger door and I slid onto a soft, black, leather seat.

"Gothic castle. Halloween parties. Vamp-mobile. Aren't you afraid you'll be outted by some overzealous groupie?"

Yeah, if word gets out you're vamp, the kinky, weird and genuinely awestruck fans won't leave you alone. Some vamps go for that sort of thing, but the downside is that with notoriety you get hunters eager to put another notch in their stakes.

"It's called 'hide in plain sight,' Glory. You should see me in my Dracula costume at Halloween."

Damian drove like he'd moved, assured, easy. He glanced at me and grinned. "Thanks."

Here we go. Maybe I could nip this in the bud. I *can* read minds, but I don't because it's usually too much information, if you know what I mean. And it really irritates me when other vamps poke into *my* mind uninvited.

"Message received, Glory." He reached over and patted my hand. "It's a bad habit so I may slip once in a while, but I'd like to be your friend."

Friend. I didn't have to be a mind reader to see that Damian was interested in more than friendship. Hey, I was flattered. Damian was hot. Of course he was probably only intrigued because Blade had had me. So what?

After I'd mourned Blade for the thousandth time, I'd be ready for someone in my life. Damian wasn't a cowboy, but the whole man in black, vamp thing was working for me. And he was an old vampire. He reeked of power behind his careless attitude.

When we pulled up in front of Freddy's, the front door flew open.

"Glory! Come inside. You, too, Damian." Freddy was paler than usual and his hair was on end.

"What is it?" We both hurried up the walk. Derek, CiCi and Freddy were gathered around Flo who sat slumped on the couch, sobbing like her heart was breaking and babbling in Italian. Valdez stood guard by the door.

Damian knelt in front of Flo and spoke to her in soothing tones in her native language. *"Dios mio!"* He pulled her up and wrapped his arms around her.

Freddy pulled me aside. "He'll calm her down. They've known each other forever."

"But what happened?"

Flo turned and looked at me, her cheeks wet with tears. "Trevor. I found him. He's *morto.* Dead."

"My God!" I sank onto the nearest chair, my knees weak. "What happened?" Trevor. I hadn't exactly fallen in love with the vampire, but he'd seemed harmless enough.

"My fault. I should have felt the hate. Warned him." Flo shuddered and pressed her face against Damian's chest. She wailed something in Italian.

"What did she say? Was it Westwood?" I couldn't breathe. Vampire hunters. Here in Austin.

Damian patted Flo's back and swallowed. "Westwood? Not unless he stakes with a wooden cross."

"I smell cat. If that Sheba followed me here . . ." Valdez's nose twitched and his tail quivered on point.

"Will you quit obsessing about Sheba? CiCi wouldn't let her follow you." Poor Valdez. He'd been beyond patient, but Sheba had stuck to him like a burr the whole time we'd been at CiCi's. It was as if the cat had sensed the one entity that didn't want her and decided to torment him. Or was it love?

"Love? Gag me. I'm just making sure you're not in danger."

"This building allows pets. Someone's sure to have a cat. Get over it. A cat isn't a danger to *me*."

"I ain't afraid of no cat." Valdez plopped on the loveseat Freddy and Derek had just dragged in from the U-Haul.

"Maybe you should be." Derek grinned and nodded to the closed door across the hall. "Werecat. Good looking redhead during the day, but by night . . . hello, kitty."

Shape-shifters. Why was I not surprised? But I was cool with it, just happy to be moving. After Trevor's death, I'd had three choices. Hustle my butt to Blade. Too wimpy. Barricade myself in Freddy's house with his mother. Way too wimpy. Or carry on with my plan while staying alert. I picked door number three. No way was I letting some vamp-hungry religious nut dictate *my* moves.

And who should come riding to my rescue but Damian. Who happened to own a building in the trendy warehouse district. With, surprise, surprise, an empty shop on the ground floor and apartments on the top three. With excellent security, of course.

Was this all just a little too convenient? If Blade had his hand in this, I'd kill, well, at least *try* to kill him. But you know what they say about gift horses. So I'm moving into 2C.

Freddy and Derek couldn't wait to introduce me to my new neighbor. I've run across shape-shifters before. There'd been one werewolf who'd been a hunk in human form and more than tempting. But he kept pressuring me to shape-shift too. No, thank you, Wolfman. We'd parted ways. Talk about your ugly breakups.

"It's three frickin' thirty in the morning, guys. Is this building on fire?" A tall woman with red hair that would've made Clairol weep with envy stood between Freddy and Derek, poking them both in the chest with what looked to be lethal peach-frost fingernails. She wore a faded orange University of Texas T-shirt and plaid boxers. Her legs were a mile long and she looked like a model. I was prepared to hate her.

"Sorry, Lacy, we forgot you're a day person. Meet your new neighbor, Gloriana St. Clair. Then you can go back to bed. Glory, this is Lacy Devereau."

Lacy gave me the once over then swept the room, her eyes narrowing on Valdez, who'd leaped down to stand by my side. He growled and I grabbed his collar, though I knew from experience that if Valdez decided to bolt, he was gone.

"Back off, fur ball. I was here first." Lacy obviously wasn't talking to *me*.

"Yeah? Change, lady, and we'll see who owns this turf."

"Stop it, Valdez." I smiled and held out my other hand. "Please, forgive my, er, protector. He's got a love-hate thing with cats."

"A hate thing that says haul your skinny ass out of here." Valdez bared his teeth.

Lacy laughed and shook my hand. "All bark. I've met his kind before. And, fur ball, you have no idea what my cat form looks like." She purred and bent down to look into his eyes. Whatever they said to each other inside their heads seemed to settle things for the moment.

"Let me go. It stinks in here. I'll be on your bed if you need me." Valdez looked up at me.

"Fine." I released him and watched him trot toward my new room. He paused in the doorway to glance over his shoulder and growl. Lacy growled back, her nails suddenly claws, and he sniffed and walked stiff-legged out of sight.

"Sorry about that, Lacy."

"Not to worry, Glory. Dogs are as important to me as a flea on my backside. He bites, I scratch him right out of existence. Which is what I told him a moment ago."

Hmm. Interesting neighbor. Could she read my mind? She smiled and nodded. Peachy. All I needed was another one.

"Damian said he's leasing the shop downstairs to you. An antique store?"

"Right. Vintage Vamp's Emporium."

"Cool. I've had some retail experience and"—she leaned forward—"I'm kind of an antique myself."

"You want a job?" This was good news. I needed a day worker and, despite her rather aggressive attitude with my dog, Lacy seemed like a competent person. I looked her over. She did have a skinny butt, so I still might hate her. And her skin. Creamy and absolutely glowing despite not a speck of makeup. Shouldn't werecats have whiskers or something?

"I *need* a job. I was working in the coffee bar at a local bookstore when this idiot told his buddy he'd just dumped a litter of kittens on the side of the freeway. He was laughing." She shuddered. "Those poor babies didn't stand a chance."

"Jerk."

"Exactly. So, oops, I dropped a latte in his lap."

"Hot latte, I hope." Kittens on the freeway. I can't tolerate cruelty to animals.

"You'd better believe it. But it got me fired."

"Too bad. I've always been an animal lover. Why do you think I keep a dog around?"

"You should switch to cats, Glory. Much more interesting. Not so slavishly devoted, of course."

Time for a subject change. "Where are Freddy and Derek?" Not that it mattered. The U-Haul was empty and we'd already arranged for one of Derek's mortal friends to turn it in tomorrow.

"They hit it as soon as they introduced us. Probably bringing down their prey as we speak. Maybe you should join them while you've still got darkness." Lacy yawned and stretched. Yes, she did have a kind of cat persona going on.

"We don't call it prey. And I haven't fed that way in years." Obviously vamps and werecats have a different mind-set.

"Too bad." Lacy looked around the room. "So how about that job? I could use the money and I do know a thing or two about old stuff." She walked over to the pile of clothes Freddy had dropped onto a chair and picked up a vintage flapper dress.

"I had one of these. Cute." She looked at me, then down at her own willowy body. "I don't think we're the same size."

I wish. "Exactly how antique are you?"

"Old enough to remember when women wore these." She pulled out a boned corset and wrapped it around her. "I'm sure a man invented this. I'd like to see one pull into a twenty-inch waist."

I was really liking Lacy. "You can work a register?"

"Of course." She tossed the corset back into the pile. "So do I have the job?"

"I'll give you a shot. I'm planning to be open twenty-four hours a day, Tuesday through Saturday. We'll have Sundays and Mondays off. Sound okay?"

"As long as you pay me enough, no problem. We can work out the details later." She yawned, a huge jaw cracker that showed some pretty impressive canines. "Sorry. I'm beat. Check with me when you wake up."

"Will do." I watched her stroll back into her own apartment and shut the door. Click. Click. Double dead bolts. Just like on my door. Nice.

The whole place was nice in a timeworn, shabby-chic kind of way. Having once been a warehouse it had high ceilings and wide hallways with great hardwood floors that creaked if you stepped just right. Someone had converted the top three floors into apartments back in the days when turquoise appliances had been the hot look. Now they were considered retro.

I'd already filled a cabinet with junk food for Valdez. Now I lugged a case of Bloody Merry into the kitchen and lined up a dozen of them in the empty fridge. Some vamps drink it hot, but, after living in Vegas and the desert heat, I've decided I prefer it cold—not that it's such a tasty treat to begin with.

"Well, that does it for the kitchen."

"Glad to hear it. May I?" Damian lounged in the doorway. He nodded toward the Bloody Merry and I handed him one. We both popped tops then he held out his.

"A toast. To new beginnings." He had a wicked smile but I couldn't read his mind. Didn't matter. Whatever he was interested in beginning, was definitely interesting to me.

"To new beginnings." We both drank and I sighed. I was getting really sick of canned jugular juice.

"What do you think of your new place?" Damian followed me into the living room. The chairs were full of clothes so he sat next to me on the love seat.

"Love it." His thigh was right up against mine. Not that there was any danger of him being overcome with lust. I looked a fright, my hair a tangle and my faded "What Happens in Vegas, Stays in Vegas" T-shirt clung in all the wrong places.

"You look great." He met my gaze and I felt his power. But I'd lived most of my life with a powerful vamp. I shrugged and looked away.

"Save the sweet talk, Damian. I'm not ready to rebound just yet."

"Blade." Damian put his can down on the marble-topped coffee table and took my hand. "I'm not going to tell you that he's not good enough for you. He's my friend. I know what kind of man he is. But maybe he's not the *right* man for you."

"And maybe you are?" I looked down at my hand resting in his. He was big, strong and masculine in a smooth sophisticated way. Very different from my Highlander who had broken men's necks with his bare hands. Damian seemed more slice and dice than rip and roar. Though Blade sliced and diced too, actually.

"Give me a chance. That's all I'm asking."

"Why? No other female vamps in Austin?" I couldn't believe this. I'm okay, but I'm no beauty queen. And I had two handsome men who wanted me? Pinch me.

"There are others. Right here in this building as a matter of fact." Damian dropped my hand and picked up his can to take a sip.

"That's handy. So why me?"

"Why not?" Damian smiled and looked deep into my eyes. I felt the pull and had to look away, fussing with my drink to avoid coming under his spell.

"Stop that. If you're serious about starting anything with me, never, ever try that mind control crap again."

Damian put down his can and touched his chest over his heart. "Would I do that?" He laughed at my expression. "Of course I would."

"Play fair with me, Damian, or there will be no play at all."

Damian leaned back, stretched his arm along the back of the couch and began to toy with my hair.

"Relax, Gloriana, of course I'll respect your wishes. I am yours to command."

Did I believe him? Maybe, maybe not, but he was my landlord so I backed off for the time being.

"Can we go down and see the shop now?" Time for a change of venue. I *did* want to see the place.

"Of course." He stood and walked to the door. "Get your keys."

Valdez stuck his head out of the bedroom. *"You going somewhere, Blondie?"*

"Just downstairs. I'll be okay with Damian."

Valdez snorted. *"You sure?"*

"Ask Blade if you don't believe me." I pulled open the door. Valdez just gave me a look and let us go.

"You don't have to listen to that dog, Gloriana." Damian had his hand on my elbow as we headed down the stairs.

"He makes me feel safe." I stopped and looked back at Damian. I decided to throw him a bone. Hunk. Interested. My landlord. Why not? "So do you."

Damian grinned. "Excellent. I'm making progress."

"Maybe." I started down the stairs again. "Tell me about this building and its occupants."

"My tenants are all special. Some nocturnals like us, others like your neighbor, shape-shifters who have a life during the day."

I stopped at the bottom of the stairs. "Your rent is ridiculously cheap. Blade isn't subsidizing me, is he?" I wouldn't put it past him. He always had his fingers in my pies. Look how he'd saddled me with Valdez.

"You pay the same rent as Lacy and everyone else here." Damian brushed my hair back behind my ear and ran his finger down my neck to touch the artery pulsing there.

"I'd hate to leave then. It's a good deal." I removed his hand and pulled open the entry door. "As long as rent is all I pay."

"Of course. Didn't I promise to behave?" He stepped aside to let me unlock the bright red door on the right side of the resident's entrance to the building.

"Not exactly." The door squeaked when I pushed it open.

"I'm sorry it's so dirty. I tried to get in a cleaning crew, but they got spooked and refused to work here."

"Spooked?"

"It's one of the reasons I got the building cheap. Years ago. It had a reputation. Some people claim it's haunted.

And I've sensed a few things." He winked. "You're lucky mortals are freaked out by it. That's why your new shop location was available."

"So how am I going to get customers in here?" Spirits. No problem for me. I had radar about such things. It would take a really malevolent spirit to scare me away. But if it was going to drive away my customers . . .

"Give it a chance. Even the cleaning crew said nothing really terrible happened while they were here. Just a few surprises. Make your shop interesting enough and customers will come. A lot of people look for haunted places. It can be a draw."

True. I stood in the middle of the shop and liked what I saw. Sure it was dirty, you could write your name on every surface in there, but it had good bones. The place had great picture windows, with discreet burglar bars behind the glass. Those were typical on a street full of warehouses that had once been part of a rough neighborhood. Now it had become trendy to refurbish the aging buildings close to downtown.

"And if this doesn't work out?"

"Full refund. I promise." Damian smiled. "I want us to stick together, we're safer that way. You'll be well protected here. Just like all my friends are."

He's hot.

The words in beautiful flowing script appeared, written on the dirty glass behind Damian's head. I blinked and they were gone. Imagination gone wild.

"It's a great space, perfect for the kind of shop I want. And Freddy says there are cameras at the entrance with alarms and a panic button in every apartment." I walked around, touching the few pieces of furniture scattered around the room.

"We must be careful." Damian just watched me, a gleam in his emerald eyes. I looked down and saw that my well-worn T-shirt hugged breasts that said "Look at us, we think you're hot, too, Damian."

"Careful. Right. A hunter with a vamp detector and a cross-wielding nut job are out to get us. I plan to be careful."

"Your shop is wired too. As is the coffee bar next door. It's run by one of the other female vampires who live here, Diana Marchand. I think you'll like her."

He used to like her. Another notch on his belt.

Different handwriting this time. Crabbed printing. The words vanished. Someone here was trying to tell me something.

I shook my head. "Diana. Fine. I'll stop by tomorrow night and introduce myself." Damian had moved closer. "A building full of vamps and . . . others. You're really into that hide in plain sight thing, aren't you?"

Honey, there ain't nothin' plain about that hunk of burning love.

I grinned. Flowing handwriting again. Obviously there were at least two spirits in here. This message didn't so much disappear as get obliterated by angry slashes.

"I believe you call it blending. We're more alike than you realize, Gloriana." Damian smiled and took my arm. "Shall we go back upstairs? I want to make sure Derek set up your television. You have cable with HBO, you know."

Watch his hands, lady.

I nodded and waved goodbye behind Damian's back before following him outside and relocking the door. Spirits. At least they definitely seemed to be on my side. I'd deal with them later.

"HBO. Great. First rule of blending is keeping up with the universe. TV is my method of choice." I headed up the stairs, sure Damian was checking out the fit of my jeans. Maybe he was a butt man. If so, he was getting an eyeful.

I unlocked my door, then stuck my head into the bedroom to let Valdez see that I was still in one piece. He lay on my bed, looking miffed. Tough. Sure, he kept me safe, but I had to have a certain amount of freedom. He turned his head away and closed his eyes.

Damian roamed around my living room, his hands in his pockets, straining the fabric over tight buns. He had a really nice build. Not muscle bound, but just powerful enough.

"Two bedrooms. One for you, one for your dog?"

"No, darling. One is for me." Florence breezed through the door and kissed Damian on both cheeks. "Did you bring us a housewarming present?"

Five

Florence and Damian. I sensed a vibe between these two. Lovers? Former lovers?

"Gloriana, you must have sex on the brain. Damian is my brother." Flo dropped her black lizard tote onto the floor. "But that is our little secret. A few other vampires know, but not many. I share this now because we are to be roomies, no?"

"Brother. Wow." I looked from one to the other. Yes, there was a resemblance. Black hair, bedroom eyes, though Damian's were a more intense green. "Why the secrecy? Most of us would love to have family still alive. Like Freddy and his mom."

"We love each other, but long ago agreed that we must have our own lives, right, *caro*?"

Damian grimaced. "You decided. I never agreed, but"— he bowed toward her—"out of respect for your strength, I gave up."

Flo clapped her hands. "A compliment. I think." She pulled off her shawl and dropped it on her tote. "You will be kind to my roomie, Damian. She's had her heart broken enough."

Damian winked at me. "Not by me. I think every person should experience a Sabatini lover at least once."

"And you've made it your mission to pleasure as many women as eternity allows." Flo had her hands on her hips.

"And you have not? Men, that is. I could name two hundred off the top of my head. And then there were the women. Lock your bedroom door, Gloriana."

"*Basta*! There were no women. But I heard a rumor about you and a very young composer in Vienna." They were toe-to-toe, eyes blazing.

"No, *cara,* that was you. What was he? Thirteen?"

"Children." I stepped between them. Now this was a new kind of sibling rivalry. It made me kind of misty-eyed. Like I was part of a family.

"I plan to love both of you."

Damian grinned.

"No, not that way, you satyr." But he was awfully cute with that wicked twinkle in his eyes.

"We'll see." He took my hand and kissed the palm, doing that fang thing again. I shivered because, sue me, it was a really erotic feeling and hit me right where I lived.

Flo smacked him on the back of his head and spat something in Italian. He got in her face and said something that must have been the worst kind of insult, because she tossed her head, gave him the Italian bird and headed for her bedroom.

"This is going to be fun." I saw Valdez poke his head out of my bedroom and give Damian the once over.

"*You ready for me to run this vampire out of here?*" My dog looked like he really wanted to have a go at it.

"I'd like to see you try." Damian showed his fangs and clenched his fists. His run-in with his sister had obviously gotten his juices flowing.

"Stop it. He's my friend, Valdez. And my dog is off limits, Damian. Hurt him and we're out of here."

Damian gave Valdez one more menacing look then seemed
to remember that he'd come here to seduce me. Maybe ripping my pet apart wouldn't exactly advance his cause.

"Pardon me, Gloriana. You are kind to take in my sister.
If she drives you insane, please don't hesitate to throw her
butt out of here."

"That's what I like to hear, brotherly love." I hooked my
arm through his and tugged him toward the door. "Just a
few hours until dawn. I've got some unpacking to do before
I can even clear my bed enough to sleep on it. I'm sure you
have people or things to do."

"You think me a savage." He speared a grim glance
toward Valdez and at Flo's closed bedroom door. When he
turned back to me, he was all charm again. "I can be. But"—
he picked up my hand again—"I can also be a lover like
you've never imagined." He pulled me out into the hall and
closed the door, then leaned me against it.

I'm easy, I admit it. A little over a week ago, Blade had
rocked my world and yet I was feeling some serious lust
here. "Are you using the vamp whammy on me again?"

"I don't need to, do I?" He put his arms around me and
pulled me against him.

Whoa. He had a growing interest in his gray pants.

"We'll be good together, Gloriana. As lovers." He leaned
down and licked my neck, just over the vein that pulsed
with the primal need all vamps feel when the urge is on them.
And, yeah, the urge was definitely in the room. My personal
basement anyway. He pressed his lips to that vein and I felt
it to my toes.

One thing I'll say for him, he didn't speak inside my
mind like Blade did. Forget Blade. I moved my head just
enough to let Damian know the biting thing was not going
to happen. Not tonight anyway. He raised his head and
looked at me, his green eyes glowing in the dim light from
the stairwell at the end of the hall.

"One kiss then?"

I ran my hands over his dark green silky shirt. It hugged his broad chest and was unbuttoned one too many. He was a *GQ* ad come to life and I wasn't about to let him go without, at least, a taste. He took my silence as a yes and swooped down.

Our lips met, explored, tasted and tested each other. It was pretty spectacular. There's something to be said for a man who'd spent centuries pleasing women all over the world. The thought hit me like a cold shower. I pushed and he stepped back.

"Not tonight, Casanova."

He grinned and bowed. "How did you know? Did Flo tell you?"

These Italians were too much. I laughed, opened my apartment door, slipped inside and then shut the door in his smiling face. Valdez turned his back on me and trotted into the bedroom. No doubt there would be a lengthy report to Blade about this.

I followed my dog and began to clear off the bed so I could go to sleep. A report that I was acting the slut in Austin. I couldn't see anything wrong with that. I put on my nightgown, retrieved my Bloody Merry and sat in bed with my current reading material. Not as riveting as the last one, *Smart Women, Stupid Choices.* Boy, I could have written that one.

This one was about running your own business. A smart choice this time. I heard Flo's door open and the tap of her high heels on the hardwood. No one had been more surprised than I was when Flo announced she was moving in and I should request a two bedroom. Yes, announced. Flo doesn't take "no" for an answer. I should ask for lessons.

I had a lot to learn from Flo and she was paying half the rent. Where she got her money, I have no idea and didn't think it was my business to ask. Now, though, I wondered if Damian supported her. Again, not my business.

She appeared at my door with her shawl draped around her neck and her tote in hand.

"What are you reading?" She plopped on the end of my bed and rubbed Valdez's ears.

I made a face. "Business stuff." I'd already offered to teach Flo to read and been set straight on the matter. She wasn't interested. Period. If I didn't like her the way she was, *ciao*. She'd said it with her usual charm. No one could stay mad at Flo. Or argue when she managed quite well on her own terms.

"You want to watch some *Sex and the City*?"

Flo was twenty-first century when it came to electronic equipment and knew her way around a DVD player. I'd turned her on to my fave show at Freddy's and she was hooked now too.

"Go ahead." I tossed my book aside. "But first I want to hear about you and Damian. Your *brother*?"

Flo shrugged. "It's a long story. Like Freddy with his mother. When Damian became vampire, I wasn't going to just turn to dust while my brother played forever." She tied her shawl around Valdez's neck and he let her. Not even a sarcastic comment. Flo did have a way with men.

"I get it. Blade's family is the same way. None of his brothers and sisters turned down the chance for immortality." I poked Valdez with my foot. "Do you need to go out before we bed down for the day?"

Valdez looked up at Flo. *"I could take a walk. What do you say, gorgeous?"*

Poor thing. When would he realize he had a dog's chance with Flo?

"Me? You want me to take you out?" Flo smiled. "Yes, I will take you. We will stop by the coffee bar downstairs and see if there is a handsome man. *Si?*" She pulled her shawl off of him and threw it around her shoulders. "And you will protect me."

"Nobody does it better." Valdez aka James Bond jumped off the bed, pulled his leash off my dresser and dropped it at Flo's feet. *"Use this. We gotta keep up appearances."*

Appearances? Hello, a dog is a dog. Valdez gave me a look that made me wonder if maybe this one wasn't. Flo fluffed her hair and wet her lips.

"How do I look, Glory?"

"Perfect, as always." Her skinny black pants and turquoise wrap top were perfect too. She had great fashion instincts. I'd invite her to work with me, but she'd made it clear that she held nothing back when she gave an opinion. Maybe not the best attribute for customer service.

"I'm surprised you're not hooked up with someone, Flo."

"Oh, I have a lover." Flo sighed as she clipped the leash onto Valdez's collar. She patted his head when he growled. "Not working out, though. He's distracted by others."

"Must have shit for brains."

"Valdez!" I'd just about spewed Bloody Merry, but I agreed with him. Flo was all that and more. Who wouldn't be satisfied with her?

"You're too kind, Glory." Flo pasted on a smile. "Yes, I read your mind still. Tomorrow I do better."

She swished out of the room, Valdez trotting at her side. My life was getting more and more interesting. I picked up my book but couldn't concentrate. Maybe a little *Sex and the City.* I headed back to the living room. "Season Four" was already in the player. But watching Carrie hook up with Big just reminded me that I was here in a cotton gown alone, sexless *in* the city. The good news was that it was by choice.

A floorboard creaked in the hall and I checked the dead bolts. Locked tight. I put my feet on the coffee table and picked up the remote again. Maybe another episode. At least my new life in Austin was shaping up to be very interesting. And the sexy Italian Casanova? Clearly a bonus.

"Hello." Time to confront my spirits and find out if they were going to be a problem. I planned to start setting things up tomorrow night, if the vibes weren't too bad down here.

My earlier encounter, if you could call it that, had seemed benign enough.

"Calling all spirits, malevolent or otherwise." I dusted off a rickety chair, sat down and waited.

"You really nailed it with Damian. Hot, but a Casanova. *So* helpful." And waited.

"Come on. Please? Haven't you been lonely here? Let me tell you about my shop. Maybe you could help me with it."

I felt the chill first. Then a woman materialized. A cowgirl. Red hat, boots and the cutest white leather outfit I'd ever seen.

"Wow! Love the threads!"

"Thanks, honey. Good thing since I seem to be stuck in them for eternity." The cowgirl looked around. "You planning to fix things up?"

"I might. If you and I can strike a deal."

"Good attitude. I was here first." She took off her hat and fluffed her gray hair. "What are you planning?"

"Vintage Vamp's Emporium." The hat went sailing across the room and vanished. I'm not afraid of ghosts. I've been part of way too many paranormal freak shows to let a ghost bother me. Shape-shifters are the worst. You try reasoning with a werewolf you just dumped.

As for ghosts, Castle Campbell had been crowded with dead ancestors. One roamed the halls carrying an ax and an enemy's head. A cowgirl was more than welcome here.

"I'm not just a cowgirl." She looked down at her fringed leather skirt. "It's okay, but not my everyday look. Just what I happened to be wearing when I went toes up."

Another mind reader? Of course.

"Whoa. Makes you want to rethink how you dress each day. I mean, what if you'd been stuck in baggy sweats and running shoes?" I looked down at my jeans and T-shirt.

"Exactly." The cowgirl looked me over. "My name's Emmie Lou Nutt."

She sighed when I giggled. I hate gigglers, but sometimes that's all that works.

"You're kidding."

"I wish. You think I wanted to be a Nutt? But Harvey Nutt was the best darn kisser in Travis County. If I had it to do over . . ." She winced and looked up. "Too late for do overs. I *get* it."

"I'm Gloriana St. Clair. Glory to my friends." I held out my hand but Emmie just looked at it.

"Look but don't touch, honey." She settled down on another rickety chair. "Now tell me about this Vintage Vamp place. I get that you're a vampire."

"True, but it's named more for my 'vamp' days. Back in the roaring twenties. I'll have vintage clothing, antiques, whatever I think will sell. I can see you've got a real sense of style."

"Thanks, honey." She got up and walked around me. "Back in my day, the only place I wore jeans was to muck out the horse stalls."

I smiled and gestured around the filthy room. "That's what I'm here to do, muck out this stall." I couldn't get a read on Emmie's age or era. The skirt hit her just at the knees.

"Would it be rude to ask when you . . . passed on?"

"Not at all. October 5, 1963. I was sixty-seven years young. I'd dressed up like this because I'd entered the peach pie contest at the Texas State Fair in Dallas. Called my entry Cowgirl Emmie's Passionate Peach Pie." She lowered her voice. "The secret's amaretto in the filling. Second place. That bitch Sheila Lee Harper stole first. I swear she was sleeping with the judge."

She glared at the ceiling. "As if my day hadn't been bad enough, Harvey drove over me pulling out of the parking lot."

"Oh, no!"

"Yep." Emmie frowned and I felt that chill again. "Harvey Nutt, don't you dare interrupt us. She's going to hear my side first."

She stood, stomped over to the window and wrote "Killer" with one finger.

"He says it was an accident. What about the rearview mirror? Did he bother to check? And we'd had a hell of a fight just that morning. The man would spend anything on a new tractor and he could *not* balance a checkbook." She underlined "Killer" three times.

"I had insurance, you know." Emmie Lou cocked her head, then looked up and made a face. "He'll be by later to tell his side. Don't listen to him."

I knew better than to take sides. "Why are you here? If you . . . passed in Dallas."

"*I* call it purgatory. This used to be a soda shop. Harvey and I met here. *Someone,*" she looked up again, "wants us to make up. When hell freezes over, Harvey!"

And she was gone.

"Wait! Are you going to be okay with this shop? Will you be trying to scare away my customers?" I smelled flowers. Roses. A pretty smell. Friendly. I took that as a yes. Interesting. And no way was I spooked.

I grabbed a broom and began to attack the dust. I felt a little sorry for Harvey, but I'd wait till I heard his side to pass judgment. For now, I had a feeling that Emmie Lou, at least, was going to like this shop.

"Everything looks great, Lacy." The store opened tonight and Lacy had been terrific the past month, working like a demon, if you'll pardon the expression. She'd scrounged up some cheap mannequins, dressed them in vintage clothes and set them in the windows. A flapper stood next to a chic fifties model in a cocktail dress complete with petticoat.

"CiCi must have arranged all the furniture and doodads again last night. They look good, don't they?" Lacy didn't look bad herself in a forties style navy and white shirtwaist and perky navy hat complete with feather.

"Great. Everything looks great." Had Freddy's mother rearranged things or were Emmie and Harvey responsible? Harvey had shown up the day after Emmie did. He'd been in plaid Western shirt and starched and pressed jeans, claiming he'd never meant to run his darling Emmie Lou down. She'd bent over to pick up a penny. Not his fault that the woman was so tight she squeaked. Emmie had appeared then and they'd vanished together, still yelling at each other.

Fortunately Lacy was as comfortable with ghosts as I was. A small vase toppled to the floor and shattered. Spirits. That was the preferred term.

"I wish they wouldn't do that." Another vase shook. "Sorry! I know. You were here first." The vase settled down.

"We *hear* you!" Lacy huffed and got the broom and dust pan.

The shop had evolved into 60 percent clothing, 40 percent everything else. When the word had gone out that I paid a fair price for vintage pieces, I'd been inundated. I wasn't the only immortal with a hoarding mentality. Fortunately, I wasn't the only one who'd decided it was time to let go of some things now too. I was proud of my store. It looked eclectic, well-organized, but crowded enough to hint at buried treasures.

I'd slipped into one of my favorite vintage outfits, a sixties lime green and orange bell-bottom jumpsuit with a zip front. I had a feeling Emmie Lou approved. Every time I looked down, my zipper was a little lower.

"Too bad CiCi can't be here when we open. She's been a big help. I had no idea she had such a head for business. As far as I know she's never even held a job."

"Could have fooled me." Lacy made a face. "She's been ordering me around like she's been a boss all her life."

"I didn't say she wasn't bossy. But she's right too often to ignore. I'm sure she'll be by later to check up on us. She, Derek and Freddy are celebrating Freddy's birthday tonight." I rolled my eyes. "Don't ask me how. Let them eat cake doesn't exactly work for us."

"Bummer." Lacy pulled a vase of beautiful blood red roses, several dozen of them, from behind the counter and set it next to the cash register. "Surprise!"

"Very nice." I moved closer. They were perfect, barely open, and the fragrance . . . Delish. The rose smell had hit me as soon as I'd walked in this evening, but I'd figured it was Emmie Lou's way of reminding us she was around and supervising.

"CiCi again? She loves fresh flowers."

"Nope. I shouldn't have read the card," Lacy handed me a small white envelope, "but you know what they say about cats and curiosity."

"I'll let you know in a minute if it's fatal this time." I pulled a card out of the envelope and recognized the bold handwriting immediately. "Success. Blade."

Blade had sent flowers? I read the card again. Apparently. All he'd sent me before was the occasional case of Bloody Merry, because he didn't trust me to keep a sufficient supply. Now red roses? Had Mara put him up to this?

"Red roses are so romantic." Lacy sighed and sniffed. "I'd like to meet this guy. Blade. Cool name."

I smiled. At times like this, Lacy made me feel every one of my four hundred plus years. She was like a teenager, crushing on every good looking guy she saw, but, as far as I knew, never hooking up with one.

"Blade likes knives, swords, daggers. And knows how to use them."

"Even cooler. Where are you keeping him?"

"Lake Charles. He has a casino there."

"Oooh. Rich *and* romantic."

"Usually not romantic." I read the card one more time. Not exactly a love note, but I'd take it. Success. Wow. This felt like a breakthrough.

Lacy wiggled her nose. "Smells like love to me, Glory. Probably *is* a breakthrough."

I'd told Lacy to stay out of my mind too many times to count in the last month. Even though she was a hard worker, I'd have to fire her if she didn't lay off. Her eyes widened and she flushed.

"Sorry, Boss. It's a habit."

I gave her a look.

"Okay, okay, a *bad* habit. If they made a patch for it, I'd be first in line."

"I don't want to waste my energy blocking you, Lacy. So just tune out. I do it all the time."

"Maybe you shouldn't—"

"And maybe *you* should." Blocking also gave me a migraine because I'd never gotten the hang of it. And if Lacy was reading this thought, she was fired. I gave her a searching look. She was smelling the roses again. *Nada.* Finally.

Tapping on the glass door. "Are you open yet?" Two women stood outside.

"Ready?"

Lacy nodded, obviously relieved to be off the hot seat.

"Okay, here goes." I took a deep breath and walked to the door. I'd think about Blade and the warm fuzzies I was feeling toward him later. Hmm. Red roses.

And Lacy? I had to admit it felt good having her here and I *had* to have a day person. She just needed time to adjust to my demands. Which were *not* unreasonable. I pasted a smile on my face. I was scared spitless.

This was big. I'd always worked for other people. Dancer, waitress, bartender—any night gig I could get. No profit, no sweat. For me anyway. Now I was totally responsible for rent, Lacy's salary and my own livelihood. This shop *had* to make it. I'd sunk all my savings into stock, fixtures and ads that I'd paid the shape-shifter in 3C to pass around in shopping center parking lots.

I flipped open the two dead bolts and threw open the door. "Welcome to Vintage Vamp's Emporium."

"The purple cocktail dress in the window. What size is it?" A blonde about my size grabbed the skirt and wouldn't let go. "Taffeta, Mel, don't you just love it?"

"Mel" was loading her arms with vintage beaded sweaters. "I want one of these in every color. They're in perfect condition. Where did you get them?"

"Here and there." I unzipped the cocktail dress. "I'm pretty sure this will fit you. The tag says size sixteen, but back in the fifties they sized things differently. Marilyn Monroe wore a twelve, but today that would be about a six. This one is about a ten to twelve in today's sizes." The truth, I swear it. And didn't I love that? I know it's just a number and retailing genius, but I *feel* smaller in a twelve.

The woman hugged the dress and followed Lacy to the dressing rooms we'd created with curtains and screens. There were no mirrors anywhere except inside those cubicles. I avoid mirrors. Nobody home, if you know what I mean.

More women pushed through the door, a man and then a couple.

"Look, honey, here's a sideboard that would be perfect in our dining room."

By the time Lacy dragged herself off to bed, we'd made enough sales to pay the rent and Lacy's salary for at least two months. I couldn't believe that at two in the morning I still had a customer hip deep in Victorian night rails, including those sexless sacks Flo had insisted I sell. The bells on the front door tinkled. Another customer?

This one was a man, his hair in spikes. He wore a long black coat and, what a cliché, black lipstick. A Goth and potential groupie. I'd had groupies before and they can be a pain, begging you to bite them, turning every night into

Halloween with their silly costumes. Sure, I'd had mortal friends in Vegas, but they'd thought I was one of them. I hadn't let a mortal in on my vamp self in *years*.

"Where are the vamps?"

"What kind of vamps are you looking for?" I gestured toward the mannequin in the window. The first flapper dress, my favorite black, had sold in an hour. This one was blue and had cool beaded fringe. I kind of hated to see it go. I'd had a lot of fun dancing in that dress.

Chicago in the twenties. Al Capone and I had been on and Blade and I had been off. Then I found out what old Al did for a living. Time for the vamp vanishing act. I'd headed to New York, a great place to get lost, if you know what I mean.

"Not that kind of vamp." The man looked pale and swayed, obviously about to faint. I hustled him into a chair.

"Are you all right?"

"I don't know. I had an . . . encounter a while ago." He looked toward the woman holding up a lace-trimmed corset, waiting until she headed into a dressing room. He leaned toward me. "A vampire." He drew out the word like the narrator in a bad horror movie.

"You're kidding. What are you on, dude?"

"Nothing. Well, maybe a little weed. But look!" He stroked his neck where I could see two bright red marks. "He bit me right here. And sucked my blood. It was amazing."

"Looks like mosquito bites to me. Where'd you score that weed?" Yeah, play the diminished capacity card. Make him wonder if he'd dreamed the whole thing. I grabbed a bottle of water from a bucket full of ice Lacy had set on the counter for our grand opening and twisted off the top.

"Drink." I looked deep into his eyes. It had been a while since I'd used the vamp whammy, but I still had him under in less time than you could say "Holy crap." What kind of irresponsible vamp was out there doing the bite and run? Left marks, didn't bother to erase memory.

And this vamp groupie wannabe was just the type to brag about his "encounter." He was already looking for his next one here. All it took was a hint to the wrong person and we'd have what amounted to a vampire witch hunt.

The man's eyes were glazed. "Keep drinking." He gulped the cold water. I pressed my fingers against his fang marks until his skin was unblemished again.

"Stop. Rest. You'll feel better in a moment."

Damn it. Some vamp was either suicidal or really, really stupid.

Six

I pulled my cell phone out of my pocket. I couldn't call Freddy, his birthday and all, so I hit the speed dial for Damian. He'd put the number in himself when he'd stopped by last night to check out the store. And insisted I call him if I had any problems. I glanced at the man staring at his empty water bottle. Definitely a problem.

"*Cara*, I knew you'd weaken. You need me." His voice was hot sex on a cold night. *Not now, Glory.*

"Can you come over here? Now? I'm still at the shop."

"What's wrong?" Now he was all business.

"Just get over here. Fast." I hit end and slipped the phone back into my pocket. I rang up a corset and a night rail for my customer.

"What's with him?" She stowed her credit card in her wallet and nodded toward my zombie.

"Bad weed. I called someone to take him home."

"What an idiot. Him, not you, honey." She grabbed her bag and headed toward the door. "These Goths." She laughed. "They actually believe in vampires and nonsense like that."

"Go figure." I showed her out the door and turned the locks. Nonsense. I wasn't insulted. It was just proof positive that I was blending successfully. I flipped the sign from Open to Closed then hurried back to the idiot's side. He sat motionless just like I'd left him. If I didn't snap him out of it, he would sit like that for hours. Cool, huh?

Kick the weirdo out. Harvey wrote on my spotless counter. He'd been doing that a lot lately. Trying to protect me. Fortunately he didn't leave smudges.

"I'm taking care of it, Harvey." I lifted the man's chin. "Look at me." I used my low, irresistible voice and he raised his eyes to mine. "What's your name?"

"Raymond Whitelaw."

"Raymond, tell me what the vampire looked like."

Ray touched his throat. "Vampire. Yes. Tall."

"Man or woman?"

"Man. Strong."

A tall man. Swell, that only fit about twenty vamps in the Austin area that I knew of.

"Hair color?"

"Light. Pretty hair. Like snow."

Now we were getting somewhere. A white haired vamp. I'd known a few and they were certainly easy to spot. But I hadn't met one here in Austin.

"You remember anything else about him, Raymond?" I kept my voice steady and calm. Ray just kept holding his empty bottle. "Think hard."

"He prayed." Ray shook his head. "Weird. Called God and Jesus. Vampires like Satan. *I* like Satan."

I felt rage boil up in me and it was all I could do not to rip Ray's throat out and toss him into a dumpster somewhere. Vamps do have a primitive side, I admit it. And when we're riled . . . Don't make a vamp mad, that's what I'm saying.

I paced the store until I'd cooled down enough to speak. Satan worshiper. Excuse me, but just because I live forever and can drink blood doesn't mean I'm a raving demon from hell. I was raised in a very religious household. Scary religious. And you don't just get over that. When I fell for an actor, my folks considered me a lost cause. After years of soul searching, I'm pretty sure I answer to a higher power, not a lower one.

I took Ray's water bottle and held his hand. He'd unbuttoned his coat and I could see a student ID clipped to his belt. What was he studying? Dumbass 101?

"Raymond, you're going to go home now. You're not going to remember anything about this night. But you *are* going to remember that vampires are good and kind. Vampires are God-fearing creatures, not demons from hell. Do you hear me, Raymond?"

Ray nodded.

"And, Raymond," I couldn't resist, more my parents' child than I'd ever admitted to *them.* "You will love God, not Satan. Satan is bad. God loves you. And," okay, I had my own agenda, "He hates black lipstick."

Ray nodded. "God loves me. Hates black lipstick." He rubbed his mouth on his black coat sleeve. He looked a fool with black smears on his face and I couldn't care less.

"Yes. Good man." I pulled him to his feet and led him to the door. I looked through the glass and saw Damian standing there. I threw the dead bolts and opened the door.

"Who's this?" My suave sophisticated seducer looked ready to tear the man's head off. So Damian had his own primitive streak. Good to know.

"Tell you in a minute." I led Raymond to the curb. "Where's your car, Raymond?"

"Don't have one. Rode the bus."

I glanced at my watch. "Oh, hell, the buses aren't going to be running this time of night. Will you take him home, Damian?" The vamp-mobile was sitting at the curb, the motor still running.

"I'll take him home if you'll come with us."

I looked up and down the street. No potential customers on the sidewalk, though the coffee bar next door had a few customers taking advantage of the Wi-Fi connections.

My first night and I had to close. Well, maybe I didn't *have* to. But I was tired, my feet ached and Damian had ridden to my rescue without question. If he wanted my company, I wasn't going to argue. Damian loaded Ray into the backseat. I locked up, stuck my keys in my pocket and settled in while Ray told Damian his address.

"He's still in a daze. I had to put him under."

"I can see that. What happened?"

I told him as he drove through the nearly deserted streets. Ten minutes later, we pulled up in front of a ratty looking rooming house for students. Damian dragged Ray out of the car, looked into his eyes, ordered him to go to bed and sleep until morning, then let him go.

"A white haired vampire. I have known a few, but none of them would have pulled a stunt like this. And none of them are in Austin that I know of." Damian looked at me, his admiration right there for me to see. "You handled this very well."

"Thank you." I basked in his approval but didn't *need* it. I was feeling pretty good about myself. Successful shop, calm in a crisis and with a handsome vamp at my beck and call. I wouldn't have had to call him at all if I'd thought about it.

Damned wimpy female mind-set. I'd worked really hard to cure myself, but slipped occasionally. Like tonight. I started to apologize for bothering him, when Damian put a finger over my lips.

"Don't say it. I'm happy to help you. And we're sticking together, remember? The man was in no shape to drive even if he'd had a car."

True. So maybe I wasn't such a wimp. Damian wore a black shirt tonight. Silky again. Not that I planned to touch it.

"We'd better spread the word that a white-haired vamp is risking all of us. He has to be stopped." Maybe my shop name hadn't been such a great idea. Ray had come straight to me looking for a vampire. Not exactly blending.

"Quit worrying, Gloriana. The vampire community here is tight. We'll find him and straighten him out." Damian frowned and put the car in gear. "If he wants to stay in Austin, he's got to play by our rules."

"Good." I felt a little better. New place, new friends. You never knew what you were getting into when you relocated. The Austin vamps seemed to have it together.

"I don't know what to make of the praying. Most vampires are afraid God has turned his back on them." Damian smiled and touched my cheek. "Not you and me, of course. How could God not love us?"

His smile was charming and I couldn't argue with his logic.

"Thank you, Damian. I hope I didn't interrupt anything tonight."

"Not anything important. Busy night?"

"Yes. Wonderfully busy. We're a hit." I kicked off my shoes and wiggled my toes. "It's hard work though. And I'm not sure I'll do enough business between now and dawn to justify staying open twenty-four hours."

"Time will tell. Give it a while for word to spread. Your shop is interesting. And there are many night creatures looking for a place to shop. Not just vampires, but mortals who work a night shift." He turned a corner and headed up a hill.

"Thank you. And you're right. There are lots of night owls, mortal and otherwise. I'm impatient, I guess. Always did like instant gratification."

Damian's eyes lit up. "My philosophy exactly. How would you handle a detour before I take you back to the store?"

"Detour?" I looked down to where he held my hand. Boy, he was smooth. Instant gratification. Was it my imagination or did everything he said or did seem to be about sex? Not that I was complaining. He turned up the winding street on Castle Hill.

"I think it's time I show you my coffin."

I laughed and brushed at my hair blowing in the cool night air. "You've just reinvented the come-on."

He grinned as he pulled into the curved driveway and parked in front of the heavy wooden front door. "Is it working? Will you come on?"

He was out of the car and opening my door before I could decide. The last time I'd been here, Blade and I had made love. Blade had sent red roses tonight.

"Are you trying to kill this?" Damian pulled me out of the car and looked down at me.

Of course he'd read my mind. He toyed with the tab on my zipper. It was low enough to show an inch of cleavage, thanks to Emmie Lou.

"There is no *this*. And I haven't killed anything in centuries." I glanced at the castle. Grand stone entry flanked by gargoyles. "I'm not staying long, but I *would* like to see this coffin I've heard about."

"It's a start." Damian pulled me toward the door.

"Wait! My shoes."

"You won't need them." He swung me up and into his arms.

"Are you crazy? I'm no featherweight, Damian."

He strode easily up the steps, reminding me that he had vamp strength. So did I, but for now I was content to relax and let him show off.

"You weigh nothing, less than a feather."

I hugged his neck. This was fun. I felt like a bride being carried over the threshold as he juggled me to open the front door. Hold it. Not a wedding night. Just looking at his bed, er, coffin.

"You have a really cool place." Which was certainly true if you were into castles. Which I was, as long as they had modern conveniences and were within minutes of a shopping mall like this one was.

"You'll have to come back some night and take the full tour when you have more time. I know you're anxious to get back to your shop."

Giving himself an out if I called a halt to things? Good. He saved his pride and I had an unwimpy excuse for rushing out of here if things got too intense.

"The shop. Yes, I'm anxious." I felt his arms cradling me and smiled. Were we really having this conversation while he held me like this? "But not *too* anxious."

"Excellent." Damian grinned and headed up the wide stone staircase. "Come to my coffin, pretty one." He growled and showed his fangs.

He played up the vamp thing like this was all a game. Which it had to be. It had been six weeks, but Damian knew I'd been remembering my last visit here. With Blade. A man would have to be a fool to compete with Jeremy Blade.

"I don't just compete, I win, Gloriana." He kicked open a door at the end of a long hall.

I'd let that comment go for now. Damian the mind reader would soon realize that I wasn't the prize in a vamp tug-of-war. Forget games. Hello, coffin. Funeral directors would have wept at its beauty. Mahogany. Brass fittings. King-sized.

"That is the most amazing bed I've ever seen." The bed slash coffin dominated the large room. A fat mattress covered with white satin sheets gleamed in the candlelight from sconces set in niches about the room. At least six pillows were propped up against the headboard and a wine, or should I say blood, red velvet comforter was folded neatly across the foot of the bed.

Damian strode into the room. "Here's the best part." He dropped me, no, threw me onto the bed. I sank into sheer, unadulterated soft-as-a-cloud bliss.

"I *love* this bed." I threw back my arms and looked up. Gilt cherubs flew along the edge of a wooden canopy lined with more white satin. A fancy coffin lid. "That thing's not going to close on me is it?"

"Not unless I press this button." He reached for the headboard.

I sat up. "You wouldn't—"

Damian laughed and kicked off his shoes. "Just kidding. Relax. Lie back." He settled on the bed beside me and we lay there shoulder to shoulder. "Cool, isn't it?"

The bed, yes. And the man? Not cool. Hot. Candlelight flickered over his Roman nose and strong chin, shadowed by a slight beard. Masculine. Powerful. Very sexy.

I rolled onto my side and propped my head on my hand, giving him a good view of cleavage if he'd just check it out. He checked and grinned. And reached for the tab again. The sound of that old metal zipper riding down my body was a total turn on. Should I stop him? He looked up, his eyes gleaming, daring me to stop him as he inched the zipper lower.

A dare? I reached for his shirt and unbuttoned it just as slowly as he was unzipping me. He had a beautiful chest, smooth, muscular. He breathed deeply as I skimmed my hands over him, stopping just short of his waist band and the bulge below it. I knew a point of no return when I saw it.

If I did this it would be just sex. A release. Some of that instant gratification we were both supposed to be into. Because I didn't know Damian well enough to make it into anything more.

"Quit thinking." Damian sat up and brushed my hair back from my forehead, reminding me that I was a windblown wreck. A horny windblown wreck.

"I can't." My mind was racing. Did Damian share his sister's appreciation of a curvy woman? I felt cool air on my breasts above my lacy low cut double *D* push-up bra. Damian's warm hand brushed down my body to my new thong panties. Flo had dared me to wear them after she'd brought home seven pairs in seven different pretty colors and thrown them on my bed. I loved them. They made me feel free and very sexy. And they were skimpy enough to distract from my tummy. I sucked it in anyway.

"You *are* very sexy. And I love voluptuous women. No skinny sticks for me." He brushed his fingers over the swells of my breasts. "I like . . . curves." He pushed open the jumpsuit. "Beautiful."

"Wait a minute." I wracked my brain. I'd had reasons why this wasn't a good idea. But his look of frank appreciation made them fly right out of my head. Maybe there was something to be said for an ancient male. Skinny used to be a sign of poverty. To look at me, you'd think I'd been a bloody millionaire.

I sighed as he ran his hands over me, murmuring compliments. I couldn't read his mind, but men tend to block everybody at first. I didn't really expect that kind of intimacy so soon. Wait. This *was* soon. I should slow things down. Our first date. Date? Who was I kidding? *I'd* called *him*.

"Relax, Gloriana. Don't make this too complicated. We'll have fun. Nothing more."

Nothing more. Fine. I wasn't ready for more. And I was a with-it happening twenty-first century kind of vamp. A woman who took her pleasure where she found it. Full speed ahead then.

"No need to rush, Gloriana." Damian leaned down to skim his tongue along the edge of my bra. "I love your breasts. Let me see all of them."

He found the front clasp of my bra and popped it open. My own vamp magic. Centuries old boobs still perky in my twenty-four-year-old body. The real deal and definitely one of my "on" buttons, if you know what I mean.

Damian growled and leaned down to kiss one nipple, sucking it into his mouth and then lightly dragging his fangs back and forth across it. Pleasure jolted through me. There's nothing like sex with a mind reader. I could draw him a mental road map to my personal nirvana. Hmm. Which should it be? The scenic route or a more direct—

"Oh. My. God." I dug my fingers into his thick hair and held on. Damian blew on my damp nipple, then moved to the other one. Oh, yes. Good move. Perfect move. Uh huh. Now do the fang thing again. If I could just catch my breath, I'd tell Damian what an incredible lover he was.

A phone rang. *Phantom of the Opera.* My phone. In my pocket. I pulled it out and threw it across the room.

"Mmm. Good choice." Damian didn't even bother to look up.

"Damian." His clever mouth abandoned my breasts to explore my stomach. His tongue dipped into my navel. Why bother holding my tummy in when he obviously loved it? He'd discovered my almost-panties and plucked the elastic with his fangs. I shivered. Another point of no return. Was I ready for this?

"I'll *make* you ready." Damian sat up and shrugged off his shirt, then pulled me close until my breasts pressed against his chest. My bones were melting. Then he kissed me and his kiss was just as delicious as I remembered. No, better. The friction of his chest against mine, the press of his arousal between my legs. I moved against him. Better and better. Damian stripped off my jumpsuit and tossed it aside.

"Answer me, Gloriana."

No! Not now.

"Beautiful." Damian stroked my stomach, then hooked his fingers on either side of my thong and eased it down, kissing a path down one leg. I lifted my foot, quivering when his tongue lightly traced my arch. I'm not ticklish, thank God, but if he wanted to work his way up . . .

He grinned and nipped at my toes. "On my way, *cara.*"

"Answer me or I will come to you."

"Stop it! Leave me the hell alone."

Damian sat up, my hot pink thong dangling from his wrist.

"What? Have you changed your mind?"

"*Where are you?*"

"I'm not answering. Go. Away." I couldn't believe Blade would *pursue* me like this.

Damian threw the thong across the room. "Son of a bitch! I hear him. What is he? Your keeper?" He looked around as if he expected Blade to materialize at the foot of the bed. Which was a possibility. Blade had a built-in homing device that could zap him right to my side no matter where I was. Damian was no more furious than I was.

"He *thinks* he's my keeper. But he definitely is *not*." But he was a real mood killer. "Get out of my head. Right now, Jerry. I'm safe. That's all you need to know."

"Gloriana has a new protector now, Blade."

Thank God Blade was in *my* head and could only hear my voice. All I needed was two possessive vamps duking it out over yours truly. But where did Damian get off declaring himself my protector? This had started as a quickie. No strings.

"If you show up here, Jerry. We're through. No more Valdez. *Nada*. Read my mind. I *mean* it." I gave Damian a blistering look as I climbed out of bed to retrieve my bra and panties. "I don't need a protector, Damian. I can protect myself."

I stepped into my jumpsuit, zipped it up and waited. Probed my mind. Blade was gone. When I picked up my phone I could see that he'd left a message. Later. Maybe never.

"That was a first." Damian lay back on the satin sheets. He must have been an outdoor man in his mortal life, because he had a natural tan. "I'm not adverse to a little *ménage à trois*, but I prefer another woman in bed with me, not a hairy Scot."

"You would." I was up to here with men, no matter how gorgeous and sexy they were. I ignored my still sizzling body parts. What had I been thinking? No question what was on Damian's mind. He was obviously still very aroused.

"Take me back to the shop."

"What did I do?" Damian rolled out of bed, picked up his shirt and stepped into his Italian loafers.

"It's not you, it's me." I shook my head. "Cancel that. Yes, it's you. That whole protector thing." I felt his hand on my back and ignored it. I was not falling under his spell again. Not until I had my own issues resolved. Which might be never. His hand moved lower and I whirled around and shoved him away.

Of course he wasn't about to just give up. He was a man, wasn't he? And he'd almost scored a minute ago.

"I misspoke, Gloriana. I meant partner, not protector." He captured my hand and pressed it to his chest. "Come back to bed. We'll do whatever you want."

Whatever I want? Hoo boy. Before you could say Casanova Freaking Sabatini, he had my zipper down and his hands on my breasts. He stared at me, willing me . . .

"Bastard!" I ripped his hands off of me and jumped back. "Don't you dare try the vamp whammy on me."

"You wanted me, Gloriana. I didn't need a 'whammy' as you call it." He stepped closer. "You *still* want me."

I would not back away. "Forget it, Damian. That ship has sailed." Not tempted. Not tempted.

"Don't let Blade do this to you, *cara*. To *us*." He pulled me into his arms and nuzzled my neck. "I can smell your desire. For me, not that Scottish son of a bitch."

And I could smell Damian's desire. But it was the scent of my blood getting him steamed up.

"You want to feed? Are you insane? Tonight is a no go, Damian."

"You're sure?" Damian held me tight and slid his fangs into my neck. He sipped me like I was a fine wine. His thought, not mine. He was in my head. Like Blade had been.

I shoved and he released me, wiping his mouth on the back of his hand. His grin was unrepentant. I slapped him with all my strength and actually rocked him back on his heels.

"Beast!"

"Aren't we all? Come back to bed, give me five minutes and I'll show you how a beast makes love. There's a lot to be said for letting our animals out of their cages." Damian rubbed his cheek, dark with his late night stubble.

"You think I should trade a Scottish son of a bitch for an Italian one? I don't think so. And I am *not* a beast." Except for wanting to pound him until he cried for his mommy. He stepped back, out of reach. Good move.

"That's some right arm you've got. Calm down, Glory."

I flipped open my phone. "I'm calling a cab."

"Cabs don't like to come here. Especially not this late." He bared his fangs, still stained with my blood. "Vampires, you know."

"Not cute, Damian." I stomped out of the room and down the stairs. The marble felt cold on my bare feet. I'd need my sandals if I was going to walk home.

"I'll take you home." Of course he'd followed me. "You're not walking. Too far and you'll get lost. You don't know Austin yet. And it's dangerous out there."

"Dangerous? I'm a blood-sucking freaking vampire, Damian." But I would take a ride. I had no idea how to get home from here. I didn't say anything. No point since Damian was reading my mind anyway. I stomped out to the car and got in. He wasn't completely stupid with lust because he started the car and drove me back to the shop in silence. He parked and put his hand on mine when I reached for the door handle.

"Don't be mad at me, *cara*. I act the beast because you're such a desirable woman." He pulled my hand to his mouth.

I swear, if he'd dragged a fang across it, I would have punched him right in his Roman nose. He raised his head.

"A man would have to be made of stone or like Frederick to not make a move on you."

"So this was *my* fault?" I jerked my hand from his and opened the car door. "Fine. I'm irresistible so you make a move. But biting when I said no, that's a violation of the vamp code, Damian. Unforgivable."

"You said no, but you whispered yes, in your mind."

"Stay the hell away from me and my mind." I slammed the car door. Oh, great. The sign now said Open and I could see movement inside. Lacy wasn't supposed to come in until six-thirty but maybe she'd come in early. I breathed and tried to calm down.

My insides were still quivering because, SOB or not, Damian knew how to rev me up. His car still idled at the curb and I could feel him watching me. He knew better than to speak in my mind, but he was probably reading it.

If I didn't go inside in exactly three seconds, he'd probably take another shot. No. I hated him. Hated Blade. Hated men in general. Let him read that. The bells tinkled as I stepped inside.

Seven

"Enjoy your night, Gloriana?" CiCi was counting out change to a customer in front of the register. The woman had a bulging bag and glanced at me, then did a double take.

"I'd say she did." The woman stuffed her change into her Louis Vuitton bag and winked before heading toward the door. "Whisker burn and love bites. And that was a good-looking man in that convertible."

"He's gay. Tonight he was experimenting with hetero-sexuality. The experiment failed." Take that, Damian! He gunned the vamp-mobile's motor, tires squealing as he drove away.

"I don't think so." The woman laughed. "But you're ob-viously pissed at him. Naughty boy?"

"Nasty, not naughty." I ran a hand over my hair and pulled up my collar. Of course Damian hadn't erased the bites. He'd been proud of them. Jerk.

"This is a great shop, by the way. Austin needed a quality vintage-clothing store. And open all night. I'm an ER doc-tor and just got off duty. Too wired to sleep, so this is prime shopping time for me." The woman waved and headed out the door.

"This great shop was closed when I dropped by earlier, Gloriana. That woman just spent three hundred dollars and we almost missed the sale. Thank God she didn't want to use her credit card. I have no idea how to do those, you know." CiCi slammed the register shut. "I thought we were to be open twenty-four hours."

We'd almost missed the sale? Obviously CiCi had decided she was my partner and maybe she deserved to be, the way she'd helped me set up. But while I was grateful to her, I was sole proprietor here. It said so on the papers Freddy's lawyer had filed for me.

"I had an emergency. I had to leave." I looked down a little late to make sure I was zipped high enough for decency.

"An emergency." CiCi plucked a red rose from the vase and waved it toward the door. "I would say so. If nasty, naughty Damian Sabatini crooked his, um, finger at me, I'd certainly never look back."

Wow. I sat down in the nearest chair. This was an interesting development. CiCi had the hots for Damian. Well, who didn't? Not Glory St. Clair, not after the past hour.

"You want Damian? He's all yours."

"No. Obviously he wants you whether you want him or not. But I'm thinking it's been a while since I've taken a lover." CiCi held the rose to her nose and sighed. "Too long. I will remedy that immediately."

A horn honked. "Freddy's here. To pick me up. You'll be all right until Lacy gets here?"

I jumped up and hugged CiCi. "Thanks for skipping the lecture and reopening the shop. I really did have an emergency. A man came in with fang marks babbling about a white-haired vamp who said prayers the entire time he was feeding. The vamp didn't even bother to erase the marks, much less the man's memory. Damian helped me take him home."

"A white-haired vampire. Yes, I know such a one. A very handsome one, in fact. But in Austin? This is news to me." CiCi walked to the door and waved at Freddy. "I'll tell Frederick about this. We must find this vampire and educate him on how we do things here. We've been able to enjoy our life because we don't call attention to ourselves." CiCi smiled and patted my cheek. "A lesson you learned long ago."

"Yes. It's a basic survival skill."

"But what is the point of surviving if you are lonely and miserable?" CiCi gave me a searching look. "Give Damian a chance to make you happy."

"I make myself happy. I'm not lonely *or* miserable. I have this shop and my friends." I grabbed the vase full of roses. "You want these? Otherwise they're going in the Dumpster out back."

"Oh, my. You have had a busy evening. Of course I read the card that came with these." CiCi sniffed, then picked up the vase. "Mmm. These are divine. But obviously Jeremiah is also on your 'I hate men' list." She headed to the door. "These will look wonderful on my dining room table."

I held open the door and waved at Freddy. "Did you see how much we sold tonight?"

CiCi laughed. "Yes, indeed. That's why I couldn't be too mad at you for leaving. You've sold clothes, my sideboard, and the customer that just left bought a piece of Sabino glass I'd consigned. We're rich!"

As if CiCi hadn't already been rolling in dough. But I agreed that it was pretty special to know you've made it yourself. Lacy bounded down the stairs and out the entrance of the apartment part of the building just as CiCi got into the car.

We both watched Freddy drive off. Lacy nodded toward the building.

"You'd better get upstairs. That mutt of yours is going nuts worrying about you. He barked for hours. Ruined my beauty sleep." She ran a hand over her hair.

"You look great, as usual." She was sticking with a vintage look. A seventies tie-dyed T-shirt and bell-bottom pants today.

"Thanks. But, much as I hate to say it, I think we're going to have to let fur face come down to the shop with you from now on."

Fur face had used his Glory radar, ratting me out to Blade when I left the shop. Blade would never have hunted me down at Damian's otherwise. Damn it. This was intolerable. I hadn't bothered to listen to my voice mail and wasn't sure I ever would. The sky was getting lighter, I felt like the living dead and I still had to walk Valdez.

"Flo walked him." Lacy made a face. "Oops. Sorry. I don't *want* to read your mind, it just happens. Now go up to bed. You look exhausted. And I think you're getting a rash." Lacy patted my shoulder.

I rubbed my cheeks, still tender from Damian's kisses. My breasts had the same "rash." I'd kept my collar up so at least Lacy hadn't spotted those marks. But I was a mess, from wild hair to aching toes.

"I *am* tired. But the register . . ."

Lacy pushed me toward the resident entrance. "I'll count the receipts for the night and lock them in the safe. We should start each morning with just a small amount of cash on hand."

"Thank you." I hugged her. "You did great last night. I'm thinking of adding a commission to your pay. If I don't have to fire you, that is."

"You won't. I promise. A commission would be fantastic." Lacy punched in the code on the keypad next to the door. "I know I persuaded you to lock up the mutt last night, but I'm serious. Flo was carrying on about something bad that happened tonight. Maybe Valdez should be here with you."

Something bad. I hurried up the stairs, making a mental list of vampires I'd met. Flo was all right, upstairs with Valdez. I'd just seen Freddy, CiCi and Damian. Damian had infuriated me, but vamps stick together. If bad things were happening, we needed to protect ourselves and figure out how to stop them.

Flo flung open our door before I got down the hallway.

"Where have you been? When I came home and saw the store was closed, I worried."

"A little emergency. I'll tell you about it later. I'm fine." I sat on the love seat and kicked off my shoes. Valdez just stared at me, his head on his paws. He was pouting next to the television which was off for a change. Flo must really be upset.

"I'm sorry I worried you. What's this trouble Lacy mentioned?"

Flo shuddered and sat across from me in one of the club chairs she'd added to the décor. My own furnishings were pretty sparse, especially after I'd decided to sell most of them.

"I was with my lover." She held up her hand when Valdez growled. "None of your business, *signor.*" She kicked off her high-heeled pumps. "I broke it off with him. I'm sick of sneaking around. I don't know why he doesn't want anyone to know he's in town. Everyone would welcome him." She looked at me for confirmation.

"Right. I'm sorry. Is that all?"

Flo sat up straight. "You think *that* is my trouble?" She snapped her fingers. "Lovers are nothing to me. One goes, another appears. He did *not* break my heart, Glory."

"Fine. So what's your trouble?"

"Tell her, green eyes. Maybe she'll get the message that I ain't stayin' locked up in this apartment another night."

Green eyes nodded. "I saw the hunter. Westwood."

"Here? In Austin? Does Blade know?" I remembered my cell phone in my pocket. Of course Blade knew. Maybe he'd actually had a reason to call me, besides to ruin my sex life.

"He's on his way as soon as he wraps up some business."

Why was I not surprised? But this wasn't about me now. Blade would want to take out Westwood himself. For Mac.

Valdez stood and stretched. *"It's almost daylight, ladies. Let's hit the hay."*

"Just a minute." I saw Flo staring at her feet as if considering whether to keep her toenails scarlet or go for pink. "Flo, look at me."

She looked up. "Pink, I think. See? You read my mind, I don't care."

"Forget that. How do you know it was Westwood? He's pretty ordinary." I picked up the photo we'd printed from the Internet. Every vamp in Austin had one.

"I wouldn't have recognized him, except he took a shot at me."

"Oh, my God!" I rushed to her side and pulled her up to give her a hug and look her over. "Are you all right? Did he hit you anywhere?"

"I saw him notch that arrow and, poof, I was a beautiful black bird, flying away into the night. The arrow hit a tree behind me."

"What the hell were you doin' out by yourself?" Valdez walked up to us and sat at her feet. *"It ain't safe."*

"You're sweet." Flo patted his head. "But I'm fine. Just worried about others who"—she gave me a look—"are afraid to shape-shift. He's an excellent shot, Glory. If I hadn't flown out of there, he'd have my fangs right now." She shuddered. "Such tacky jewelry. What is the man thinking?"

"All men are beasts. That's my new philosophy and Westwood proves the point." I pulled my phone out of my pocket. Should I listen to Blade's message? Not now. I was dead, well almost. The sky was getting lighter outside and I needed my bed and the blackout drapes in my bedroom.

I checked the deadbolts. "Let's go to bed. We'll talk about this tomorrow." I looked down at Valdez. "You ready?"

"I got my orders. I ain't leavin' your side until Blade gets here."

"Fine." I would deal with that macho mind-set later. I hugged Flo again. "I'm glad you got away from him. Valdez is right about one thing, you shouldn't go out alone after this. Westwood knows what you look like now."

"I'll be careful." Flo patted my back. When she released me, she had a puzzled look on her face.

"Sleep well." I headed for my room.

"Wait!" Flo hurried after me.

Now what? I was too tired to think. I unzipped my jumpsuit and dropped it on the floor.

"I knew it! I smelled . . . Damian. You've been with my brother." She grabbed my chin. "Bastard! Look at you. Mauled. Couldn't he bother to shave?" Then she saw my neck.

"You let him taste you?"

Valdez growled and I shoved him into the living room and slammed the door. Maybe he could hear through it, but I didn't need a third party observer right now.

"I didn't *let* him do anything, Flo. He forced me." I heard Valdez's enraged barking. Great, now Blade would know. I rubbed the marks. I should have erased them immediately, but they'd be gone when I woke anyway.

Flo muttered something in Italian. "I hope you ripped off his man part and stuffed it down his throat."

Now there was a visual to savor. "I should have. I certainly felt like it. Unfortunately it would probably grow back." God, did we have to go into this tonight? "I handled it, him, Flo. Please don't get involved in this, okay?"

"How can I not? My brother attacks my roomie?" She swept her gaze over me. "You wear a thong for him. Pah! He deserves granny pants and one of your sexless sacks."

"I didn't wear this for him. I wore it for *me*. And my sacks are all downstairs, for sale." Unfortunately. I could have really enjoyed vegging out in something sexless right now. Instead, I rummaged in my dresser and pulled out a blue lace-trimmed nightie. "You staying for the show or heading to bed?"

Flo sighed. "Bed. This has been a horrible night. I am almost killed. My lover is a jerk. And my brother . . ." More

Italian. "You can't expect me not to say anything, Glory. I would like to grind his fangs into dust. Let him try drinking Bloody Merry the rest of his days through a straw. Biting my roomie." Muttering in Italian, she pulled open the door and slammed it behind her.

Maybe she'd cool off by evening. I dropped my underwear into a laundry basket and pulled on the gown. Valdez scratched at the door and I let him in before I turned out the light. I could tell he wanted to lecture me, but I sent him a stern mental message to just shut up and go to sleep.

I lay down then felt the bed shake as Valdez jumped up to settle next to my feet. I usually like my bed, but it was a slab compared to Damian's. What a hell of a thought to go to sleep on.

World War III had broken out in my living room. Barking. Shouting in at least three languages. Would anyone notice if I just stayed in bed with the covers over my head for, say, the next year?

But I was anxious to get down to the shop to count yesterday's receipts. And how had we done during the day today? I pulled on another vintage outfit and took plenty of time with my makeup. I used to get help with my stage makeup, but for every day I do it by feel. After decades of practice, I've got it down to a science. I added a little contouring to give me the illusion of cheekbones, then reluctantly opened my bedroom door.

Silence. All nations had either declared a cease fire or they'd killed each other. No such luck. Flo had collapsed on the love seat, her head thrown back as she stared at the ceiling. Blade glowered near the front door, in his fighting stance and wearing full Clan Campbell regalia. Damian lounged in one of the club chairs until he saw me in the doorway. He leaped to his feet and winked. Valdez trotted up to me representing Fido-land. He and Jerry stared at me as if I'd suddenly sprouted horns and a tail.

"What?" I strolled into the kitchen and pulled a Bloody Merry out of the refrigerator. This silence was even worse than the yelling had been.

"Damian brought your keys, Gloriana." Blade fingered his broadsword. "He claims you left them in his bed."

Damian grinned, obviously quite happy to drive Blade insane. And what was wrong with that, now that I thought about it?

I yawned. "Is that where I left them?"

Valdez woofed. *"You got a death wish, Blondie? Anybody,"* he glanced at Damian—*"anybody could have gotten hold of those keys. Besides, you never shoulda left me up here."*

I reached down to rub his ears. "Sorry, pup. When you're right, you're right. From now on, you can stay in the shop with me."

"I should hope so. None of us need to take foolish chances." Flo had finally found her voice. For a woman who usually chattered nonstop, she was being very subdued now that the shouting match had stopped.

"How are you feeling?" I moved closer and put my arm around her. "You look like hell."

"Compliments. That's all I needed."

To my horror, Flo welled up and fled to her bedroom. She slammed the door on a sob.

"Whoa. Was it something I said?" I looked at Damian. He shrugged again.

"I don't know what her problem is. She and Blade were busy yelling at me about those keys." He strolled over as if to put an arm around me. I gave him a look that stopped him in his tracks. He threw up his hands. "Women!"

"It's not just women, Damian. Flo's obviously still upset about last night." Could Damian really not know about his sister's near miss?

"Why?" Damian smiled at me. "Is my sister saying I shouldn't date her roommate? You won't listen to her, will you, *cara*?"

"You're not the center of the universe, Sabatini. This isn't about you. Florence has good reason to be upset." Blade didn't seem surprised by the brother-sister thing. Of course he'd probably been reading minds right and left.

Damian looked at me. "All I know about is Gloriana's encounter."

"What encounter?" Blade grabbed my arms and made me face him.

I wondered if I could sharpen the wooden spoon I'd seen in a kitchen drawer and use it to shut Damian's big mouth, permanently. Blade was on the protect Glory warpath now. Which I didn't need. Damian had better get a clue if he had any notion of getting something going with *me*.

"Let me go, Blade." I gave him a hard look. "I don't respond well to manhandling, remember?"

Blade stepped back and held out his hands. "Fine, but again, what encounter?"

"No big deal. A man wandered into the shop and had been with a vampire. I freaked because the vamp hadn't erased the man's memory or the fang marks on his neck. You know how I feel about blending." I sipped my drink. "I sure don't want my shop to become a magnet for vamp wannabes."

"*It's that name.*" Valdez had decided to put in his two cents. "*I told ya, Blondie. You're just askin' for it.*"

"Nonsense. The name is clever, Gloriana." Blade gave Valdez a look and the dog lay down and lowered his head to his paws.

Clever? Wow. But maybe a little too clever if my shop turned into a Goth hangout.

"So what's wrong with Florence?" Damian glanced at her closed bedroom door.

"She's upset about Westwood, Sabatini. He shot at her last night. If she hadn't shape-shifted, he would have killed her." Blade scowled at Damian like he should have been protecting his sister instead of frolicking in bed with me.

"*Dios mio!*" Damian swore and strode down the hall to Flo's room. He jerked open the door and went inside. Italian. Loud Italian. He slammed the door so at least the volume was muted.

"Are you starting a relationship with Damian, Gloriana?"

I didn't owe Jerry an answer, but saw no point in playing games.

"I doubt it."

"Then come home with me." He stepped closer.

"Because Westwood's in town?" I moved away to sit on the love seat. "No way. I'm staying here. I'll take Valdez down with me from now on, but the shop had a great start. I think it's going to be a moneymaker."

"You could open a shop like that in Lake Charles instead. I'd feel better if you were close."

I sipped my Bloody Merry, grateful for the energy it gave me. Blade just stared at me. I was *not* caving. Even though I could practically *feel* his frustration.

"I haven't lived close to you in decades, Jerry, and we've always had hunters to deal with." I held up my hand when he opened his mouth to argue. "I know. Westwood's more high tech than the others, but I'm sure not abandoning my shop to chase you to Lake Charles and hide inside your casino. Sorry, Jerry. You mean well, but I'm staying."

"If you won't go there, I'll have to come here."

"What?" I put down my can.

"You heard me. I'll move here, to Austin."

"You'd really do that? For me?" This was serious. "What about your business?"

"I've already had offers. I'll just sell it." He sat down on the chair across from me, his elbows on his knees as he stared at me.

I stared back. Seeing him in his plaid always reminded me of other, more primitive times. Some of them pretty

damned good. If only he didn't look so absolutely hunky . . .
Not a factor.

"You aren't going to do this for *me*. Uproot your life. Forget it."

"I'm not going to forget it. Besides, I was ready to move
on." He sat back and crossed his legs. Naughty man, he'd
flashed me. And did I look? You bet. His family jewels were
just as impressive as the rest of his package.

"You sure you want to come to Austin? It's totally unnecessary. I have my own life. Friends."

"So do I. Mara will be happy to come with me. She's obsessed with taking out Westwood."

"Of course. This is about Westwood." Thump. Well, there
went *my* ego. Time for a strategic retreat. I glanced at the
clock and got to my feet.

"It's been swell, but I'm going downstairs now. You can
wait for Damian and Flo to come out if you want. But I've
got a business to run." I hurried into the bedroom to grab
my purse and keys. Valdez sat next to the door with his leash
in his mouth.

"You're not goin' without me, Blondie."

"I know. You're coming." I turned to Blade who, ever the
gentleman, had jumped to his feet. "My day worker, Lacy,
has been on duty by herself since six this morning. I probably
need a third person, a third shift. I don't know yet. Maybe I
should close from six in the morning until noon." My mind
raced with possible solutions.

Better to think about business than the man who stood so
close I could have reached out and touched his face, a face
which looked freshly shaved. It would be smooth except for
the occasional rough spot, that mirror thing again. I remember shaving him, back in the day. He'd loved the attention and
had showed his gratitude in some very clever ways . . . No, I
was getting sidetracked. Business. I had to relieve Lacy.

Blade stepped even closer. "You're serious about this store,
aren't you, Gloriana?"

"Of course I am. I'm finally getting why you've always owned your own places." Blade has a string of businesses all over the world. He'd start one, decide to move on, then keep a percentage while he set up something else in a new location. No wonder he's rich. "I'm sure you'll make a profit when you sell your casino."

"Yes, I will. But I don't give a damn about that." He brushed my cheek with his thumb. "I'm worried about you. You're in danger here, Gloriana. Please be careful."

I fiddled with Valdez's leash to keep from leaning into that touch. No, I was *not* that needy.

"Thanks for your concern. But I'll be okay." I patted Valdez's head. "I've got my guard dog, Damian's security system complete with panic button, and my friends." I smiled and pocketed my keys Damian had left on the coffee table. Leaving my keys had been careless of me, but I'd been so upset . . . I narrowed my eyes.

"Wait a minute. Last night." I stomped my foot. "Don't. Ever. Speak. Into. My. Mind. Again." I punctuated each word with a finger stab into Blade's hard chest. He didn't even flinch. Which made me *really* want to hurt him.

"It was an emergency. Valdez reported that Westwood was here in Austin and that Florence said the shop was closed when she came home. She was worried when you weren't upstairs either." Blade grabbed my hand and held onto it when I tried to wrench it free. "I didn't know where you were, Gloriana."

"And you have to know where I am every minute of every day? Why not just lock me in the Campbell dungeon?" I looked down at his hand which had tightened around mine. "Oops. I forgot. You lost the keys to the dungeon when you called your father—"

"That's enough. I'm only trying to keep you safe. It's my obligation." I swear if a vamp could stroke out, Blade would be on his way to intensive care.

And I wasn't far behind him. Obligation? Not exactly a declaration of undying love. And wasn't I an idiot to want one? After all this time? I took a breath and looked down at my hand, just about mangled by his.

"Let go, Jerry." I wiggled my fingers. "Seriously. Do you keep track of all the other vampires you've turned during your long and not so illustrious career? Heard from Katie lately?" Oh, boy. Call nine one one. Blade was going to blow. Mr. Wonderful had made a few mistakes in the past. I hadn't been the first woman he'd turned. Or the first one to decide he wasn't her lord and master.

"Leave Kaitlyn out of this." At least he finally let go of my hand.

I could see his struggle to contain his anger. If I had any sense, I wouldn't goad him. But I was sick of being sensible, sick of being controlled. I mean, he'd interrupted me in bed with another guy. It doesn't get any worse than that. If that made me an ungrateful bitch, so be it.

"Katie seems to have figured out how to be free of your control. Maybe I should give her a call. You got her number?" I whipped my cell phone out of my purse.

"Damn it, Gloriana. Why do you fight me?" He crushed me in his arms, purse, cell phone and all.

I felt the scratchy wool of the plaid tossed over his shoulder against my cheek and voted against an undignified struggle to put distance between us. Forget getting away from *that* iron grip.

"Give it up, Jerry. You can't keep me safe. You can't control me or every nutcase out to stake a vampire. Not and leave me any kind of life of my own." I looked up and met his gaze. "And, news flash, Jerry, I'm going to have a life of my own." Why did I waste my breath? I'd have as much luck convincing Valdez to eat Alpo. I pushed.

Blade was stony faced. But he did let me go.

I wrenched open the door. And came face-to-face with a white-haired vampire carrying a hot pink Kate Spade purse.

Eight

"**You!**" I grabbed his shirt and jerked him into the apartment.

"What the hell?" I swear he started to cross himself.

"I know this purse. It belongs to Florence."

"Is Florence here? Do I have the right apartment?" He looked down at the purse. "I'm just returning this."

"Who's this?" Blade was fingering his broadsword again.

The vampire stiffened. He was a pretty tough looking dude. I never could have pulled him inside without the element of surprise.

"I could ask the same. I'm looking for Florence da Vinci. Is this the right apartment or not?"

"She lives here. What's it to you?" Maybe I was crazy, but I got up in tough dude's face. This jackass had been going around snacking on students without taking the proper precautions. He narrowed his gaze on me. Another mind reader. Why was I not surprised? Everyone did it but me. And could I read his? I actually tried and hit a brick wall. Of course not.

"Florence and I are, were, close. She left this at my place last night." He held out the purse.

I took it, handling it with the respect it deserved. Florence has a terrific purse collection. One I was planning to raid as soon as I had some place special to go.

"You let a defenseless woman go out alone last night?" Blade had abandoned his broadsword to pluck a dagger from his shoe. "Haven't you heard vampires are in danger here?"

"Perhaps *you* are in danger, Scotsman. Not many men have pulled a knife on me and lived to tell the tale." The vamp slipped his own dagger from his sleeve. Slick. He tossed it from hand to hand like he'd welcome a little street fight. Valdez growled, obviously eager to join the fray. In my living room? Not tonight. I glanced at the clock. I *had* to get downstairs.

"You boys play nice." I laid the purse on the coffee table and opened the door. Valdez came with me, though he gave Blade a lingering look like he was hoping to be invited to participate in the action.

"Blade, explain to our guest how we blend. Nicely. And tell him what happened to Flo after she left him last night." I slammed the door and headed down the stairs. They couldn't kill each other unless one of them packed a wooden stake. Not my problem. I'd had it up to here with men.

I got to the shop. At least one part of my life was on track. Lacy was ringing up a sale. The woman at the counter gasped when she saw Valdez and I quickly stowed him in the store room. He growled when I slammed the door in his face, but business is business.

Two other women were checking prices on my selection of vintage handbags. I needed more but Flo had already refused to part with any of hers.

Flo. Obviously the white-haired vampire was her lover, ex-lover now. He was handsome, looked in his midthirties and his hair was platinum, not white. It was easy to see why

Flo had been attracted. He had an edgy quality, but most male vamps did. And that just added to their attraction.

Freddy came into the shop just then. Not edgy. But a welcome sight. I could send him upstairs to referee. Though I knew from past experience that he had a wicked temper himself when riled.

"Why do you want me to go upstairs? And I've worked on anger management. It takes some serious shit to make me blow." He had a pile of clothes over his arm.

"Blade and the white-haired vamp I told your mother about are upstairs circling each other with knives." I heard a customer gasp. "Sorry, ma'am. Figure of speech. They're cutting up veggies for the potluck later."

Freddy grinned. "And I forgot my wok?"

"Good comeback." I lowered my voice. "I know they can't kill each other, but I'd hate to have to get blood out of the carpet."

"I'll go up." Freddy looked down at the clothes in his arms. "Mother thought you might want these." He looked around. "I don't see a men's section, but these are good quality, hardly worn." He made a face. "From my zoot suit period."

"You've got to be kidding!" The customer at the register whirled around. "My husband would kill for a zoot suit." She looked him over. "And he's about your size."

Freddy grinned and nodded toward me. "Bring him back, I'm sure Ms. St. Clair will have it ready to sell by the end of the night."

"You bet I will." I took the suits into the back room and hung them on the spare rack there. Freddy followed me, nodding to a sulking Valdez. My dog didn't speak, not with customers still fairly close by. I'd warned him about that too many times to count.

"I heard you had a date last night. Damian?" Freddy fingered a fox collar I'd picked up from a fellow vamp cleaning out her closet.

"Another reason you need to go upstairs. Damian's up there too, with Flo, but Blade knows Damian and I had a little"— I grinned—"fun last night. Of course Damian's doing everything he can to rub it in. As if Blade really cares who I have fun with." Oops. My grin slipped and unfortunately I sounded bitter.

Freddy smiled. "You deserve some fun and Damian's hot. But then so's Blade." He shook his head and tossed the fox back on the table. "I should be so lucky as to have two hunks wanting me for fun and games."

"Fun interruptus. Blade sent me a mental telegram at the worst possible time. Threatened to show up. And not for fun either. Because he thought I was in danger."

"Danger?" Freddy put his hand on my shoulder. "What's happened? Why would he think that?"

"Ask him. Upstairs." I patted his hand, then shut the storeroom door again and headed to the counter. Lacy had sagged onto a stool. "How are you doing?"

Lacy looked up and yawned, a real jaw cracker. "Sorry. If I didn't know better, I'd think I was dying, I'm so tired. But overall it was a great day. We sold a ton of stuff. Look around."

Sure enough, there were significant inroads into our stock. I could definitely squeeze in a men's section.

"Go home, go to bed. We need to talk about a better schedule for you. Maybe hire someone else."

Lacy sighed. "Yeah. I thought I was Wonder Woman, but turns out I'm more human than I thought." She stretched, a sinuous motion that was pure cat. "And I still need to," she glanced at a customer, "um, eat."

"Go, then." I pushed her toward the door. "I'll count receipts, put away our excess cash if there is any."

"There is. It was a great day." Lacy looked Freddy over. "Your mom says you're gay. You sure?"

Freddy laughed and hooked arms with her. "Sure. But I'll walk you upstairs. Glory's afraid there's murder and mayhem going on up there."

"Sounds interesting." Lacy looked back at me and winked. "Any eligible guys involved in the action?"

"They're *all* eligible. Help yourself." I picked up a stack of receipts.

Lacy made a face. "Wouldn't you know I look like hell?" She fluffed her hair.

"You could use a little blush." Freddy nodded toward the counter. "Mother left some makeup here in case of emergencies."

"You *are* gay!" She patted his cheek. "Thanks. I know about the makeup. Give me a minute." She grabbed a gold brocade bag from behind the counter and headed toward the dressing rooms.

"Lucky. She can actually use a mirror." I looked down at my fifties pencil skirt and twin set. Red. Which Blade had always said was my color.

Freddy grinned. "You know you look good. So who's it going to be, Blade or Damian?"

"Probably neither. Good looks aren't everything."

"But they don't hurt." Freddy patted my shoulder. "Give the guys a chance. See what develops."

"The only thing developing with either of them right now is hand-to-hand combat. I really need you to go upstairs and check for survivors. Okay?"

"On my way." Freddy smiled as Lacy emerged, looking like she'd just taken a twelve-hour nap instead of working all day. Did I really want her to help herself to the men upstairs? A customer approached with a vintage Gucci bag. Whatever. Blade infuriated me. Damian infuriated me. Even white-haired no-name vamp infuriated me. I was making money. Not infuriating at all.

Lacy and Freddy left and I was too busy to spare them a thought. I waited on customers. Rearranged things to make room for my new men's section and counted money. No way was I giving up the store just because Westwood had come to town. And, wow, I really could afford to hire someone else.

The store was empty when the bell tinkled on the front door. Derek.

"Freddy was upstairs last I knew."

"I'm not looking for Frederick." Derek ran his fingers through his hair. "I'm looking for a job."

"Here? You want to work for me?" I looked him over. He was dressed right for a college student. Vintage rock band T-shirt, faded jeans and running shoes. A decent look in this college town. Of course he was to-die-for handsome.

"I've had retail experience." He strolled over to the rack I'd just set up in one corner. "Frederick's suits." He sighed and glanced at the tag. "A bargain. Man, I wish I'd known him then."

"You know him now. So why do you need a job?" Were the von Repsdorfs in financial trouble? They'd always lived well, but, unlike Blade, Freddy didn't own businesses or seem to work. Certainly CiCi never had.

"No financial problems. Freddy has investments. I want my independence." Derek made a face. "Sorry, I know you hate mind reading, but you're so easy to read."

"Unfortunately I'm used to every vamp I know browsing through my brain. I can relate to your need for independence." Poor Derek was probably on an allowance. He looked up. Got it in one.

"What I really need is another day person. But I guess I could use you for a few hours. We could try eight till midnight a few nights a week. I'm putting Lacy on commission and it's adding up to a fair amount. How about minimum wage plus that?"

"Really? You'll give me a shot?" Derek grinned. "And I know a little about women's fashions too. One of my former boyfriends was a drag queen. He had a fabulous wardrobe. You should have seen him do Marilyn Monroe." He fingered a fifties shirtwaist and looked wistful.

"What happened to him?"

"Killed crossing a street in New York City." Derek dropped the dress and moved on to the nightgowns. "Mortal obviously. We'd talked about making him vampire but he was still weighing the pros and cons."

Pros and cons. Turning vampire was really all about trust. You were literally dying when you changed. And you had to know the vamp turning you wouldn't just suck you dry and leave you for dead. They had to infuse you with their own blood, at no little risk to themselves, to give you immortality and all those vamp powers that I'd been determined to squander for so long.

I'd trusted Blade like that. So very, very long ago. And I'd been so crazy in love I'd never really thought the whole vampire thing through.

"I'm really sorry, Derek. But at least you and Freddy found each other."

"Yeah." Derek straightened a stack of hankies. "So when do I start?"

I looked around. "It depends. How do you feel about spirits?"

Derek looked startled. "I'm not like Trevor if that's what you're getting at. I'm not into alcohol."

Dumb ass appeared on the wall behind Derek's back. Harvey.

"Not alcohol, Derek. Ghosts. We have a situation here." I gestured toward the wall, but the words vanished.

"Ghosts? Cool." Derek looked around. "Helloooo."

Emmie Lou appeared next to the nighties. "Hello, cutie."

"Great outfit." Derek grinned and winked.

"Thanks, hon." Emmie Lou did a little twirl.

"She's taken, fella." Harvey appeared just after a crocodile handbag flew through the air and bounced off Derek's head.

"Whoa. Back off, Grandpa." Derek picked up the purse and slung the strap over his shoulder. "She's safe from me. I'm gay and I'm in a committed relationship."

"Figures." Emmie Lou made a face and disappeared.

"Keep it that way." Harvey vanished.

"Unbelievable." Derek set the purse back on the shelf. "This is going to be fun."

The bells on the front door tinkled. A new customer. The man made a beeline to my new men's section and began examining each seam in one of the zoot suits. He flipped open a cell phone and punched in a number. Probably going to describe the suit to a friend. He held out the phone. Now he was taking a picture. Modern technology. Gotta love it. I turned back to Derek.

"You want to start right now?" I glanced upward. "I'd like to see what's happening upstairs."

"Sure." He nodded toward the customer. "If I'm lucky, I'll score my first big sale."

"If you need my help with a credit card or anything, my cell phone number is by the register." I patted my pocket. Yep, I had it with me. "Any real problems, there's a panic button under the counter near the register. The police promise to respond in five minutes or less."

"Now you're scaring me." Derek grinned, leaned closer and showed his fangs. "You really think I need the police to protect me?"

I shook my head. "Behave. And, Derek, the customers are off limits if you know what I mean."

Derek straightened. "I'll be a good boy. I want this job."

"You got it. Back in a few."

Derek waved and strolled over to chat with the customer. The man snapped the phone shut and put on some tinted glasses to read the price tag I'd pinned on the sleeve. He'd probably want a discount. Most customers at vintage stores seemed to think we liked to bargain. And I wasn't above it. Derek could call me if he needed a price check.

I headed upstairs. No sign of Lacy or Freddy inside the apartment, but Flo sat on the love seat, looking tragic and beautiful in black, her hair pulled back in a chignon. Blade and Damian were talking in the kitchen. No blood in sight unless you counted the cans of Bloody Merry sitting on the counter next to them.

The white-haired vampire sat in a club chair staring at Flo. I didn't have to read minds to know things weren't going well between the two of them. Which was fine with me. This yahoo had two strikes against him in my book.

"Where's Freddy?" I sat next to Flo.

"He left. Something about an appointment." Flo wasn't exactly exuding enthusiasm. "He probably didn't like all this tension." She glanced at the man sitting across from us. "Or the company."

"Company, right." I met white-haired guy's bright blue gaze. Hmm. He had some serious mojo going on. I blinked when I felt like smiling at him. He had a lot of nerve trying to whammy me in my own home.

"We didn't get introduced earlier. I'm Flo's roommate, Glory St. Clair."

The man leaped to his feet. "Richard Mainwaring. Sorry I can't say it's a pleasure to meet you." He glanced at Flo. "Maybe I should leave."

"Maybe you should. Especially if you're going to be rude to my roomie." Flo sniffed and lifted a white lace handkerchief to her eyes.

"Sorry, Glory." He didn't *look* sorry. Then he turned back to Flo. "I never should have let you leave last night."

"You couldn't have stopped me." Flo rose to stalk to the door. She flung it open. "Leave. Austin. Texas. The United States. The world." She laughed. "Oops, sorry, you'd have to die to do that and we all know *that's* not going to happen."

"You're not as sorry as I am." Mainwaring glanced toward the kitchen. Blade and Damian had stopped talking to give him the evil eye.

"I guess someone explained how we do things here, Mainwaring. You're welcome to hunt, but you must erase fang marks and memory. We want to keep a low profile. It's safer for all of us." I glanced at Blade. "We've got enough danger around us without attracting more hunters."

"I get it. Though I don't know why you think I'd do a thing like that. You've got the wrong vampire." Mainwaring stepped into the hall. "Good-bye, Florence."

"*Ciao,* Ricardo. Have a nice life. Or not." She flounced back to the love seat and sat, crossing her legs so that her short skirt displayed a good bit of thigh.

Mainwaring was headed down the hall when an orange and white cat strolled past him. Thinking of Valdez and his cat hatred, I slammed the door then remembered I'd left the dog downstairs.

"Who's minding the store?" Damian handed his sister a can of Bloody Merry.

"Would you believe Derek? He wanted a job. To earn his own money. I could relate to his need for independence." I felt Blade's eyes on me. At least he wasn't trying to send me mental messages.

The fact that he was still here, though, meant he and Damian had come to terms. What kind of terms? Was Blade really staying in Austin? Or had he handed me off to Damian? Like little Glory couldn't survive without a male protector. I glared at both men.

"I hope at least one of you tore a strip off of Mainwaring for sending Flo out alone last night."

"Of course." Damian sat next to his sister. "Though Florence is notorious for ignoring good sense."

"Hah! You almost wept you were so worried about me." She patted his knee. "I think our men are sweet to want to protect us."

Jerry walked over to stand beside me. I could smell him. Okay, I'm still susceptible. And, with his knees showing in his plaid, he was a Highland hunk.

"Sweet? I don't think so." I eased away from Blade, but I could *still* smell him, that combination of old wool and male that had turned me on for centuries. A knee-jerk reaction on my part. I didn't want to go down that road again. I really didn't. But sometimes enhanced senses can be a curse instead of a blessing.

Damian grinned. "I can be sweet. If that means I care what you think. Tell me anything, Gloriana. Order me to do anything. I am yours to command." He looked at Blade. "Not the other way around."

"That's a terrific offer, Damian. I'll think about it." I put my hand on Flo's shoulder. "You okay?"

Flo covered my hand with hers. "I'm fine. I know you're anxious to get back to the shop."

"I am. So if the knife throwing is over, I'll get back downstairs. Valdez is down there with Derek."

"I'll walk you back down." Blade opened the door. He was smiling. Of course he'd picked up on my sensory overload. He leaned down and sniffed. "New shampoo, Gloriana? I like."

"Mango and grapefruit. I can't eat but I can smell." I was babbling.

"Good night, Gloriana. Or would you like for me to wait for you here?" Damian laughed when Blade threw him a dirty look.

I ignored him. "Flo, are you *sure* you're going to be all right?"

"Of course. I'll have a new lover by this time next week." She sipped her Bloody Merry.

"It's not your love life I'm worried about." I walked over to stand in front of her. "Look at me, Flo." I waited until she did. "You had a near miss last night. You're bound to be shook up."

Flo laughed. "I love your English. I must watch more TV. Glory, I'm not shook up *or* down. I'm fine. Go, work. Have a good night."

"You could come down with me."

"No, thank you. I have my brother here. And there is still something he and I have not discussed." She quit smiling. "With Ricardo here, I forgot. But now I remember that I must kill my brother." Flo gave Damian a look, reminding me of how mad she'd been the night before.

I squeezed my eyes shut. *Block, damn it.* I had to shield my thoughts from Blade. If he knew Damian had bit me without permission . . .

I looked up, a giant headache settling between my eyes. Blade didn't react except to give me a searching look. Hah! I'd blocked, but wasn't sure it had been worth it. The pain stabbed me again, the vamp version of a migraine. Damian jumped up and started edging toward the door. He probably deserved Blade's wrath, but I really didn't feel up to a resumption of hostilities right now.

"My sister exaggerates. A slight disagreement, nothing more. There will be no killing, but maybe I should hit the road."

"You hit nothing, Damian, until Gloriana and Jeremiah have left and you and I have a talk." For a little woman, Flo had a seriously dangerous look. Thank God she and Damian both blocked everyone as a matter of course. Blade was giving off the frustration vibe again and I could almost feel him trying to slip inside my brain. Boy, was my head killing me. But the block held.

"Fine. I only obey you now because you have had a near miss and you *are* shook as Glory says." Damian looked resigned as he walked over to sit in a club chair again.

"Flo, don't you think it would be better if we just forgot about last night? I'm fine. You're fine. Right?" I don't know why I cared what she did or said to Damian. He grinned at me and Blade's hand on my elbow tightened. Okay, so I kind of liked being in the middle of a handsome-man turf war.

Flo gave me a tight smile and nodded. "Of course you're fine. Men are nothing to us. But Damian must listen to his sister's"—she gave him another murderous look, *"concerns."*

"Right. But no killing, Florence. You'll mess up the apartment. See you later." I glanced at Blade. His hand was firm on my arm as he guided me out the door.

"I'd like to know why Valdez let you leave without him."

"I had to shut him in the stockroom. Some of the customers get nervous when he's around. He *is* a big dog. Not everybody's a dog lover."

"Damn it to hell, Gloriana. How can he protect you from a storeroom?" Blade threw open the door at the bottom of the stairs. "He must be by your side. At all times."

Valdez and Derek met us at the door. The dog bared his teeth and Derek held on to the dog's collar like that was the only thing holding him up.

"What's happened?" I looked around the shop. No customers. Derek had a card in his hand.

"This." His hand was shaking as he held out the card. "I didn't find it until the man left. He'd stuck it in the breast pocket of Freddy's gold suit."

"This is big, boss. If Glory had let me out of the back room—" Valdez gave me a withering look—*"I could have torn him apart and ended this thing here and now."*

Blade snatched the card before I could take it. "Bloody hell!"

I looked down. A business card. Expensive. Gold lettering. With a bold black signature at the bottom.

"The hunt is on. Westwood."

"My God. Westwood was here?" I felt Blade's arm go around me and didn't object. It kept me from falling to the floor in a heap.

"You saw him, Glory. The man looking at suits. That was Brent Westwood."

Nine

"We need a mortal to help us."

Everyone stared at me like I'd uttered blasphemy. Have I mentioned that vamp men think they can handle *anything*?

"Why would we involve a mortal in our business?"

Blade really needed to change into different clothes. The plaid thing was like a red flag saying "I'm weird, check me out." And of course Westwood had seen him before. My stomach knotted. No more talk. We needed action.

"A mortal might be able to figure out how Westwood is IDing us." It seemed I had to spell out everything. "Maybe someone who could infiltrate Westwood's organization."

"Glory's got a point. If we knew how Westwood made us as vampires, that would help us avoid detection." Derek was still shaking and I led him to a chair.

Damian strode over to the door, flipped the dead bolts and turned the sign to Closed. He'd stopped on his way out of the building when he'd seen us gathered around Derek.

"We need a plan. Now that we know he's on to Derek, we can use him as bait."

"Thanks a lot, Damian." Derek put his head between his knees. "I think I'm going to throw up."

I rushed into the back room and wet a cloth. I laid it on the back of his neck. "Relax, Derek. No one is going to use you as bait." I gave my macho vamps a stern look. "And that guy saw both of us. Maybe he knows I'm vamp too."

"Exactly. Discussion is closed, Gloriana. You're coming home with me now." Blade grabbed my arm.

Would he ever learn that ordering me around never got him what he wanted? Probably not. And it made me sad. Because we, as a couple, were definitely over in that case.

"I'm not going anywhere. This Westwood character isn't going to ruin the best move I ever made." I gestured around the shop. "Vintage Vamp's is my creation and a success so far. I'm not about to tuck my tail between my legs and skulk off into the night."

"Blade's right, Glory. You should get out of here." Derek sat up and put the cloth on his forehead. "Westwood aimed that camera phone at both of us. He has our pictures."

Damian cursed in Italian. "You can move into my castle, Gloriana. I'll hire guards. They can escort you to and from the shop and stay with you—"

"She's not your responsibility, Sabatini." Blade still held my arm. Like I was shackled to him.

Valdez barked just before someone knocked on the door. Blade dropped my arm and whipped out his broadsword.

Damian looked through the glass. "It's Diana Marchand. She runs the coffee shop next door. I'm going to let her in. She knows a lot of mortals. Glory's right. Only a mortal is going to get close enough to Westwood to figure out how he's identifying us."

Glory's right. Beautiful words and all too rare in my lifetime. Damian flipped open the locks and let Diana in. I'd met her while I was setting up the shop. I'd been way too busy to do much more than say hi and wave, but I liked her. For one thing, she was vamp like me. Turned on a day when she should have been at a Weight Watchers meeting. Plump, short and with a southern belle thing going on.

She called her place Mugs and Muffins. I'd heard more than one customer call it *Jugs* and Muffins. One look at Diana and you know why.

"What're y'all doing over here?" Diana's wide-eyed gaze was fixed on Blade. Well, he did stand out. He slid his broadsword back in its scabbard and bowed in her direction.

"Jeremy Blade, madam, at your service." He looked around the room. "Do you know everyone else here?"

I really wanted to smack him. For being here. For looking like a Highland throwback. For moving closer to Di and eyeing her "jugs" appreciatively.

Diana knew a great marketing tool when she saw one. She and her waitresses wore low-cut spandex tops over lacy edged bras in contrasting colors. I had to admire her entrepreneurial spirit. And hate her Dolly Parton–sized attributes. Tonight they were showcased in black lycra with just a hint of pink lace.

"Gee, Jerry, this isn't a soiree at the castle." I think I could have stripped naked and Blade wouldn't have been able to tear his gaze from Di's assets.

"She's got you there, Blade." Damian laughed as he flipped the deadbolts again. Of course he'd read my mind. Men love female rivalry and pray for a cat fight. Can you tell I'm down on men?

"Be nice, Damian." Diana looked around. "Sure, I know everyone else here. So what's up, Glory? I have customers who are waiting to get into this shop. Not that I'm complaining. They're drinking my coffee while they wait for y'all to open again."

"An incident, Diana. You know about Brent Westwood?" Damian slung his arm around her.

"Hands off, hot stuff." Diana lifted Damian's hand off her shoulder and smiled sweetly. There was obviously a story there.

Damian frowned and moved closer to me. I shook my head and he stuck his hands in his pockets.

"Sure I know about Westwood. I've got that vampire-killin' lowlife's picture right next to my cash register." She looked at me and ignored Damian. "Why? What about him?"

"He was here. He left this." Blade handed her Westwood's card.

"Oh, my God!" She leaned against Blade and fanned her cheeks with the card. "So close!"

I swear, if Diana swooned, I was leaving her on the floor. She rallied and winked at me as Blade helped her into a chair.

"Are you all right?" Damian moved in until she put up her hand like a stop sign.

"I'm fine, sugar. As you would see if you checked a little higher." Diana looked at me and rolled her eyes. Of course Blade stayed close, positioned for a good view of that pink lace bra. He'd always had an appreciation for a full-figured woman. Diana was just his type. Fine. I *did not* care.

"But what I don't understand"—Diana looked at the card again—"is why he would warn whoever his target was that he was hunting them."

"Me, Diana, he left the card for me." Derek shot to his feet. "I've got to call Freddy. Maybe it's time for us to move on. Blade's right. Running is the answer. If this guy got MacTavish, screw it. I don't stand a chance." Derek pulled out his cell phone and hit the speed dial. He moved to the back of the store and started talking rapidly.

"Running is not the answer. I never said that." Blade ground out the words.

"No, that would be cowardly." Damian jingled the change in his pockets. "Does Blade look cowardly to you, Diana?"

"No, indeed." Di smiled and gave Blade a look that made him puff out his chest. You had to give the girl credit, she had both men eating out of the palm of her hand. I should take lessons. Not.

"He probably left the card to put us on the alert. Westwood likes the hunt. Here, we're sitting ducks. No sport in that." I saw Blade nod, his face solemn. He was probably reliving the night he'd lost Mac. I started to move closer when Damian stepped between us.

"You should close this shop, Gloriana. Why present such an easy target?" Damian put his hand on my shoulder.

"This shop pays my bills, Damian." I shrugged and he moved his hand. "Can we get back to Westwood?"

"But if this sorry so-and-so's got some kind of new technology, how are we going to fight that?" Diana said this to me.

"Mortals." I was getting really tired of men. Was everything a competition? This danger should unite us. Vamps against Westwood. Damian nodded and even Blade looked thoughtful.

"Mortals?" Diana looked puzzled. Could she actually be a vamp who didn't read minds? I suddenly wanted to hug her.

"We need mortals to get close to Westwood and find out how he can tell if we're vampire. Then we can try to counteract whatever he's got." Not all vamps are comfortable around mortals, but Diana's coffee shop swarmed with them. "You know any who might help us?"

"I've got some mortals I do business with from time to time." Diana glanced toward her shop. "Tony Crapetta is over there right now drinking one of my special grande triple mocha lattes. You know him, Damian."

"How is a man who likes sissy drinks going to be of help in this situation?" Blade had just stepped in it, big time.

"Sissy drinks?" Diana looked him up and down. "If you weren't a freak prehistoric vampire, you'd probably kill to taste my triple mocha latte."

Well, that love affair was over. And if Blade didn't get rid of that broadsword, I was going to find a wooden hanger and test my vamp strength.

"She's right, Blade. I do know Tony Crapetta. He's got connections that could help us." Damian moved out of the way when Diana stood and walked toward the door.

"I don't like using mortals." Blade frowned.

Damian sneered. "Quit being all muscle and no brain, Blade."

"By God!" There went the hand to the broadsword again.

"I've had enough of this. Can you get Tony to come over here, Di? Does he know you're vampire?" I stopped her at the door.

"He knows. He saw me change once. I could have wiped his memory, but I decided he might be useful. He knows about Damian, too." She smiled at Damian. "That was before we split."

"You broke my heart, you mean." Damian put his hand over his alleged heart. "But she's right about Tony. He's done a few jobs for me too. And he knows I'll rip his throat out if he crosses me."

"He's scared to death of vampires, but also thinks it's cool to work for them. A groupie." Diana shook her head. "I told him I wouldn't use him for feeding as long as he kept our secret. But you should see what he wears around his neck. In case I get overcome by bloodlust." She winked. "I don't have the heart to tell him I satisfy my thirst with a canned drink."

Derek had come out of the back room, still looking shaky.

"Are you going home?" I guessed I was losing my employee already. Too bad. I had a feeling Derek would be a great salesman.

He nodded. "Frederick is coming to pick me up. Sorry, Glory."

"That's okay. You've had a scare. Like I just told the gang here, I think we're safe in the shop. This Westwood character warned you for a reason. He probably plans to stalk you." I had to swallow. "Or me. For sport."

"Brave, Gloriana." Damian gave Blade a look. "What a woman."

Brave or stupid? Whichever, I wasn't going to just run or roll over and play . . . dead. I pushed down the urge to cry, maybe against one of the broad strong masculine chests so readily available. I hadn't survived this long, much of it on my own, by being a wimp.

"I'm reopening. I'm not going to let Westwood scare me away." I looked at Derek. "No offense, Derek."

"You're right. What's wrong with me? I'm not usually such a coward." He ran his hands through his hair, then threw back his shoulders and got a combative gleam in his eyes. "I love my life here. I don't *want* to start over, damn it."

I turned to Blade and Damian. "Why don't you get Diana's mortal and take him upstairs? See if he has any ideas on how we can get the scoop on Westwood's technology. Valdez and I will stay down here and run the shop."

"I don't like it. Come upstairs with us." Blade put his hand on my shoulder.

"No. And can't you change into a pair of jeans or something? That outfit screams 'Stake me.'" I looked around the store. Vintage jeans would be a big seller. And old band touring T-shirts. Freddy had left his zoot suits, but I didn't see that as much of an improvement over a plaid and a kilt as far as maintaining a low profile went.

"Come to my castle, Blade. I have something for you to wear. As Gloriana wants, we must call a truce between us."

Damian gave me an admiring look. If he just hadn't been such a jackass last night. Nope. Couldn't even think about that.

"Jerry, Damian is willing to be civilized, are you?" I touched his hand and waited until he finally loosened his grip on that sword with his other hand.

"Aye. Civilized. But we can meet here."

"The castle. You need clothes and I have cash there to give Tony. He'll want some money up front to help us. Westwood shot at Florence. I'll pay anything to get that bastard." Damian unlocked the door. "Go get Crapetta, Diana. Tell him I'll make it worth his while."

"Yeah, money talks with Tony." Diana smiled at me. "You're really opening?"

"Why not?" I flipped over the sign. "I've got my guard dog and hopefully customers will swarm around me. Westwood can probably buy himself out of a lot, but I bet he doesn't want to get the law on his back."

I looked outside, but everything seemed fairly normal for this time of night. A good thing since my tough talk was just that. Talk. God, Westwood had been here. Close enough to take my picture. And what was he going to do with that? Somehow I didn't think he was into scrapbooking.

"See? No sign of Westwood with his bow and arrow."

It was quiet. Too quiet. I glanced at Derek and he jumped up to turn on the radio, an oldies station. Elvis sang "Heartbreak Hotel." It figured.

"I'm open. Go. Plan. Let me know what you decide." I actually batted my eyelashes at both men. "I'm so glad I've got such big strong men to take care of me."

Derek snorted, turning it into a cough when both Damian and Blade gave him a dirty look.

"I'll stay here with her. When Freddy gets here, I'll send him to the castle. He can help you guys plan." Derek stood next to me. "Glory's right. Westwood could have already taken us out here if that was his game. Leaving the card ramps things up a notch. He's done the ambush gig, maybe he wants his 'prey' "—Derek shuddered—"to *know* it's being hunted."

"You're creeping me out, Derek." I squeezed his arm and felt it trembling. "I, for one, am not 'prey.' I say we hunt the hunter." If I kept saying the right things, maybe I could stave off the major meltdown I had coming to me. At least until I was alone in my bedroom with the covers over my head and my dog between me and the bad guys. I lifted my chin and gave the group my Glory-the-brave glare.

"Hunt the hunter. I like that." Damian smiled at me. "Our new motto."

"And if Westwood wants the chase, he'll get one. We're going to work on defense too." More tough talk. I was on a roll. Blade moved closer, tuned in as always to my distress.

"It's not going to be easy. He's got that hunter mentality, Glory, and unlimited resources. Checking surveillance tapes, we saw that he'd been in the casino with his equipment at least five times before he took his shot. He stalked us and waited until we were outside. Mac was caught off guard and didn't have time to shape-shift." He touched my shoulder until I looked up at him. "You know that's how Florence saved herself last night."

"I know. I'll try. Really." Didn't Yoda in *Star Wars* say there is no try? But *doing* absolutely stymies me. I'd think what I wanted to be, just like Blade had tried to teach me. But then I'd feel just the beginning of some kind of change and freeze. I don't *want* to change. It creeps me out. But I can't deny that it's a vamp's best defense mechanism.

Di was back with a man in tow and quickly introduced everyone Tony didn't already know. I don't know what I expected, but Tony Crapetta wasn't it. He was a small man draped in gold chains, a large cross visible on his hairy chest where he'd left his pale blue nylon shirt unbuttoned way too low.

His eyes lit up when he saw my zoot suits. "I didn't know you had men's clothes in here. You got any leisure suits? *Saturday Night Fever,* baby." He tapped his chest. "Disco King."

"Gee, sorry, Tony. Not yet. But we'll keep our eyes open. Check back with us." Derek didn't laugh but I could tell he was thinking the Disco King thing was a stretch. More like "Disco Duck."

"I didn't bring you over here to shop, Tony, darlin'." Diana flipped the sign to Closed again. "Glory, you and I are going to be in on this. I told the people next door to get free refills. You'll reopen in thirty minutes."

"You will be in on it, lass. But Sabatini's right. We'll need some things from the castle." Jerry walked up to Tony and looked him over. "We expect discretion, Crapetta."

"Yes, sir, Mr. Blade." Tony fingered his cross. "Mr. Sabatini here can tell you I don't flap my yap." He was wide-eyed, but forged ahead. "Miss Diana tells me you've got a job for me."

"Right." Damian pulled Tony out the door. "Let's go to my house. I'll lay everything out for you there."

Diana made a sound of protest as Blade, Damian and Tony climbed into the vamp-mobile.

"Let them go, Diana. I've got an idea." I waited until the car pulled away from the curb. "Let's go back to the coffee shop."

Diana crossed her arms. "Fine. But if you think I'm playing the little woman while they—"

"Give me a minute. We may be little." Okay, maybe not so little. "And we may be women, but we can come up with our own plan, don't you think?"

Valdez was right on my heels.

"I'll stay here, Glory. Freddy will be here any minute." Derek stuck his head out the door and looked around.

Diana grabbed my arm. "The dog can't go inside, Glory. The health department would shut me down before you could say scat."

"I go where she goes, Blondie."

"Gee, I thought *I* was Blondie." I patted his furry head. "We won't go outside until you check things out. Then you can watch me through the window. You won't miss a thing." I squatted down and looked him in the eye. "And thanks for not ratting Damian out to Blade. About that thing last night."

Valdez showed his teeth. *"I'd like to bite that creep where it would hurt the most if you know what I mean. But we got more serious worries now. You seem to handle Sabatini pretty well by yourself."*

"Thanks." I stood and saw Diana gaping at Valdez. When he "talks," anyone around can hear him too. "It's complicated."

"Yeah. I imagine so. But if he decides to bite Damian you know where, I want a front row seat."

I laughed. "You're going to have to tell me what happened between you two some day."

Diana grimaced. "What can I say? The man's incapable of sticking with any woman for very long. But he's a lot of fun if you're not looking for more."

"Mr. Right Now, not Mr. Right."

"You got it." Diana sighed. "I'm over Damian, I've moved on and I'm seeing someone else."

"Good." I pulled open the door. Valdez finished checking the surrounding area. When he sat down, I figured we had the all clear. And Freddy was pulling up in my, I mean Blade's, Mercedes convertible. Jerry's just evil enough to leave my dream car here with Freddy to torment me. I was *not* caving in, even though my Suburban was currently DOA in the alley behind our building. Transmission problems. I looked around the shop. I'd have to sell a hell of a lot of clothes to bring that vehicle back to life.

Di and I slipped from my shop to hers. Mugs and Muffins was small but spotless. Great smells. Coffee. Muffins. And she sold Bloody Merry. Big freakin' deal. Did I mention the muffins? Three tables were occupied by what looked like students with laptops. I checked them out. One woman who wore vintage cat's-eye glasses was staring at her computer and biting her lip. A computer geek if ever I saw one.

"Excuse me." I tapped her on the shoulder and she jumped.

"Oh, hi. You own the shop next door. I love your stuff."

"Great glasses. I'd like to carry things like that."

"Estate sale. I'm an addict."

"Hmmm." I had another idea, but first things first. "You studying computer science at school?"

The woman laughed. "No, I'm teaching it. I know, I know. I look young. But I'm old enough." She looked past me. "That your dog? I love dogs."

I saw Valdez staring a hole in the glass. "He's okay." He glared at me. "Give him a muffin and he'll be your friend for life."

"Good to know." Diana came closer. "I hope we're not interrupting you."

"No. I'd just decided to pack it in. Why?"

"Well, I, we, have a technology question. Would you mind coming over to my shop with me?" I saw her uncertainty. Maybe a little incentive. "If you help us, I'll let you have any item in the store for fifty percent off."

"Cool! My name's Miranda Anderson, by the way."

"I'm Glory St. Clair and this is Diana Marchand who owns this coffee shop."

"Sure. I recognize her too." Miranda smiled. "Give me a sec to shut down my computer." She looked up as Diana set a cup next to her.

"Free refills tonight, Miranda. Take it next door with you." Diana smiled and tapped her fist against mine as Miranda stuffed her laptop into a book bag. "Girl power, Glory."

"Exactly." Di, Miranda and I went back to my shop. Derek and Freddy were talking next to the register.

"This is ridiculous. You don't need to work." Freddy saw me make a face. "Stay out of this, Glory."

"I'm not in this." I pushed Miranda and Diana ahead of me into the stockroom. I gave Valdez a mental message to guard the store, then closed the door. Diana and I exchanged looks. There were two ways to do this. One. Tell Miranda everything and then erase her memory. The drawback? What if she needed time to do research? Better to try subtlety first.

"Here's the deal, Miranda. A man has what looks like a cell phone. He points it at someone." I gestured toward Diana. "Like Di here. And he can tell if she's human or . . . not."

"Or not?" Miranda's eyes widened. "Like a zombie or something?"

"Theoretically, yes." Diana smiled. "How would you do that? Tell if someone was a . . . zombie. We're thinking of writing a murder mystery. Looking for a twist." Di winked at me. I loved the way she'd caught on.

"Cool. That's a weird application, but easy enough." Miranda sat on the edge of the battered table I'd shoved up against one wall. "Humans. Like us." She smiled. "Have a pretty constant body temperature. You know, approximately ninety-eight point six. Someone dead wouldn't have the same heat. Maybe no heat at all if they'd been dead a while."

"And a cell phone could read body temp from across the room?"

"Well, not a regular cell phone. Instead it would have to be like the scopes on the guns police use on those TV cop shows. Heat seeking devices. Infrared probably. Expensive. I doubt the Austin cops have them." She pulled out a notebook and began to jot down notes. "Cool concept. Yeah, it could be done." She tapped her teeth with her pen.

"Night vision goggles use that kind of technology. A hunter might use those. Combined with the heat seeking scope, he could do a job on night creatures. But I can't see why anyone would go out looking for the walking dead. How creepy is that?"

Diana made a face behind Miranda's back.

"Beyond creepy. But a neat idea for our book." I kept my smile firmly in place. "Thanks, Miranda. You want to shop now or can I write out a fifty percent off coupon you can use later?"

"That's it? That's all you want?" Miranda's eyes gleamed behind her cool glasses.

"Well, I may have an idea. You ever consider shopping at estate sales for someone else? I'm a night person. So I could use someone to find more vintage clothing for the shop during the day."

"You mean a picker." She grinned. "My mom owns an antique store in Galveston. I've been finding stuff for her for years."

"So you've had experience. Better and better. If you want to do it for me instead of her."

"No problem. She's not really into the clothes. I'd love to be your picker. And you'd pay me. Right? For shopping? Mom kind of feels like I owe her. Six years of college and still going."

"Sure I'd pay you. But if you're a college professor—"

"Teaching assistant. Slave wages while I work on my doctorate." She yawned. "I'm usually a day person myself. And I'm fading fast. Give me the coupon. I'll come back another day. Or night. So we can work out the details."

I opened the door. Valdez sat there with an accusing look. I stepped around him and grabbed a sales pad from by the register. I quickly wrote out a coupon while Miranda patted Valdez's head.

"What a sweet doggie." She made kissing noises. "Aren't you just the cutest thing?" She reached in her pocket and pulled out a piece of muffin wrapped in a paper napkin. "You hungry?"

Valdez was too busy scarfing down what looked to be a chocolate chip laden treat to answer. Plus he knew better than to communicate with anything more than a "woof" in front of mortals.

"He's always hungry." I handed her the coupon. "Thanks, Miranda. You were a big help and I look forward to working with you in the future. We may have more questions later." I looked at Diana. "As we get further into the book."

"Sure." Miranda dug into her book bag. "Here's my card. Call me." She slung the bag over her shoulder, cast a longing glance around the shop, then headed to the door. "I'll be back."

"Arnold Schwarzenegger she's not. Cute glasses though." Derek grabbed the sales book. "I just sold a zoot suit. Cha-ching." He turned to the man standing behind him.

Diana pulled me back into the stockroom and closed the door. "Now what? We can't change our body temp, Glory." She sighed and sat on the table. "We're doomed. Westwood's a billionaire because he owns over a dozen high tech companies. What if he decides to make and sell these vamp detectors? Every hunter on earth will be on us like white on rice."

"We need to think." Body temperature. "I don't even know my body temperature."

"Good point. There's an all night drug store two blocks over." Diana jumped off the table. "I'll send my kitchen guy, my *mortal* kitchen guy, over there to pick up a thermometer." She put her hand on my cheek. "You're warm, sort of. Feel me."

I touched her forehead. I remembered my mother doing that when I was little. One of the few caring gestures she'd ever made. Of course if I dared have a fever, she'd dose me with some awful potion she got from God knew where. The cure was usually a lot worse than the illness. It was a miracle children had survived at all back then. And way too many of them hadn't.

"You feel just like me, Diana. We should have felt Miranda. But when I used to feed from mortals, I remember they felt really warm."

"Yes, their blood's almost hot. You handled Miranda just right. We didn't have to erase her memory and she'll be back if we need to ask her more questions." Diana opened the door and we headed back into the store. "I'll let you know when I get the thermometer. We'll check the three of us, you, me, Derek, and figure out an average temp."

"And then figure out a way to raise it." I picked up a Sharper Image catalog Lacy had left behind the counter. "Battery operated heating pads. Do they make such a thing?"

Derek came back with a credit card. "Give me a minute with a computer and the Internet and I can find out." He grinned. "I'm sorry I was such a wimp earlier, Glory, Diana. You ladies have inspired me. I told Freddy to go to the castle. And to get used to me working because I was going to do it whether he approved or not."

High fives all around. Diana left and a pair of women in scrubs pushed through the door. A night shift for mortals had ended. I glanced at the clock. Just a few hours until dawn. At least we knew Westwood liked the chase. He wouldn't try to get us in our sleep. But I wondered how the men were progressing. There was nothing wrong with a two-pronged approach.

"Hey, Derek." He was flirting with the women. He strolled over to my side.

"A guy's got to do what a guy's got to do. Am I a natural salesman or what?"

"Definitely. When you get on the Internet, check on Kevlar vests." Did I mention I watch a lot of TV? Including cop shows. "See if they can be penetrated by a wooden arrow."

Derek's eyes gleamed. "Will do, boss. What was I thinking? Run? Hell, we'll stay and fight. Freddy's a crack shot."

"And Blade never misses with his knife."

"There you go." Derek leaned closer. "And I've heard that our Italian friends know a thing or two about poisons."

"So we're not defenseless. And Westwood is crafty, not crazy. He sure won't make a move when we've got customers." A good-looking guy in boots and work shirt, who smelled like B negative, pushed open the door. Hmm. I probably wouldn't even have noticed if I'd had a Bloody Merry in my hand. But Derek's eyes lit up. I sent him a mental reminder that he would *not* use my customers for feeding. At least not while they were in the store.

I stepped into the storeroom and got a can of Bloody Merry out of the fridge. When I'd fortified myself with a deep swallow, I headed back into the shop. I looked around and finally relaxed. The thought that Westwood, the fang collecting son of a bitch, had been in my store had almost ruined it for me. But I was getting over it. We had quite a crowd for four in the morning. And wouldn't you know the radio began a Queen set with "We Are the Champions"? Valdez put his paws over his ears.

"You know," I said patting Derek's cheek, rough with his morning beard and barely warm. He would only get cooler as we got closer to dawn. "We'll make Westwood sorry he ever started this hunt."

Ten

"I've moped around here long enough. I'm ready to live again." Flo made this declaration as she bounced on the foot of my bed. "Get up, Glory."

"Forty-eight whole hours. That was fast." I sat up and pushed my hair back. I still felt a little tired.

"Life may be long for us, but I still don't waste a minute." She handed me a Bloody Merry. "Valdez says Westwood came to the shop the other night. Are you still freaked out?"

"Sure." I sipped my drink and felt the familiar surge of energy. "But, like you, I'm not wasting time on it. I need to get down to the shop."

"It's Sunday. You're closed today."

"Yes. I forgot." I lay back and set the can on my night-stand. "Good. Maybe Derek will have time to do that re-search we talked about."

"I know you want to fight Westwood. And that's a good thing." Flo wandered over to my closet and pulled out a black leather mini skirt. Not my best look. Too much thigh. "But I want to have fun. Forget for a while." She put it back and dug out a blue top with a vee neck. My color. She nodded and laid it on the bed. A print blue and red sequined circle skirt that hit me midcalf landed on the bed next.

"We need to go out. Show we're not afraid. Spit in Westwood's eye."

"Jerry and Damian would stroke out if they knew."

"Me, too, sweet cheeks. Forget it." Valdez jumped up on the foot of my bed.

"Down! You'll wrinkle Glory's outfit." Flo pushed him off the bed. "And we do not obey our pets."

"Pets?" Valdez bared his teeth. *"You want a little demo of what this 'pet' can do?"*

Flo clapped her hands and I groaned. Now she'd done it.

"Yes! Show me a trick."

"It's not a trick. It's defense, for Blondie." Valdez shook his head, seemed to gather himself, then growled, the sound sending shivers up my spine. His teeth seemed to grow longer, kind of like a vamp's did. Then he jumped. No, it was more of a leap. From one side of the room to the other, clearing the bed by a good foot and a half.

"Ta da!"

"Magnificent." Flo laughed and headed out to the living room. "Someone is knocking. We have company. Get dressed, Glory. We take Valdez with us wherever we go."

"I could do more, but I've got orders not to tear up your place."

"Glad to hear it." I shut the bedroom door and got busy in the bathroom. Mortals say life is short, live every day like it is your last. Vamps say life is long, live every day like it is your first. So I was going out. Cautiously, but I was going out. So what if I had a body temperature of sixty-two point five? That was a good thing. It helped me live forever. That and my slow heartbeat, which Diana and Derek and I had also checked last night.

I've had a lot of years already. Wasted years to hear Flo tell it. Maybe it was time I got into my vamp thing. Developed more powers. Flo could give me lessons. She'd love that. I still wasn't sure about the shape-shifting, but there were other things. I stepped into the living room to find Lacy with Valdez and Flo.

"Our first day off, boss. I found someone to work days with me." She nodded toward the hall. "If you approve."

"She has a new boyfriend, Glory." Flo lifted her can as if in a toast. "Bring him in, Lacy. We'll let you know what we think."

Lacy gave Valdez a look. "He's mortal. And he thinks we're all just regular folks. Okay?"

"She means we must behave. Got it, Valdez?" I went back to the bedroom for my Bloody Merry and finished it off. "Bring him in." I was pumped, ready for anything.

Anything but Palmer Ryan Dexter the Fifth. For some reason I'd imagined Lacy with the casual type. Not that he wasn't good looking. He was. Even dressed like Gatsby, from the ascot down to the saddle shoes. That was a plus when you wanted to work in a vintage-clothing store. The slicked down hair was a little much and I swear Valdez actually smirked when he saw Ryan, as he asked us to call him. He wore tinted wire-rimmed glasses and looked at Lacy adoringly. A little off center, but a winner if he worshiped Lacy.

"You ever worked retail before?"

"Sure. I've helped in my dad's stores every summer since I turned sixteen." He glanced at Lacy. "He owns fifty-seven SuitMasters." He and Lacy laughed like hyenas. "Can you believe it?" He looked down at his own pin-striped suit with wide lapels. Obviously vintage. "If you can't find a suit for seventy-nine ninety-five, you're not at SuitMasters."

"I've heard those ads." Flo smiled at Ryan. "I don't think you wear one of your father's Sunday specials."

"Naw. He and I don't agree on what we like." He looked at me. "Your store is really cool. I'm studying fashion merchandising at UT. I think the experience of working in a store like yours would be invaluable." He held Lacy's hand. "I want to start my own clothing chain."

"Wasn't there a SuitMistress store too?" Flo stared at Ryan intently.

Ryan winced. "Yeah. Not one of my dad's best ideas. Women didn't dig his cheap suit concept. My stores will be different. Quality vintage."

"You want me to groom my competition?" I kept my hand on Valdez's collar.

"No competition. I'll have to go home to Houston after graduation. I know the territory there. That's where I'll start." He kissed Lacy's cheek. "Lacy and I just met, but I'm already thinking she'd like Houston."

Lacy actually flushed and gave Valdez another look when he made a rude noise. "Can we give him a try, Glory? I could really use the relief."

He was certainly qualified and who was I to trample on young love? Of course Lacy was actually about three hundred years old, but she was enjoying Ryan. It might even develop into something worth moving to Houston for.

"Sure. You can start Tuesday. Lacy, you can train him, right?"

"Right. Thanks, Glory." She hugged me, then pulled Ryan toward the door. "Bye, ladies." She pushed Ryan into the hall, then turned to hiss and rake her claws in Valdez's direction.

"She could do better." Valdez barely waited until the door closed.

"I thought he was cute. Couldn't really get a read on him, though. Some mortals do that with thoughts, like, what you call it, white noise. No matter. He looked harmless enough." Flo tossed her can into the trash and fluffed her hair. "Let's go."

"Blade wants Glory to stay here."

"Blade is not my lord and master." I put my hands on my hips. Yeah, I was a little scared to go out, but I knew what Westwood looked like now. And if we stuck together and went someplace really crowded . . . And what was this about

Ryan? I hadn't tried to read his mind, but Flo didn't seem to think it was a big deal. Still . . . Maybe I shouldn't hire him.

"Ryan's fine. And I know just the place for us. Great music. Lots of people. And the last place a scumbag like Westwood would ever think to look for a vampire." Flo picked up her Fiori bag. Green and blue, a perfect match to her green pants suit. Her shoes were blue lizard. I needed new shoes. But who had time to shop?

Maybe tomorrow night I'd hit the mall. These brown sandals were okay, but it was almost October and the nights were getting pretty cool for bare toes. Surely Westwood wouldn't pull anything in a mall. I desperately needed new boots.

I picked up a shawl and slung it around my shoulders. My own purse was a vintage tooled leather from Mexico. Very *in* right now. I was thinking about selling it.

"It's your day off, Glory. Quit thinking about the shop. Let's go." Flo gave Valdez a look. "Staying or going?"

"Going. I can't let Blondie out of my sight, remember?" Valdez grabbed his leash and dropped it at my feet. *"Blade is going to kill me."*

"He knows you can't stop me, Valdez." I clipped on the leash and dug out my keys. I locked the dead bolts, then dropped the keys in my purse.

"How are we getting wherever it is we're going? My Suburban is dead, you know." I should have thought about this before we headed out. Forget the bus. No dogs allowed. A cab? I'm sure a big tip would get Valdez on board. Flo didn't drive. That pesky reading problem.

Flo waved a set of keys in my face. "I have one of Damian's cars. He left it here for us to use when I told him your car quit. He wants you to drive me."

I debated for exactly one second. "Sure, why not?" If we were lucky, it would be a sexy model. A convertible. Or one of his vintage Mustangs.

It was parked in the alley next to my car. It was vintage all right. A Town Car. Black. Four doors. A mile long and built like an armored car. Were those tinted windows bullet-proof? It would have been right at home in front of a funeral procession.

"Cool car." Valdez approved and what does that tell you?

Flo made a face. "I told him I wanted a sports car and you see what he gives me. Brothers! Pah!"

"Well, we should be safe anyway." I started the engine and it did purr like a very well maintained machine. "Where to?"

"Turn right at the corner. It's a surprise." Flo settled back and clicked on her seat belt.

We only had lap belts. The car was that old. Ten minutes later we were in a parking lot overflowing with pickup trucks, battered economy cars and a few other relics like what I was not so lovingly calling "the hearse." I swear you could see the gas gauge go down when you pressed on the accelerator.

"What is this place?" Valdez stuck his head over the bench seat.

"The Moonlight Church of Eternal Life and Joy. I come here every Sunday night that I can." Flo's look said she dared either of us to say anything negative. Not me. I like churches, though I can't say I got to see the inside of one very often. Forget Sunday mornings. At least the name seemed like a sign.

"Yes, a sign, Gloriana. Eternal life. Us. Joy. Us." She looked at Valdez. "You're going to have to wait outside."

"Yeah, yeah." He huffed. *"Sure. A church. No one would think a vampire would set foot in one."*

"I'm in. You say they have good music?" I'd discovered hymns centuries ago and modern ones are cool. Rock and roll. I'd listened to them on the radio.

"The best." Flo opened her door and hopped out. "Very joyful." She let Valdez out the back. "You listen by the door, mister. You will learn something."

"Oh, great, now she's worried about my soul." Valdez trotted by my side as we walked up to the church. We got some looks. Not because of the dog, he lay down beside the door, out of

the way. I figure we got some looks because we'd dressed up.
I was surprised at the number of men and women in jeans
and T-shirts. There seemed to be a bottleneck at the door.

"Churches are more casual nowadays." Flo whispered as
we waited to get inside. "Not like they used to be. And of
course this church is special, for night creatures like us."

"Cool concept." The Campbells had a private chapel, but
keeping a priest to serve a family of vampires had proved prob-
lematic. At least one Campbell brother had enjoyed terroriz-
ing the neighborhood *and* the priests. Not all the Campbells
were into blending. I haven't seen any of them in decades.
Hopefully they've wised up.

I've never lost the urge to pray for my soul. Maybe vampires are damned. But I don't want to believe it.

Except for the fact that our clothes were cuter than ninety
percent of the congregation, we were blending nicely.

"Welcome to Moonlight, friends." A man acting as greeter
smiled and waved us into the large sanctuary. The walls soared
above us to a glass ceiling that framed the clear night sky.
Clever lighting made it possible to appreciate the view.

I looked around as the church filled. Huge TV screens
flanked a stage that held rows of singers in maroon choir
robes. A five-piece band was set up on the floor in front of
the stage. They were playing a peppy melody that had me
slapping my thighs as I followed Flo to seats near the back.

"Hmmm. I think we're not the only vampires here tonight." Flo looked behind her and nodded to a woman in a
large brimmed pink hat.

"Seriously? All I smell is Chanel No. 5." I turned and
smiled at the same woman. "Nice scent."

"Thank you, dear. Ooo. Here comes Pastor John." The
middle-aged woman put her hands to her breast. She was
stylishly dressed to match her hat in a vintage Chanel suit if
I wasn't mistaken. I'd have loved to slip her a business card.
Wouldn't I like to dig into her closet?

I turned and caught my first glimpse of Pastor John. He was tall and handsome in an obviously well-tailored charcoal suit. His blond hair was brushed back from his high fore-head, but all that was a frame for the sheer joy on his face. He seemed lit from within, smiling, waving to people in the crowd who stood and called out to him. He gestured to the band and the peppy music stopped.

"Welcome, friends of the Moonlight. We're here tonight to celebrate life, celebrate our blessings and to banish our worries."

I was hooked. His joy, his message, his big hands stretch-ing toward us as we prayed to the Creator who seemed non-denominational. Everything he said and did pulled me in until I could hardly sit still. Finally he asked us to stand and sing with him. Another upbeat song. The words scrolled across the screens and I sang.

Flo gave me a look and I piped down a little. Okay, not a singer. But I couldn't just shut up.

"Love lifted me."

"Oh, my God! Glory!" Flo yanked on my skirt and I looked down at her.

Down? I was, okay, I guess you could say I was levitating. Yep. Hovering about six inches off the floor and rising.

Firm hands landed on my shoulders and I dropped like a rock.

"Uh, thanks." I shook my head and looked back.

"Behave, my dears, or don't come back." The hat lady's lips were tight, but her blue eyes twinkled. "Blend, Gloriana."

"I—" Okay, I was speechless. She knew my name. Was obviously one of us. And her English accent took me straight back to home. I blinked, suddenly homesick. Which was stupid considering how long it had been since I'd thought of myself as anything but an all-American vamp.

Flo patted my hand. "It's okay. Nobody noticed except"—she looked back and smiled—"our new friend."

Everyone sat down. Song over. I was blown away. Who knew I could actually come off the ground? How cool was that? A power that I didn't know I had, but which could be tremendously useful. Useful? Hell, this was a freakin' miracle.

I felt a sharp poke in my back. Of course pink hat was reading my mind. Cursing in church was a clear no-no. I remembered that much from my childhood.

A lay preacher took over the pulpit to make announcements about upcoming activities. Lots of stuff going on, all of it at night and much of it involving nature. I'd already learned that Austinites were really into protecting the environment.

"What does he mean? Sky clad?"

Flo frowned and looked around. She suddenly clutched my arm. "Hate!"

Announcements over, a soloist sang about God's love and meeting him in the great beyond. Now *she* had a voice. I kept my feet firmly planted, but swayed to the music.

"I feel hate, Glory."

"What?"

"Someone here is full of hate and it's coming at *us*."

"No." I glanced around. Everyone near us was smiling, moving to the beat of the music. "Look. Everyone's happy."

"Not everyone." Flo shuddered. "We must get out of here."

"But the service isn't over yet."

"Now, Gloriana." Flo pulled me out of the pew and toward the door. I glanced back and saw a man. White hair. Richard Mainwaring? Here? He was staring at me with a look that was all too easy to read.

"Do you see him? Richard?"

Flo looked back over her shoulder. "Ricardo? He is the one?" She shook her head sadly. "I don't like seeing him like this. He can be very . . . dangerous."

I glanced back at Richard. Definitely dangerous. Flo pulled me out the door. Valdez jumped up, on high alert.

"I don't know why he is hating you, Glory."

"Who's hating Glory?" Valdez looked ready to take a chunk out of someone.

"Calm down. Nothing's happened. And maybe he's hating *you*, Flo. You *did* break up with him." I could hear the music faintly through the closed door. Too bad. But I would be coming back here. No way was I letting a perv like Mainwaring keep me from doing what I wanted.

"Ricardo loved me. Still loves me." Flo got into the car and dug in her purse for a hanky. "But he is troubled."

"He's in church. I'd say that's a good sign." And now that I thought about it, even though he'd denied it, he had to be our praying vamp. I hope he'd learned to use discretion and his vamp powers to erase memories if he was determined to feed from mortals. Otherwise someone was going to have to pound some sense into him.

"He is ashamed to be vampire." Flo huffed. "Which is an insult to me, is it not?"

"I can relate to Richard's attitude." But I'd decided to quit being negative. "He's stuck, Florence. Like we all are. I, for one, am ready to make the best of it."

"I know. Ricardo has secrets too. Things he wouldn't share with me. But he was a wonderful lover." She glanced back at Valdez. "Very unselfish, if you know what I mean."

"Unselfish?" I suddenly had an X-rated movie in my head. "Lucky you." I started the car. "Where to now? It's early yet."

"Blade wants you two at the castle." Valdez put his face between us. *"It's a meeting. He's gonna get Tony's report on what he's found out."*

"Someday you're going to tell me how you and Blade communicate."

"The same way you and I do, Blondie. It's a mental thing. Just long distance." Valdez's ears pricked up. *"That Mainwaring creep just came outside. He's trouble."*

"I'm afraid you're right, Valdez." Flo looked at me. "Let's go to the castle."

Flo was clearly still spooked after her brush with death. And I didn't blame her. The soothing quality of the church service was wearing off and I was once again one of those hated demons from hell. I got us out of the parking lot and on the way to Damian's. Fortunately Valdez gave me directions. I was still learning my way around Austin. The dog kept looking over his shoulder.

"Is someone following us?"

"*I don't think so.*" He faced front again. "*Take the next left and you'll see it.*"

The castle was lit from top to bottom. Like for a party. Damian, in black cashmere sweater and jeans, clearly host, greeted us at the door. He was charming with a capital "C" and I had to remind myself that it was calculated down to the last smile.

But he was the only one smiling. It was a pretty somber bunch gathered in Damian's living room. About twenty vampires. Fifteen men. Five women. CiCi was there. Freddy and Derek. Diana. She introduced me to the others, but their names were a blur. Except for Marguerite, a twentysomething brunette with the kind of bee-stung lips women get collagen for nowadays.

Marguerite was with Kenneth Collins, one of the few black vampires I'd met. He was suave, sophisticated, and it took him about two minutes to work the fact that he'd lived in Paris for most of the twentieth century into the conversation.

Flo rushed up and kissed Kenneth on both cheeks then began chattering away in French. Marguerite made a face and pulled me aside.

"Call me Margie. Kenny and I are from Atlanta, Georgia originally. You can imagine why we headed to France when we did."

"He's really handsome. I can see why you followed him."

"No, honey. You've got it backward. I made Kenny and he followed *me*. I've been vampire since 1843. He joined me in 1904." She kept her eyes on Flo and Kenny.

"You knew Flo in Paris?" Flo had definitely known Kenny, the way she was hanging on to him.

Margie's smile was brittle. "Oh, yes. We were all pretty wild back then. Our salons were filled with mortals begging to be tasted." She lifted her glass of Bloody Merry. "This pig piss doesn't do it for me."

Wow. Nothing I could say to that. Besides, I was still pretty buzzed about floating earlier. Could I float now? I looked down at my feet and tried to concentrate. Nope. I looked up and told myself to float, damn it. Nothing.

Margie was watching me curiously. Of course, another mind reader. She could probably float at will. Time for a subject change.

"I like your outfit. Vintage?" She wore a long skirt similar to mine.

"Thanks. It's from my flower-child period in the sixties. I hear you own a vintage-clothing shop."

"Yep. Vintage Vamp's Emporium." I dug in my purse and pulled out one of the business cards Derek had made for me on his computer. "Come by and shop. I give fellow vamps the family discount."

"Super." She licked her full lips and glanced at Kenny again. "You have any corsets? Black or red lace? Kenny loves me in a corset."

Flo had moved closer to Kenny and they had their heads together, laughing as if at a secret joke. Margie apparently decided enough was enough. "Florence, honey, what ever happened to that handsome Spaniard you used to sleep with in Paris?"

Flo turned to Margie. "Ricardo or Pablo?"

"Ricardo was English, wasn't he? The Spaniard was an artist. I had such a crush on him." Margie was obviously dealing out payback. Kenny's mouth tightened.

"Pablo Picasso. Wild times in Paris, eh, Kenny? I left Pablo when he started painting me with three breasts." She looked up at Kenny. "Do I look like I have three breasts?"

Margie looked ready to pull out some hair. I decided it was time for a distraction.

"Flo, who's that handsome man over there, the tall one with CiCi?" Flo looked and got a competitive gleam in her eyes.

"Come. I introduce you. Au revoir, Kenneth." Flo kissed Kenny good-bye, a totally unnecessary gesture since we were only going across the room. Margie's hands fisted.

"See you two later. Come by the shop." I let Flo drag me across the room. Freddy's mom kept her hand on her vampire's arm and made it obvious that she'd put her search for a new lover into high gear and Flo wasn't going to interfere.

CiCi and Flo were sniping at each other when I wandered away to park myself next to Diana. "I feel like I'm at a singles' mixer."

Diana nodded toward the door. "And here comes another hot guy."

Blade walked in and looked around.

"*Your* hot guy?"

"Nope. We're both free agents." Blade smiled at me but didn't stop to speak to me. Well, hell, we weren't so free that he could practically ignore me. I know, I'm perverse. I've done nothing but push Blade away. So when he stays away? I resisted the urge to send him a mental message. He was busy speaking to each vampire individually, obviously acting as a leader. A role he was born for.

A waiter in a tux circulated around the room with fresh crystal goblets of pig piss, I mean Bloody Merry, on a silver tray. I'd passed the first go round. This time I snatched one and sipped gratefully. I was *so* not going to think about the last night Blade and I had made love. Here. Right upstairs.

Or the night Damian and I had checked out his coffin and each other. Here. Right upstairs. I drained my glass and grabbed a second. At least the waiter was a distraction. How long had it taken Damian to find a Lurch look-alike named Lex Luther?

"People. Can we start this meeting?" Blade. Impatient as always.

Damian nodded. "Bring him in, Luther."

Luther opened a door and Tony Crapetta strutted into the room. The strut was marred by the visible shaking in his knees. And then there were the crosses . . . He had at least six of them around his neck. Religious medals too. He clutched a rosary in his hand and looked nervously around the room.

Diana rushed forward. "Darlin', relax. We're all friends here." She looked around and grinned. "Who wants the first bite?"

Eleven

"Oh, Jesus, Mary and Joseph." Tony crossed himself and sank to his knees.

"Diana, behave." Damian gave her a stern look and pulled Tony up to shove him into a chair. "No one's going to bite you, Tony."

"I might." Another woman walked in from the entry. Her red hair pulled back to show killer cheekbones, Mara MacTavish was dressed in expensive black, cut down to there. She was tall, model thin and a reminder that life is *not* fair. She strolled over to Tony and ran her fingers through his thin brown hair. She stared into his eyes and licked her lips.

"Mmmm. O positive. Am I right?"

"Our Father—" Tony gasped and closed his eyes.

"Wimp." Mara looked at Blade. "Are we so desperate for help that *this* is what we use?"

"Yes." Blade gestured for Mara to sit, but she just shrugged.

"I don't believe it." She looked around the room. "Gloriana. Frederick. Countess. I don't know the rest of you. Well,

Florence of course. Everyone knows Florence. I'm Mara MacTavish."

"I don't like the way she said that, Glory. Is she calling me a slut?" Flo clutched her crystal goblet. "How would she like to wear a little Bloody Merry?"

Blade looked over at us. Of course he'd heard Flo, every vampire in the room had heard her, including Mara. That lady just smiled and walked to Blade's side.

"Florence, Mara, can we get on with this?" Blade pulled out a chair which Mara ignored.

She frowned at Tony who was busily saying a rosary. "I think you're wasting our time with this sniveling mortal."

"He's not as useless as he looks." Damian took Mara's hand and pulled it to his lips to give her a fang job. Never let it be said that he wasn't an equal opportunity letch. "Damian Sabatini, Mrs. MacTavish."

"You fang me again, demon, and I'll knock your choppers down your throat." She jerked her hand back to her side.

"Whoa. I like this woman," Diana whispered.

I had to admit Mara was rapidly becoming my heroine, despite what *had* been a slam against Flo. Mara was taking control of the meeting. And the men hated it. Blade was obviously sending her mental commands to cool it. She ignored him.

Damian wasn't taking rejection well. He turned his back on Mara and focused on Tony, jerking him to his feet in mid-Hail Mary.

"Get up. Be a man. Tell us what you found out today."

"Yes, sir, Mr. Sabatini." Tony wiped his forehead on his sleeve. He was sweating as if it was a hundred degrees in here instead of a cool seventy.

Blade stepped forward. "Report."

"Yes, well, Brent Westwood's got a ranch just north of town. He's made that his headquarters. Surrounded himself with hired muscle and high tech security."

"Why Austin?" A dapper man, sort of a scholarly type with a neat mustache and goatee, stepped forward. "There are a lot more vampires in New York City or even San Francisco."

There were murmurs of agreement around the room.

"Westwood started his fortune with a computer company in Austin. He's owned the ranch for years. I got a contact on the inside." Tony let go of his rosary long enough to pull a paper out of his pocket. "The guy says Westwood got a call a while back that there was, uh, a coven of you people here, two dozen or more."

Flo marched up to him. "We're not witches, you oaf. We don't do covens or clubs or even gangs." She threw up her hands and snatched the paper. "What's this? Your grocery list?" She handed it to Blade then turned to examine Tony like he was something stuck on her high heel. "I can smell your fear. Is it because you plan to betray us?"

"No! No, ma'am." Tony swallowed and held his rosary in both hands. "It's a list of names, ma'am. The hired muscle Westwood's got inside." Tony put the rosary up to his neck.

"I wouldn't bite you if your veins were pure champagne." Flo flounced back to my side. "Mara's right. Is this the best we can do?"

"Flo, some cities do have covens," Diana felt compelled to say. Flo gave her a withering look. "Not in Austin, though. Obviously."

Tony wobbled and Blade shoved him into the chair again.

"What are we supposed to do with this list?" Blade glanced down at it.

"I figured you might get to one of Westwood's goons. Pay him off to take out Westwood." More murmurs. Some vampires actually whipped out their checkbooks.

"I don't like it." Mara looked around the room. "Are we going to rely on mortals to take our revenge?"

"I got other stuff. Valuable information." Tony obviously saw his fat paycheck shrinking. "My contact says Westwood's got pictures. He's keeping a kind of shooting gallery." Tony looked around the room. "It's his hit list."

I shuddered. I bet I could name five on Westwood's list. Blade looked at me and moved closer. Mara stepped between us and grabbed Blade's arm.

"I have an idea."

"She would." Diana had just decided Mara was not so hot.

"Some of us can shape-shift. We go in as a flock of birds, though bats are common enough around here."

"They are." The scholar spoke up. "Millions live under the Congress Avenue bridge downtown."

"Okay, then." Mara walked over and patted the man's cheek. "You do the bat thing, honey?" She gave him a sultry look. "I'm sorry I don't know your name."

"Jason. Jason Morgan." He grinned. "Actually, I run with them sometimes. There's a great place called The Devil's Hole a few hundred miles from here—"

"Fine. Who else is up for a flight?" Mara looked at me. With pity? Or disdain? "Not you, of course, Gloriana. I know how you feel about shifting."

"I'd like to shift *you*." Flo, my new champion.

"I'm sure you'll have fun spying on Westwood." I looked at Diana. "Di, Derek and I are working on a more technical approach."

"Technical?" Blade looked interested.

"We think we've figured out how Westwood's vamp detector works. It's got to be a heat seeking device." Derek stepped forward with a sheaf of papers in his hand. "He can make us because we don't give off enough heat."

"So?" Mara looked around the room. "We can't raise our body heat, you know." She glanced at me, then touched Blade's cheek. "Just slightly warm. Perfect for a healthy vampire. Heat us too much and we die. That's why sunlight fries us."

"Not necessarily. Fire doesn't do us permanent harm." Derek wasn't giving up. "I'm no scientist, but I'd say there's something special in the sun's rays that gets us." Other vamps nodded.

Mara frowned. "Whatever. We still need to take out Westwood."

"I'm not disagreeing with you, Mara." I touched Derek's arm to show my support. "But Westwood's not the only one out to stake us. We need to be able to protect ourselves."

"I get that. But right now Westwood's our biggest threat." Mara had her fierce warrior woman face on. "I say we fly out there. We may get lucky. Get the drop on Westwood." Mara grabbed Blade's arm. "This man, at least, can change in an instant, tear Westwood apart and problem solved."

"Westwood's pretty well protected." Tony shrank back when Mara glared at him. "Good plan."

"Sure. Go, Mara. Just watch out for the guano, bat girl." I was pretty proud of that zinger until Blade shot me a warning look. "Oh, excuse me. Who's going with them?" Five more vamps stepped forward, including Flo.

"No, honey, stay here." I grabbed her arm.

"The bastard shot at me, Glory. I get a chance to rip his throat out, I take it." She walked over to Damian. "What are we waiting for?"

"I'm staying here." Damian came over to my side. "I want to see what Glory's got."

"I'm still going." Flo tossed her hair and looked around. "Is this it?"

Tony jumped up and pulled another paper out of his pocket. "Here. A map. I marked the ranch with a red X. You guys can really change into bats?"

Mara took the map. "Vampires have many powers, mortal. You'd be smart to remember that."

"Yes, ma'am." Tony sat again and groped for his rosary.

Diana and I stayed out of the way. I'd had visions of being the heroine tonight. Screw that. At least Damian was being attentive, his hand on my shoulder as Derek laid out his papers on a mahogany table.

"This vest thing has possibilities, Glory. Let them go." Derek grinned at me then turned to the vampires not eager to go batty. "Come look at this, people. There's protective gear available. Glory's idea."

"I told Blade you had brains and beauty." Damian's hand slid up to my neck to lightly stroke my jugular. I shivered and tried to ignore him without making a scene. Mara had done enough of that tonight.

The others crowded around us. But I managed to catch Blade's eye.

"Be careful, Jerry."

"And you stay safe, Gloriana."

I nodded, message received. Then he and the rest of the bat patrol stepped outside. Oh, God, what if Westwood shot at bats too?

"Forget the bats. Feed with me, Glory." Damian pulled me away from the crowd.

"Are you nuts?" I gestured toward my empty goblet. "I've fed."

Damian pulled me out into the hall. "How can you live like that? Don't you ever thirst? For say," he glanced back at Tony Crapetta who seemed afraid to move out of his chair, "O positive?"

I didn't want to think about it. Of course I could smell Tony's blood surging through his veins. The other vampires didn't spare us or Tony a glance, too absorbed in Derek's research. My gums swelled and I leaned closer to Damian.

"We can't."

"Yes, we can." He leaned closer and kissed my neck. "And after we have satisfied that urge"—he touched my breast, ever so lightly—"we can satisfy another."

Why hadn't I knocked Damian on his ass? I shook my head.

"Not going to happen, Sabatini."

He just smiled and looked into my eyes. Tony had worked up the nerve to approach us. Clueless.

"Uh, Mr. Sabatini, is there anything else tonight?" He wiped his hands on his pants. "There's the little matter of payment."

With him so close I swear I could hear Tony's heart pumping.

"Come to my library, Tony, and I'll give you cash."

"Where are you going, Blondie?" Valdez had followed us to a door down the hall.

"Nowhere." I tried to head back to the living room. Damian stopped me with a touch on my hand.

"Order him back to the living room." Damian didn't spare the dog a glance.

"Will not." I couldn't seem to look away from Damian's glowing emerald eyes.

"Yes, you will." Damian smiled and opened the door.

"Go back, Valdez. I'm okay here." Why had I said that? *"Blade ain't gonna like this."*

"Blade doesn't have to know." I ignored Valdez when I felt Damian's hand on my elbow, guiding me inside. The door shut gently behind us and I was in a library.

"Valdez?"

"He must obey you." Damian was still smiling.

"Of course." Something was off here. I didn't meekly follow Damian anywhere. I didn't trust him.

"Trust me, Glory." His soothing voice shooed away my misgivings and I couldn't remember why I'd ever resisted him.

I looked around the library. Wow. It was a feudal lord's dream come true. Old and obviously expensive tapestries hung on the only wall not covered by built-in shelves. A heavy carved desk and massive red velvet armchairs faced an unlit fireplace. Of course no feudal lord had ever had books like those filling every inch of the shelves. Thousands of books, most leather bound. A few sat in glass cases. Treasures that were so old you wore gloves to touch them.

Damian had Tony in a trance. The man just stood there, motionless while Damian watched my reaction to his library.

"I'm very proud of it. I've been collecting for . . . centuries."

"I can see that." That's right. Concentrate on books. "Flo's missing a lot. Not reading."

"You believed her?" Damian laughed and walked up behind me. "She plays the helpless female to perfection. And if you tell her I revealed her secret"—he licked a path up my neck to behind my ear—"I will have to kill you."

I shivered and turned in his arms to look up at him. Was he using the vamp whammy on me? He had to be. I didn't—My eyes closed as his lips met mine, sucking away any thoughts of resisting. Casanova kisses. Mmmm.

I kissed him back, sending him a mental message that if he bit me again against my will, I'd have to kill *him*. He pushed me down to the rug. I felt heat and realized he'd started the fire in the fireplace with just a look. Neat trick.

My blouse was open and my bra. Another neat trick. Wait a minute. I shouldn't—Damian kissed my breasts and sucked a nipple into his mouth. I had a random thought and struggled to focus on it. We weren't alone. I looked over Damian's head to see Tony staring at us. Staring, but not seeing. Okay, it was kind of a turn-on. That and knowing that over a dozen vamps were down the hall and Valdez was less than twenty feet away.

Had Damian locked the door? Who cared? Damian pulled up my skirt, his hand pressing against me in a way guaranteed to break me apart. No. Wasn't breaking apart for him. Wasn't—He stroked me with clever fingers and I sighed. How had I gotten so lucky? With all those other beautiful female vamps to choose from, the most handsome man at the meeting had wanted Gloriana St. Clair.

Most handsome? I tried to open my eyes and couldn't. Instead, I pulled Damian's head up to kiss him again. His taste intoxicated me, otherwise why would I rake my fangs over his lips until I settled at his throat? I asked the question and he pressed my head to him, inviting me to feed. So I did, while he ran his hands over me, kneading my breasts and pushing his enormous arousal against me. He really wanted me.

Casanova. This had to be some kind of vamp whammy. I didn't do this. I didn't—Oh, the taste. Rich, warm, flooding my mouth until I tore myself away from drinking to rip open his shirt. I had to have him, his body. I opened his zipper and held him before I raked my fangs down his swollen length.

He gasped and lay back as I crawled over him with a wildness I'd never felt before. I shook my head. What was wrong with me? I wouldn't—I pulled up my skirt and jerked aside my thong to take him inside me. His thrust filled me, sending me close to the edge. I bit back a shriek of ecstasy.

Slow down, think. I couldn't think of anything beyond prolonging the pleasure. I looked over my shoulder to see Tony, still staring.

"We have an audience."

"I think an audience makes you hot. You *were* a performer." Damian pushed into me again, holding onto my breasts with both hands. He played my nipples like a virtuoso and my body hit high *C*. Insane, this was insane. I didn't even *like* Damian Sabatini.

"*You* make me hot," I whispered as I leaned down to bite him again. I felt the first waves of a major orgasm crashing over me. I fed and felt Damian's hands on my ass, clutching me, urging me on. I needed no urging. I couldn't stop. Faster, harder, oh, God I can't—

He drove into me, touching me deep, deep, deeper inside until I gasped and sat up. This had to stop. I didn't want this. Suddenly still, Damian reached up and held my face in his hands.

"You *do* want this, Gloriana. You *own* me. Punish me."

Yes, I wanted to make him suffer. So I rode him hard, punishing him and pushing toward my own satisfaction. I glanced down and his eyes met mine. He was in pain. He wanted to taste me.

"No." I wasn't so far gone with orgasm number two that I didn't remember he *should* hurt.

"You're killing me, Gloriana."

"Then die, vampire." I gripped him with my thighs and moved faster. Damian thrust one more time, groaning as he came. I lay there, quivering inside and out. Damian ran his hands down my back to grip my ass again.

"Woman, you are magnificent."

I just lay there. What had just happened? Who was this woman lying on top of Damian Sabatini with rug burns on her knees and postorgasmic quivers streaking through her limp body?

Damian touched my cheek. "Look at me, Gloriana."

I found the will to refuse. Look at him? Face what I'd just done? I rolled off Damian and sat up. Suddenly I felt Tony's eyes on me. He was smiling.

"Damn it!" I jumped up and reached for my blouse. "Put him back under, Damian. Right. Now."

"Holy moley, lady." Tony clutched his crosses. "You vampires sure know how to get it on. If you could do it without the fang action . . ."

"Damian . . . I'm warning you." I snapped my bra closed and buttoned my blouse.

Damian lay back, obviously very well satisfied. "And if I don't obey you?" He had the nerve to grin.

"This will never happen again." For the life of me, I couldn't figure out how this had happened at all. I turned on my heel and strode to the door. I put my back to it and crossed my arms over my chest. My breasts were still tender and my almost-panties were damp. Had Damian used a whammy to give me those multiple orgasms? No wonder women found him irresistible.

"Take care of him, Damian."

"I'm too weak." He held out his arms. "Let me feed from you."

"No way. Hit Mr. O Positive there."

Tony yelped and looked wild-eyed toward the tall windows since I blocked the door.

"Fine." Damian got to his feet, finally bothering to tuck in and zip his pants. He had such a great body, his shirt hanging open to show ripped abs. His pants rode low. No underwear. Damian stopped and grinned at me.

What the hell was I doing admiring him? He'd done something to me. I wasn't—

"I'm waiting. Wipe his mind clean. Right now."

Damian grabbed Tony on his way to the window and looked deep into his eyes. "You will remember nothing about this night except"—Damian pulled a wad of bills out of his pocket—"that I paid you and you went home."

"You paid me."

Damian looked at me and winked. "I could use a pick-me-up. You want to join me?"

"No, thanks." I opened the door and ran into Valdez, who sniffed, then growled at the door when I shut it.

"The guy's a user and a loser."

"Of course he is." I patted his head and fought the urge to cry into his soft fur. What had I just done? And now I smelled like sex. Oh, God, please let no one else notice.

"You want me to tear him apart?" Valdez growled at the closed door. *"Open up."*

"No. He might hurt you." Damn it, I had to go back to the living room.

"I'll take my chances."

My eyes filled with tears and I shook my head. "He's not worth it." I took a deep breath, pasted on a smile and forced myself back into the living room.

The living room . . . I rubbed my eyes and, hello, the bat patrol was still in the room discussing strategy. Tony still cowered in his chair and Damian grinned and winked. What the hell had just happened to me?

I heard Derek explaining the virtues of Kevlar. Apparently I *hadn't* gone to Damian's library, *hadn't* had mind-blowing sex with an audience. I sent Damian a mental message to go screw himself since screwing me was *never* going to happen.

"What do you think, Glory?" Diana was obviously waiting for me to answer. What did I think? That Damian Sabatini was a dead man.

Twelve

Twenty-four hours had passed since the bat patrol had returned with the bad news that Westwood wasn't taking midnight strolls around his property. Apparently he knew enough about vampires to stay locked inside his ranch house after dark, surrounded by thugs armed with stakes, guns and anything else he thought might slow down what Westwood considered a predator.

Twenty-four hours had passed since Damian had used the whammy on me and I was still freaking out. Damian had taken mind control to a whole new level. Could other vamps alter reality so completely? This could be good defense. Something I should learn to do. But not with Damian as teacher. I was avoiding him like the bird flu. And if I did have to be in the same room with him, I was throwing up a block the size of Mount Rushmore.

At least Diana, Derek and I had been a hit with the non-flying vampires. Derek had found out that wooden arrows couldn't come at enough velocity to penetrate Kevlar, even if Westwood started using a crossbow.

Some vamps were already ordering Kevlar vests. Others who hadn't been spotted by Westwood yet were investigating heat generating devices. We'd found battery operated socks that hunters wore, surely there were other heaters we could wear on our chests. Maybe a battery operated T-shirt. Of course in summer this might present a problem. Austin has really hot summers.

The female vamps had decided to work on developing a Kevlar bra. You knew I wasn't going to wear a bulky vest, didn't you? I mean how many pounds would that add? But a bra, with ample coverage over the heart region. That might be workable.

I'd ordered some Kevlar material from the Internet. Expensive and when it came I'd have to find a seamstress. But I'd already developed a cover story. Worked with a knife thrower in the circus. Sometimes he missed.

Unfortunately it would take at least a week to get the fabric and I had this one night off before I would be back in the shop again. I could lock myself in my apartment, but how wimpy was that? And new boots were calling my name. So Diana, Flo and I decided to head to the nearest mall.

"Forget it, Blondie. You're not going anywhere without me." Valdez hopped out of the car before I could shut him inside.

"I see a sale sign." Flo tugged on my arm.

"And I see a sign that says service animals only." Diana patted Valdez. "Sorry, fella, that means you stay in the car."

"Not necessarily." I looked around the dark parking lot. As long as I had Valdez by my side, I knew no one could sneak up on me. I dug in my purse. Yep, the sunglasses a customer had left in the shop were in there. I put them on and grabbed Valdez's leash.

"See? I'm a service animal."

"Just behave. If I have to play blind, you have to play serious guard dog."

"Don't I always?" Valdez pulled me toward the entrance. *"Let's get out of the open."*

Flo and Diana followed us. And didn't I feel like a fool groping for the door?

"Would one of you lead the way? Flo, take us to the nearest shoe store with a big sale going on."

"You got it, girlfriend." Flo stepped out with Valdez right behind her.

Diana grabbed my arm like she was steering me through the crowd. I got a few sympathetic looks and felt like a total fraud.

"What color boots do you want? High or low heels? Ankle or knee high? Suede or leather?"

"Gee, Diana, I'm blind not dumb. I can tell the salesman—" I was sounding bitchy. This blind thing was going to be a pain. "Sorry." I gave Diana a rundown of what I was looking for.

"Here we go." Flo stopped in front of a store with a Sale sign, then stepped inside. "Please excuse my blind friend and her guide dog. Poor thing hardly ever gets to go shopping."

Poor thing? Valdez took exception to the salesman blocking the aisle and showed his teeth.

"Uh, sure, guide dogs welcome." The man backed away and knocked over a display of evening shoes.

Apparently metallics were in and I stopped myself just before I picked up a particularly cute pair of bronze sandals. I groped my way to a chair.

"Valdez, sit." I smiled and pushed Valdez's butt down until he sat, unfortunately on my left foot. "Ouch!"

Diana took his leash and shoved him off me. "She wants a pair of brown suede boots, knee high, medium heels, size seven and a half. Right, Glory?"

"Sure. Thanks." I took off my left shoe and rubbed my toes, sending Valdez a mental message to behave.

"Feel this boot, Glory. Isn't that just the softest thing?" Flo pushed a boot into my hand.

Valdez jumped up and started barking wildly.

"Oh, my God!" I dropped to the floor. Diana crawled under a table and Flo scrambled behind the counter with the bewildered salesman.

"Is it Westwood?" Diana reached out to drag me under the table with her. Yep, her vamp strength was working.

Thank God we were the only customers in the store. "Valdez, what is it?" I watched him sniff around the floor, then sit down and scratch his ear.

"False alarm. Damned boots are lined with rabbit fur. I thought I smelled cat."

"Thanks a lot." I crawled out and stood. "Flo, do your thing, honey."

She grinned and put the salesman under a whammy. He silently headed to the storeroom to find my boots. Diana dusted off her jeans and shook her head.

"You scared the life out of me, you hound. You better be dang sure we're in danger before you go off like that again." Diana was paler than usual.

Hey, my heart was pounding too. Flo collapsed in the chair next to me.

"Valdez, you must understand. Shopping is serious business, especially a shoe sale." Flo fanned her cheeks. "No noise now unless you see a man with a bow and arrow."

"You're cramping my style, lady."

"Consider yourself cramped." I pushed him back down, careful of my feet this time, just as the salesman came out with three boxes. And wasn't that a treat, going through the whole charade of trying on and groping my way around the store? But I did feel safe. And Flo and Diana both agreed that my new brown boots were cute and a bargain.

Diana fell for some Prada pumps. And at half price, how could Flo resist the Ferragamo slides? Three pairs in three colors.

We were headed for the hearse in the parking lot when Valdez barked again and knocked me flat on my back, my package and purse flying in two different directions. Diana cried out and grabbed her arm. An arrow stuck out of it.

"Down. Everybody down." Valdez hit Flo and she landed on her behind just as another arrow whizzed past us.

"Dios mio. What's happening?" Flo crawled over to rescue the three pairs of shoes flung across the pavement.

"Damn it, woman. I said stay down." Valdez barked and other shoppers heading to their cars paused to watch. A few seemed inclined to come help us, but Valdez's wild barking and growls discouraged them. He finally stopped and sniffed the air. We heard tires squeal like a car couldn't get out of the lot fast enough.

"All clear. He's gone." Valdez stayed by my side as I got to my feet.

"Diana, are you all right?" I helped her up. She was bleeding and I wrapped my sweater around her arm. We both stared at the arrow.

"Hell no, I'm not all right." Diana took a shaky breath. "It hurts like the Devil." She put her hand on the shaft and pulled, her face going white.

"Stop it, Diana. Leave it alone." She was swaying and tears streamed down her cheeks.

"Can't. It's got to come out." She sniffed and wiped away the tears with the back of her hand. "Just break it, Glory, then pull it out."

I swallowed. Obviously I can deal with blood, but I hated to hurt her even more.

"Can't be helped, hon. Just do it." She bit her lip and looked around. More people had stopped to watch. A security guard was headed toward us. "Flo, take care of him, will you?"

"No problem." Flo got to her feet and limped toward the guard. I could see she was using the vamp whammy on him. He just stopped and stared unseeing while I pulled Diana to the other side of the car. Thank goodness it was fairly dark. My guess was that Westwood had taken out the light we'd parked under. He'd obviously followed us to the mall, then waited for us to come out.

He'd taken a big chance hitting us in such a public place. A bystander could have called the police. But being a big game hunter, he probably got off on taking chances. I looked around to make sure I didn't need to erase some memories. I saw Flo take care of the few shoppers closest to us. No one else seemed to realize what had happened and went on to their cars.

"Glory, come on. Get this arrow out of my arm."

"You sure you want me to do this? It's going to really hurt."

Diana was obviously in some serious pain but she nodded, biting her lip.

"Here goes." I grabbed the arrow. I'd have to break off the feathered end and then push the arrow through her arm.

"Quit thinking about it and just do it." Diana had tears running down her cheeks again. "And tell Flo to pick up my new shoes."

Shoes? To hell with shoes. I had to do this quick. I sucked in a breath and snapped off the feathered end. One sharp tug and I had two pieces of really bloody olive wood arrow to dispose of. I thought I was going to be sick.

"You're *not* going to be sick, Glory. You did fine. And keep the arrow. Put it in one of the shopping bags." Diana wrapped my sweater back around her arm. "We might want to study it later."

"Good thinking." I couldn't quit shaking. Diana had pulled herself together and was now fairly calm. "We've got to get you home."

Flo walked up to us lugging all of our shopping bags. "I've taken care of our witnesses." She looked at Diana. "Wow, you already took out the arrow?"

"Glory did it." Diana leaned against the car. "Valdez saved us. I moved when he jumped at Glory. If I hadn't . . ." She swayed and I reached around her to open the car door.

"Get inside." I looked around the dark parking lot. The mall was closing. Flo stuffed our packages in the backseat.

"Valdez, you're our hero."

"Just doing my job." Valdez looked at me. *"You okay?"*

"Sure I'm fine. It's Diana we should worry about." I helped her into the front seat. "Flo, watch and make sure we're not being followed."

"Will do, Glory." Flo reached over the seat to pat Diana's shoulder. "Let me touch your wound, Diana. I think I can heal it."

"Really? You *think*? You're not sure?"

"Not one hundred percent."

Diana winced when another car leaving the lot passed us, flooding the interior of our car with light. She held her arm and shook her head. "Then wait until we get home. I just want to get out of here."

"Good idea." More and more cars were pulling out of the parking lot. If Westwood was still around, he might try to take another shot.

"Yeah, get us out of here. But I think Westwood's gone." Valdez looked around. *"I've got his scent now. He's not getting near us without warning again."*

I pulled out of the parking lot. The arrow was in a bag on the floorboard under Diana's seat. It gave me the creeps. So did the near miss we'd just had. A few inches to the left and Diana would be dead, a new trophy for Westwood's necklace.

"He missed worse than that."

"What do you mean, Valdez?" I was glad we lived so close to the mall. A few more minutes and we'd be home, safely locked in.

"I mean, he wasn't aiming at Diana, Blondie. He was aiming at you." Valdez put his head over the seat and nudged my cheek. *"He didn't know Diana was vamp. He's got your picture, remember? It was dark. She's blond, you're blond. And about the same size."*

"Oh, God." I was shaking so badly I had to pull over. No traffic to speak of. If Westwood was following us, I was being pretty stupid. But I didn't want to hit a tree or another car either. I breathed through nausea. I had to drive. Flo couldn't and Diana wasn't in any shape to. I gave myself a minute to melt down, then sucked it up and put the car in gear again.

And I drove, on automatic pilot, as my mind raced. He'd been trying to kill *me*. This was real. Suddenly immortality seemed like the best gift Blade had ever given me. And I was damned if I was going to let Brent Westwood steal it away from me.

We pulled up in the alley and parked. Valdez got out first and sniffed until he gave us the all clear. Then we hurried into the back door, Flo punching in the security code. Diana lived on the third floor. We took her to her own apartment and sat her in a kitchen chair.

"Now I'm not sure this will work. But I do think I can heal you." Flo pulled off her own sweater and rolled up the sleeves of her green silk blouse. "Just like all of us, I heal fang marks. But I've also taken off scrapes, cuts, minor things before." She held out her leg. "I had a bad scrape on my knee when I fell in the parking lot. You saw me limping. See? I touch. I healed."

"That's amazing." I was constantly surprised by Flo's powers. It seemed like a new power had shown up every week since she'd moved in with me. Though considering what her brother could do . . . Not thinking about that now. Diana was still bleeding.

Flo pulled the wrapping off Diana's wound. "This is pretty bad. Maybe you should sleep it off."

"Go ahead and try. What could it hurt?" Diana was really pale. "It already stings like a son of a bitch."

I walked into her kitchen and got a can of Bloody Merry, popping the top before handing it to her.

"Take a swig. It should help."

"Good, Glory. Now you watch me. If this works, you will want to know how to do this." Flo glanced at me and grimaced. "With luck, you won't have to."

She placed her hands on either side of Diana's arm and pressed, staring down at the wound and obviously concentrating all her energies. "I'm *seeing* it healed. Like we do with fang marks."

She continued pressing and I thought for a minute that it wasn't going to work.

"Concentrate *with* me, Glory, Diana. *See* it healed. Put your hands over mine." Flo was using her vamp whammy voice and I couldn't have disobeyed her if I'd wanted to. Which I didn't.

I stared and saw the wound closing. Yep, it really did. Right in front of our eyes.

"Wow. That is so cool." Diana touched her arm and smiled. "No pain, nothing."

"You did it, Flo." I hugged her and blinked back tears.

"*We* did it, *cara.*" She pulled back and looked down at Valdez. "You saved us, doggy. We go home and have dip and chips, yes?"

"*Yes.*" Valdez wagged his tail and trotted toward the door. "*You'll hand feed me?*"

"You bet, *signor.*" Flo picked up our packages. You'd think none of this had fazed her except that her Italian accent had gotten thicker. "I think our shoes are okay too. A triumph. That Westwood bastard, we beat him."

I was still shaky. And the sight of my blood-soaked sweater on the table didn't help. I picked it up and dropped it into the kitchen trash can. I stood at the sink and washed my hands. I should take the trash with me. Diana didn't need to see it when she woke. "I'll chuck this mess in the trash bin out back, Di."

"I'm okay. Leave it there, Glory. I'll take it out tomorrow." Diana stood and hugged me, then Flo. "Girl power rules."

Girl power. No. Vamp power. Yes. I'd just seen a miracle with it. I was pumped. I wasn't wasting another day denying my potential. My next night off, Glory St. Clair was starting power lessons.

Flo just looked at me and smiled. "You got it, girlfriend."

When not dodging arrows, I still had the store to run. The next night I was adding up receipts when the bells on the front door tinkled. Damian.

"Get out." I battened down the hatches on my mind. No vamp whammy would creep inside tonight.

Valdez barked. Had he read my mind enough to know what Damian had done to me? But I was blocking now. Both of them. And I had the headache to prove it. Valdez just didn't like any man who came sniffing around me. Any man who wasn't Blade.

For a minute I was tempted to let Valdez do his thing. No, I could and would handle this. I gave my dog a mental command and he settled down by the door with a growl. He still kept his eyes on Damian.

"Gloriana, *cara*." Damian came toward me, hands outstretched. I turned my back on him. As far as I knew vamps had to at least make eye contact to put on the whammy. Of course Damian's power level was off the charts if he could put wild monkey sex in my head.

"You blew it with me, Damian. Give it up."

"I was playing with you, Glory. Giving you a fantasy." He came up behind me and touched my shoulder.

"Back off. Do *not* touch me."

"What was the harm? We played a little game." He was so close I could feel his warmth, all seventy or so degrees of it. "You were amazing and we had fun."

"*You* had fun. I should have known you were faking me out." Oh, I wanted to confront him face-to-face. "Trust me. When I'm in the throes of a screaming orgasm, I don't think how lucky I am this handsome man picked poor unworthy me to be his lay."

"I never thought you unworthy." His voice was coaxing. He was trying to whammy me again.

If I stuck my fingers in my ears, I'd just look stupid. I walked over to the radio and turned up the volume. The oldies station was doing a Beatles set. "A Hard Day's Night." Definitely.

"Gloriana. Of course I would choose you. You are desirable, passionate, all woman."

"And you are a first-class creep." Blocking him might not be enough. I didn't trust him not to try to pull another stunt. I got as far away from him as my little shop would allow. Damn it, he was making me look like a fool.

"Let me make it up to you. Please." He touched me again. Of course he'd followed me. I scooted away from him to sort through a stack of sweaters.

"Not listening." I refolded a hot pink one, then put it aside. It would look great on Margie and she was supposed to be by later.

"I'm not giving up, Gloriana. Ouch!"

I turned to see Damian take a glancing blow on the forehead from a depression glass bowl before it hit the floor and shattered. Next, a Coach purse hit Damian on the shoulder. For once I was glad my spirits were around.

Get lost, loser. Harvey in bold letters on the counter.

"What is this?" Damian rubbed his head. A lump was forming. Too bad it would be gone tomorrow.

I grinned. "I have guardian angels, Damian. I suggest you get out before they knock over that bookshelf behind you."

Sure enough, the shelf trembled. Then three books came at Damian. Direct hits.

"Stop it. I'm leaving." He leaned down to pick up the books. "Remember my library, Glory?" Grinning, he set them back on the shelf. "I have great respect for books."

"But not for women." I shook my head. "You ever put that kind of whammy on me again and I'll personally see to it that every female vampire in Austin gets a picture of your penis. The one the size of my little finger." I walked over to open the door.

"It is not—"

"Doesn't have to be. I can get a picture of anything on the Internet. And unless you want to go around with your dick hanging out to prove otherwise, you'll be a laughing stock."

Damian held up his hands. "You win. For now. Perhaps I went too far."

"Perhaps?"

"Okay, I did go too far. But I'm not giving up, Gloriana. You saw. We can be great together."

"Did I say little finger? Maybe I meant little toe." I laughed at his expression. "Poor Damian and his teenie, weenie, wienie. Enormous in his own mind. How pathetic is that?"

Valdez jumped up and did one of his patented "I'll eat you for dinner" growls. Damian couldn't get out fast enough. I slammed the door behind him then looked down at the pieces of glass on the floor and picked up the purse.

"Thanks, Emmie Lou and Harvey. Next time could you stick to nonbreakables? That guy's not worth the price of the bowl." I went to the stock room to get the broom and dust pan. Men. Why did I bother?

Thirteen

I'd just swept up the last of the glass when something told me to look up. Blade. And the bells on the front door hadn't made a sound.

"Would you not sneak up on me? I've had a rough night." I stuck the broom and dust pan back in the storeroom. Valdez greeted Blade like an old friend. Which he was.

"You mean *last* night? When you went shoe shopping?" Blade had no shopping gene whatsoever.

"I guess the furry snitch here told you all about it."

"Yes." Blade just stared at me. "You could have been killed, Gloriana."

"I know." Oh, shoot, my voice wobbled. Yeah, I was still shook up and being alone in the shop didn't help. Westwood had been in here.

"Come here, Gloriana."

As if I wanted to resist. I moved into his arms and let him hold me, resting my head on his chest. I could feel his strength. Around me, where his arms wrapped around my back. And inside my mind, where he murmured comforting words.

I didn't cry. But it was tempting. I saw words appear on the wall behind Blade.

Nice catch. Emmie Lou.

This one's a keeper. Harvey.

I stepped back and pushed my hair out of my eyes. I needed a haircut. A new hairdresser. Maybe I'd go red. Vamp magic let my hair grow just like a mortal's did. I was a mess. My mind was a mess.

"Glory, you look great." Blade smiled. "But I liked your hair best when it came down to"—he reached out to run his fingers down to the tips of my breasts—"here. And do *not* go red."

My nipples peaked and I swayed toward him. Wait a minute. Mind reading.

"Could I have a little privacy please?" I looked down at Valdez who stared up at both of us. "Both of you need to stop reading my mind."

"Yeah, right." Valdez trotted over to the door and lay down beside it. I didn't know whether to be glad we didn't have any customers or worried that my business was falling off.

"I like your shop." Still smiling, Blade headed over to the rack of men's suits. He hadn't missed my reaction to his touch. No way. But he knew me well enough not to push.

"Thanks. I just added the tuxedos and there's a leisure suit I'm sure will end up in Tony's closet if he comes by and sees it."

Blade had stuck to jeans tonight. Which looked good on him. Very good. He turned and glanced at Valdez. "I understand your business is doing well."

"Yes." I wiped my hands on my skirt. Sixties mini with coordinating sweater set. Blue to match my eyes. You'd almost think I knew Blade would be stopping by. Which I'd suspected. No way would Valdez fail to report last night's incident.

"Thanks, by the way."

"Thanks?" Blade looked at me.

Gee, maybe I'd surprised him.

"For Valdez. I know I complain, but, clearly, he saved my life last night." I looked at the dog sitting calmly by the door and he blurred. Oh, shit, I was going to cry.

"Glory." Blade pulled me into his arms again. "Och, now, lass. You're safe."

"But for how long?" I was getting his shirt wet. A nice shirt. Beige. Snap front. Western.

"We're doing all we can to fight him, Glory." He patted my back until I stepped away and grabbed a tissue from behind the counter.

"What are you doing? Be careful, Jerry."

He pulled out the paper Tony had given him last night. "I'm working on this end. Seeing if we can bribe one of Westwood's hired guns. All I need is one unguarded moment." Blade wiped a tear from my cheek. "The bastard will be stopped."

"Did you hear about the Kevlar?" I pulled his hand from my cheek and held on to it. "Vests are made of it, for law enforcement agencies. It stops bullets, arrows. Sails are made out of it too. Because of its strength." Speaking of strength. Blade had some serious muscle in his upper arms. He was definitely bulked up more than Damian.

"I'm supposed to wear a vest? Like I'm afraid to be staked?" Blade shook his head. "That sounds cowardly."

"No. It's a precaution." I should have known a Highlander would resist this kind of technology. "Think. You used to use a shield. And body armor. It's the same thing."

"When you put it like that. But I only wore those things for battle. Not every day in case a danger leaped out of the bushes." His mouth tightened.

"You did when you were at war. And that's what this is, Jerry."

Blade looked thoughtful.

"Just think about it. Until we can neutralize Westwood." I couldn't take my eyes off his mouth. I wanted to kiss him.

To compare to last night. Not that there had really been a last night. Just virtual sex with Damian.

"You had sex with Damian?" Blade's chin jerked up and he looked around like he wanted to punch or tear or rip something or someone apart.

"No! I mean I thought I did but it was a trick. One of Damian's stunts. A mind game." Oh, God. I should have known Blade wouldn't stop reading my mind.

"Do you *want* to have sex with Damian?" Blade's hands were fisted. "He's seduced many, many women, Gloriana."

"He won't seduce me. Not after last night. He pulled some kind of whammy." Why didn't a customer come in? And I had the distinct feeling that Emmie Lou and Harvey were all ears.

"I know I have no right to even ask you about this. You've made it very clear that you're on your own." Blade turned away as if he couldn't bear to look at me.

"Jerry." I put my hand on his shoulder. Like iron.

"Damian's not for you, Gloriana. But I know you're a passionate woman." He whirled around in one of his vamp moves. "And that you don't want to be committed to me. But if you need . . . release, I will always be available to you. No strings, as you wish."

Oh, gee. The back was much easier to deal with than the front. His x-ray eyes raked over me. Need release? What? Use him instead of a vibrator? And was passionate woman another way to say whore?

"By God, you are *not* a whore." He jerked me into his arms and took my mouth, kissing me until I grabbed his hair and opened my mouth to taste all of him. The doorbell tinkled. Oh, great. *Now* I get customers.

"Sorry." A deep male voice.

Blade tore his mouth from mine because I simply couldn't.

"Collins." Blade put me away from him. All business. "What's wrong?"

I smoothed my hair and pulled down my sweater. I couldn't remember Blade reaching under it, but obviously one of us had felt up my breast.

Kenneth Collins stood just inside the door, looking around. He was obviously upset. "Have you seen Marguerite? She was supposed to meet me next door. At Diana's coffee shop. Then we were going to come here."

"No, she's not here. Maybe she's running late." I put some space between me and Blade because he was seriously interfering with my thinking.

"Her car's outside. But Diana hasn't seen her." Kenneth started toward the back of the store. "Maybe she's in the dressing room."

"No. No one's here." I looked at Blade. "Maybe you should help Kenneth look outside." I had a queasy feeling in my gut. Nowadays when a vamp went missing, it was only natural to fear the worst.

"Outside. Yes." Blade put his hand on Kenneth's shoulder. "You check the vacant lot across the street and I'll go around back and look in the alley." Blade and I exchanged a look. "Have you tried to call her, with your mind? She *is* your mate."

"Yes! That's the first thing I did. We always communicate in our minds." Kenny took a shuddering breath. "She's not answering me. I'm afraid—"

"Maybe she's mad about something. Not answering on purpose." I reached for the Open sign and flipped it over. "I'll help you look."

"No, you will not." Blade turned the sign back over. "We have enough to worry about without you presenting a target."

"Okay, then." I recognized that this wasn't the time to quibble over whether I'd take orders or not. What Blade said made sense. "If she shows up, I'll tell her to call you, Kenneth."

"Thanks." Kenneth headed across the street. From the look on his face, I could tell he was calling Margie in his mind. He also pulled out his cell phone and hit the speed dial. I held my breath and listened, but didn't hear another cell phone ring.

"I don't like this." Blade said what I was thinking. "Unlock the back door and I'll go out in the alley. I can't imagine Margie would be back there, but it can't hurt to look around. Be sure to lock the door behind me."

"Jerry, be careful."

"Of course." He touched my cheek, then stepped outside.

I locked the door behind him and leaned against it. The front doorbells tinkled. Customers? I hurried out in case it was Margie. No such luck. Just a pair of night owls shopping for antique furniture. I tried my best to work up enthusiasm for a Victorian washstand, but I was almost relieved when the two left without buying.

I really wanted to close, but another customer came in, so I occupied myself with shop business, ringing up a sale, answering a phone inquiry. An hour went by and I was going crazy. I was alone when I heard pounding on the back door.

"Who is it?" I wasn't about to just open the door, even with Valdez at my side. At least he wasn't barking. Good sign.

"Blade. Open up." I turned the locks. Blade stepped inside and looked around. "Are you alone?"

"Yes. No customers at the moment."

"Put the Closed sign up and lock the front door." He had such a grim look that I got sick to my stomach. I didn't say anything, just walked over to flip the deadbolts and the sign.

"Bring her in, Kenneth." Blade stepped aside.

Kenneth staggered through the door with Margie in his arms. He was crying, his dark cheeks wet. Margie was limp and, oh, God, a wooden cross stuck out of her chest.

"My baby girl." He wept as he laid her on the floor. "How can she be gone? We were supposed to have forever together. Who would do this?"

I held on to Blade, not sure what to say. There were no words of comfort adequate.

"We'll find out. This must stop." Blade pushed Valdez out of the storeroom and closed the door. "Whatever it takes. We'll find out."

Kenneth looked up and his eyes hardened. "Westwood?"

"No, this hunter has struck before. Two vampires in Houston were staked this way the night MacTavish was killed in Lake Charles."

I had the presence of mind to pull out a fifties vintage chenille bedspread, a pretty rose color, and hand it to Kenneth. "Why don't you wrap M—Margie in this?"

Kenneth just stared at me, obviously in shock. "Would you leave me alone with her first?"

"Of course." I pulled Blade out of the storeroom and shut the door again. He put his arms around me and buried his face in my hair.

I couldn't let him go. Oh, God, he was shaking. I rubbed his back. How horrible to find Margie like that. She'd been so beautiful, so alive. Full of vamp power. Valdez pressed his warm body against my skirt. We were like a huddle of shell-shocked soldiers after an assault.

Blade raised his head and touched my cheek. "It could have been you, Gloriana. You see why I want you to be careful?"

"Yes. I'll be careful." I didn't want to think about Kenneth saying good-bye in my storeroom. He'd been with Margie for over a hundred years, but that was nothing compared to the time I'd spent with Blade. I brushed Blade's jaw with my fingers.

"*You* stay safe." I patted his chest. "And if I say wear a vest, damn it, wear a vest."

"I don't understand why Margie was in the alley. How did someone lure her there?" Blade ignored my demand and was already into his "Find the enemy and eliminate it" mode. "And what do the crosses mean? I know mortals think we can't tolerate them, but to stake with a cross, that's strange."

"Do you think it could be another vampire? He denied it, but Richard Mainwaring, Flo's lover, I mean ex-lover, matches the description of the praying vampire. The one who fed from the Goth who came to my shop that night. The vamp prayed while he fed. Like he was asking forgiveness or something. Maybe he's got a hate on for other vampires."

"A vampire taking out his own?" Blade stared at the closed storeroom door. "Why? And Marguerite wasn't exactly a rogue vampire. She was as into blending as you are."

"Exactly. So who would know she even was vamp, except another one? Or someone with one of Westwood's vamp detectors."

"I hope to hell Westwood's not selling those things." Blade looked really, really grim. "Another vampire. Maybe. But I don't see a motive."

"It could be another vampire." I hoped I wasn't sending Blade in the wrong direction. I rubbed my aching forehead. None of this made sense. But hate crimes never did. "Listen, I may be all wrong. But when Flo and I saw him at church, Richard looked at me with so much hate—"

"Did he threaten you?" Blade's fingers bit into my arms. Yes, he was still holding me and I wasn't about to push him away.

"No. He didn't even speak to us. But Flo broke up with him because he was sneaking around, didn't want anyone to know he was in Austin. That's suspicious right there." This find-the-perp mode was contagious.

Blade let me go to pace in front of the storeroom. "I won't ask what you were doing in a church. But, Glory, why would Richard be killing other vampires? He's a very old vampire himself."

"He's decided he hates what he is. And he hates *us*. Flo says he doesn't want to be vampire anymore. But we can't kill ourselves. That vamp code thing." The vamp code's not written down anywhere, but there are some unwritten rules. Don't bite another vamp without permission. Hah, Damian! Never deliberately endanger another vampire. And we keep our secrets. It's a close knit community and when one of us is attacked, we all go on high alert and do whatever it takes.

"It's not just code, Gloriana. I knew a vampire once who tried to commit suicide." Blade looked grim, obviously remembering a bad time. "He couldn't do it. Even though you know vampires are fearless."

"Most of them anyway." I grabbed Blade's hand and made him look at me. "What happened?"

"He simply couldn't put a stake to his own heart. He begged me to do it."

"No!" I squeezed his hand. "Who was it, Jerry? Anyone I know?"

He shook his head. "He died before I met you."

"You didn't—"

"No, but he had no trouble finding a hunter to oblige him."

Blade turned away, obviously not interested in sharing any more about this with me.

I shivered and picked up a paisley challis scarf to throw around my shoulders. Had I really wasted years with my own suicidal thoughts? Am I dumb as dirt or what?

"I have no idea if Mainwaring's the one who killed Margie, but you should question him."

The storeroom door opened and Kenneth came out with Margie wrapped in the bedspread. He didn't say anything, just walked to the door and waited for Blade to flip the locks to let him out. He walked out into the night. A few quiet words and Blade stepped outside to open a car door. Blade came back in and put his arm around me.

"Where will he take her . . . body?" I nervously pulled the glass door closed and locked it. We could still see Kenneth as he tenderly placed Margie's body in the backseat of his car. It was really late and the street was deserted, thank God.

"I'm sure he'll find a place."

Vampires don't exactly buy cemetery plots and plan funerals. You think you'll live forever. And when a vamp does die, it's usually horrific and a loved one or another vampire will take care of burying the body. We don't melt like the Wicked Witch of the West. Or turn to dust. Instead we get a lonely unmarked grave. Forget about a headstone. What would you put? Born 1580, died 2000-and-something?

"What happened to Mac's body, Jerry?"

He looked at me and let me see his pain. "I don't know. I had Mara to deal with." He looked down at his black boots. I knew he must have a knife tucked in one. "That's another mark against that bastard Westwood. He takes fangs and then God knows how he disposes of the body. I went back later . . ." He ran his hand over his face. "No sign of Mac."

I wrapped my arms around him again. "How horrible for you." I leaned back and looked up at him. I've never seen Blade cry. Not in hundreds of years. And he didn't cry now. But his face could have been carved from stone.

"If something happens to me, Jerry, cremate me. Take my ashes back to England. Scatter them around the Globe." I didn't have to say it was where I'd met Jerry. He knew. Grief makes me sentimental, I guess.

"You won't die, lass. I'll see to it." His hold on me tightened and he rested his chin on my hair.

"You can't promise that, Jerry." I saw Kenny's car pull away from the curb. "You just can't." I looked back in the store room. The wooden cross lay on the floor in a puddle of blood. Kenny must have pulled it out.

That did it. I ran to the bathroom and was violently ill for the first time in decades. It's pretty harsh since our stomachs are basically empty.

When I came out, glad I'd had a toothbrush back there, Blade had cleaned the linoleum. He carried one of my shop sacks. The cross.

"What are you going to do with that?" I couldn't bear to think about where it had been. Margie. I swallowed, hard.

"It's evidence. I'm no forensic scientist, but I can hire one. I'll take it to one for analysis. Maybe he can discover a clue that will help us find this killer and punish him."

Vigilante justice is the only kind vampires can get. And Blade had obviously nominated himself as leader of the posse.

I kissed his stiff jaw. He grabbed me and kissed me with all the emotion that he kept pent up inside him. I leaned into him, savoring his taste and his strength. Finally Blade pulled back.

"I don't suppose you want—"

I put a hand over his mouth. I don't think he meant to be insensitive. It's just that Jerry is such a guy. Naturally he'd think sex would be a great comfort for both of us.

But passionate woman or not, I wasn't ready to climb into Jerry's bed. It was a slippery slope. Next thing you knew, I'd be sleeping over. And he'd figure I'd come to my senses and had decided to give us another chance. I just wasn't ready. And wasn't sure I'd ever be. But, damn, the man could kiss.

He was staring at me, the bag with the cross between us. "Go. See what you can find out. Keep me posted." I unlocked the front door to let him out.

"I will." He strode toward his car without a backward glance.

Well, shoot. He could have at least begged a little. There were still a few hours until dawn but I saw that pink sweater I'd set aside for Margie and didn't have the heart to reopen the shop. I called Valdez and locked up. Another dead vampire. Weren't we supposed to live forever?

Fourteen

Blade called another vamp meeting. I got Ryan to take care
of the shop so Derek and I could go. Valdez too, of course. He
wasn't letting me out of his sight. Not that I was objecting.
Flo met us there, with Damian. We were in Blade's new house
this time. An English manor style place in an affluent older
neighborhood.

Damian and Blade had obviously declared a truce in the
interest of vamp unity. Derek told me that Damian was rent-
ing the house to Blade, one of Damian's many properties in
the city.

The vast living room was sparsely furnished but a fire
blazed in the stone fireplace. Mara seemed to have taken on
the role of hostess, directing some of the male vampires to
bring in chairs from the dining room. This time there were
almost thirty vamps present. A coven? A herd? A flock? I
was still plenty freaked out about Margie. Valdez, our furry
sentinel, settled near the front door.

Kenny sat in an armchair and received condolences. This
seemed more like a wake than a meeting. If someone broke
into "Amazing Grace," I was going to lose it, big time.

I had a killer headache. I had vowed never to be in the same room with Damian without blocking him and was sticking with it. I stood with Derek and Freddy and waited for someone to start things. I didn't have long to wait.

"People." Blade held up his hand and the room got eerily silent except for the crackling of the wood fire. "We have another danger in our midst. Do any of you know who could be staking vampires with a wooden cross?"

There was a murmur of speculation. Flo stepped forward. "I know you think Ricardo did this, but he would not."

"Who's Ricardo?" This was said by a vamp I hadn't met. Short, stocky, probably a weight lifter in his former life.

"Richard Mainwaring." Blade looked at me. "He seems to hate vampires, some of them anyway. I tried to find him, to question him, but no luck so far."

"Why would Richard kill my Margie? We knew him in Paris, but . . ." Kenny stood and looked around. "You should be looking for mortal hunters instead. We don't kill our own. We don't."

"But we can." Damian walked over to Kenny and gave him a sympathetic look. "We can't kill ourselves, but we can kill our own kind. Anyone who can wield a stake can. The wooden cross suggests our killer thinks he's got some kind of holy mission. Mainwaring's been seen attending church services."

"I go to church." Another man spoke up.

"So do I." A woman this time. One I hadn't met yet. "And I sure wouldn't go out looking for other vampires to stake. It doesn't make sense."

"Ricardo is troubled. He thinks maybe we are demons from hell." Flo had her chin up, but it wobbled a little. I walked up to put an arm around her.

There were angry murmurs around the room. Obviously some vampires are evil, but this group seemed civilized, more likely to form a book club, than a posse. We all were civilized and into blending. We condemn the kind of risky behavior rogue vamps revel in. Of course rogue vamps don't attend meetings either. Richard Mainwaring sure hadn't shown.

"People." Blade held up his hand again. "Just watch out for Mainwaring. He's about Damian's size with white hair. Easy to spot. But we've had no luck tracking him down. Approach him cautiously and never alone."

"I still don't think—" Flo sighed. "We shouldn't be hasty. We have no proof that it's Ricardo."

"No, we don't." Mara had planted herself by Blade's side. "And, frankly, while I'm sorry for Kenneth's loss, I doubt the cross killer is as well organized or as well equipped as Westwood. Stay in pairs and I doubt this religious fanatic will approach you."

Mara's eyes blazed and even I had to give her credit for being bloody beautiful in her hatred. "Westwood is stalking us. Treating us like trophy animals. He has . . ." she swallowed, "He has Mac's fangs around his neck. We *must* stop him."

"You're right, Mara. So what are we doing about him?" I stepped forward, pulling Diana with me. "Diana, Flo and I were ambushed outside a mall the other night. We know it was Westwood because Diana took an arrow in the arm." I looked over at Valdez who had raised his head and was studying the crowd. "My guard dog saved us."

Valdez sat up as everyone turned to look at him. "*I've got his scent. He ain't gettin' close to Blondie again.*"

"What scent?" The new woman again.

We'd skipped all the niceties this time and no one had bothered to introduce us. There had been crystal glasses of Bloody Merry set out on the dining room table, but clearly this was a business meeting.

Diana pulled the pieces of arrow out of her purse. She'd washed them but the wood still had a distinct odor that our enhanced sense of smell would be able to pick up easily.

"This is it, folks. Olive wood. It's Westwood's arrow of choice. Take a whiff. If you smell this, do a shift and get the hell out of there." Diana looked at Blade. "The cross that killed Margie wasn't olive wood, was it?"

"No. It's still being analyzed, but it didn't have this odor."

Everyone crowded around Diana and she passed the pieces around. While the sniffing and exclaiming were going on, Damian appeared beside me.

"Gloriana."

"I'm not speaking to you. Remember?" I turned my back. God, but my head was killing me.

"You're blocking me. Don't you trust me?" His voice was soft in my ear.

"Hell, no. And I won't look at you either." I kept my back to him. "That was a mean trick, Damian."

"But fun." He touched my neck, just a tickle. Trying to get me to turn around? Not in this lifetime.

"You have a warped sense of fun." I heard a noise. A grunt. I turned around.

Blade had pulled Damian up by his shirt and was in his face. "Leave her alone, Sabatini. Try your tricks on some other unsuspecting female."

"Jerry, I was handling it." I smiled. "But if you want to beat the hell out of him, go ahead." I turned my back again.

"Is this meeting going to degenerate into a brawl?" Mara. "Blade, tell the group what we found out about Westwood."

That got everyone quiet. I turned in time to see Blade throw Damian across the room. Of course Damian landed on his feet and kept grinning. I had a really strong feeling that Flo's brother never would have bothered with me if he hadn't seen me with Blade. Competitive bastard.

"Westwood has a vulnerability." Blade took the center of the room and looked around. "He hires men who will do anything for money. So if we want someone inside, we can buy him."

"To do what? Spy?" Flo looked around the room. "Would anyone object if we arranged for a little something to be added to his dinner?"

"Poison the bastard." A man.

"I like it." A woman.

"Too quick though. I'd like to see him suffer." Mara, of course.

"And while you're waiting for your chance at a ringside seat, some of our own are in real danger." Freddy had his arm around Derek. "I say the sooner the better."

"Bottom line is we all have to be careful." Blade was definitely the leader here. "Use your sense of smell, then be a moving target. No one can hit a vamp at warp speed." More murmurs. Nods all around.

"What about paying off one of the goons?" The body builder. "Not all of us can afford to pony up what it might take."

"Don't worry about that." Freddy looked at Derek. "I'll pay whatever is necessary."

"We'll decide who pays later. I'll move ahead as I can." Blade turned to Kenneth. "Now I think we should adjourn this meeting. Anything you'd like to say, Kenneth?"

A eulogy. Oh, God, I didn't think I could take it. But Kenny just shook his head.

"I'll say something." Flo stepped up to Kenneth. "Marguerite was a woman who loved life, never wasted a moment of it and spent it with a lover who adored her. May we all be so blessed." She raised her glass. We all did the same. As a eulogy, it was enough. One thing was becoming crystal clear in my aching brain. I had to get with the power lessons ASAP. No way was I going to be anyone's sitting duck.

"Flo." Another Sunday night. My roommate was flipping through channels looking for something to watch. We'd talked about going out, but were still a little too freaked out for that. No church. I had a feeling Blade and Kenneth would be hanging around the Moonlight Church of Eternal Life and Joy looking for Mainwaring. I couldn't forget the hate

Richard had aimed at me. He'd certainly looked capable of killing another vampire.

Flo and I'd been moping around for over a week. I'd wanted to start power lessons sooner, but between my work and Flo's always active social life, I hadn't even had a chance to mention it to my roomie.

Another reason I'd delayed, Damian had stopped by twice. I'd retreated to my bedroom and left him with Flo. He hadn't stayed long. And I was glad for that. Even with a door between us, I'd blocked him. Too bad a vampire can't take Excedrin.

Flo figured I was still mad about him biting me without permission. That worked for me. Blade had also come by, to question Flo, to give us progress reports. Which had added up to he knew nothing and the bribery scheme with one of Westwood's guards was a delicate operation that would take time.

My Kevlar had arrived. Unfortunately it only came in a weird brownish gray. I'd already found a seamstress thanks to Miranda and been measured for my bra. And wasn't that fun? Let's just say the numbers were, uh, impressive. It's a good thing I'd ordered plenty of fabric. The bra would be ready in a few days. Diana and Flo were waiting to see how mine turned out. Flo wouldn't wear anything ugly, but I was already thinking that if we could dye it black and add some lace . . .

I put down the book I'd been reading—*How to Get What You Want and Keep What You Need.* Easy to see why it was a best seller.

"Flo, listen to me, I've had an epiphany."

"And you sold it?" Flo put down the remote. "Tell me it wasn't one of those cute little bracelets. Just once I'd like a lover who buys me good jewelry."

Valdez winked. I swear he did.

"No, not *Tiffany,* Flo. An epiphany. A revelation. I figured something out about myself. This is *big.*"

"So what did you figure out?" Flo pulled out polish remover and attacked her nails. "I hate brown polish. What was I thinking? Red, pink, coral. From now on, I want pretty colors."

Was it too much to ask for an attentive audience? Like I said, this was big. Flo put down her cotton ball and looked at me.

"Spill, girlfriend." She grinned. "Love the CW."

"Maybe we should cut back on the TV watching."

"No, I'm learning more English. It's fun." She focused on me. "I said spill."

Now I was embarrassed. Even Valdez had quit scratching his left ear to stare at me. "It's about me and Blade. Our relationship." I got up and paced the living room.

"This should be good." Flo sat back and put her bare feet on the coffee table. "He's been dropping by a lot lately." She looked at Valdez. "And I don't think he's coming to see us. Right, doggy?"

"Hey, he doesn't need to check up on me."

"Forget Blade. This isn't just about us. It's about the whole vampire culture."

"We have a culture?" Flo picked up her cotton ball again and doused it with remover. "I'm way past worrying about that stuff. I had my artist period. A few composers. A rock star in the sixties. But now—"

"Will you stay with me here?" I wrinkled my nose. My enhanced senses kicked in again, unfortunately. "And please quit giving Valdez bean dip."

"Don't tell her that. You should see the way she scoops up some on a chip and slides it into my mouth." Valdez walked over to lean his head against Flo's knee. *"She's my hero."*

"Ooo, doggy." Flo fanned her face. "Glory's right. Maybe onion dip, *caro*." She rubbed her bare foot against his chest, then pushed him away. "Sit by Glory, guard her."

"Thanks a lot. Maybe you should guard both of us from the next room." Obviously Flo wasn't interested in my big reveal. Who else could I tell? I don't keep a diary, you never know when it might fall into the wrong hands. But I was bursting to share.

"Reveal!" Flo pushed Valdez away again. I swear he was trying to look up her pink miniskirt.

I sat down. "Okay. I realized that Blade treats me like a helpless female because I've been *acting* like one."

"*Cara*, I could have told you that centuries ago. When we met in Campbell Castle." Flo gave in and stroked Valdez's head. "'Oh, Jeremiah, I can't shape-shift. What if I get stuck?' I heard you."

"Shape-shifting is scary. I may have a bat's hearing and a bat's night vision, but does that mean I want to hang upside down in a cave, eat mosquitoes and give up cute shoes?" There, surely Flo couldn't argue with that logic.

"You don't have to be a bat. I prefer birds, cats—"

"*You're breaking my heart, Florence.*" Valdez lay his head on her feet.

"I'm not ready to shape-shift. But I'm ready to embrace being vampire. No more whining about what can't be changed." I looked down at the book I'd tossed on the coffee table. "This is about power, Flo. I want to explore my powers."

Flo's eyes lit up and she winked at Valdez. "No whining. Good. And we know you embrace vampires. Especially one in particular."

"Forget embracing. Think power. For defense. Okay? We start with some little things and work our way up. Baby steps."

"Of course. I will be your mentor. And I think you have more power than you know. Remember in church? You were singing up and going up, without even trying. Even I have to concentrate to move like that."

"I don't want to make a fool of myself." That floating business *had* been pretty cool.

"Of course not." Flo jumped up. "What do you want to learn first? There are so many things."

"Okay." I had a mental list. "First, how do you move so fast? You know, here one second, over there the next?"

"Like this?" And before I could blink, Flo was behind me.

"Yes! How do you do that? Blade, Damian, even Derek does it."

"Easy. Just focus on where you want to be and, voilà, you're there."

"Focus." I looked around.

Valdez hopped up on the love seat. *"This is going to be good. We got any popcorn?"*

I stuck my tongue out at him. Then I looked past him to the kitchen. Kitchen. I concentrated and, bam!

"Uh, Glory." Flo and Valdez were looking up at me. "Did I mention you need to see the exact spot where you want to be?"

"You don't think I picked the top of the refrigerator?" I reached behind me. "See? The microwave popcorn is up here."

"Nice save, Blondie." Valdez wagged his tail and watched me climb down. Maybe I should have put on a different outfit for this. My long blue skirt got tangled in my legs and I fell into Flo's arms. Thank God for her vamp strength or we both would have landed on our butts.

"You'll get better. Give me that." She grabbed the popcorn and stuck it in the microwave. "Come here." She steered me to our front door. "Now look at the love seat. Your usual spot. *See* yourself there. Just like you were a few minutes ago."

I felt her hands on my shoulders. "No cheating now, Flo. I've seen you move everything from a purse to that chair over there."

"No cheating. You do this all yourself." Valdez barked, the microwave beeped and she let me go. "Think now. The *exact spot* where you want to be. Picture it. In your mind."

I closed my eyes. I could hear Flo dumping popcorn into a bowl. Warning Valdez that it was hot. I made myself tune them out. And I saw myself. Sitting on the love seat, usual spot. I opened my eyes. Hello, I was there.

Flo clapped.

"Way to go, Blondie." Valdez caught a fluffy kernel in his mouth when Flo tossed it. *"It's good defense. Some slimeball gets the drop on you, blink and you're outta there."*

"Wow! I did it." I picked up my book and closed my eyes. I was in my bedroom, lying down with my book in my lap.

"Practice, Glory." Flo went back to her nails.

I sat up. Specific. The bedroom floor was not exactly my pillowtop. But I was making progress, gaining powers of my own. Could I move anyone or anything else? I laid my book on the bed, closed my eyes and saw it on the coffee table. I opened my eyes.

"Bravo, Glory! You go, girlfriend."

I *had* to get my "girlfriend" turned on to some new TV shows. But her admiration was the real deal. And how cool was that?

I walked to the bedroom door and stared at Valdez, *seeing* him on the end of my bed. *Nada.*

"You're not moving me, Blondie." Valdez quit eating pop-corn long enough to look at me. *"And whatcha wanna bet Flo here don't go either?"*

"Don't try it, Glory." Flo brushed Pink Persuasion polish on her left thumb and examined it critically. "I'm not your book to land, plop, on a table."

"Okay, okay. You're both off-limits." I walked back into the living room. "Could you move a mortal? Like Westwood?"

Flo shook her head. "I don't think so. It's better *you* move. Like Valdez said. If you can't shape-shift, at least you can get behind him, run like the wind."

"Yes, that's good."

"There are other limits, Gloriana." Flo frowned. "I wish there weren't. But only very old, very powerful vampires can move *through* walls and doors. I've only known one who could do that."

"Okay. So I need to see a clear path."

"Right. And if you're being held by anyone, mortal or vampire, you won't be able to move either. It interferes with the energy flow you need. Of course I would hope you could knock a mere mortal over on his ass with your vamp strength."

"I would hope." I sniffed and stared at Valdez's bowl. That popcorn smelled *so* good. I know I've vowed to adjust my attitude. But that smell . . . That was the worst about being vampire. Not being able to eat.

Flo looked up. "You want to eat?"

"Sure." I sniffed the air. "Doesn't this delicious smell bother you?"

"Some vampires can eat." She added color to her little finger and held out her hand, flapping it to speed the drying like she hadn't just uttered magic words that could make my whole existence into nirvana.

"You're toying with me." I picked up a kernel that had landed on the coffee table. "You think I could learn to eat? Can *you*?"

Heaven on earth. Eat whatever you wanted and then, vamp magic, you wake up the next morning still exactly the same weight and size. This was *huge*.

"I tried it once." Flo made a face and began to work on the nails on her right hand. "Not for me."

"Why not?" I got up and went into the kitchen to pull out Cheetos from Valdez's stash. I hugged the bag to me. I left it unopened. If I smelled and couldn't taste . . .

"Are you hungry?" Flo had finished with the polish, now she waved both hands in front of her.

I thought about it. Hunger, real hunger that starts in your churning gut. Nope. Hadn't felt it since the change.

Bloodlust. That's another hunger altogether. It's centered more in your, don't laugh now, nose. You smell the blood coursing through a mortal's veins, hear it pumping their life force through their bodies. Your fangs run out, ready to rip when the craving becomes an obsession. Then you feed—either from a person or a canned substitute.

"I'm not hungry. It's a mental thing. Like if someone said you absolutely could not wear cute shoes ever again. You were doomed to wear clunky orthopedic shoes and athletic socks forever. And you could look at Ferragamo slides, touch them, even smell them, but you could never, ever wear them."

Flo looked startled. "Even my lover Dante couldn't have imagined such a level of hell. Better to get staked tomorrow."

"Exactly. See? Do you wonder I get depressed once in a while?"

"Once in a while?" Valdez bumped his head against my hip. *"Until we got here, Blondie, you were lower than my blood sugar when I need a Twinkie fix."*

"Excuse me? What do you know about blood sugar?" I looked from Valdez to Flo.

"My fault." Flo grinned. "We watched the Health Channel while you were in the shower last night. When I saw the program was about blood sugar . . ." She shrugged.

"I've never found human blood to be sweet." I said. "But even I wouldn't mind a treat now and then."

Valdez bumped me again. *"You gonna open those Cheetos or what? I think I'm havin' a sinking spell."*

"You'll live. Give me a minute." I sat down next to Flo. "Valdez is right about one thing. Between my sucky love life and my lack of crunch, I've been down for centuries."

"Then we must do something about it. The love life may be complicated." Flo got out her clear top coat and began on her left hand again. "You don't want Damian, he's no good for you. You've had Jeremiah, he drives you crazy. Was there anyone at the meeting the other night who made you hot?"

Hot? I'd spent the whole evening with a headache the size of Kansas. Blocking Damian was wearing on me, but I sure wasn't going to give him a shot at playing virtual sex games again.

Flo looked up, her eyes narrowed.

"Forget my love life." I ripped open the bag of Cheetos. I put one to my nose. Inhaled. Oh, God, was there ever a better smell? I put it to my lips. The texture. I'd heard Valdez often enough crunching his way through a bag. To bite into something with texture . . .

"Wait, Glory." Flo snatched it out of my hand. "Before you do this, I must warn you."

I swear my eyes watered. So close . . . "What? Is it like poison? Will I . . . die?" Yep, I was truly over that "Woe is me, I'm immortal" crap.

"No, but you might wish it so." She popped the Cheetos into Valdez's mouth. "I remember . . . I had a lover. Ari was a handsome Greek who owned his own island in the Aegean." She sighed.

"But he was mortal and didn't want to know I was vampire. I read his mind. So I pretended I was mortal too. Staying in my own room all day because I preferred the nights. Cooler, less interruption from the staff." She waved her hand. "Details. Anyway, I went so far as to eat with him. I would pretend of course. Push my food around my plate." She smiled at Valdez. "Drop some bites down to his little dog."

"I knew I liked you, Flo." Valdez wagged his tail, but his eyes were on that Cheetos bag.

"One night he insisted he hand feed me tidbits from his plate. He thought he was being sexy." Flo shuddered. "I chewed. I swallowed. I suffered agony. Pains in my stomach. I could not stand. I told him it was food poisoning. From something I'd eaten in my room before dinner."

"That's terrible." I fondled the Cheetos bag. "How long did the pains last?" Was I hopeless, or what?

"Days, Glory. The healing sleep didn't fix me. Can you imagine? From a few tidbits." Flo looked at the bag. "Worth it?"

"Maybe not tonight." Not with Westwood gunning for me and a business to run. I couldn't afford to be laid low for the sake of a few Cheetos. Could I? "Maybe we should work on my love life first."

"Love." Flo clapped her hands. "Now you're talking, girl-friend."

"I still haven't met a cowboy." I threw a handful of Chee-tos into Valdez's popcorn bowl, then reluctantly returned the bag to the kitchen.

"Why a cowboy?" Flo really seemed interested.

"I've been partial to Stetsons and boots since my Califor-nia gold-rush days. I'm not much of a singer—"

"I can vouch for that." Valdez had polished off his Cheetos.

"Would you not interrupt?" I gave him a look. "Anyway, back then I could have howled like Valdez and sex starved miners would toss gold nuggets in my direction. Of course they loved checking out my boobs in low-cut gowns."

"Use what you have, I always say." Flo sighed and leaned back. "Is this a love story?"

"Of course." I picked up a throw pillow and hugged it. "One miner in particular, the hat and boot type, caught my eye and swept me off my feet. Randy O'Banyan."

Flo rubbed her hands together. "Was he a good lover?"

"Incredible." I squeezed the pillow. "And full of fun. Like your Ari, he never knew I was vampire, though I fed from him. Young, healthy, O positive." I never used to think twice about feeding from a mortal. You get an incredible high. Then I got a conscience. Thought maybe I was taking advantage . . .

"Glory, mortals have plenty of blood. They never miss what we take as long as we aren't greedy." Flo grabbed the pillow and tossed it across the room. "Are you going to fin-ish this story?"

"Okay. Randy and I'd meet every night for mind-blowing sex, with a little bite action on my part. Then I'd zap his memory and he'd go off to the mines every day. Un-til a mine shaft collapsed and buried him."

"No! You should have made him vampire, Glory." Flo wiped away a tear. "This reminds me of my lover in St. Petersburg. I waited too long and he was killed. Ungrateful peasants."

"I don't make people vampires, Flo." And that was one power I had no interest in picking up. "So I cried for weeks. Refused to hunt. I was so weak, I figured I might just die. And that was okay with me. I *loved* Randy."

"Of course you did." Flo patted my hand. "I have had many wonderful lovers. And lost many. But you must feed. Keep up your strength."

"That's what Blade said when he found me." I got up and headed into the kitchen to get a Bloody Merry. All this talk of feeding . . . I took a deep swallow and told myself for the thousandth time that it satisfied me. Yeah, right. I settled on the love seat again. "You know Blade has this uncanny telepathic ability where I'm concerned."

"I call it love." Flo looked wistful. "A great love. He is your life mate, Gloriana."

I wasn't about to get into the love versus possessiveness versus responsibility argument now. "Whatever he is, he came roaring into town. He scooped me up, literally, along with the Valdez du jour." I looked at my current Valdez. "A fierce protector who never talked or read my mind. I loved that dog."

Valdez gave me a reproachful look. Okay, that was mean. He'd saved my life, a little over a week ago.

"I'm sorry, Valdez." I smiled slightly. "I love you too."

"You'd better. He saved us both. Eh, doggy?" Flo rubbed Valdez with her bare toes and he was glad to turn to her, presenting me with his backside.

"What did Blade do after he scooped you?"

"He took us to a villa in Mexico. He was alternately sweet and bossy, forcing me to feed from him until I got my strength back."

"Your hero! He must really love you to be so generous."

"He was generous like a fox. You know feeding makes hot, hotter. And with the right person . . . One bite and I was jumping his bones. Again and again. God, I'm so freaking easy where Blade is concerned."

"Of course you are." Flo willed me to meet her gaze. "So are you going to just sit back and let Mara have him now?"

"Quit doing the whammy, Flo. I don't know." I picked up my book from the coffee table. "I don't know what I want. That's part of my problem."

Flo smiled. "I think you *do* know what you want. And that's your whole problem."

Fifteen

Whether I wanted him or not, Blade showed up the night I was going for my bra fitting.

"Florence tells me you're making your own protective gear and are supposed to pick it up tonight." Blade stood at the door jingling car keys. "Let me go with you. I want to see this Kevlar."

Why not? Through Flo, I'd arranged to use the hearse. Hey, Damian *owed* me. But this was better. Flo didn't need to be running her mouth about me to Blade, though. Matchmaking, no doubt.

"Can Valdez stay here? The seamstress got a little"— I looked down at my dog, who was wagging his tail and grinning at Blade—"nervous around him. She's got young kids."

"Sure. Stay here, Valdez." Blade waited for me to grab my purse.

"It's not far." We walked downstairs, stopping at the threshold to sniff the outside air. In a little over a week it had become a cautious habit. No olive wood, thank God.

We stepped outside and of course Blade had driven that Mercedes convertible. I held out my hand. "I'll drive."

Blade grinned. "I think you want this car. And Florence tells me the last estimate to fix your old car was over a thousand dollars."

"Flo's been a busy girl, hasn't she?" Flo and I were going to have a little chat as soon as I saw her. She was out tonight with Kenneth Collins. Not a date. Way too soon for that. But Kenny was lonely and Flo *is* good company when she's not being a blabbermouth.

I got into the driver's side and adjusted the seat. I did love this car and the cool fall night was perfect for the top to be down. The drive lasted less than ten minutes, darn it. I'd found this seamstress through Miranda, my technical expert and picker. She'd come in to spend her coupon and hung around long enough to get a feel for what I wanted for the shop.

I pulled up in front of the small wood frame house. Now that we were here, I wondered if this was a good idea. Blade had been quiet during our drive, watching my hair blow in the breeze. I could still feel his gaze. Warm. Sexy thoughts. What would he think when he saw me in the bra?

"Let's go in." He got out and walked around to open my door. "And I've seen you with and without a bra. I prefer without."

I took his hand and let him pull me up. Definitely sexy thoughts. "I told Kim that I needed this bra because when I'm not running the shop I work with a knife thrower in the circus. That's you. And that he misses. Obviously not you."

Blade leaned down and pulled a knife from his boot. "Good idea. Maybe we can test this Kevlar."

"Not on me you don't." I grabbed his arm and pulled him up the walk. "But maybe we can get a piece of extra material, put it on one of my mannequins and see how it works."

"Good idea." He put the knife back. He was still going with the jeans and western shirt look. Had Flo told him my cowboy fantasy? He looked up and winked. Of course she had.

I rang the doorbell and the door opened immediately.

Kim was a stay-at-home mom who did sewing to supplement her husband's income as a teaching assistant. He worked with Miranda at the university. A baby cried and Kim looked frazzled. A two year old clung to her leg.

"Hi, Glory. Come in. It's ready." She smiled at Blade. "Are you her partner?"

He put his arm around me. "When she lets me be. I'm Jeremy Blade."

"Oh, good name for a knife thrower." She darted a glance toward the back of the house where cries had turned into screams. "It's right here on the couch, Glory. Try it on in the bathroom. I've got to deal with the baby."

"Sure, go ahead." Kim hurried off, the two year old stuck to her like a burr. I picked up the Kevlar bra. We'd decided a sports bra style would work best with Velcro down the front. Cute, it wasn't, but not horrible.

Kim had lined it with cotton since Kevlar doesn't breathe. If we really were the walking dead, that wouldn't be a problem. But vamps do breathe, slowly, but with real lung action. So Kevlar wasn't exactly comfy to wear.

"Try it on, Glory." Blade sat on the couch and crossed his leg over his knee. "Let me see."

No point arguing. It was what I was here for, after all. I stepped into the bathroom, pulled off my sweater and bra and set them on the closed toilet lid. I slipped my arms into the bra and adjusted it until it fit snugly before closing the Velcro. Forget the mirror on the back of the door, my bra and skirt showed, I didn't.

I looked down. The bra fit tight enough that a slice of cleavage showed. Not totally sexless. But was my heart protected? I stepped outside.

Blade stood and walked around me. "The back's good. High enough to keep you safe. But the front . . . " He traced the edge of my bra. "Wrong angle and you're staked." He dipped his finger between my breasts and pulled. He was thinking like a warrior, obviously.

"Sturdy. I'd like to test this fabric with that piece of arrow Diana's got. Just to make sure it can't penetrate." His finger still rested in that vee.

"Flo won't wear one. She's not into ugly."

He finally let me go. "Not ugly. Though, like I said, I like you best without a bra. The color is odd and I don't know how it will look under your clothes."

I looked down again. "Maybe if I added lace . . ." I headed to the bathroom. "I'll put my sweater on over it. See how it looks."

In the bathroom, Kim's two-year-old looked up from washing my sweater and bra in the open toilet.

"Oh, no! Stop that!"

"Mommy!" He dropped them into the water and ran out of the bathroom.

I just stared at my soggy clothes. Blade came up behind me and put his hand on my shoulder.

"Oops."

We stepped into the hall as Kim came running. "Noah! What have you done?" She grabbed a toilet brush and fished out the sweater, tossing it into the tub. The bra was trickier, but it finally landed with a plop.

"Glory, I'm so sorry. I'll buy you new ones."

"Don't be silly. Just wash them and I'll get them when I come back with my friend Diana." I touched my bra straps. "It's perfect, Kim. Diana's going to want one and probably a few more of my friends will too."

Kim looked at Blade standing behind me. "You throw knives at *all* her friends?"

Okay, this was making us sound like a weird cult or something. The old knife throwing ritual. And of course Blade oozed the kind of charisma that could sweep a woman right into his own personal harem. Was it time for the vamp whammy? I looked down at Noah, still clinging to his mother's leg. I don't believe in doing that to kids. Better to leave town, pick up a new identity . . .

Blade grinned. "I think her friends watch too much TV. Cop shows. Glory's starting a fad. Bulletproof bras."

Kim laughed. "Oh, I get it. Work out at the gym in one. A guy comes on to you and you shoot him down—'Hey, buddy, you don't want to mess with me, I've got on my bulletproof bra.'"

We all laughed.

Kim looked me over. "Fits good, but should probably be higher in front." She put her finger in the middle just like Blade had. "You want to leave it here? I can add an inch or two on top."

"No, I like it like this. But make me another one and it can be higher." I put my hand across my chest to show her where. I glanced at Blade. "Jerry's not that bad a marksman. But we'd like to take a piece of cloth with us. Just to use as target practice." I held onto Blade's arm. "He doesn't believe he can't throw hard enough to cut through it."

Kim walked into her dining/sewing room combination and picked up a one foot square. "It's easy to cut with scissors, but that's not the same as a stabbing motion. If this stuff stops bullets, it's bound to stop a knife." She gave me a sympathetic look. Like, gee, couldn't you do better than as a knife thrower's assistant? I wouldn't be surprised if she tried career counseling on my next visit if I came without Blade.

"Let me get you something to wear home."

"Good. Thanks."

Blade leaned down to whisper in my ear. "You don't need a blouse."

"It's cool outside. But if you want to put the top up and turn on the heater . . ."

"Never mind."

Kim came back with a large black T-shirt. The Austin Annual Bat Festival. Austinites love their bats because the bats eat literally tons of mosquitoes. And I'd already learned that, in Texas, almost anything was an excuse for a festival. I'd have to offer to buy the T-shirt from Kim. An early Christmas present for Mara.

"This is Dan's. I didn't think mine . . ." She flushed.

"Right. You're a size two and I'm . . . not." I pulled the shirt over my head and got an envelope out of my purse. "Here's what we agreed on. In cash. That okay?"

Kim grinned. "Perfect. And keep the T-shirt if you like it. Dan's got six of them. One for every year we've been in Austin."

"Thanks, it's cool."

"I'm going to experiment with dye on the Kevlar. See if we can't sex it up a bit some way or other."

"Great. You've read my mind." And how nice to know that she really hadn't.

"Call me when you're ready to bring your friends by."

"I will." Blade and I said our good-byes and walked to the car. "How does the bra look under this shirt?"

Blade stopped me and turned me around. "It smashes you. Not flat, of course. But I don't see your usual curve." He opened the car door and helped me in. "Are you in a hurry to get home?"

I took a deep breath of the cool night air. Fresh. Sweet. Nonthreatening. "I could take a ride." I started the car. I *loved* it. And wasn't going to turn down a chance to drive it a while longer.

"Come home with me. So we can talk. Without others around." He got into the car and slammed the door. His eyes gleamed in the darkness.

"Just talk? Do I look stupid?"

Blade brushed my hair back behind my ear and traced a path down my neck. "Not at all. We'll do what you wish. Talk or . . ." He kissed the spot behind my ear that he knew drove me wild. "More."

I shivered then groped for sense. "Is Mara living with you?" That could certainly be a deal breaker.

"Yes, but she's not there. She's in Lake Charles. Closing up my house there."

"How helpful." I sounded jealous. No surprise there.

"It helps her to stay busy. She's still grieving, Gloriana."

"How long will she be staying with you?" Not feeling pity for Mara. She didn't invite it with her "screw you" attitude and I wasn't in the giving mood.

"I don't know. She can't live alone. It's too dangerous. I like the security in your building, but Damian says there are no vacancies."

"You checked?"

Blade put his hand behind my neck and turned me to face him. "Yes, I checked. Mara and I are not a couple." He smiled and kissed me lightly on the lips. "You and I are. I'm just sorry you and Mara don't get along."

Don't get along. That was like saying the American Revolution had been a minor skirmish.

"I get along. Mara's the bitch." I put the car in drive.

"Mara's a bitch because she's in pain. MacTavish was the love of her life."

Great. Now I felt small. Like *I* was the bitch. "Give me directions. I still don't know Austin."

"Drive until I say turn. It'll be a right. But quite a way from here." He kept his hand on my neck, a warm gesture of possession. I shouldn't allow it. Shouldn't go to his home for what was surely more than talking. I stopped at a red light and glanced at him.

"We're not a couple."

"But we're friends." He gestured. "Turn here, it's in the next block. Just come inside. Maybe we'll watch a DVD."

A DVD. Somehow my relationship with Blade had never included something so mundane, so . . . ordinary. I liked the concept. Maybe this was just a date. Less than a date. Two friends hanging out.

I pulled up in front of the large stone house where we'd met to mourn Marguerite. He'd left lights on.

"Pull into the driveway. We can go in the back door."

We both went on high alert as we climbed out of the car. Blade punched in a code on the pad by the back door, the alarm beeped and we were inside. We looked at each other and breathed a sigh of relief.

"I hate this." I looked away from his intensity. He wouldn't pull a whammy, but he read me much too easily. "At least you have great security and a nice kitchen. A real waste." It was one of those designer jobs, all granite countertops and stainless steel appliances.

Blade grinned. "The advantages of being vampire. You never had to learn how to cook."

"Neither did you. Modern men share household duties." As if Blade could ever be classified as modern. Metrosexual to him would mean a quickie on a bus.

He grinned, obviously mind reading again. I ran my hand over the cool granite. He didn't say a word, just planted a little picture in my mind of the two of us on a cracked leather seat doing the wild thing between stops. Hoo, boy. That *had* been him planting the picture, hadn't it? I gave him a searching look. He looked as innocent as a decadent male can manage.

"You didn't get much of a tour last time you were here. Come upstairs." He took my hand and tugged me toward the staircase.

"I think not." I knew exactly what would be on the second floor. I've watched my share of home decorating shows. With a designer kitchen comes a designer master bedroom, make that a suite, with a luxurious bathroom complete with a Jacuzzi tub and steam shower. A girl can resist only so much. I was safer downstairs.

"Come on. The TV and DVD player are in my bedroom. I know you like HBO. Flo told me you have some favorite shows."

"Aren't you two just the best of buds?" Calling myself all kinds of an idiot, I let him lead me up the stairs. I *wanted* to see his bedroom and safety is highly overrated. He stopped in front of a closed door at the top of the stairs.

"I apologize in advance. I haven't slept in a coffin in centuries."

"You *never* slept in a coffin." But he did sleep raw and in a king-sized bed. He pushed open the door.

"Maybe we should go back downstairs. We can sit and talk. Drink a Bloody Merry together. Like old friends."

"Are you afraid to be in my bedroom with me?" He gestured toward a plasma TV hung on the wall across from the foot of the bed. "See? I have a TV."

"Sure." In a vamp magic move, Blade had my T-shirt off and eyed my bra.

"I want to study this Kevlar. As a scientist."

"You were never a scientist."

"True. But I love modern technology." He put both hands on the bra. "Velcro." He ripped it open, the sound a bizarre kind of turn-on. "Easy on. Easy off."

I reached for his shirt. "Snaps." I popped them open. "Easy on. Easy off."

We just stared at each other. Had I come here to have sex? Probably. Almost getting killed makes me horny. So I was looking for a little affirmation. I'm alive, almost. I want to *feel* alive. And maybe I want some of that release Blade had offered. I looked down at my skirt and *saw* it on the floor around my feet.

"Gloriana!" Blade laughed and pulled me to him. Skin to skin. Nice. "Where did you learn to do that?"

"Flo." I leaned against him for a moment, then pushed back to walk away from him. I wore a bright red thong. I looked over my shoulder. "How do you like *these* panties?"

"Is that what they are?" Blade eyes gleamed. "What else have you learned, Gloriana? Has Flo told you how she pleases her many lovers?"

I turned and put my hands on my hips. So maybe I was posing a little. Judging from the way Blade's jeans bulged, I was having the desired effect.

"Do you think I need lessons in pleasing a man?" I walked slowly up to him and brushed my nipples across his chest. I dipped one finger into his waistband. He sucked in a breath when I popped open the snap there. "Are you complaining about previous performances?"

"Do you take me for a fool?" He pulled me into his arms and kissed me hungrily, as only Blade could. I wrapped my arms around him and *saw* his jeans and boots in a heap next to the bed. I slid my hands down to cup his bare buttocks. Bingo.

"Gloriana." He picked me up and carried me to the bed. "You're magic."

"And don't you forget it." I pulled him down on top of me and we made love. Not wild monkey sex, but can't-pleasure-you-enough sex. Our timing, our moves were as perfect as centuries of practice could make them.

"Lie back, Gloriana. Let me love you." Jerry held my hands over my head and nuzzled my breasts, suckling first one and then the other until I moved my legs restlessly.

"Does that please you?" He blew on a damp nipple then looked up at me.

"You know it does." I reached for him.

"No. Keep your hands there, above your head. Tell me where to go next."

Next. He knew where I wanted him next, but I smiled and decided two could play the waiting game.

"Kiss my calves, then the back of my knees."

Jerry slid down me, "accidentally" dragging his warm mouth and tongue over my stomach and curls on his way.

"Roll over. I want to do this properly."

I rolled and gripped the brass headboard with both hands. Properly? There was nothing proper about the way Jerry spread my legs and explored my backside while he kissed a heated path where I told him to.

"Taste me, Jerry. You know where." I felt his warm breath on my inner thighs.

"Do I?" His hands were under my hips, lifting me. His tongue flicked across my sensitive flesh. "Am I in the ball park?"

Cute. Maybe Jerry *had* been watching some TV. "Lover, you're hitting a home run." I clutched the cool metal until I feared I'd bend it. "Oh . . . yes!"

He wouldn't stop until I shuddered, unbearably sensitive to his touch, my legs quivering. Finally, he rolled me over and gathered me in his arms.

"Was that to milady's satisfaction?"

I yawned and stretched, rubbing my toes up his hairy leg. " 'Twill do." I looked down to where his erection nudged my hip. "But we seem to have a bit of a problem. My knight's lance is unsheathed."

Jerry grinned and threw his own arms over his head. "Mayhap my lady has a remedy?"

I ran my hands over his hard body, then crawled on top of him. Oh, God, but he could fill me.

"Better?" I moved just enough to take him deeper.

"Getting there." He pulled me down to kiss me, his tongue stroking mine as I began to move. When I finally collapsed on top of him, I was wasted. Inside out and upside down. As a release it had been a dandy. And Jerry had the cat-who-ate-the-canary kind of smile that told its own story.

"Stay with me tonight, Gloriana. Sleep in my arms while the sun's out."

I sat up and looked down at my forever lover. Tender feelings washed over me. The very feelings that scared the hell out of me. Blade picked up my hand and kissed my knuckles.

"Stay, lass."

"Flo and Valdez will freak out if I don't come home."

"Call them. Tell them you're with me." He sat up and reached for me, cupping my breasts and kissing each one in turn. "Don't be afraid of staying. It doesn't mean I own you."

Trust Jerry to cut to the chase. "I'm not afraid." And trust me to rise to his bait. I'd dropped my purse on the floor next to the bedroom door. I *saw* my cell phone in my hand and it was there.

"What made you decide to learn this now?" Blade shook his head. "You're dazzling me."

"You ain't seen nothin' yet." I hit the speed dial. Flo wasn't home but I left a message which I knew Valdez could hear. I *saw* the phone into my purse, then lay back. Maybe I should go home, but the bed was comfy and the man seemed inclined to pleasure me again before the sun came up. I was staying put.

I woke suddenly. Jerked awake by the touch of cold steel on my breast. Mara stood over me. She held a knife in her hand. One of Blade's stilettos.

"I could cut out your heart. No vampire can survive that."

I glanced at the pillow next to me. "Where's Blade?" I'd managed to say that pretty well. Like I wasn't inches away from death.

"Downstairs on the phone with our Westwood snitch." She smiled and flicked the sheet off of me. "I will never understand your appeal to him. You are . . ." She made a face. "Fat."

I *saw* myself behind her. And my fat ass was out of reach. I laughed, high on my power and the look of utter bafflement on Mara's face. I *saw* the stiletto on the floor, but her grip tightened and it didn't move out of her hand. Can you say power struggle?

"You weren't really going to kill me, were you?" I pulled on my new bra and skirt. God knows where my thong had landed. "Blade would be . . . vexed." I'd never liked Mara. She'd been a Campbell favorite, the noble daughter of a neighboring clan. How does an English actress stack up next to that? Like a rust bucket next to a Ferrari.

"No, I wouldn't kill you." She tossed the knife on the bed. "I'll leave that to Westwood."

"Gee, thanks." I found my T-shirt and was about to slip it over my head.

"Wait! That's your Kevlar, isn't it?" Mara stepped closer. She had the knife again, clever girl. "How about a little test?" The bitch put the blade against the fabric and pushed.

"Mara! Stop that!" Blade grabbed her wrist and the knife landed on the carpet.

"Relax, Jeremiah. I was only playing." Mara put her hand over his and smiled up at him. She wore low-riding skinny black jeans and a T-shirt that hugged her breasts and left a nice strip of bare skin showing at her narrow waist. Everything about her was better than me. Outside, inside. I hated her. Hated myself. Hated Blade for returning her smile.

I jerked the shapeless T-shirt over my head. "I need to go home now. Shall I call a cab?" I plucked my cell phone from my purse.

"I'll take you home." Blade picked up the knife and hid it . . . somewhere in one of his lightning fast moves. "Mara, I'll see you later."

I headed down the stairs. I threw up a block to keep Blade from reading my mind. I'd been a damned fool once again. Mara was living here and obviously eyeing Blade as a MacTavish replacement. What man wouldn't choose her over me? My head hurt and my heart ached. I sure didn't need Blade's pity. I had enough of my own to wallow in.

Sixteen

Blade dropped me off, inclined to follow me upstairs until his cell phone rang. Business. I waved good-bye, blew him an air kiss to show that Mara's bitchy possessiveness hadn't gotten to me. No sirree.

I unlocked the apartment door and Valdez trotted up to me.

"Thanks for the night off. Flo took me out with her." He followed me into the kitchen.

I popped open a Bloody Merry.

"I could eat."

"Flo didn't feed you? Where is she?" The apartment was silent.

"I'm not supposed to say." Valdez plopped his bottom on the linoleum and watched me dump Cocoa Puffs into his bowl. I topped it with milk and held it just out of reach.

"Excuse me? Whose dog are you, anyway?" I knew he could do one of his tricks and get to the cereal, but I also knew he shouldn't be allowed to keep secrets from me.

"You got me. She's with Richard Mainwaring."

"Oh, my God!" I slapped the bowl on the floor, splashing milk everywhere. "How could you let her go with him?"

"He's okay." Valdez was busy licking up the spilt milk before diving mouth first into his bowl.

"He's not okay. He could be staking other vamps with crosses, for crying out loud." This was bad. Had Blade left yet? I looked out the window but his car was gone.

"He's not staking other vamps. He said so and Flo and I believed him. I have a b.s. detector, you know. The guy was telling the truth."

"I thought she went out with Kenneth Collins." I walked down the hall and flung open Flo's bedroom door. The usual chaos associated with her decisions about what to wear. But the bed was made and that told the tale.

"She did. But that ended early. So we went out looking for Mainwaring. And found him."

"Where are they?"

"His place. Flo dropped me off here and went with him. He's a tough dude. No one will get by him. She musta spent the day with him too." Valdez had cleaned out the bowl. *"Seconds?"*

"No. I'm so glad you and 'Ricardo' bonded. I can't believe you let Flo leave with him." I watched Valdez rub his face clean on the living room rug.

"You think anyone can stop Flo from doing what she wants?" He gave me a long suffering look. *"Both of you females are stubborn as hell."*

Was I going to stand here trading insults with my *dog*? I stormed off into my bedroom. Valdez was just another macho male in a furry body. Had Mainwaring done some kind of whammy on both Flo and my dog to get them to accept his story so completely? And if he wasn't the religious psycho staking vamps, then who was? I showered the smell of sex off my body, taking a minute to reminisce about the pleasure Blade had given me and three minutes to seethe about that bitch Mara before worry about Flo took the upper hand.

I pulled a hot pink fifties circle skirt and white twin set with pearl buttons out of my closet and stepped into the loafers that went with it. I dragged my hair into a ponytail and tied a white scarf around it. Now I looked like a teen-ager. Which made me feel marginally better. Mara had been close to thirty when she'd turned vampire and I'd been a young looking twenty-four. Yeah, I was bitter. Right now, if Mara and I had a bitch-off, I'd win, hands down.

"Come on, you worthless hound." I threw my stuff into a cute fifties Lucite box purse which I would never sell and unlocked the door. "We're going down to the shop."

Ryan was working the evening shift. At least nights were getting longer as the season changed. Which is a really good thing in the vamp world. Not that Texas seasons seemed dramatically different from each other. But the nights were cooler and my sweater felt good. So did the hours stretching out ahead of me.

I stuck my worry about Flo onto my mental to-do list and plastered a smile on my face as I entered the shop. Ryan looked up from straightening a stack of sweaters. And, yes, that stack was shrinking every day. My business was boom-ing and I had good help.

"How'd it go today?" I stuck my purse in the storeroom and picked up a pile of receipts.

"Sold that leisure suit to Tony Crapetta. He said you told him he could have a family discount?" Ryan squinted at me through his thick glasses. He'd stuck with the Gatsby look, this pin-striped suit a dark brown.

"Sure. Twenty percent." I tapped in some numbers in the calculator next to the register. "You've got a nice commission coming this week."

"I know." Ryan gestured around the shop. "I tried to call you about the discount, but your cell phone must have been off. So I just gave it to him. I hope that was okay."

Cell phone off. Yes, I'd turned it off at Blade's, after I'd called home. Lacy knew enough not to try to reach me during the day, but we hadn't made a big deal out of that to Ryan.

Of course common sense should tell him I had to sleep most of the day if I worked all night.

I looked at him and focused, trying to read his mind. Flo was right. White noise. Weird.

I wondered if Lacy could read his mind. Maybe not. And that would be part of his appeal. No random thoughts interfering during sex like "Check out those thighs" or "Will this woman ever come?" The worst? "Why won't she just blow me so I can go home and catch the end of the game?" Been there, done that. Another reason I usually swear off mind reading.

"You don't have to call me about discounts. I have the price I paid for each item in the inventory list in the computer. The program Derek set up for me. Just look up what I paid, use your best judgment. I like to get at least double what I paid to cover costs." And wasn't that computer technology the coolest thing? I looked around and saw some empty spaces crying out for new merchandise.

I hoped Miranda would come by with her latest finds from the weekend estate sales. Austin has lots of old homes, old families and great sales to hear Miranda tell it. I got a little wistful for a moment, but that was useless. I'd never be able to check them out for myself. Estate sales didn't go on at night. Period.

"Something wrong?" Ryan was still squinting at me. "You're quiet."

"I'm okay. Do you need new glasses? You look like you're straining your eyes." I reached for the glasses and Ryan jumped back, out of reach.

"No! I mean, I've got really bad eyes. Can't see worth a damn without the glasses and not much better with them." He adjusted the frames and looked down at Valdez who was studying him intently. "What's up with the dog? I don't think he likes me."

"Valdez is probably jealous. He knows you're with Lacy. And he really likes her." I grinned at Valdez's snarl. "Of course that's conjecture. He's just a dumb dog." Valdez turned and trotted to sit by the front door, obviously miffed. Too bad. He'd let Flo go off with a dangerous man. I hated to, but I was going to call Damian as soon as Ryan left. Someone had to check on Flo.

"You can leave now, if you want to. I've got it covered."

"There's a customer in the dressing room." Ryan glanced back at the curtained area. "I'll wait until she gets out. Commission, you know."

"Hey, head out. I'll make sure you get the credit." I put my hand on his sleeve and he jumped. Gee, he was really uptight. Surely he didn't have a clue that I was anything but a night owl, did he? But weird people came in the shop all the time. Shape-shifter friends of Lacy's. Vampires who wanted to sell their old clothes.

I was going to play this by ear, but I might have to let Ryan in on my little secret if he was going to keep working here. Of course that might send him screaming for his life. My real problem was that I didn't know Ryan that well. I'd hired him on Lacy's say-so and she'd known him about five minutes at the time. So far all the books balanced, and the son of the SuitMasters mogul wouldn't need to steal anyway.

Ryan had been thinking over my offer. "Thanks. I'll go home and change. I'm supposed to meet Lacy here later. Tell her I'll be back by nine. So we can go out to dinner."

"Will do." Out to dinner. What a concept. I watched him leave, giving Valdez a wide berth. The curtain moved and a woman stepped out of the dressing room. "That looks great on you!" I smiled and got involved in a discussion of the mini versus maxi skirt debate. The woman had great legs. We went with the miniskirt and Ryan got his commission.

An hour zoomed by, with customers, a vampire with an armload of clothes and Miranda all stopping by. I had a good assortment of stock to tag and inventory and was alone in the shop doing just that when Lacy came in.

"Yoo-hoo! Ryan, love dumpling, are you back there?" Lacy sauntered into the back room. "Oh, Glory. Hi." She turned red. "Where's Ryan?"

"I let love dumpling off early." I glanced at the clock. "He went home to change and will be back in a few minutes."

Lacy picked up a fifties sundress. "Cute stuff. Miranda?"

"Yes. I think I'll keep the summer stock back here until spring. I got in a great fur coat a while ago." I held it out. "Chinchilla. Feel."

"Mmm. Soft. I had a chinchilla once." Lacy smiled, her canines gleaming in the light. I had a feeling she wasn't talking about a coat.

"Let me ask you something. About Ryan."

"He's working out, isn't he? I know he's enjoying it here." Lacy grabbed a pink lace teddy. "Mine. He'll love this."

"Can you read his mind?" I leaned against the table.

"I don't know. Well, no, when he has on his glasses. And I refuse to try when he's got them off." Lacy got a dreamy look. "I can't tell you how many lovers I've lost because of the whole mind-reading crap. Some thoughts just kill the mood, you know? There's a lot to be said for mystery."

"I agree. Blade never lets me read his mind. Not unless he's got a message for me." I had a feeling I was getting my own dreamy look. "Never mind that. Ryan *is* mortal, isn't he?"

"Of course he is." Lacy held the teddy up to her, then tossed it down. "Too big." She found a black one and checked the tag. "This will work."

"Earth to Lacy. This is serious, Lacy. Why can't we read Ryan's mind? Any thoughts?"

"Well, he wears those thick glasses, everywhere but in bed. I usually look in a mortal's eyes to read minds. The windows to the soul, you know." She shook her head. "Don't ask me to read his mind in bed, Glory. Even though he says he's blind as a bat, I don't want to go there."

"Have you showered with him? Surely he'd take the glasses off to shower."

"No, we haven't done the shower thing yet." She bit her lip. "Tonight. I'll get him in there tonight and see if I can read his mind, if you really think it's necessary. What are you worried about, Glory?"

"I don't know. Maybe I'm getting paranoid. But with so many people out to get us, I'm entitled. I'd just feel more comfortable if you could read Ryan's mind, make sure he doesn't have a clue about who or what we really are."

"I've thought about telling him the truth." Lacy really had it bad. She was swaying to the ballad on the radio, the teddy clutched to her breast.

"Snap out of it, Lacy. Most mortals can't handle the truth."

"You're right." Good-bye dreamy look, hello worry.

I felt low for bringing her down. Maybe Valdez was right. I was a downer.

"Enjoy Ryan while you can. If you decide we can trust him, we will." I patted her shoulder. "Can you make someone immortal?"

"Werecats are born, not made. So when I mate with a mortal, I'm setting myself up for eventual loss." Lacy sighed.

"Blade or Damian could turn him for you. If you thought he'd want to be vampire."

"Really?" Lacy lit up. "So we could be together forever?"

"Just a thought. I haven't asked them, but even Flo can turn mortals. Not me. I don't do that." I heard the bells tinkle on the front door. "It's a personal thing."

"Right." Lacy put the teddy in her purse. "Take this out of my pay, will you? That's Ryan. I'd know his smell anywhere. See you later." She headed out into the shop, stopping in the doorway. "And, Glory, I'll let you know what I find out."

"Thanks. And consider the teddy a gift. Enjoy." I smiled. Young love. It had been so long since I'd felt that first flush of infatuation. Way too long. But I'd had an incredible night with Blade. Infatuation wasn't nearly as great as the real deal. Oops.

If I wasn't careful, I was going to end up in a threesome with Mara and Blade. Not going to happen. Mara had to go— I didn't care where—before I'd fall into bed with Blade again.

I picked up my cell phone and hit the speed dial for Damian. Voice mail. I left a message that I needed to talk to him and hung up.

The door opened and bells tinkled. Vampire. A woman I recognized from the wake for Margie walked in carrying a pile of clothes. Wheeling and dealing kept me busy for the next hour. I was alone when the door opened again and Damian came in.

He was grinning of course. Like I'd called him asking for more sex, the real thing this time.

"Sorry to disappoint you, Damian, but this is about Flo." I threw up a block. Maybe I was getting used to pain, but it wasn't as much of an effort as it had once been.

"My sister is in trouble." Damian lost his smile. "What's happened?"

"I don't know that she's in trouble, but she and Valdez tracked down Richard Mainwaring last night." I glanced at Valdez. When Damian had crossed the threshold, the dog had jumped up and looked ready to take a chunk out of my visitor at the slightest provocation.

"Did she kill him?" Damian's fangs shot out and I shivered. Whoa, this man could go from charming seducer to homicidal vamp in less time than it took me to blink.

"No. He's not our guy." Valdez bared his teeth. *"Flo and I believed him."*

"You believed him." Damian looked down and snarled. "My sister who thinks with her"—he said an Italian word that probably meant a female body part—"and a dumb mutt believed him."

"You want to take on this dumb mutt, asshole?" Valdez morphed into his attack mode and I stepped back.

"Stop it!" I said bravely from behind the counter. "A customer could come in."

"So we'll erase some memory." Damian and Valdez had locked eyes and it looked like neither one was giving an inch.

"Valdez, I forbid you to attack Damian." My dog knew the rules. He couldn't disobey a direct order from me. No matter what. He glared at me, almost *willing* me to change my mind. I shook my head.

"Can you tell us where you saw Mainwaring? Where Damian might look for Flo?"

Valdez sat and scratched his ear. *"Maybe."*

"Damn it, let me rip out his throat, Glory. You will be well rid of this mangy beast."

Valdez just wagged his tail, obviously not concerned. Hey, I was concerned enough for both of us.

"Tell him, Valdez. Where do you think Flo and Mainwaring went?"

"He's got a garage apartment on Lamar Street. Yellow with brown trim. It's on a corner."

"Address?" I put on my sternest look. "Damian is not going to drive up and down Lamar, which my customers tell me is one of the longest streets in Austin, looking for brown and yellow houses."

"You got that right." Damian looked like he really wanted to kick my dog.

"Don't even think about hurting this dog, Damian. I mean it." I stepped between them.

"Sixteen twelve Lamar." Valdez pushed his head under my hand. I swear he was grinning at Damian. Like he'd won or something. Jerk.

"North or South?" In Austin that made a difference.

"South. Satisfied?" Valdez scratched his ear. *"When you gonna pick up some more flea shampoo?"*

Damian spun on his heel and headed for the door.

"Let me know what you find out," I said to his back. He nodded and disappeared into the night.

"You could have been more helpful."

"I told you. Mainwaring's okay. If I were you, I'd worry more about Sabatini."

Food for thought. But now the evening stretched out endlessly. The hours crept past, especially the ones when no customers showed up to distract me. At one point I popped over to Diana's to get a Bloody Merry. Diana wasn't there. So I paid and returned to my lonely post.

The bells on the door tinkled and I looked up eagerly. Blade and Mara.

Blade looked around. "Are you alone?"

"Yes, it's the slow time of night." I walked out from behind the counter. "Welcome to my shop, Mara." See? I can be gracious.

"It is . . . quaint." Mara strolled over to finger a fifties cocktail dress. She was still in her tight jeans but had thrown on a leather jacket against the chilly evening air. "Good quality, but why on earth would anyone buy used clothes?"

"You'd be surprised." I really liked that jacket she wore, talk about quality. "You ever want to clean out your closet, come see me. I pay a fair price."

Mara's nose went up like she'd just caught a whiff of something nasty, like my lack of class. "I donate my castoffs to a worthy cause."

"I'm glad you can afford to do that." I *wasn't* going to let her get to me. Of course she'd never had to work a day in her life. From privileged birth to wealthy husband. I glanced at Jerry. My own fault I hadn't snagged a rich husband of my own.

"Mara, didn't you want to say something?"

I swear Blade's stern voice had all the authority of a father chiding a naughty child. Mara's chin went up and she looked inclined to argue. Then she met Blade's gaze. Whoa. He was steamed with her. On account of *me*?

"Gloriana, I apologize if I frightened you earlier. With the knife." Mara made it sound like I was a wimp who couldn't handle a little joke. "You know I wasn't really going to hurt you."

"Do I? Know that?" Sure I was going to make her squirm. She didn't mean a word of what she'd just said and obviously just wanted to keep Blade happy. Did I want to keep Blade happy? Not enough to just roll over and accept this pseudoapology.

"Gloriana, Mara's truly sorry." Blade had his hand on her arm. "Aren't you? And it won't happen again. Will it?"

Mara winced and it was all I could do not to happy dance. Don't you love it when the good guys come out on top?

"I understand that Jeremiah esteems you, Gloriana. And that if I want to stay with him, I must esteem you as well." Mara had her lady of the manor gig going.

I could either keep resisting and sound like the low-born chit who'd played the Globe, or try on my own dignified lady of the manor act. Oh, what the hell.

"Thank you, Mara. I accept your apology." I smiled at Blade. "Is this the only reason you came by?"

"No, we have news." Blade let Mara go and moved closer to me. "We have a man inside who's willing to help us. With Westwood."

"That's great. What are you going to do? Poison Westwood?" I glanced at Mara. "Hit him from the air when he's vulnerable?"

"I'm still working out the details." Blade frowned. "Poison seems like the coward's way out."

Mara smiled. "Yes, it does. We want a fight. We want to stare into Westwood's eyes when the life leaves his body."

"That may be your idea of fun, Mara, but if we can stop Westwood with something as simple as arsenic in his spaghetti, then I think we should do it. Before he kills again." I put my hand on Blade's arm. "I know you want a fight, Jerry, but think about all the people who are already on Westwood's hit list. Get this over with quickly. So we can go about our lives without looking over our shoulders constantly."

"You have a good point, Gloriana." Blade leaned down to drop a kiss on my lips. "We must go. Mara and I are meeting our man tonight. I'll let you know what happens."

"Great. Thanks." I watched them leave. And of course Mara couldn't resist sending me a hate-filled look over her shoulder. Once a bitch, always a bitch. Boy, did I need a distraction.

"Hey, Harvey, Emmie Lou. Are you hanging around tonight?" Yep, I was that desperate for company. Valdez had practically danced around Blade the whole time he'd been here, but now he snoozed by the door. He looked at me for a moment, then went back to his nap. He was used to the spirits and obviously didn't see them as a danger so he ignored them unless objects started flying around the room.

"Sure, honey. We're always hanging around." Emmie Lou materialized next to the designer scarves. "We just keep out of sight when you've got customers. Out of respect."

"Well, thanks." I smiled.

Harvey appeared next to the men's suits. "Can't believe that feller bought that polyester leisure suit today. Hell, you just wait till summer. Ain't nothin' hotter than polyester."

"I'm sure you're right. But business is business." I stepped closer and glanced at Valdez. "Can you two come into the stockroom with me? I want to ask you something."

"Sure, sweetpea." Emmie Lou twirled her skirt as she headed that way. "Harvey, shake a leg."

"That woman's so dang bossy." Harvey glowered. "But I'm comin'."

"Thanks." I followed them inside and shut the door. Valdez probably could hear us anyway, but I doubted he'd bother to listen. I wasn't planning to let Blade in on my concerns. I could handle this situation, if it *was* a situation. "I want to ask you about Ryan."

"That youngun's got a screw loose." Harvey looked at Emmie. "Am I right?"

"Sure are. Plays with bugs."

I don't know what I expected, but bugs? "What do you mean?" I looked around. "We don't have bugs."

"Sure do. There's one there in the corner. On the top shelf." Harvey nodded toward the metal shelving. "Cockroach the size of your thumb."

I grabbed the can of Raid. I hate bugs. I'd insisted on an exterminator before I'd even considered this space. Yeah, yeah. I'm a blood-sucking vampire and I'm terrified of bugs. Go figure. I crept closer and could just see antennae peeking out from the top shelf. When I lifted my hand, it scuttled away. I aimed and sprayed, chasing it around the shelving until it didn't even twitch.

"Ryan should have killed it. I'm not entertaining anybody's pet bugs." I wasn't getting near it. Disposing of the body would be a good job for bug boy when he came to work tomorrow evening.

"Don't know, honey. All's we know is that he used to play with it every time he came into work. Talked to it too." Emmie Lou waved a hand over her face. "Can't you open that door? That stuff's not exactly Evening in Paris."

"Right." I jerked open the door into the shop. I'd been trying to ignore the smell, but it was about to choke me.

"You better get the spider too, while you got the can out." Harvey headed back into the store. "It nests right up here, next to that set of Shakespeare you bought off Miranda." Harvey gestured, then made a face. "Those books were a waste of money, if you ask me."

Emmie Lou shook her head. "Harvey never did appreciate fine literature. His idea of a good read is a paperback Western."

"And what's wrong with that? Zane Grey. Louis L'Amour. Geniuses."

"You'd be surprised what a first edition Zane Grey goes for, Emmie." I'd enjoyed getting into old books along with the clothes. Of course that remark only fueled the fire and they started shouting at each other.

I ignored Emmie Lou and Harvey as the argument escalated. Of course I had my own fond memories of Billy Shakespeare. I'd only done a few of his plays, but had worked my way through reading the rest of them over the years. I looked up at the shelf.

A spider crouched on the edge. I shuddered. What would Billy say? "Out damn spot." Something like that. I crept up on it, can at the ready, but it scurried out of sight. I wasn't about to spray my books, so I figured I'd tell Ryan to kill the creepy crawly. I turned back to Harvey and Emmie. She was about to throw a crystal wine glass.

"Stop!" I didn't think I could take it away from her. So I just looked at it until she put it back. "Thanks. Any more bugs?" I held the can out in front of me and scanned the room.

"Ain't seen any." Harvey looked relieved to change the subject. "What's got you so riled? Those itty bitty things don't even bite. Why, I remember the time I got caught in a bee hive. Now that's no treat, I can tell you."

"I don't want bugs in my store. I know *I* wouldn't shop where there are roaches and spiders." Or where I found the screeching owner perched on the counter with a can of bug spray.

"We'll keep our eyes open, honey. If we see any more, we'll let you know." Emmie gave Harvey a look. "Everybody's got phobias, Harvey. You got that thing about Ferris wheels."

"Now, Emmie, no need to bring up ancient history." Harvey looked embarrassed.

"Can I ask you both a favor?"

"Sure, honey." Emmie winked at me. "Harvey's ready for a subject change. Whatcha need?"

"I need you both to watch Ryan when I'm not here. Just see if he does anything else strange or suspicious." As if playing with bugs wasn't strange enough. I put the spray back in the storeroom and looked out the open back door. The smell wasn't that bad, but it wasn't exactly the perfume Emmie Lou had mentioned either. Nope. The back door had to be locked and double bolted. Security first.

"What do you think he's up to, Glory?" Emmie Lou came closer. "Stealing?"

"No. I don't see any signs of that." I looked at both of them. "Have you let him see you? I didn't warn him about the two of you."

"No. Lacy asked us not to. He's her boyfriend, you know. And we really like that girl, so we've kept out of sight." Emmie Lou frowned. "You think he's cheating on her?"

"Now, Emmie, there you go again. Not every man's a cheater. I sure wasn't." Harvey ducked behind the suit rack when Emmie Lou whirled around.

"So you say, Harvey Nutt. But there was that checker down at the Piggly Wiggly—"

"I don't know what he's up to. Just watch him, okay? You can be my eyes and ears."

"Like a detective." Harvey hitched up his pants. "We're your spies. You hear that, Emmie? We got us a job."

"Yes." I smiled at him and a still fuming Emmie Lou. "Are you okay with that, Emmie Lou?"

"Sure, honey. Anything for you. You've treated us real nice." Emmie cocked her head. "People comin'. Let's go, Harvey."

They both vanished just as Valdez barked once and the door swung open. Damian, Flo and Richard Mainwaring pushed inside.

Seventeen

"I can't believe you sent my brother after me like I'm a foolish teenager, Glory." Flo's eyes glittered. "He humiliated me."

"I did not." Damian grinned at me. "Caught the two lovebirds with their pants down. Learned a new position." He winked. "So the night's not a total loss."

Richard Mainwaring glowered. At me, at Damian, even at Valdez. But when he looked at Flo, his face changed. He'd been bit by the love bug, for sure. A new position? I looked at Flo and she actually flushed.

"Wait a minute. You're convinced this vampire isn't staking with a wooden cross?"

"I would *never* do such a thing." Mainwaring looked down at Flo. "I confess I *did* feed from that goth a week or so ago. Didn't erase his memory." He shrugged. "Hey, he was going to have a story to tell his freak friends."

"How generous of you." I liked the fact that Richard seemed to adore Flo, but he was just a little too casual about blending for my peace of mind. "What about the praying?"

"I was a priest before I became vampire."

"I cannot believe God wanted you to be celibate, Ricardo. A mistake." Flo held on to his arm.

"Mistake or not. I always ask God's forgiveness when I feed from mortals." Mainwaring put his arm around Flo. "I feel like it's a sin, but I can't seem to stop."

"Ricardo, it's in your nature. God made you so, God forgives you." Flo leaned against him.

"Oh, please." Damian moved closer to me and I remembered to throw up my blocks. "God didn't make you, Mainwaring. Some other vampire did. Centuries ago."

"Damian, be nice. Ricardo and I are in love. Deal with it."

"Florence, I can handle your brother." Mainwaring moved Flo away from him. "You want to take this outside, Sabatini? See who's stronger?"

"If I have to kill you, my sister will be mad at me. And if you accidentally kill *me,* Florence will never forgive you. Am I right?" Damian looked at Flo. When she seemed inclined to think it over, Damian shook his head. "Save your strength for our enemies. If you're not staking other vampires with a cross, then we're back to square one."

A customer pushed open the door, took one glance at our group which practically vibrated with hostility and stepped back outside.

"Wait!" I ran after her. "Come in. These folks were just leaving. Right, guys?" I pushed Damian out the door. I thought for about half a second about doing the same with Mainwaring, but the hard look in his eyes nipped that idea in the bud. "Come back. We should have more Halloween costumes next week."

Mainwaring and Flo stepped outside, stopping beside the keypad and obviously heading upstairs to our apartment.

Damian held open the shop door and, with a charming smile, bowed to the female customer.

"Please, lovely lady, come in and look through the merchandise. You will love this store."

The woman flushed and stepped inside.

Damian leaned close to me and whispered, "B positive, yum."

"Good night, Damian." I nodded toward the door then turned to the customer. Damian stood there a moment. I could smell him, vampire, male. Not unpleasant unless I associated those things with his bad habits. The virtual sex had been hot, but had been a sleazy thing to do. I turned and let him read my disgust.

Damian grimaced, the bells tinkled and he was gone. I got into helping my new customer, but I couldn't totally relax. Flo and Valdez may have decided to trust Mainwaring's word, but I wasn't convinced. He'd sent those hate messages at church. Strong enough that Flo had noticed and hustled us out of there. Strong enough to motivate him to kill fellow vamps? I shivered and looked up at the ceiling. I hoped my instincts were wrong. If they weren't, my roomie was in big trouble. No, make that danger.

"I couldn't do it, Glory." Lacy prowled the shop like a caged tiger.

"He wouldn't get in the shower?" I was learning way more about Lacy's sex life than I wanted to, but I had a nagging feeling my security was at stake. Oops. At stake. Gee, I hate vampire jokes.

"Of course." Lacy flushed. "He's got a great body, absolutely nothing to be ashamed of on *his* part. So we're in the shower, the water's just right, but I just couldn't make myself read his thoughts. Ryan's insisted he's not put off by my flat butt, but what if he hates it?"

A flat butt, what a body issue. I didn't have to look back to know my own butt was *ass*tronomical.

"So what about after the shower? When you got dressed? Couldn't you take a chance and read his mind then?"

"I got up my nerve and reached for his glasses, but he got all antsy. Had to go, early class, a bunch of excuses that a few minutes before hadn't existed. I'm afraid he's got another girlfriend. One with a nice ass like yours." Lacy was still pacing.

Have I mentioned how much I love Lacy? "Come back into the storeroom with me." Valdez still snoozed by the door. In the hours just before dawn, we were never busy. I should probably close, but it gave me time to catch up on paperwork.

Lacy plopped on a chair in the storeroom. "It smells funny in here."

"Bug spray." I nodded toward the shelf. "Ryan ever talk about his bug fetish?"

"What?" She sat up straight. "That's ridiculous. He's not into bugs." She looked thoughtful. "Though I have to admit he's got a hard-on for old comic books about superheroes that I find a little weird. Did you know there's a vampire *hunter* named Blade in one series?"

"Lacy, concentrate here. You want to know why Ryan's acting funny about his glasses. You want to know if he has another girlfriend. And I think his glasses are keeping us from reading his mind. They're so thick."

"Maybe they *are* blocking us." Lacy got a gleam in her eyes. "Do you think we can work together to get them off him? I would like to know about that girlfriend situation. I haven't used my cat strength on him yet, but he *does* work out."

"I can hold him long enough for you to get his glasses off, then I'll try to do the whammy. If I can get him under, we can ask him all the questions we want. And I'll be able to read his mind. So will you."

"Why do you want to read his mind?"

"I told you. It's just a funny feeling I've got. We needed help in the shop and you immediately met Ryan who's perfect for it. Coincidence?"

"Stranger things have happened. I call it synchronicity. The universe provided Ryan just when we needed him—a lover for me and a clerk for you." Lacy winced. "You're right. I've lived too long to believe in coincidences. But I really think Ryan's legit. He's a great salesman." She sighed. "He's sure sold me."

"Obviously. And I hope you're right, Lacy. But since we both have questions, I think we need to take a shot at reading his mind." Now I felt guilty. I'd gotten Lacy worked up and I had absolutely no proof that Ryan was anything but a lucky hire for me.

"What if it doesn't work? What if he gets mad at us?" Lacy's eyes filled. "I love him, Glory."

"We blame me. I'm a crazed woman, determined to give him a makeover. Have to see what he looks like without his glasses."

Lacy giggled. "Yep, I think that'll play. He likes you, but he does wonder about some of your friends."

"*I* wonder about some of my friends. So what do you say? Are you in? Do we take down Ryan together?"

"Sure. When is this intervention going to take place?"

"Monday. When we're closed. Tell him I've got another commission check for him. About nine o'clock here in the shop."

"That's still a few days away. In the meantime, I'll keep working on those glasses. I hate to see us use violence."

I patted Lacy's shoulder. She *was* a little bony. "I'm sure it's just my raging paranoia. Ryan's probably fine, just into a few weird hobbies."

"I hope you're right. I can deal with bugs and graphic novels. But if he's cheating . . . He swears we're exclusive, but he's been out of pocket a few evenings and gave me vague excuses." Lacy slid off the stool and walked to the door. "Damn it. I'm freaking out. I'm going hunting before I relieve you here. See you in a few."

I watched her snarl at Valdez, who didn't even bother to look up, then she was gone. An intervention. I glanced up at the shelf where the cockroach still sat in a puddle of spray. Maybe I'd get some answers to questions I wasn't even sure I had.

• • •

"Are we going to church tonight, Flo?" I was still in my robe and lounging on the love seat while sipping my wake-up Bloody Merry.

"I asked Ricardo to take us. Do you mind?" Flo was brushing out her long dark hair.

"I think *he'll* mind, Flo. I'm not his favorite person." Well, shoot. I'd really looked forward to going to church and sitting through the whole service this time. "Are you sure you trust him? He hates me."

"I know, Glory." Flo frowned and set down the brush. "I don't understand it. He hates Damian too. Which I do understand. My brother is not popular with other men."

"Casanova wouldn't be. But I've done nothing to Richard except chew him out for failure to blend. He needs to get over it." And I needed to get over my mistrust if Flo and Ricardo were going to be a couple. He was here almost every night when I got home from the shop. So Valdez—who seemed to tolerate Richard better than I did—and I had to hang out in the living room with the TV loud enough to drown out the sounds coming from Flo's bedroom or give up TV and hole up in my bedroom. Obviously watching me read wasn't Valdez's entertainment of choice.

"I'm sorry we disturb you, Glory." Flo got a faraway look. "We will go to Ricardo's place from now on. I promise."

"I don't want to run you off." Maybe I should put up a block to Flo. This mind reading was really getting to be a drag. But at least we were communicating.

"I've been inconsiderate. But if you would just decide on a lover of your own, you could make your own noises." Flo looked me over. "Are you going to get dressed? Please don't stay home because of Ricardo."

I should just decide on a lover. The Florence da Vincis of the world could do that. Just decide and the man would worship at their feet or any other body part that needed attention. I got up and went into the kitchen to get a fresh can of Bloody Merry.

I really didn't want to spend an evening with Richard. He made me uneasy. No matter how devoted he seemed to Flo I knew he still hated me, and was that fair? I was nice to him when he came over. Well, maybe nice is an overstatement. But I tolerated him for Flo's sake.

"I think I'll stay home. The service is carried on one of the local stations, isn't it?"

"TV's not the same as being there, Glory. Please come with us."

I turned on the TV and found the guide channel. "No, look. It's on later. This way I can enjoy my night off, relax and still hear the great music." I grinned. "And if I float during the hymns, then only Valdez will see me."

"Now I feel bad. I'll call Richard and tell him that I'll stay home too."

"No, you don't." I walked to my bedroom door. "I'm going to shower and wash my hair. I'll expect you to be gone by the time I get out." I looked at Valdez. "It's steak night, pup. Rib eye, rare." I'd learned over the years that my dog needed red meat at least once a week. Not the dog food variety either. The rest of the time, he was happy to chow down on whatever junk food we had in the cupboard.

"There you go, Flo. Blondie and I will hang out here. I'll eat and she'll float. No problem."

"Fine. But I will go to Ricardo's after the service and spend the night and day there." Flo winked. "Maybe you invite Jeremiah to come over."

Tempting thought. He'd called to let me know he was working on the poison angle. Unfortunately, his guy inside was a lot like Tony Crapetta, scared of vampires, but willing to take their money. Blade wasn't going to hand over a dime until he was sure he would get what he paid for.

"Don't worry about me. I've got a book to finish reading. Some hand washing to do." I grinned. "At least the thongs you make me wear don't take long to dry."

"Have you washed the Kevlar vest yet?" Flo hadn't been impressed, even though I'd made her try it on. It had almost fit her, she's got a pretty generous bust herself, but she didn't like the way it made her look. Like Blade had said, it did tend to flatten us.

"I washed it. I don't suppose you'd consider wearing it under your clothes tonight. Westwood's out there, not to mention the religious nut."

"No, Ricardo will protect me. And I don't think Westwood has my picture. Both times he shot near me, it was dark. Not like when he aimed at you and Derek."

"Gee, thanks for reminding me." A night holed up in my apartment with excellent security was sounding better and better. "Have fun. Say hi to God for me." I headed for the shower.

I'd bathed, thrown on my bat T-shirt and jeans and had just settled down with *Shape-shifting for Dummies* (just kidding) when there was a knock on the door. Valdez jumped up and growled.

"Who is it?"

"Damian."

"Flo's not here."

"I don't want Florence. Can I come in? Please."

"Why?" I looked at Valdez. He looked ready to take a hunk out of Damian if I let him in. Not that I was against the concept.

"I need to talk to you about my sister. I'll be on my best behavior. I swear on her life."

He sounded serious. Of course I didn't trust him as far as I could throw him.

"Don't let him in." Valdez punctuated this with some really ferocious barking.

"Hush. Lacy's sleeping across the hall." I got up and threw the dead bolts. "And don't attack unless I give the word."

"What's the word?" Valdez was showing all his teeth.

I shook my head. "Would you relax?" I pulled open the door. "And, Damian, you'd better not try anything weird." I threw up my mental blocks anyway.

Damian smiled. "I am never weird." He brushed against me as he came inside.

"What's this about Flo?" I sat in one of our club chairs and watched Damian try to avoid Valdez. Not easy. My dog was right on him, never more than six inches away.

"Can't you put the beast away?" Damian had a hunted look. "At least order him to back off."

As much fun as this was to watch, I did want to talk to Damian about Flo and Richard. "Okay, Valdez. Go sit by the door. I'll let you know if I need you to take a chunk out of Mr. Wonderful here."

I leaned back and crossed my legs. "Damian, sit. You too, Valdez." Both beasts gave me a go to hell look. Too bad.

"Gloriana, you look wonderful tonight." Damian settled on the love seat.

"You are so full of it." No makeup, shapeless T-shirt and barefoot? A raving beauty I wasn't.

"What I am full of is lust for you, Gloriana." Damian struggled to keep his charming smile going and sniffed. "What do I smell? Have you been cooking? Florence told me you want to eat."

"I'm not eating yet. It was steak. For the dog."

Damian sniffed again and leaned toward me. "And lavender."

"Good nose, Sabatini." I'd tried a new soap Lacy had brought when she'd gone to the store for Flo and me. We were low on a lot of supplies. I hated to be scared to even go to the supermarket. Maybe after Damian left I'd slap on the Kevlar and hit the all-night grocery store.

"You're still blocking me, Glory." Damian slouched, playing the poor rejected lover. "Don't you trust me?"

"It'll be a cold day in hell before I trust you again, Damian."

"You wound me." He put his hand on his heart.

Too bad he was so damned good-looking. Everything Damian said and did was calculated to be completely charming. And it worked. Five o'clock shadow for the masculine touch. Silky shirt open low enough to showcase his toned body. Loafers without socks to hint at his sophistication. Well-cut trousers giving more than a hint of impressive male attributes. I doubled my block. Too much dwelling on his package was a bad sign.

"What about Flo? That's the only reason I let you in here, Damian. I'm worried about her association with Mainwaring. They're out again tonight."

"Ricardo's fine. Not a problem," Damian said it almost by rote.

"*Great guy.*" Valdez stood and padded into the kitchen. "*Any steak left?*"

"No." Okay, this was getting weirder and weirder. "When you two agree on something, the planets are out of alignment. I'm convinced Ricardo, as you call him, has done something to both of you."

"What could he have done?" Damian yawned, obviously unconcerned.

"Mind control, Damian. Something you're very familiar with."

"Don't be ridiculous. No one controls my mind." Damian stood and looked at Valdez. "The dog, sure. Anyone could make Rover roll over." He got a crafty look and he and Valdez locked eyes. "Forget it." He sat down again. "Why do you think Ricardo could do this, what do you call it, oh, yes, whammy on me?"

"Listen to yourself, Damian. 'Ricardo's great. No threat.'"
I frowned. "When you went after Flo and him the other night, you were furious. Did all that anger and mistrust just melt away?"

"I got to know him. He adores my sister."

"But he hates *me*." I stood and walked over to sit beside Damian. "I know I'm not Miss Perfect, but I've done absolutely nothing to provoke such all out hatred."

"Of course not, Gloriana." Damian picked up my hand. "I'll talk to Ricardo. Explain that we must love you." He smiled and kissed my knuckles. "He will be like a brother to you."

I jumped up. "I don't want him for a brother!" Damian was obviously not getting it. "He may be stronger than you, Damian. Or maybe you let down your guard around him."

Now that got his attention. "I never let down my guard." Damian finally looked thoughtful. "But if you're right, which you're not, then Florence isn't safe with him."

"She says he loves *her*. But the rest of us . . ."

"You seriously think he could be staking vampires with a cross? That he killed Trevor and Marguerite?" Damian shot to his feet. "And my sister is sleeping with him?"

"I don't know what to think. So far whoever's staking doesn't leave witnesses. We need proof and obviously we're not going to be able to read his mind."

"No, I tried." Damian began to pace. "He *is* powerful. You sure he won't hurt Florence?"

"I'm not sure of anything." I was almost sorry I'd started this. I hadn't really learned anything new and now Damian was fired up. "Why did you come over tonight?"

That stopped him in his tracks. "Halloween. It's next week. I want you to come to my party."

"I could use a party."

"Of course you could. So many worries." Damian moved closer and took my hand again. "And you could be my hostess. Some say that is an honor."

An honor. Only Mr. Super Ego Damian Sabatini would say such a thing. I extricated my hand and put the coffee table between us. It was a wimpy move. I was blocking. My head ached, but it didn't kill me. I wasn't afraid of Damian's power over me, was I?

"I don't think so."

He pouted until he saw it wasn't working. I've known way too many bad boys in my time to fall for their games. But the term "bedroom eyes" could have been invented for a guy like Damian.

"I promise you'll have a good time. I play Count Dracula and everyone comes in costume. Lots of mortals too, eager to donate a pint or two if you wish to feed from the real deal."

I glanced at the two empty Bloody Merry cans on the table between us. It was taking more and more of the stuff to silence my inner beast. Which, sorry, but that's what it is. Not that I'm ashamed of it or anything. It's a fact I accepted a long time ago. Like my gambling addiction, I know that it'll never go away, but I don't have to give in to it.

"Sounds like a swell time, Damian, but I think I'll pass."

"Mara and Jeremiah will be there. I already talked to her. She says Jeremiah will be wearing his kilt and, when I told her about the costume contest, she promised to blow us all away in something sexy."

Manipulative bastard. Of course he wouldn't hesitate to use the old jealousy card. And of course it was working.

"You're kidding. You have a costume contest? Isn't that a little . . ."

"Juvenile?" Damian grinned. "Perhaps. I don't know about you, but my childhood didn't feature fun and games. I'm making up for it now." He was on my side of the coffee table. "We'll play, Gloriana."

"Play" was whispered in my ear and my imagination filled in the blanks. Have I mentioned that I've always had a soft spot for bad boys? And I wondered about Damian's childhood. I was pretty sure he and Flo came from privilege. Poor little rich kids? I figure we all came with some baggage.

"Let me think about it. The party. Not the hostess gig." I patted his cheek. "That implies a relationship between us that doesn't exist."

"Yet." He took my hand and sucked one of my fingers into his mouth before I realized what he was up to.

I jerked my hand away and staggered when Valdez leaped between me and Damian.

"Did you call me, Blondie?" Valdez growled at Damian.

"You go too far, dog," Damian snarled.

"Calm down, both of you." I kept my hand on Valdez's collar. "This is about the time of night Margie was killed. Why don't we go down to Diana's coffee shop and see if she's got any regular customers who might have seen something or someone that night?"

"Good idea, Blondie. Put on your Kevlar first." Valdez bumped me toward my bedroom door. *"Sabatini doesn't need to come with us."*

"Yes, I do." Damian was eyeing my chest.

I wasn't wearing a bra, but the T-shirt was doing a pretty good job of hiding that fact. That's one reason I've always loved black. It hides a *lot*.

"I want to see this Kevlar that Flo told me about. She thinks it's ugly, but I want her to wear it too."

Did I really want to parade in front of Damian in my Kevlar bra? Why not? I could handle Damian and I wanted Flo to wear one too. Maybe she'd actually listen to her brother if he agreed that it wasn't all that ugly. I had my second one now. It hadn't taken to dye, but Kim had discovered she could use fabric paint on it. I had to give her credit for imagination, even if my seamstress had gone a little nuts on this first experiment.

"Wait here and I'll put it on." I gave Damian a stern look. "This isn't for your entertainment, Damian. This is a security issue."

"I won't be entertained." He grinned and crossed his heart. "I swear."

I couldn't keep from grinning back. My inner slut was having a great time flirting with such a hottie. Of course I realized that if I hadn't been playing hard to get, Damian would have moved on long ago. He'd started this pursuit as a "Get Blade" maneuver. Now it was a "Get Glory to admit she wants me" deal. I wasn't admitting anything, but I did slap on some makeup while I was in my bedroom.

When I came out in my bra with my T-shirt over my arm, Valdez was staring at Damian. But Damian was staring at me. His mouth dropped open. "What is that all over your chest?"

Eighteen

I looked down ruefully. "Bull's-eyes. Can you believe it? My seamstress was making a little joke. I'd told her Blade threw knives at me and sometimes missed. She painted on targets."

"And this Kevlar really repels knives and arrows?" He moved closer to touch the fabric. "It's not heavy. I thought it would be thick. Like chain mail."

Valdez growled. "Valdez, stay by the door. That's an order." My dog subsided with a sniff. "Kevlar heavy? No, but that's a common misconception." Interesting. I think Damian had served his own time as a warrior. He had the same look of concentration Blade had gotten when he'd examined my first Kevlar bra. This one was higher in front and it made me feel very safe. Safe from stakes anyway. Damian had his hands on the Velcro.

"Nope, that stays closed. What do you think? Is it too ugly for Flo?"

Damian traced the fabric above my breasts. "I like more of a plunge, but it's the woman underneath that matters. Keeping your heart safe. *That* is beautiful."

Oh, gosh. Just when I'd figured Damian for an unre-
deemable jerk, he said something like that. Then his clever
fingers stroked the bumps of my nipples.

"Cool it, Damian." I backed up and ignored the shivers he'd
started. "Do you think you can get Flo to wear one of these?"

"I'll try. Without the targets, of course." He grinned, obviously happy he could make me back up. Not to mention,
make my nipples stand at attention.

"You need to wear one too."

He moved close again. "Ah, Gloriana. You *do* care."

"Vamp to vamp. We all should wear one as long as Westwood is using us for target practice." I held up my hand.
"Look, but don't touch again, Sabatini. If you want a vest
made, I can give you my seamstress's number. Call her and
she'll fix you up."

"Is Blade wearing one?" Damian actually backed off
when I jerked my T-shirt over my head.

A sore subject. Of course he wasn't. These macho males.
Impossible.

"Not yet. But he's thinking about it." I grabbed my purse.
"Let's hit the coffee shop. Ask around. Unless you've got other
plans."

"My other plans would be carrying you to your bed and
showing you some more screaming orgasms. For real, this
time." He gave me his patented "I'm too sexy for my fangs"
look.

"Then we're going downstairs." I shoved past him and
picked up Valdez's leash. "The three of us."

"She doesn't want you in her bedroom, Sabatini." Valdez pressed
himself against my legs while I clipped on the leash.

"I can speak for myself, Valdez." I opened the door.
"Let's go."

Damian made an excuse and headed for parts unknown.
He wasn't interested in any activity with me that didn't
involve the mattress mambo. I've got rhythm and didn't
doubt for a minute that I could dazzle Mr. Sabatini with some

of my creative moves. But Damian was going to have to work a little, no, make that a lot, harder before he'd get on *my* dance card.

Diana was behind the counter when I got downstairs. Valdez settled at his usual post right outside the door after he'd given me the all clear for the dash from the front door to the coffee shop. First the coffee shop, then the grocery store. I still had the keys to the hearse and a list of things Flo needed, including a new bottle of nail polish remover. I could definitely rationalize using Damian's spare car.

"Hey, Glory." Diana grabbed a can of Bloody Merry. "I was just going to take a break."

"Good." I looked around. Only two customers, both mortals, sat at tables. One was reading the newspaper, the other stared at a laptop screen.

"I'm here about the night Margie was"—I lowered my voice—"found out back."

Diana gulped her drink, then sat at a vacant table as far away from the customers as she could get. "Horrible. Poor Kenneth."

"I was thinking poor Margie. She was supposed to meet Kenneth here that night. Did you see her?"

Diana stared down at her can. "Can't say that I did."

"Mind if I ask your customers if they saw her?"

"Are you playing detective?" Diana looked grim, which was appropriate under the circumstances.

"Blade and Kenneth are investigating, but I wanted to help." I sat across from her. "I still think Richard Mainwaring might have done it."

"Any proof?" Diana asked the question I'd been asking myself for days.

"No." I shook my head. "But who besides another vampire would know Margie was one?"

"There are plenty of supernaturals who hang out around here who would have no trouble spotting a vamp. Shifters, werecats, a few others that I've gotten vibes from." Diana set down her can. "Some are pretty edgy but Margie wasn't the kind of vamp who made enemies. Not like Trevor, who probably got careless, drank from the wrong person, place or thing, and didn't bother to cover his tracks."

"It does seem likely that the same person staked both Trevor and Margie." A fact that just confused the issue as far as I was concerned. "Did Trevor and Margie know each other?"

"Sure. They'd both been in Austin a while. Been to Damian's annual Halloween parties."

"Speaking of, are you going this year?" Nothing like going from death to party talk. I've never claimed to be Miss Sensitivity.

"Wouldn't miss it." Diana smiled. "You *have* to go. Damian throws an amazing party. And there's always a surprise."

"What kind of surprise?" If it involved mind control, I was *so* not going there.

"Last year Damian had a magician saw him in half. I was hoping it was permanent, but no such luck." She sighed. "But the year before he brought in wonderful flamenco dancers and a guitarist from Spain. Fabulous."

"Somehow it doesn't seem right to party hearty so soon after Margie . . ."

Diana shrugged. "It's what we do, Glory. Life goes on."

"Or not." I couldn't shake the feeling that I should *do* something.

"Come on, Glory. Lighten up. Margie wouldn't expect anything else." Diana patted my hand. "Besides, you'd only met her once. Why the fixation?"

"She was killed right behind our shops, Di. I'd be stupid not to be a little fixated with figuring out who did it and why. Knowledge is power and can help keep us safe."

"Good point. Okay then. Maybe Westwood does the cross thing too."

"I doubt it. He's really into hunting with his bow and arrows." I studied Diana's pale arms above her black bustier. "Your wound ever give you problems?"

"Nope. As you can see, it's as if it never happened." Diana smiled. "Vamps rule. We help each other. That's why I don't think another vamp would kill his own."

"Are you kidding me? Get real, Di. Vamps love, hate and get even if we're crossed. And with abilities that make us a hell of a lot more lethal than mere mortals." Abilities that, short of shape-shifting, I was working on in my spare time.

"You're right, Glory." Diana sipped her drink. "Kenneth's supposed to come by tonight. The poor guy's really lost without Margie. When he gets here, I'll ask about Margie's relationship with Mainwaring. I agree Mainwaring does seem a little intense."

"See? I'm not crazy. Margie knew Richard from Paris. She might go with him willingly. And because he thinks we're demons from hell, he killed her."

"That's quite a stretch." Diana put down her can. "Margie was a nice woman who just happened to be vampire, not a demon from hell or anywhere near there. I've known plenty of reckless vamps who deserve a stake more than she did."

"I give up then." Like Damian had said. Back to square one. "So I guess Richard's probably not the killer. Flo says not. Damian says not." I glanced toward the door. "Even Valdez says Richard didn't do it."

"Well, if the dog vouches for him . . ." Diana got up. "*Someone* took her out and they're still out there somewhere. You got on your Kevlar under that T-shirt?"

"Yep. I'd be crazy to go out without it. But . . ." I looked down. "It's not exactly a Wonderbra, is it?"

"Nothing can make you flat chested, Glory, but your curves aren't curving."

"You mean I look lumpy, dumpy and fat. Thanks for the reality check." When you can't see yourself in a mirror, you can pretend you're hot stuff even if you're not. Hey, I look down, I see cleavage. That's hot, isn't it? But I avoid looking at my backside. You know why.

"Hey, reality right now, honey, is we wear whatever keeps us safe. I've got my own vest in back. To change into before I go outside." Diana stretched. "Back to the computer. Payroll. I'll be in the back if you need me."

"Thanks." I got up too, but it only took a minute to find out that present customers hadn't been in Mugs and Muffins the night Margie was killed.

"I think I'm wasting my time, Valdez. No one knows anything about anyone." I picked up his leash. "Let's hit the grocery store now."

"Can we call reinforcements?" He trotted along beside me. *"You know they won't let me inside unless you want to do the blind thing again."*

"Sure. I'll drive up, park, hop out and then go blind." We were in the alley now, the hearse just a few feet away. "Not going to happen. I'm okay to go to the store."

Valdez stopped suddenly and looked around. He morphed into attack mode. *"Get behind the car. Now."*

"Oh, God!" I ran to crouch between the hearse and my dead Suburban. "Come here, Valdez. What are you doing?" Sure I had on my Kevlar, but I didn't want to test it up close and personal right now. Not ever, if truth be told.

Valdez growled then barked frantically. *"Stay down!"* He darted toward the end of the alley.

"I *am* down. What is it?" I hoped this was one of his cat frenzies and not because he'd smelled olive wood.

More really ferocious barking. Anyone who didn't back off in the face of that had a death wish. Or a really lethal method of defense. I unlocked the passenger door, crawled into the car and began honking the horn frantically. Wait. Had that been a yelp? I quit pounding the horn and listened. Silence. I rolled down the window an inch.

"Valdez!"

The back door to Mugs and Muffins flew open and Diana and her two helpers poured out. Diana had thrown on her

Kevlar vest, had her fangs full out, and was armed with a broom. Her helpers each held a frying pan.

"Get back!" I yelled. From the light of the open door, I could see something move near the back door of my own shop. "Valdez! Are you all right?"

"All clear, Glory. Tell Diana and the others to go back inside."

It had sounded like Valdez's voice. It *had* to be his voice. Who else talked inside my head and sounded like an extra from *The Godfather*? I cautiously unlocked the car door.

"You sure you want me to send them inside?"

"Just do it. Now." Valdez almost barked the order.

"What is it? Is something wrong?" Diana jabbed the air with her broom. I didn't doubt for a minute that, with her vamp strength, she could do some serious damage with that broom.

"False alarm. I'm fine. Thanks for responding, though. You just never know."

Diana waved the broom. "We stick together. Let me know if you need me later." She touched her wide-eyed workers' shoulders. "Relax, darlings. You saw nothing, heard nothing, except Glory honking her horn and Valdez barking at a stray cat." She pushed her employees back inside and slammed the door. I heard the dead bolts click shut.

"Okay, what's the deal? Valdez, are we talking cat here?" I still wasn't ready to just walk out into the open. "Or something or someone more threatening?"

I kept low and the dark lump by my shop's back door moved again. The security light above the door was out. Westwood's work? He did seem to favor working in the dark. Night vision goggles probably.

A whimper. *"Help me. I'm wounded."*

"Wounded! Oh, my God!" I *saw* myself at the back door and I was there, looking down at Valdez stretched out on the concrete, an arrow sticking out of one of his back legs. "You've been shot!"

"*Westwood. I don't think I can walk and I'm losing blood.*" He groaned and lifted his head, his eyes gleaming in the dark. "*I think he's gone, but help me get inside. Then lock the door in case he comes back.*"

"Valdez, puppy." My voice broke and tears ran down my cheeks. I rubbed his head, then quickly unlocked the back door.

"I'm sorry, but this will hurt." I gently slid my arms under him. "I'm going to lift you now." He weighed a ton, but I don't have vamp strength for nothing. I cradled him against my chest and carried him inside. I laid him carefully on the table in the storeroom, then rushed to lock the back door.

I wiped away my tears then turned back to him.

Valdez moaned and looked up at me. "*I'm fading fast, Glory. It's been swell knowing you. Say good-bye to Florence for me.*"

"Stop it. You're not going to die. He hit your leg, not your heart." I hoped I was right about the dying part. He was bleeding pretty heavily. I grabbed a wad of paper napkins someone had left on the table and mopped at the blood seeping from around the arrow. I used another napkin to dry the last of my tears, then focused on the arrow sticking out of his flank.

It didn't take vamp powers to figure out this was Westwood's work. Olive wood smell, same kind of arrow that had hurt Diana. A paper was tied around the end of the shaft.

"Damn it. Westwood sent us a note. Hasn't he heard of the U.S. Postal Service?" I rubbed Valdez's head. "I'm so sorry."

"*Me too, Blondie.*" He licked my hand. "*Could you call me puppy one more time? I liked that.*" He groaned. "*I just wish I had time for a farewell bag of Cheetos.*"

"You'll have a lot more than a farewell bag, puppy." Oh, boy. I *had* to stop crying and get a grip if I was going to get both of us through this. "You're not going to die, damn it." I wiped my eyes again and studied the wound. The arrow seemed stuck, like it had hit the bone.

"I'm going to pull out the arrow. Then heal you. Like we did with Diana, remember?"

"Hold on, Glory." He rolled his eyes at me. *"Flo did that. I don't think—Ow! Ow! Ow! Damn it!"*

I'd gotten out the arrow. Now it was time for some vamp magic. I pressed my hands on either side of the wound and concentrated.

"Heal!" I sounded like a televangelist at a prayer meeting. And it wasn't working. I pressed harder.

"Hello. That hurts, Glory." Valdez's leg quivered. *"Maybe you should call Flo."*

"She never leaves her cell phone on when she's at church or with Richard." I tried to beam my thoughts to the bloody wound. Was it closing? "Maybe I should get Diana."

"No, you can do it, Blondie." Valdez lifted his head. *"I'll concentrate with you this time."*

No time to wonder why Valdez thought *he* could help. "All right. On three. One, two, three." I pressed and stared and prayed and, would you believe it, that wound closed. Vamp magic at its best.

"Fan-damn-tastic! We did it." Valdez moved his leg tentatively. *"Help me down."*

"Wait! Let me clean you up." I ran to the bathroom, washed my bloody hands, then wet some paper towels. I held one against my eyes for a moment and said another prayer. Thank you, God.

"Glory." Valdez still sounded weak.

"Coming." I hurried back and gently washed his dark fur. I ignored the smell of fresh blood. Even from a dog, it had a certain aroma that I couldn't deny got my fangs swelling against my gums. But I'm civilized and way beyond giving in to my more primitive urges. At least where blood is concerned. Now if Westwood crossed my path, I'd unleash my beast.

"Are you sure you're okay?" If I didn't have Valdez's completely unmarked and damp hairy hip right in front of me,

I wouldn't have believed it. I'd healed him. What a rush. What power. And how long had I denied I even had power? No more. I rocked.

"How does that feel?" I tossed the bloody towels in the trash.

"Okay, I guess. Lift me down and I'll see if I can walk. I sure could use a Twinkie about now."

I picked him up and he laid his head on my shoulder.

"You're my hero, Blondie." He licked my cheek before I set him gently on the floor.

"No, you're *my* hero. You went right after Westwood."

"But I didn't get him." Valdez shook himself, then looked at his back leg.

"Careful now. I'm not Flo, you know. You may not be completely healed."

"Don't sell yourself short, Sweet Cheeks. This is what I call a freakin' miracle." He walked slowly around the room. *"Not even a twinge. But I'll feel better once I get a Twinkie fix."*

"Soon. All the Twinkies you want." I picked up the paper that had been wrapped around the arrow. I didn't want to read it. "What kind of message could Westwood be sending me?"

"Open it, Blondie. We got to know. And I'm sending for Blade." Valdez lay down on the floor. *"I'm not hurting, but I'm weak all of a sudden."*

"You're probably in shock and don't call Blade. We don't need him."

"It's my deal, Blondie. I've got to report." Valdez groaned. *"I'm having a sinking spell. I did lose a lot of blood. We got any snacks around here? I bet Ryan has a stash behind the counter."*

I raided the drawer where either Ryan or Lacy had stuck some peanut butter crackers. I sniffed them and wondered for the thousandth time how it would feel to crunch again. Can you tell I *really* didn't want to read Westwood's love note? I threw it on the table and hand fed Valdez until all the crackers were gone.

"Any better?"

"*Yeah, thanks. Got any Coke to wash them down with?*" He wagged his tail. "*Now I'm parched.*"

"How about bottled water?" I opened the fridge I'd put in when we'd set up the shop. "You should probably have a Bloody Merry. To replace the blood you lost. I'm getting one for myself."

Valdez shuddered and sat down with a thump. "*Put the water in a bowl. I ain't no blood sucker. No offense, Blondie.*"

"Excuse me?" As much fun as it was to see Valdez back to his usual self, I was still stalling. I dumped the water into a bowl and listened to Valdez lap it up. I took a deep swallow of my Bloody Merry before I finally picked up the note again. My stomach churned as I unfolded it. I looked at Valdez then read it out loud.

"Don't try your vampire tricks on my men. I'm watching you *and* my spaghetti. Westwood."

Banging on the front door. Blade stood outside. I was shaking as I let him in.

"What is it, Glory? Are you all right? Valdez just said there'd been an incident at the shop." Blade held me away from him and looked me over. "Are you hurt?"

"No. Westwood shot Valdez." I sat abruptly in one of the overstuffed chairs CiCi had consigned just last week. I was having one of Valdez's sinking spells. Between the concentration I'd used to heal Valdez and the note . . . I still gripped it.

"*I sacrificed myself for your lady, Boss.*" Valdez came to stand next to the chair. I sank my fingers into his soft fur.

"You look all right to me, Valdez." Blade knelt in front of me. "You're pale, Glory."

"*She's shook up. She healed me. See for yourself. The bloody arrow is still on the table in the store room.*" Valdez looked up at me and I swear he was smiling. "*It was a near miss. But we're okay. She called me her puppy. What do you think of that?*"

Blade jumped up to go into the storeroom. When he came out, he was as pale as I felt. "Are you wearing your

Kevlar? Did the arrow hit you anywhere?" Blade knelt in front of me again.

"He never even got a shot at me. And I *do* have on my Kevlar." I held out the note. My hands were surprisingly steady considering my insides were quivering nonstop. "He sent us a message, Jerry. I think we've got a spy in our midst."

He opened the note and read it. "Son of a bitch. You're right. Spaghetti. But no one was here when you said that except for me and Mara." He looked around and grabbed a small plastic bag from the counter.

He went into the back again and I heard him drop the arrow into the bag. I saw stars and put my head between my knees before I passed out. Valdez was right. I was still really shook up.

Blade came back into the room. "Gloriana, lass, breathe. Are you all right?"

"I'm okay. Just a little dizzy." I felt his hands on my back and made myself take even breaths until the room stopped spinning.

"Hey, what about me? I took an arrow in the hip for your woman."

I sat up. "He's right, Jerry. Valdez was shot to carry a damned message. I hate Westwood."

"And you healed the dog, all by yourself. God, Gloriana, I had no idea . . ." Blade squeezed my shoulder. "You're incredible."

"I helped. Added my power—"

"Valdez, thank you. You can believe me when I say you'll be rewarded in good time." Blade gave the dog a speaking look. "Now go sit by the front door. I want to talk to Gloriana."

The dog sniffed but turned around and headed for the door. He put on a pitiful show, head down, limping.

"Wrong leg, puppy." I gave Blade a dirty look. "Can you cut the dog some slack, Jerry? He *saved* me."

"Right. And I'm grateful, of course." Blade crouched in front of me again and took my hands. "But about this note.

Think, lass. Did you tell anyone about our conversation the other night?"

"You think *I'm* the leak?" I shoved him away and stood. Amazing how I could go from incredible to dumb as dirt in a heartbeat. The room spun for a moment so I held on to the chair. "What about Mara? Maybe she's a blabbermouth. Or did *you* say something to someone?"

"Of course not. I don't know what to think." Blade ran a hand through his hair. He was letting it grow and it reached his collar. The natural curl was probably annoying him, but it was very appealing to a susceptible woman. Which I was *not* at the moment.

"It would be nice if, just once, you'd realize I'm not an idiot." It felt good to get *that* off my chest.

"Lass, of course you're no' an idiot." Scottish Blade put his hands on my shoulders. Okay, maybe I'm a little susceptible. But I hate it when he tries to *charm* me.

"Knock it off, Jerry. Speak American." I lifted Jerry's hands off my shoulders.

"I'm sorry, Gloriana." He looked down at the note again.

He obviously didn't have a clue how to handle me after all these years. And how cool was that?

"The question on the table is how could Westwood know such a detail? Spaghetti, right?"

"Right. The three of us were alone here. Along with Valdez." Blade looked around the shop, like he'd see a spy hiding behind the counter.

"Westwood's a technology freak." I could see the bookshelf next to the counter. "Bugs! Oh, my God. How stupid. We've got bugs!" I would have smacked myself in the forehead, but I was more than a little unsteady.

"Sit down, Gloriana. You're obviously still upset." Blade tried to guide me back to the chair. "Call an exterminator tomorrow."

"Look up there, on the top of the book shelf." I stayed put. I wasn't going to be *guided* anywhere. "There's a spider.

It ran when I tried to spray it, but I bet it's back and look-ing right at us."

"Fine. I know you hate spiders. I'll kill it." Blade grabbed a book.

"No! Grab it. I don't think it's real. I just realized, I've never seen a single web around here."

"Sit down, lass. You've had a rough night."

"Oh, great. Now I'm an idiot again." I walked over to the shelf. Oh, God, what if this was a real spider? I shuddered but slapped my hand over it before it could get away. Hard metal or plastic crunched under my palm.

"Hah! Here's your spy." I dropped it into Blade's hand.

"What the bloody hell is this?"

Nineteen

"A bug, Jerry. The surveillance type. A mini version of the spies in the sky you have in your casino." At last my hours spent at the poker tables in Vegas were paying off.

"By God, I think you're right." He set it on the counter. "It moved?"

"It must have motion sensors. Damn Westwood and his technology. I thought it was a real spider. It's probably still working." I grabbed it and stuck it in a drawer, then headed for the storeroom. "Here's another one. I sprayed the hell out of this one. I hope I stopped it." I pointed at the roach.

"Son of a bitch!" Blade grabbed it and stared at it for a moment. "Cutting edge technology. Mini cameras and microphones." He held it up. "Westwood, if you're listening, this is your fate." He dropped it to the floor and ground it under the heel of his boot. "Damn it! I should have expected this. The bastard owns the kinds of companies that make this shit." He stomped the bug again, then picked it up and threw it against the wall.

I stepped up behind him and wrapped my arms around his lean waist. I could feel his tension. There's nothing sexier than a strong vampire in a fury. And this one wore cowboy boots, black leather. A Scottish cowboy. To please me? He turned. His arms went around me and his eyes darkened.

I was too wiped out to resent the mind reading or to bask in the glow of Blade's interest. Of course he could just be revved up in general and I was getting the fallout. Sometimes I think too much.

"I need to get Valdez upstairs. He's got a box of Twinkies up there with his name on it." That earned me a woof and Valdez stood and stretched before trotting to my side. I reluctantly backed away from Jerry.

"Wait. Someone planted these bugs. And there may be more." Blade prowled around the room. "Valdez, you look low, I'll look high. Anything that might be a small camera or microphone."

"You're wasting your time, Jerry. We need a professional to come in and sweep for bugs."

Blade stopped examining a shelving unit to look at me. "Sweep? How do you know about such things?"

"I watch cop shows, Jerry. Bring one of your security experts from Lake Charles here. He'll know what to do."

"But who could have planted them? Westwood himself? He was in here."

"True." I looked around. "But not in the storeroom. I had Valdez locked in there, remember?"

"*I shoulda knocked that damned door down.*" Valdez sat and looked back at his leg. "*Next time, I take Westwood down or die trying.*"

I shuddered. "I don't want anyone dying on my account. It's bad enough you took an arrow for me." I still got queasy remembering. The arrow embedded in his flesh. The blood. And now this . . . invasion. Damn it. How long had Westwood been spying on us? What had he seen and heard?

"All in the line of duty, right, Boss?" Valdez looked at Blade.

Jerry finally gave Valdez an approving look. "Above and beyond the call of duty. Well done."

Valdez wagged his tail and pressed up against me. I needed his warmth. This near miss had chilled me to the bone.

"*I'm* the one who should have taken out Westwood. Hell, I'd seen his picture. I should have recognized him."

"You weren't expecting him to be so bold, Gloriana. And Derek didn't recognize him either." Jerry put his hand on my shoulder.

"He won't slip by me a second time." I felt violated and sorely pissed. I had an idea who might have planted the bugs, played with them, even talked to them. Tomorrow night I was getting some answers.

"Tomorrow night? What's happening tomorrow night?" Jerry squeezed my shoulder. "Your shop is closed, isn't it?"

"Yes, it's closed." Of course Blade was still reading my mind. "Now hush. This place isn't secure." I pulled open the drawer and grabbed the bug. "I'm going to stomp this one too."

"No. Give it to me." He wrapped it in one of my plastic bags and stuck it in his pocket. "I want my security guy to check it out. I'll have him here tomorrow. Give me a key and I'll make sure this place is swept clean before nightfall."

"Good. Spidey there might have some little friends." I sighed, suddenly exhausted. "Let's go upstairs." No way could my apartment be bugged. Ryan had only been in there once, for less than five minutes and never alone.

"Ryan?" Jerry waited until we were outside and I was locking the shop door. I handed him the key.

"I've got an extra key upstairs. Come on up and I'll tell you my suspicions. To be on the safe side, get a locksmith to come tomorrow too. We need to change the lock on the shop."

Valdez, Jerry and I were silent as we trooped upstairs. When we were inside and Valdez was chin deep in Twinkies, I sat on the love seat.

"Lacy and I are planning a little intervention with Ryan tomorrow night." I looked at Blade. Big mistake. He was so focused on me that for a moment I lost my train of thought. "I'll let you know if I find out anything useful."

"This Ryan works for you. You think he could be our spy?" Blade grabbed my hand. "I should be there. You'll take no chances, lass."

"I'm more than able to handle Ryan. Let me take care of this, Jerry. And Valdez will be there with us." I turned to give the dog a look. "You can't deny he's bound to tell you everything that goes down. It's his deal." And what a pain in the butt that was. Jerry still held my hand. Okay, so I was glad he was here. He could make me feel safer than anyone else ever had.

"What happened earlier, Jerry? Did your man inside show up for your meeting?"

"No, he didn't. And his phone was out of service when I tried to call."

"Obviously Westwood got to him. Or maybe he was a plant, to learn your plans." Call *CSI,* I was on a roll with my investigative skills. A little late, though. We'd been spied on, betrayed. It was a miracle Westwood hadn't succeeded tonight. Jerry jumped to his feet.

"If my contact wanted my plans, he would have shown up tonight." Jerry looked as pissed as I felt, fired up again and pacing.

"Maybe the guy chickened out when it came to meeting a real semi-live vampire face-to-face."

"Semi-live?" Jerry stopped in front of me and pulled me up against him. "Does this feel semi-live to you?"

As an ego boost, Jerry's bulging jeans were proof I still did it for him. You think it's freaky that we could even think about sex at a time like this? Hey, vamps are sensual creatures. All the vamps I've ever met have an unusually active libido. And Jerry and I are no exception.

Now about those bulging jeans . . . I looked at Valdez, but he'd turned to stare out the window at the street, obviously ordered to give us privacy.

I leaned against Jerry for a moment. "You're obviously way more than *semi*-live, Jerry, but it's close to dawn. I'm ready to curl up in my own bed."

Blade ran his hands down my back to pull me flush against him. "I could curl up with you."

I wrapped my arms around him and breathed in eau de Blade. Tempting. He was still palling around with Mara but I doubted he saw her as any more than his best friend's widow. And I sure couldn't blame Jerry if Mara had her eye on Scottish vamp husband number two. I was really drained from the whole hellacious night, but when his arms tightened around me, I knew I wanted him in my bed.

I tugged him toward my bedroom. "Valdez, you set for the night?"

Valdez turned around. *"Sure, Blondie."*

Jerry gave the dog a look before he followed me. I shut the bedroom door and leaned against it. Jerry glanced at the double bed, unmade of course.

"Pillow-top mattress."

"Excellent."

"I should change the sheets." I pushed away from the door.

"Don't bother." He pulled me into his arms and laid his cheek on my hair. "We've slept on far worse."

I reached up and traced his firm lips. "I remember a cave once. With furs on the hard stone floor and neither of us complaining." We'd been new to each other then. Never sated. We'd ridden his father's lands to where Jerry had arranged to give us privacy. God knows there was none in Castle Campbell.

I unbuttoned his shirt and slid it off his broad shoulders. I don't think I'll ever tire of exploring his solid strength.

"And our first. Against the door in your dressing room at the Globe." He pulled my T-shirt up and off, then dropped a kiss on the swell of my breast. "Not my finest moment."

I blinked back sudden tears. He remembered our first time. I'd sure never forget it. God, I'd been so wild for him. He'd shown me pleasure I'd never dreamed existed. And then he'd used his fangs . . . I shivered, remembering.

"They took the cost of that ripped bodice out of my pay, you know." I smiled and circled his nipple with my fingertip.

"I was in a bit of a hurry. In all things." Jerry stared down at me, suddenly solemn. "I know you've regretted becoming vampire for me, Gloriana."

I laid my hand over his lips. "No regrets. You gave me eternity, Jerry. In case you haven't noticed, I'm pretty fond of modern conveniences."

"Such as?" He ran his thumbs up my neck.

"Mercedes convertibles." I kissed his smooth chest.

"I knew you wanted that car." He grinned, ripping open the Kevlar bra. It hit the carpet.

"It's a sexmobile, who wouldn't want it?" I dragged my fangs across his shoulder and up to the vein pulsing in his neck. Forget the car. I wanted to taste him. He moved his head just a bit, enough to tell me not yet.

"What else do you like?" He trotted out an evil grin I recognized.

He was a mind reader, he knew damned well what I liked—him, inside me, taking me hard against the bedroom door. I shook my head. Now who was moving too fast? He rubbed a leisurely spiral around my aching nipples. Okay, slow could work too.

"Cell phones." Thunk. His belt hit the floor.

"You can call me in your mind and I will always answer you, Gloriana." My jeans pooled around my ankles and I kicked them away.

"Zippers." I pushed down his and stroked the erection straining his white cotton briefs. Yeah, ancient Scottish vampire wears Jockey shorts. Progress.

"I'll not argue with that one."

"Hot showers."

"I've always liked you"——he slid his hand inside my black lace panties——"wet."

I flushed from my head to my toes, then shoved his jeans and briefs down until they were around his ankles. I dropped to my knees in front of him.

"There's much to be said for ancient pleasures." He groaned, his fingers in my hair.

"And primitive males." I traced the length of him with my tongue. He lifted me and held me against him for a moment before he set me on my feet. I wobbled, then grabbed his hair as he kissed a path down my stomach to the curls between my legs.

"But you're a modern woman." He pushed me back onto the bed and spread my legs. "You love those television shows."

"H.B.Oooh." One of his clever fingers had found my hot button.

"I've never understood why you would be content to watch actors pretending to have sex when you can be"——he lifted my hips and pushed into me——"participating."

"Yes." I grabbed his buttocks, holding him close. He was right. To hell with modern anything. This, this was what I wanted, had always wanted. To be his, to feel the pressure of him touching me so deeply, I could hardly breathe.

Orgasm number one thundered through me and I knew the best was yet to come. It always happened like this between us. I dug my nails into his shoulders when he stroked me and, oh God, tasted me with his fangs. I think I blacked out and probably screamed. By the time he thrust into me, shouting my name, I was definitely participating.

• • •

I woke up alone unless you counted Valdez curled up on the foot of the bed. There was a note. Jerry had obviously left before dawn.

If you need me, call me. Jeremiah.

I indulged in a few tears. Okay, so I'd earned them. His note, while brief, meant he trusted me to handle Ryan on my own. This felt like a breakthrough. We'd been so close, and not just physically connected. For the first time in almost forever I couldn't work up a hate for being Jerry's "woman."

"I got my orders, Blondie. Tonight, that Ryan gives you grief and he's dog chow."

Well, hell. So much for Jerry's trust. As long as his right-hand dog stuck to me like glue, I'd never be truly independent. I sat up and wiped my eyes.

"And if I tell you to back off and let me handle Ryan?"

Valdez jumped off the bed and stretched, then trotted up to nudge my hand with his cold nose. *"Handle him, Blondie. Rip him a new one. Whatever. But he tries to hurt you and all bets are off."*

I sighed and stroked Valdez's head. "This is going to break Lacy's heart."

Valdez snorted. *"Tough. Cat lady is the one who got you to hire the creep."*

"Ryan had us all fooled, Valdez." I tugged on his ear. "Even you, my friend. Even you."

I heard the key in the lock and took a deep breath. I'd given Lacy a new key before I'd come down to the shop. I didn't think Ryan was dangerous, but I had on my Kevlar, under my sweatshirt, just in case. If he worked for Westwood, he had to know I was vampire. He'd be stupid not to carry a stake around in case of emergencies. Like if I was suddenly overcome by blood lust and drank him dry.

Not a bad thought. I was furious that he'd used Lacy to get to me. She didn't deserve that kind of betrayal and, damn it, neither did I. At least I knew we'd found the only two bugs in the shop thanks to Jerry's security expert.

"See? She's here waiting for us." Lacy's smile looked like a death mask. Ryan didn't notice. He glanced around the store and again I noticed that he was uneasy being around me. A little part of me had hoped I had this all wrong, for Lacy's sake. Oh, well, she'd had centuries of love experience. This was surely not the first time she'd been deceived.

Her eyes met mine. If she'd been betrayed this time, she was making damn sure it wouldn't happen again.

"Hi, you two. I've got the checks in the storeroom. Come on back." I'd set up the area carefully. I didn't want us to be visible from the street, so I'd put a couple of chairs in the storeroom. Valdez was lying across the back door and I gave him a thumb's up as I led the way.

"I thought you paid on the first. That's not until Wednesday." Ryan smiled. "Of course I can always use the cash."

"Can you?" Lacy slammed the storeroom door and locked it. "You seem pretty flush to me."

"What's going on?" Ryan backed away from her until he bumped into a chair. He held on to it.

I didn't blame him. Lacy mad was a sight to see. She wasn't in cat form, but I swear her eyes glowed and her hair almost stood on end. Even her nails seemed to grow longer.

"Glory and I have a little problem, Ryan. You." Lacy pushed him into the chair, but he popped right back up.

"Hey, watch it. This is a new suit." The jerk actually stroked the front of his black jacket. "New to me, anyway. Brooks Brothers. Can you believe it? Nine dollars and ninety nine cents at the Salvation Army store."

"Pay attention, Ryan." I put my hands on his shoulders and shoved him down in the chair again. I kept them there and felt him go rigid. Click. He was finally getting that he was in deep shit here.

"What did I do?" He looked at me, then Lacy. "Come on, baby. I told you I didn't mean to be late. My dad caught me on the phone just as I was leaving. The usual lecture on keeping up my grades."

"Your dad on the phone or Brent Westwood?" Lacy's smile had all the charm of a lion contemplating a late night supper.

"Westwood?" Ryan tried to jump up, but I held him in place. He was no match for vamp power, especially when I was steaming. "I don't know what the hell you're talking about."

"Sure, you do. Played with any bugs lately?"

"I still don't know what you're talking about. Let me go, Glory." Ryan struggled against my hands, his face red. "Lacy, sweetie. You know me better than this."

Lacy snatched his glasses off his face. "Do I? I'm about to find out."

"No!" He made a grab for the glasses but Lacy stepped back and held them out of reach. "I can't see. You know that." He tried to pry my hands off his shoulders, then kicked, connecting with my shin.

"Damn it!" I'd had enough. I stared into his eyes. In seconds, he was still, unable to resist the whammy. And I could read his mind. So could Lacy. I could see from her stricken expression.

"Say your thoughts out loud, Ryan," I ordered. I knew this was harder for Lacy to hear than it was for me, but we'd deal with it together. I was fighting for my life and the lives of my friends against Westwood. We could lick our wounds later.

"Lick *our* wounds?" Lacy hissed and looked at me with narrowed eyes.

"Sorry." I really could use some sensitivity training. My wounds were nothing compared to Lacy's. I'd liked Ryan, she'd actually thought she was in love with him.

Ryan chose that opportune moment to blurt out his thoughts. "Oh, God! Oh, God! Got to get out of here before the blood sucker takes me out. Not worth it for a little nookie. Lacy's got to be a freak too, hanging around with vampires."

"A freak?" Lacy wiped at her eyes. "I'll show you freak. I've had better sex with—"

"Too much information, Lacy." I held up my hand. "What about the glasses?"

Lacy made a face and looked through them. "Why don't I rip them apart?"

"Hold it! Let me see those." I took them and held them up to my eyes. Clear if a little distorted. Like everything wasn't quite right. It was a miracle Ryan could walk around in them. I examined the ear pieces. There'd been a show just last week on the Discovery Channel about surveillance equipment. And I was holding one clever piece of it.

"Sorry, Lacy. As Valdez would say, this guy's a Grade A asshole."

"What is it, Blondie?" Valdez got up and nudged my hip.

"His glasses must be the same kind Westwood uses. To protect him from the vamp whammy. But the worst part . . ." I aimed the glasses at Lacy. "There's camera equipment in the earpieces. Video and audio, I'm sure. The signal's being sent to another location." I put my hand on Lacy's shoulder. "Smile, you're on Candid Camera."

Lacy gasped and looked at them in horror. Then at Ryan. Horror became hate. "You bastard! You've been recording every moment we've been together. Sometimes you even kept them on in bed."

Ryan just stared into space, but his brain was busy and, per my orders, he was still saying his thoughts out loud. "Got my glasses. Now I'm toast. I shoulda brought my stake with me, but it made a bulge in my new suit. All Dad's fault. He never should have ordered suits from a country he couldn't spell. Velcro instead of zippers. No guy's going to wear a suit with a Velcro fly. Ten million bucks down the crapper and Westwood holds the paper. Had to do this to wipe out the debt so we can start over. Promised me. At least I get to keep the sex videos. Planted a camera with a view of her bed. I'm a love machine and Lacy's skinny butt can sure move—"

Lacy hauled off and slapped Ryan. His head snapped back, but he didn't try to get away. I had too strong a hold on his mind for that. But he was thinking . . .

"Help. Help. Help. Help. Glory's gonna bite me and suck me dry. Westwood's creepy. Obsessed with vampires. Now I'm screwed."

"Is someone watching the tape right now, Ryan? Will someone try to come save you?" I glanced at the back door, securely locked but an army with a battering ram could take it down, no problem. Valdez jumped up, suddenly on high alert.

"No. I'm a dead man." Ryan closed his eyes.

I put my hand under his chin. "Look at me, Ryan. You won't die if you tell me about spying for Westwood."

His eyes popped open. "Spying. Right. Tapes. Video feed goes to my setup in the trunk of my car. Go through the tapes later, keep what I want and then e-mail Westwood anything to do with vampires. Wants to take out more vampires. Like . . . you. We checked you out with the vamp detector. Lacy's okay, Derek's not." He closed his eyes again and tears leaked out. "Don't kill me. Please don't kill me."

I'd almost feel sorry for him if he hadn't used Lacy like he had. He was right that I could bite him and suck him dry. Tempting. I'd squeezed his chin until you could see my fingerprints on his skin. To hell with it. I let him go and stepped back. It would be way too easy to just rip him apart. I could smell his blood pumping through his veins. He was young, healthy, but damned ordinary, O positive. I took another step back.

"Isn't Ryan just a friggin' techno genius?" Lacy turned her back on him. "I can't believe I was so gullible. I practically forced you to hire him, Glory. But he seemed perfect."

"Don't blame yourself, Lacy." I put a hand on her back. "Obviously the whole deal was a set up. Ryan was clever. Believable. And he *is* a good salesman."

"What happens now, Blondie? You want me to take him out? Or do you want to do the honors?" Valdez looked like he really wanted to sharpen his teeth on this well-dressed loser.

"No one's taking anyone out." I glanced at Lacy. She was nodding, like, sure, Valdez, tear him limb from limb.

"Ryan, where are the videos of you and Lacy in bed?" I grabbed his chin again and he opened his eyes.

"My place. Downloaded into my computer. Gonna start a web site. Lovemachine dot com."

"Please drain him dry." Lacy looked ready to explode. She picked up a chair. "Or let me pound him to a pulp."

"No." I grabbed the chair after a little struggle. "Think of the fallout."

"Like me on the Internet doing the wild thing with this dickhead?" She wiped her eyes. "Hey, asshole, you got backup copies of those videos anywhere?" Lacy was nothing if not quick on the uptake, though she obviously was disappointed not to be able to do more violence.

"Laptop too. In case desktop crashes. Don't want to lose them. I was pretty spectacular. Made you scream—" Ryan got another right to the jaw and slumped over this time.

"I bet that felt good." I put my arm around Lacy. "You got a key to his place?"

"It's in his pocket." Lacy shoved her hand into his pants pocket and pulled out a key ring. "I'll go through his car and take everything in the trunk. Then I'll leave the keys in the ignition. It'd be a shame if someone stole that beater."

"Right. Just take his apartment key off the ring."

"Will do." Now that Lacy was a woman with a mission, she'd lost her defeated look and had fire in her eyes.

Immortals are resilient. We have to be. 'Cause you know there *will* be a tomorrow. Might as well make the best of it. "You'll take care of his computers? Both of them?"

"Sure. I know a nice spot on Lake Travis where I can send everything Ryan treasures to hell." She smirked and I had the feeling more than computers were going to a watery grave.

"Good. I'm going to wipe this night from his mind and plant the suggestion that he can't work for Westwood anymore. That he lost his special glasses and there's no such thing as vampires anyway. Plus he has to drop out of school and go home to Houston tonight."

"You're letting him off easy, Blondie." Valdez grabbed the sleeve of Ryan's Brooks Brothers coat and tugged. The rip made Lacy and me smile.

"He's going to be very sad about that." I rubbed the dog's ears. "Get the pants too."

"My pleasure." Valdez shredded the knees of those elegant trousers, then sat back to admire his work. *"I'd lift my leg on him, but I don't want to mess up your shop."*

"It would almost be worth it." I sat on the table. Damn but I hate being a sucker. Why hadn't I questioned the fact that the perfect clerk had appeared the day I needed him?

"I'm leaving now. You're going to keep Ryan here until I call with the all clear, aren't you?" Lacy's hands were still fisted. "Maybe I should hit him again."

"And maybe you shouldn't. It might make you feel better, but I want him to go home to Houston sooner rather than later. He can't do that if he ends up in the emergency room." I patted her shoulder. "Head out, Lacy. He'll stay here until I take the whammy off."

"What about the glasses? Do you think they're still recording?" Lacy picked them up and looked at them. "I could toss them in the lake too."

"No, leave them. I think Blade will be interested in the lenses if nothing else. They kept us from controlling Ryan and reading his mind and apparently Westwood and all of his men wear them. You're going to destroy the receiver." I looked them over. "And I bet if I close the ear pieces, the video and audio shut off."

Lacy sighed and looked at Ryan. He was still handsome, even though he looked like he'd lost a fight. He'd have a black eye tomorrow and his beloved suit . . . it would make a good dust rag.

"I can't believe I was so taken in by him. I should have known . . ."

"What? You're a beautiful woman, Lacy. Smart. Accomplished. Naturally men are going to come on to you."

"Not beautiful. Not smart. And the only thing I'm accomplished at is turning into a cat that"—she glanced at Valdez—"isn't exactly king of the jungle."

"You sound like you need cheering up. Tomorrow night. Halloween. You and I are going to Damian's party. And we're both going to look so sexy, the men will trip over their tongues pursuing us."

Lacy smiled sadly. "Why not? But what about the store? Now we don't even have Ryan to help out. And I'm sure Derek will be going to the party."

"We'll close the store. One night only. Tuesdays aren't that busy anyway. And we need to hire more help. I'll go next door and see if Diana can recommend anyone."

"Good. Now I'm off to collect and destroy evidence." Lacy had traded sad for mad.

"Are you going to look at the tapes first?" I know. None of my business. But I *had* to ask.

Lacy flushed. "Of course I am. Is that perverted?"

"Not at all. But destroy them afterwards, Lacy. Westwood will know Ryan's compromised when he doesn't get a report. He might send someone to search your place when you're not around. The hunter seems to have no end of resources and surely has the technology to bypass any alarm system." Now wasn't that a thought to send chills all through me? "Though he really has no use for the tapes. He's probably current on what's been going on. He wouldn't expect anything from the nights we're closed."

"I don't like the fact that Westwood's so determined to stalk you." Lacy stared at the glasses I'd tossed on the table. "The man's obviously got a screw loose."

"No argument there." I shivered and walked out of the storeroom. "I could lock myself in my apartment and hide under the covers. Or I can go on living." I grabbed a shawl and wrapped it around me. "I've got Valdez and my friends. We're all on high alert."

Lacy sighed. "It's not fair. You're good people. Drink that canned stuff. I've never seen you hurt anybody. Not even Ryan tonight when I know you wanted to."

"Yeah, I did." I leaned against the counter. "But I'm not the animal Westwood takes me for."

Lacy wiped at her eyes, back to sad again. "He used me to get to you. I'm so sorry, Glory."

"Not your fault." I opened a drawer and pulled out a box of tissues. "But you can make it up to me. Come with me to Damian's party tomorrow night."

"How can I say no?" Lacy took the tissue I held out to her and blew her nose. "I'll have to work on the party mood."

"Do that. And come up with a killer costume."

"What are you wearing tomorrow night? You got a costume in mind?" Lacy toyed with Ryan's keys. "Maybe I'll help myself to one of Ryan's vintage suits. His favorite Gatsby look. Worn without anything underneath, it should come across as sexy."

"Sounds good." I glanced at Valdez. "Maybe I'll pull out one of my Vegas costumes."

"Can't wear Kevlar under those little bits of nothing, Blondie. It ain't safe."

"It'll be a big party. Westwood couldn't think of showing up there. He'd be surrounded by vampires, shifters and way too many people who'd dearly love to take *him* for a trophy." I smiled sadly. "Damian has good security and Blade will beef it up even more once he knows we're all going to be there. I say we plan to have fun and forget all this danger and deception for a few hours."

Lacy shook her head and glared at Ryan one more time. "I may never forget, but I'll be there." She turned to Valdez.

"I say we make fur face here wear a costume. A cute little kitty mask."

"Bite me, cat girl."

"You wish, dog breath."

I pushed Lacy toward the door. "Call me when you've got the computers and, Lacy . . ." I gripped her shoulder for a moment. "I'm serious about tomorrow night. Eight o'clock. We'll ride over together."

"Fine." She grimaced. "I'll be sexy. I'll be fun. And I'll be on high alert in case Westwood shows up with a death wish." Lacy flipped open the deadbolts.

"There you go. Be careful out there." I heard her lock the door again from the outside while I went back to check on Ryan. He still sat slumped where I'd left him. I probed his mind. He was regaining consciousness, but the whammy would hold him in place until I released him.

"Let's go next door, Valdez. I need to find another day worker now that Ryan's out of the picture. And this time I'm checking references."

"Don't blame yourself, Blondie. The kid had us all fooled. Those glasses are something else. Be sure you give them to Blade." Valdez trotted by my side to the front door. *"Maybe you should wear some around Sabatini. The guy's put the whammy on you more than once."*

"Glasses would be cheating. I don't need them anyway. I can block Damian. Now that I know what he's capable of, I do it automatically." How much did Valdez know about Damian's sex mind games? The dog woofed and I figured it was more than I wanted him to.

I opened the front door and Valdez stuck his head outside and sniffed.

"All clear. But make it snappy."

"No problem." I stepped into the coffee shop and inhaled the sweet scent of muffins baking. Blueberry? The coffee didn't smell too bad either.

"Glory, over here." Flo waved at me. She was with Richard Mainwaring. This night just kept getting better and better.

Twenty

Mainwaring. I either had to make my peace with him, or prove he was a stone cold killer. I threw up a block and strolled over.

"Hi, you two. I was looking for Diana."

"She and Kenneth just left. She was taking him for a ride. To cheer him up." Flo exchanged a look with Richard. He'd stood as I approached, the perfect gentleman. And, for once, he wasn't glaring at me.

"Join us, Gloriana. Florence tells me I owe you an apology." He actually smiled as he held out a chair. He really was handsome if you liked the white blond hair and sky blue eyes thing. But those eyes clearly saw too much. I ramped up my blocks.

"Apology?"

"You think Ricardo hates you, Glory. At the church, he gave you a look, remember?"

Remember? I'd never forget it. "I just don't understand, Richard. What have I done to you to make you care about me one way or another?"

"A misunderstanding." Richard picked up Flo's hand. "Florence had just moved in with you, then immediately broke up with me. She didn't intend it so, but it seemed to me that you had poisoned her against me."

"I could hardly do that, Richard, when I'd never met you."

"Which is what I told him. I wanted him to socialize with us, come to meet my roomie." She squeezed Richard's hand. "But he was being secretive. Not wanting to go out at all. That's why I broke up with you, Ricardo. I like to go out, dance, have fun. You weren't giving me that."

"I know that now, sweetheart." He leaned over to kiss her cheek. "I'm a private person. And I didn't come to Austin by accident. I had my reasons," he glanced at me, "for not rushing to join the vampire community."

Reasons. Like the fact that he hated being around us? Oh, not Flo, obviously. I tried to probe his mind. Nothing. But I wasn't getting the hate vibe either. So we were making progress.

"Ricardo has never understood my brother's lifestyle." Florence smiled at him. "Of course who does? Damian dresses as Dracula on Halloween. It took me years to get used to the idea that he wasn't just asking to be staked."

"He calls it hiding in plain sight. Blending." At least Damian and I had that philosophy in common. I glanced at the cans of Bloody Merry on the table. Florence had poured hers into a glass and was using a straw. She didn't like to mess up her lipstick, a beautiful gloss tonight the color of ripe strawberries. It matched her red sweater and skirt. Mortals probably thought she was drinking an exotic juice.

I felt frumpy, dressed in black sweats with my Kevlar on underneath and running shoes on my feet. Dressed for battle, actually, in case the intervention with Ryan had somehow gone wrong. Of course it was hard to think it had gone right either. Finding out you've been had doesn't exactly inspire a party and balloons. Speaking of parties . . .

"Are you going to Damian's Halloween party tomorrow night? Diana tells me his parties are not to be missed."

"We'll be there. Right, Ricardo?" Flo toyed with her straw, but her eyes were fixed on Richard. This was obviously a test of their relationship.

"Yes, it's time I revealed myself."

Flo was smiling, so he'd passed her test, but I still wasn't ready to embrace Mr. Mainwaring.

"A lot of people already know you're here, Richard. We had a meeting . . ."

"Where Florence defended me. She told me about it." He put his hand on hers. "I swear I didn't kill Trevor or Marguerite." He looked at me directly. "I swear."

"All righty then. I'll see you both at the party tomorrow night." And didn't I sound like an idiot? I should be relieved my roomie's lover wasn't a psycho killer. Or was he? Flo began to chatter about Damian's parties, past and present.

Despite his swearing, I figured Richard still had secrets. All vamps did. It comes with the territory. Even I had some. Back in Las Vegas, I'd been secretive as hell out of necessity. I knew now I'd been way too isolated. No wonder I'd gotten in trouble with the gambling. Surrounded by mortals with no other vamps to relax with. On my guard all the time. Inadvertent fang action, stuff like that, and I had to spend all my time erasing memories. And wasn't that a drag?

Back then I couldn't go around with a can of Bloody Merry in my hand all the time either, at least not without a Koozie covering the label. I called it my energy drink. But if you don't have the blood sucking habit, I imagine it would freak you out to taste it. That's when I'd learned what I could and couldn't drink. Alcohol, no. Water, yes. But I don't handle bubbles well. Forget sodas. My system goes nuts. I could belch the "Star Spangled Banner" without taking a breath.

"Glory, are you listening to me?" Flo tapped her red nails on the table. "What are you wearing tomorrow night? I told Ricardo about your Kevlar. He wants me to try it. And Damian has been nagging me too." She looked down at her clingy sweater, then over at my smashed boobs. "Can I borrow your vest with the targets on it? I find it amusing."

"Sure. I'm not wearing Kevlar tomorrow night. My costume is way too skimpy."

"Now I'm jealous." Flo pouted prettily. "You will be sexy and I will be—"

"Safe, Florence, darling." Richard's eyes fixed on her lips. "You must stay safe. And I know for a fact that you look sexy in anything. Even wrapped in a bed sheet."

"Especially wrapped in a bed sheet, you bad boy." Flo pulled his hand to her lips and nipped at his knuckles. "Pardon us, Gloriana. We are full of passion for each other. Like two teenagers, yes?"

I stood and smiled at them. Wasn't this a treat? I not only was a third wheel here, but I was being reminded in the most graphic way possible that my own love life was a suck-fest. Sure, I could sleep with Blade again, but that would only complicate things. Or I could bed Damian and not complicate things nearly enough. I hated the way I felt. Jealous, out of sorts and, watching Richard stare at Flo's lips, horny enough to actually consider calling Blade.

Richard looked up at me and winked. He was reading my mind! Through my block. Just how old was this vampire?

"Florence, would you excuse me a moment? I think I'll walk Gloriana to her door. To make sure we have peace between us."

"Thank you, darling. Of course." Flo gave me a serious look. "Have an open mind, Glory. Ricardo's in my life now. I would hate to have to find a new roomie."

"My mind is way too open right now, Flo. And you won't have to find a new roomie on *my* account." I nodded toward the door. "I've got my dog, Richard. I can make it upstairs just fine."

"Please. Humor me. I have something to tell you."

If it was a passionate declaration of his love for Flo, he could spare me. He gripped my elbow and propelled me toward the door. When we got outside, he gave Valdez a look that had my dog tucking his tail between his legs. I shivered. Okay. What the hell was going on here? Richard punched in the code that Flo had obviously given him and held the door open so I could enter the apartment building. He shut the door in Valdez's face. Dog out, us in. I couldn't believe Valdez had allowed it. And he wasn't even barking. Freaky.

"Stop right here. I can get upstairs on my own. As soon as I get my dog inside where he belongs." I looked around. No one was above us on the stairwell or in front of the mailboxes that took up one side of the small lobby. "What is it you want to tell me, Richard?"

"I know you still think I may have been staking vampires with a cross."

Well, that laid it all out. "Have you? Former priest. Praying over your drinking buddies. Even Flo says you think we're demons from hell." Well, if I wanted to earn my own piece of holy harpoon, I was doing a whale of a job. Sorry, I get a little pun happy when I'm nervous. Have I mentioned how tall and toned Richard is?

"I've struggled with what I am, what we are, for a long, long time." Richard stepped back and leaned against the wall. "And I won't hurt you, Gloriana."

I released the breath I hadn't known I was holding. This was one scary dude. Powers off the charts or my name wasn't Gloriana, uh, uh, oh right, St. Clair.

"We are what we are, Richard. I've struggled with it too. And wasted a lot of time denying my own power." I *saw* myself at the top of the stairs. And I was there. In front of my own apartment door. I turned around. Of course Richard was right behind me.

"I know you're Florence's good friend. That you love her as she deserves to be loved." Richard put his hand on my shoulder and I couldn't have moved an inch if my life depended on it.

"Yes, I do love Flo. She's a wonderful friend. I've been worried about her. Because of your . . . secrets." Damn it, I was *not* going to cry. But it was clear as glass that Richard really did love my roomie. His eyes met mine and he let me see the truth of that.

"My secrets are my own. I promise I'll not harm you or any other vampire. Unless that vampire is threatening someone I love." Again, he let me see that he meant it. As solemn as a vow. Of course, he'd taken the vows to be a priest once too. Obviously he'd discarded the celibacy vow in a big way.

"I'm a man, Gloriana. I love God. I've never stopped. But I was not meant to serve Him inside the Church. So I chose immortality. And to serve Him in my own way." Richard's hand tightened on my shoulder for a moment and I winced. The man was damned strong.

"You sound like some kind of holy crusader."

"I have been." Richard finally let me go. "Are we good now?"

"Good? If you mean do I believe you're not staking other vamps . . ." I lifted my chin, "Not yet. Sure, you let me see your thoughts, but you're stronger than Blade, stronger than any vamp I've ever known. I could be under a whammy here and I wouldn't have a clue."

"You're very clever, Gloriana. I'm glad you're Florence's good friend and champion." He smiled. "You *are* her champion, are you not?"

"Yes, I am. So don't hurt her, Mainwaring. Or you'll have to answer to me." I had to give the man credit. He didn't laugh his ass off at my bravado.

"I will never hurt Florence. We'll be together until she decides to move on."

"There you go. So why don't you go back to her? And send up my dog." I pulled my keys out of my pocket. "I don't appreciate all this show of power. Valdez will sulk for a month that he let me down."

"I'll erase his memory. He'll come bounding up those stairs and think he's been with you every moment. Satisfied?" He kept looking at me.

Satisfied? Not really. I had more questions now than ever before. But I *was* clever. So clever I realized he'd respected me enough not to erase *my* memory. So I wasn't going to ask my questions. Not tonight anyway. But I wanted answers.

I watched him walk down the stairs and saw Valdez pass him, tail wagging like they were old friends. Nothing could have made me more uneasy than that little bit of action. I hope Flo knew what kind of man she was involved with, because I sure as hell didn't.

I waited until I was sure Mainwaring had left the building then headed down the back stairs. I hated going out the back. The alley had proved to be a vamp hunting ground. But I still had to deal with Ryan. Wipe his mind, plant a suggestion and send him on his way.

Fortunately all the security lights were working again and Valdez and I got inside the storeroom before my cell phone rang.

"I just left Ryan's apartment. I've got every piece of computer equipment he owned in the back of my car."

"Great. I hope no one saw you." As far as I knew werecats couldn't do a whammy and wipe memories.

"It's cool. I sneaked in, loaded up and sneaked out." Lacy giggled. "After a detour by a paint store. Ryan's precious vintage wardrobe is officially history."

"What color?" Nothing like a good revenge scenario to lighten a dark mood.

"Red. The color of that lying SOB's blood. You ought to drain him dry, Glory."

I looked at him, sitting peacefully under the whammy, eyes closed as he waited for my next order. I was feeling more sick than bloodthirsty. The idea that he'd recorded all of our conversations . . . Well, maybe I could come up with a little blood lust. But I wouldn't. Westwood thought vamps were animals. Ryan apparently was on board with that. I was way above the animal level and I sure as hell didn't want to put my teeth anywhere on Ryan's body.

"Thanks, but no thanks. How are you doing with all this?"

Lacy sighed. "It felt good at first, but now I'm just tired and—"

"I know. The man's a dirtbag. I'll send him home to Houston and you'll never have to see him again."

"Thanks, Glory." Lacy hung up and I turned to Ryan.

"You've been robbed, Ryan, and you want to go home to Houston to finish your degree. You won't work for Westwood any more. Let your father take care of his own mess."

Ryan nodded. I was guiding him out the back door when Valdez got in on the act. He grabbed a chunk of Ryan's pants and ripped out the seat.

"Red silk boxers? Good thing you like red, bug boy."

The dog spit out the fabric and snorted. *"Damned sneaking son of a bitch. We should throw him in the lake with his laptop tied to his ankle."*

I patted Valdez's head and shoved Ryan outside. "Too easy. Let the creep explain to his daddy how he screwed up in Austin. He'll remember just enough to know he won't be showing his face here anytime soon."

"Can't say I'm sorry to see that young'un gone." Harvey appeared in the storeroom.

"You didn't like bug boy?" I pulled a Bloody Merry out of the fridge and headed into the store to collapse into the comfy chair that still hadn't sold. I could definitely use some down time and it was only an hour until dawn.

"He was jealous of Ryan. Because I thought he was cute." Emmie Lou sat on the counter.

"Cute is, as cute does, Emmie Lou." I nodded at Henry. "Henry and I agree. Good riddance. Ryan was a slimeball."

"Poor Lacy. She sure deserves better than that." Emmie glanced at her spouse. "I guess there's worse things than cheating."

"Here we go. I never cheated." Harvey paced the length of the store. He stopped by the ladies' underwear and held up a red and black lace bustier. "Course if you'd ever worn something like this, I wouldn't even have looked at that checker at the Piggly Wiggly. Not that anything happened there."

Emmie Lou hissed, I swear it. "You hear that, Glory. Thirty-nine years of marriage and he thinks I should come strutting into the bedroom dressed like a high-priced hooker." She hopped off the counter and walked up to Henry.

"Let me tell you something, mister. If you'd still kissed me like that Mr. Blade kisses our Glory here, you'd have had me prancing in front of you like a show girl every night. I married you for your kisses, then you got stingy with them. Your tractor got more affection than I did."

Kissed like Blade. I tuned out the Nutts' never-ending fight and thought about being kissed by Blade. We'd always had the hot-for-your-body thing going for us. But it wasn't enough for the long haul. One thing that watching Harvey and Emmie Lou bickering had taught me, was that you could talk a thing to death. What really mattered was action. Behavior.

Reality check. Blade's behavior toward me had been . . . caring. Rushing over to check on me whenever Valdez called. Hey, Valdez sticking to me like a leech. Those things proved that Blade cared about me. But Blade also "cared" about Mara, "cared" about his family, despite the current rift. Was I just one more obligation to him?

But when he kissed me it was easy to imagine that we still had the mystical connection that had pulled us together in the first place. I never would have become vampire just for hot sex. I'd felt back then like I'd met my, don't laugh now, soul mate.

Some people don't figure vamps as being human. I know we're *more* than human. Along with enhanced senses, immortality and the potential for powers off the charts, we *feel* things more intensely. Hate, love, sorrow and, the worst for me, guilt. Is it any wonder our relationships tend to be complicated?

Blade had given all that to me, along with a libido that wouldn't quit. I like sex, *need* sex on a regular basis. Seeing Flo and Richard all touchy feely had brought that fact home big time. I strolled over to the lingerie section and picked up the bustier. I knew how to show off my assets and downplay my defects. I'd wear this tomorrow night and see what happened. I didn't doubt I'd have some opportunities—Blade, Damian, maybe somebody new. If I got a chance to have a good time, I was going to take it.

"Come on, Flo, pull!" The bustier laced up the front but lacked two inches before it would cover me decently.

"Just one more inch." To hell with decency. I grabbed the strings. Thank God they were industrial strength. "I'll lay down on the bed. Flo, you get on top and don't hold back. Use your vamp muscles this time."

"I don't know, Glory. If I do get it that tight, you're going to suffer." Flo shook her head.

"This from a woman who wears four inch stilettos? We suffer for beauty. Now get up here and do your thing."

Valdez looked up from the bowl of dip he was licking clean. *"I should sell tickets. Guys would pay good money to see you two like that."*

Flo had climbed on top of me, her knees on either side of my waist. She held the strings in her hand, looked over at Valdez and grinned. "Only if I kiss her on the lips first."

"Ewww! You two cut it, oof, out." Flo had jerked on the strings and I would have gasped except I was permanently through breathing.

"One more . . . Got it!" Flo tied a bow, then frowned. "Better make it a double knot." She looked down at me. At least I think she did. Everything was kind of blurry.

"Hello? Stay with us, girlfriend. Can you breathe?" She climbed off me.

Breathe? Maybe, maybe not. I managed a nod and held out my hand. Flo pulled me to a sitting position. I was a little off center while I tried to adjust to the vise around my middle.

"You're really out there, girlfriend." Flo glanced at Valdez. "Is she turning blue or am I imagining it?"

"I don't know about her color, but I think she's going to blow. Cut her loose, Flo."

"Don't." Wheeze. "You." Gasp. "Dare." Sigh. I blinked the room back into focus and managed to stand.

"You should have a Bloody Merry." Flo pressed a cold can into my hand.

"No! Can't. Bloats me." I staggered into the living room and glanced down. Whoa. Talk about your ripe melons.

"Wear something else, Blondie." Valdez nudged my hip. *"You don't look so hot."*

"Au contraire, puppy. I look sizzling." At least I hoped that was the effect of my tits galore. "I just need some blush." I walked carefully into the bedroom and stroked some Fiery Rose on my cheeks. My spray-on tan had faded until I was pale again.

Of course the fact that I hadn't let myself drink any Bloody Merry since waking had also added to the pale, "I'm undead," look. But fasting seemed to be the only way I could lose any weight. Temporary, but every ounce helped. I dipped a little blush into my cleavage. If the men in my life didn't fall over in lust, then I was going into a nunnery.

"I don't think convents accept vampires as novitiates." Flo picked up my blush and dabbed at her own cheeks. "This Kevlar. I should have worn something low cut."

"You look cute." Which she did. Flo had on the Kevlar bra with the bright yellow targets. She'd paired it with skintight black satin capris and four-inch heels with rhinestone buckles. There was a knock on the door.

"Lacy's here." Flo threw open the door. "Check out Glory, kitty girl."

"That's quite a costume." Lacy looked me over. "The Devil with, um, major bazooms."

"I'm a minion, a minor demon from hell, not the big guy." I had put on a very short skirt made of layers of red and orange silk with my bustier. The skirt looked like flames and had originally been part of my costume during my stint as a barmaid at the Hot Spot, a bar in the hotel where I'd eventually gotten work in the chorus of the revue playing the main stage.

Cute little horns and a tail had carried on the theme and they were part of the junk I'd hauled with me to Austin. Damian and I were both hiding in plain sight tonight. Well, not much of me was actually hiding.

"My brother will love it. Especially if you pop right out of that thing."

"Thanks a lot. Are we ready to go, Lacy? Flo, are you waiting for Richard?" I hadn't asked before, glad Flo had been around to help me into my costume.

Flo studied her long red nails. "No, he's meeting us there. I'm mad at him. He's getting mysterious again."

"I believed him last night, if that helps. I don't think he's staking other vamps." I picked up my black satin cape lined with red and tied it around my shoulders. I still wasn't breathing much, which made serious inroads on the sexy feeling.

"Good to know. But, Flo, it sounds like you and I *both* need new boyfriends." Lacy looked very sexy in Ryan's suit. The trousers were slung low on her hips and the jacket was held closed by just one button. There was plenty of bare skin above and below that button.

"Blade's here." Valdez stood and there was a knock on the door.

"Why?" I flipped the dead bolts. "We were just leaving."

"Ask him yourself." Valdez gave me a look then sat down again.

I opened the door and Blade stood there, resplendent in Campbell plaid complete with broadsword. My heart jumped around in my chest. I'd always loved the way Blade looked in clan regalia. Tonight he had the whole "I'm ready to slay the world for you" look going on.

"Why are you here? We're on our way to Damian's party."

"I know. Valdez told me."

"Where's Mara? She told Damian she'd be coming with you."

"She'll be along. I have a guard assigned to her." He looked at Flo and nodded approvingly. "Good idea, Florence. Gloriana, where's your Kevlar?"

"I'm not wearing it tonight." I threw back my cape and let my cleavage shine. And was Blade looking? You bet he was. Good news that I rated Blade's personal attention tonight while Mara got stuck with a bodyguard.

"Living dangerously, are you?" Blade moved closer, his fangs just showing beneath his smile. "Or perhaps you've been developing more of your powers. Any new tricks to show me?"

Hmm. He was obviously remembering the now-you're-dressed, now-you're-naked number I'd pulled on him. I wouldn't mind another round. I smiled back and let him read the possibility. Lacy cleared her throat and Flo shook her head.

"Gloriana is keeping secrets from us, Jeremiah. She's been working on her powers without me." Flo smiled sadly. "I just hope you don't have to use them tonight, Glory."

"I don't think Westwood will try anything at a party where he'd be surrounded by vamps." I glanced at Flo. "And it doesn't hurt for a woman to have a few surprises up her sleeve, does it?"

"Not at all. I just hope you're right about Westwood. But we'll be well protected, Jeremiah." Flo grabbed a black fur shrug and pulled it on. "Damian has a security force and his grounds are surrounded by a ten-foot fence. I can't see Westwood climbing a fence, can you?" Flo patted my arm on the way to the door.

"I have my own security there too." Blade was definitely giving me the eye. I was a naughty girl and trailed a finger across the top of my lace bustier.

"Then we should be fine." I picked up my black satin clutch. "Let's go."

"Not yet." Suddenly solemn, Blade blocked the door. "I have news. About the cross that staked Marguerite."

Twenty-one

There went the party mood. "What about it, Jerry?" I had a feeling I didn't want to hear this. Lacy and Flo sat on the love seat.

"I've been in contact with vampires in Houston. The crosses used there were identical to the one that took out Trevor. And another vampire was staked in Dallas last week. Same kind of cross."

Nothing like a vamp network. Blade had always maintained connections with other strong vamps.

"Who was killed in Dallas? When? What night?" Despite her blush, Flo was pale. Did she wonder at all if this was Richard's work?

"Thursday night. Sebastian de Ville. You knew him, Florence."

"Of course." She bit her lip. "In London. Many years ago. This is terrible." She gave me a look. "Ricardo was with me last Thursday night, Glory. Does that make you believe in him?"

"I told you I believed him, Flo. But it's good to have proof." I let Flo read my aggravation that she still read my mind whenever she felt like it, then shrugged. "If you know where he was every minute last Thursday, Flo, then we should *both* feel better."

"But what about Margie?" Flo put her hand on Blade's arm. "Wasn't the cross that took her the same?"

"No, it wasn't. And that's what's bothering me." Blade did look serious. "My expert traced it to a local store here, but they've sold dozens of them."

"But surely not sharp enough——" Lacy looked at me.

"No. Someone sharpened one end." Thank goodness Blade didn't whip out the cross for us to study.

"Poor Sebastian. He was a poet. Very gentle. So undeserving of such an end." Flo stepped back and dabbed at her eyes with a lace hanky she'd had tucked between her breasts. The Kevlar was my size, not Flo's. She could be carrying a change of clothes in there. "But what does this mean, Jeremiah?"

"Obviously Marguerite wasn't killed by the same group staking other vampires in Texas." Jerry stood with his feet firmly planted, hands behind his back, every inch the Highland warrior.

I'd like to see some religious fanatic try to take *him* out. Wait. No, I wouldn't. Blade seemed invincible but we were all vulnerable in some way. Blade's weakness, if you could call it that, was his protectiveness. He'd be taken out riding to some damsel's rescue. I prayed I wouldn't be that damsel. I eased closer until I could lay my hand on his arm. Solid. I wanted to believe he'd be here forever.

"Someone else killed Margie? A copycat?" I glanced at Lacy. "Pardon the expression."

"No problem." Lacy shrugged. "I didn't know Margie. Did she have enemies?"

"I'd only met her once myself." I looked at Florence. "Flo, you knew Margie better than we did. What do you think?"

"If she wasn't killed because she was vampire," Flo locked eyes with Blade, "then I would suspect a lover's quarrel."

"Kenneth?" Blade was taking Flo's outrageous suggestion seriously.

"Or someone who wanted Kenneth for herself." Flo tucked her hanky between her breasts again. "He or she will not get away with it. Glory, you thought all along it might be another vampire. I'm afraid you might be right." She squared her shoulders. "Kenneth will be at Damian's party. I'll question him myself."

"For God's sake, be careful, Flo. If he staked Margie then he's capable of anything."

"I have on your Kevlar, Glory." Flo had a hard look in her sea green eyes. "And I have powers Marguerite and Kenneth never bothered to develop. If he killed her so he could be with another woman . . ."

Lacy frowned. "There's nothing worse than a lover who betrays you."

"Exactly, girlfriend. I took Kenneth as enough of a man to ask for his freedom." Flo's eyes misted and she took a deep breath. "But Marguerite made him. She might not have wanted to release him."

"Slow down, Flo." I could practically see the lynch party forming. "Wait until you talk to Kenneth before you jump to any conclusions."

"Florence and I will question him together. And we'll know the truth when we hear it." Blade strode to the door. "Ladies, allow me to drive you to the party." He opened the door, then bowed at the waist.

A party. I felt like I was on my way to another wake. I wasn't about to turn Blade down, though. I had a gut feeling that something bad was going down tonight. I *had* been working on my powers and if I could help make things right, I would.

Could Kenneth have killed his own life partner? We'd already figured out Margie wouldn't have been in the alley unless she'd known her attacker or been forced there. And with her vamp strength, only another vamp or half a dozen mortal men could have forced her to go anywhere.

"Jerry, how do you know it wasn't the same group that did the other vampires? Maybe they ran out of their stake of choice and had to improvise."

Jerry stood up straight, his face grim. "The group was led by a religious fanatic. My friends in Dallas caught him and his followers. Before justice was served, the man admitted to his killings. Only one in Austin, a man who appeared drunk, obviously Trevor."

Before justice was served. Ye Gods. I sure didn't want a blow by blow of *that* confrontation.

"Maybe he was lying."

Blade put his arm around me and guided me out the door. "No, Gloriana, he wasn't lying. You know a mortal can't lie when a vampire orders him to talk."

"Oh, yeah, the whammy." I glanced at Lacy. We'd both seen the truth of that with Ryan. She looked good, if a little ragged around the edges with a bitter twist to her lips. She'd piled on the makeup tonight. Like she didn't want us to notice that she'd spent the last twenty-four hours crying and had probably skipped sleeping altogether.

I let Valdez out then locked the door. Despite the colorful costumes and the jaunty orange and black kerchief around Valdez's neck, we were a pretty somber bunch trooping downstairs and out to Blade's car.

But you can't keep an immortal down for long and the mood lightened as we reached the small Mercedes convertible. Blade had parked in front. He and Valdez were obviously alert and kept looking around as we stepped outside.

"You're kidding. You expect me to ride back there with that mangy mutt?" Lacy glanced meaningfully at the front passenger seat.

"Oh, no, you don't. I've got shotgun." I held back the seat so she could climb in. Blade stood behind me, still obviously very watchful. "Valdez had a bath yesterday and I ran out of his usual flea soap so—"

"*So I smell like a damned fruit salad.*" Valdez had been sulking ever since. "*Talk about animal cruelty.*" He hopped into the backseat. "*You think I want to sit next to a kitty wannabe?*"

"You 'wannabe' singing soprano, fur face?" Lacy sniffed, her hands on her narrow hips.

"I'll sit next to you, doggy." Flo got in next. "But put the top down, Jeremiah. I never should have given Valdez that onion dip."

Lacy squeezed in the tiny backseat, still grumbling. Blade helped me into the front, slammed the door and strode around the car. He'd offered me the keys when we were coming down the stairs, but I didn't dare drive. Between lack of oxygen and the horrific idea that Kenneth might have . . . Impossible. Margie and Kenneth had been a couple for over a hundred years. Surely they could have just decided to go their separate ways, like Blade and I had. No one had to resort to murder to end a relationship. No one civilized anyway.

"Don't fash yourself, lass." Blade took my hand and held it while he drove slowly down Sixth Street. The area was party central on Halloween night and people in every kind of costume imaginable thronged the sidewalks, sometimes moving the party into the street. Music changed by the block—country, rock, heavy metal. Something for everyone on a street lined with clubs, restaurants and bars. I welcomed the cold air as I indeed "fashed" myself over a love affair gone wrong.

"We don't know anything yet, Gloriana." Blade stopped at a red light and pulled my hand to his lips. "But some lovers are more possessive than others."

Was that a slam? A not so subtle reminder that I'd cut Blade loose without fighting for our relationship? Maybe if we'd tried harder to make it work . . .

"Hindsight, Gloriana. All we can try to control is our present and, to some extent, our future." The light changed and Blade dropped my hand to begin negotiating the climb up the narrow streets of Castle Hill.

Gee, wasn't he Mr. Philosophy all of a sudden? But he was too right.

When we finally pulled up to Damian's iron gates, a security guard checked our names on his guest list then waved us through. The castle was ablaze with lights. White tents were set up on the expansive lawn and the lights of the Austin skyline provided a spectacular back drop.

Control my future? I was living moment to moment, waiting for the next arrow to fly or cross to come at me. I'd been working on a little self-defense, but hadn't really tested it. I hoped I never had to. I glanced back at Flo, safely wrapped in my Kevlar vest. Maybe I'd been stupid to go for sexy over safe. But as we drove up to the house, I could hear lively music coming from the wraparound porch and laughter from a group clustered in front of a tent.

Party time. And vamps do know how to have a good time. I determinedly shoved all my worries to the back burner as Blade parked the car behind the house. There were already over a dozen other cars there.

Damian grinned when he saw me. I threw up a block, wincing when my head throbbed. Damn it, I wasn't going to be *controlled* by anyone.

"Gloriana." Damian stepped behind me and removed my cloak. "Ravishing." He dropped a kiss on my bare shoulder. Okay. I watched Blade's reaction and preened a little.

"You might be cold without your cape, Gloriana." Blade wasn't smiling.

"Nonsense. The night is a bit chilly, but the tents are heated." Damian handed my cape to a hovering servant and nodded to Lacy. "Welcome, Lacy. Another beauty." He hooked arms with both of us and headed toward a large white tent. "I have a surprise. A new synthetic blood that I swear tastes like it's fresh from the source." He patted Lacy's hand. "And would kitty enjoy a little milk punch?"

Lacy laughed and kissed his cheek. "If you weren't my land-lord, I'd show you what I think of milk punch. I assume you have an open bar. I'll take a Scotch and make it a double."

"Damian, is your sister invisible?" Flo stepped in front of us. "Aren't you going to greet me?"

"Sorry. I was distracted." He squeezed my hand. "Wel-come, sister dear. I recognize the Kevlar. Good choice. Your lover is inside. In my library coveting my latest acquisition, a Thomas Aquinas manuscript. Breathtaking illuminations." Damian looked at me, though his eyes never got above boob level. "I'll show you later, Gloriana."

"Damian." Flo wasn't budging.

"Your lover is waiting, Florence. Shouldn't you join him?" Damian was staring at my breasts as if hoping they'd pop free of the bustier. Which would almost be a relief. But what was a little pain when you could make hunky vamps pant?

"In a moment." Flo tapped her foot. "Look at me, Damian."

"What?" Damian dragged his eyes to his sister's face. "Whoa. You look steamed. What's going on? Has Mainwar-ing done something?"

"No, not him." Flo glanced at Blade. "Have you seen Kenneth Collins this evening?"

"Not yet. But I saw him last night, driving a new Jaguar. Grief seems to agree with him. He also contacted my realtor about a new home in the hills."

"Will you let me know when he gets here?"

"Sure. Whatever." Damian patted Flo on the shoulder then moved her out of the way. "It's party time, ladies."

Flo shook her head. "Jeremiah, you should come with me. Talk to Ricardo. He may be able to help us with Kenneth."

"If you're sure you'll be all right, Gloriana." Blade ignored Damian as thoroughly as Damian ignored him.

"I'll be fine." I squeezed Damian's arm. "Anyone aims a stake at me, I'll throw Damian in front of me."

Lacy laughed and I eased away from Damian in case he'd lost his sense of humor.

"You *are* a little devil, aren't you? No one will be aiming stakes here. Security is as tight as Jeremiah's ass."

"By God!" Blade put his hand on his sword.

"Ignore him, Jerry." I smiled at Blade. "Damian hates to be ignored. Go with Flo. We'll see you later."

Damian reached up to straighten my horns and gave me one of his smoldering looks. "Later I will show you my dungeon, Gloriana. Where I put bad little girls."

Blade and Valdez snorted in unison. Both turned away. Blade to follow Flo into the house and Valdez to settle next to the door of the tent.

"I haven't been a little girl for a long, long time, Damian." I smiled and fiddled with the ties of his black satin cape lined with red. Damian was Dracula incarnate in the cape over a black tux, snowy shirt and bow tie. His hair was brushed back from his forehead and his fangs were full out. The overall effect was definitely sexy. "As for being bad . . . the night is young. I could go either way."

"Come play with me, Gloriana." Damian was doing his best to do the whammy on me. I could feel his intensity. But my blocks were strong and holding. I do so love to feel my own power.

"Maybe later. You have more guests arriving. Go play host." I gave Damian a finger wave and sauntered into the tent, making sure to twitch my devil's tail. A crowd was gathered around a steaming fountain in the middle of the tent. The new synthetic blood poured out and could be caught in crystal goblets. The smell was pretty amazing. I was heartily sick of Bloody Merry. If this stuff tasted as good as it smelled, I was switching brands. My fangs ran out and I looked around to be sure no mortals were going to gasp and point.

Not to worry. Among the vamps and shifters, the mortals looked twice as weird, scary even. I'll take natural vamp fangs over deliberately sharpened teeth any day.

Lacy immediately latched on to a good-looking shifter. This one had a slight wolf smell to him, a werewolf. You'd think a kitty would avoid her natural predator, but then Lacy was gulping Scotch like it was water and had a "What the hell" look to her. I got the feeling she could take care of herself. She was definitely on guard against predatory men.

I drifted around the room, greeting the vamps I knew. CiCi was a very sexy Glinda the Good Witch. Her companion, the handsome vamp she'd latched on to at the meeting, struggled with a Tin Man costume that clanked and seemed on the verge of falling apart. Freddy was the Cowardly Lion while Derek dribbled straw as the Scarecrow. The capper was Sheba, her kitty self draped over CiCi's shoulder, a dog mask over her face, clearly impersonating Toto.

"What is this? The vamp cast of *The Wiz*?" I looked around. "Where's Dorothy?"

"I knew we forgot someone." CiCi frowned and looked me over. "I don't think you would do, Glory, unless you lost the *Girls Gone Wild* look and we found you something a little more . . . innocent."

"Don't let her get her hooks into you, Glory. You look great. Unlike some of us." Derek shuddered and pulled a straw out of his hair. "I don't know how I let CiCi talk me into this."

"Mother is very persuasive when she puts her mind to it." Freddy's yellow tights didn't leave nearly enough to the imagination and he made a pretty impressive lion. His mother tapped Derek with her wand.

"I think we'll win the prize this year, Derek. Be patient," CiCi said sternly. "Where's Valdez? Sheba would love to see him." The cat hopped down and stretched, the mask slipping down to hang around her neck. Her blue eyes gleamed as she looked around.

"Sitting outside the tent." I grinned, imagining Valdez's reaction to the Toto costume. Tin Man's funnel hat fell off with a clank and I left the group arguing about how to get it to stay on short of the nail gun a glowering Derek proposed.

"A prize?" I smiled at the body-builder vamp I'd met before. I couldn't think of his name. Tonight he was Hercules, his skimpy costume showing off a seriously buff body.

"Sure. Damian is famous for his costume contests. Last year a Lady Godiva rode up at the last minute on a horse." Hercules laughed. "Of course she won, especially when a breeze showed everyone at the party that she'd taken the riding naked through the streets part seriously."

"Sorry I missed it." I looked around.

"If you'd been here, Gloriana, *you* would have won. You look hot." Hercules moved closer. "Can I get you a drink? Damian's imported the good stuff. Fangtastic. From Transylvania."

"Thank you. I'd love to try it." Maybe just a sip wouldn't hurt me. I took a cautious breath. Hercules' eyes bugged and his jaw dropped. He almost backed into a tray of glasses on his way to the drink fountain. I looked down to make sure I was still decent. Barely. But got to love the boobs-galore effect.

"Forget him." Damian was back in the tent and handed me a full goblet of his imported synthetic. "Taste. Tell me what you think."

I smelled. Mmm. AB negative, much better than Ryan, the sneaky spy. I allowed myself just a taste. Have mercy. This was enough like the real thing that I could close my eyes and imagine . . .

A kiss brushed my lips, deepened. Leave it to Damian to take advantage of a blood lust moment. I leaned into it. The man kissed like an artist. Red, green, yellow and violet swirled behind my closed lids. His hand slid around my neck—

"Mr. Sabatini, Mr. Sabatini."

I leaned back with a sigh. "You're being paged, Mr. Sabatini."

We both turned to stare at Tony Crapetta. Typically clueless, the mortal had interrupted just when things were getting interesting.

"What is it, Tony?" Damian picked up a goblet of his own and took a deep swallow. "This had better be good."

"The guards down at the gate caught a guy trying to get inside who's not on the list. Maybe you should do your mind reading thing on him. See if Westwood sent him."

Damian got a look that made even me shiver. "You're right. I'm coming. Stay here and take care of Miss Gloriana. See that she gets whatever she wants." He winked at me. "I think I'll take Hercules with me. In case we need to get physical with our gate-crasher."

"Sure, boss. I'll stick to Miss Gloriana like glue." Tony looked at my drink and grimaced. "You mind if I get me a real drink first?"

Damian nodded and Tony headed for the bar. After a short discussion with Hercules, Damian strode from the tent. He was followed by Hercules, who sent me a mental "catch you later" message before he disappeared. I'd better ramp up my blocks if a guy I'd barely met could communicate with me. A shame, really. I wanted to relax and have fun, not give myself a headache. I decided to forget blocks as long as Damian was out of the way.

I looked around at the crowd. I saw more than one witch, though CiCi was the only one who hadn't gone over to the dark side. Then there were the Draculas. Most of them were mortals who'd painted their faces white and their lips red with fake blood dribbled at the corners of their mouths. Yeah, right. Like we're pigs who slobber our supper and never use a napkin.

There was a flash and a puff of smoke as a wizard turned a startled man, dressed as an Elizabethan courtier, into a frog. The wizard glanced at me and shrugged, like "What are you going to do," then walked away. Oops. I'd say Froggie had made Wizard mad about something. Apparently Froggie's date, a ringer for Queen Liz I, wasn't going to just let this go. She picked the creature up and headed outside, hot on the heels of the Wizard. No one paid attention to her screeches of rage.

Various vamps that I'd met at the meetings we'd held recently smiled and nodded to me. It was definitely nice to be part of what Richard had called the vampire community.

"I'm back, Miss Gloriana." Tony had a stiff drink in his hand.

I probed his mind. Nervous. Sticking with the vampires, no matter how much Westwood offered him. He wasn't the idiot everyone took him for. He wanted to live, in Austin, for a long, long time. Maybe forever if he got up the nerve to ask one of the fang masters to turn him vampire.

"Mr. Sabatini sure throws a quality party." Tony took a swallow of his drink and sighed with pleasure. "What say we check out the next tent?"

"Sure. Why not?" I walked beside him to the door of the tent and looked around. There were three other tents scattered around the lawn. The band I'd heard when we arrived was set up on the porch that faced the breathtaking view. The band played a song that sounded familiar and a few couples danced on the stone terrace. Small tables held candles and the flickering lights were very romantic. And here I was with Tony Crapetta.

"See that band? They just had a hit single on the country charts. Last year it was a rock band. Not the disco that I like to groove to, but I'd be glad to dance with you if you want, Miss Gloriana." Tony held out his hand. "Mr. Sabatini dropped a bundle bringing this group here for a private party. A shame to waste good music."

Tony was wearing a vest suit straight from the seventies, bell-bottom pants and a full sleeved shirt with a wild print. He could have been a contestant in the dance contest in *Saturday Night Fever* except for the six crosses nestled in his chest hair. He did a little John Travolta move and that sealed the deal as far as I was concerned.

"Thanks, Tony. Maybe later. Let's explore the next tent before we do any dancing." I'd have been smart if I'd just danced with the Disco King. Because the next tent held a horrifying sight. Was Damian trying to ruin me? I stopped in the doorway. Paranoia. Damian couldn't have known about my little problem. Nobody in Austin knew. Except for Valdez.

"What's wrong, Miss Gloriana? See? There's blackjack, roulette, poker tables. Free chips so you don't have to lose your own money." I felt Tony's hand on my back, urging me inside. "Then there's a prize table if you want to cash your winnings in for some pretty nifty things. Last year I went home with a DVD player."

Here it came—the rush, the adrenaline flow I'd tried to forget, but had to admit I'd missed. The music outside was just so much noise compared to the symphony inside. The rattle of chips, the cry of the winner and the moans of the losers as someone got twenty-one almost brought tears to my eyes. The roulette wheel whirled and the crowd gasped as the ball fell and danced around the circle. I edged closer. What number had hit? If it had been seven black, my lucky number . . .

"What the hell's going on here?" Valdez bumped my hip. *"Not going in there, are you?"*

Tony stared bug-eyed at Valdez. "Did that dog just talk?"

"No, you imagined it." I hit Tony with the whammy, then gave Valdez a stern look. "You know the rules, Valdez. Cool it around mortals. Now I have to erase Tony's memory and I've only been here a few minutes."

"Whatever. Just stay out of that tent. You can take care of Crappola later."

"If I want to gamble, I'll gamble. This isn't the real deal. It's just for fun."

"You can't have that kind of fun, Blondie. You go nuts and you know it." Valdez actually stepped between me and the roulette table.

My fault. I never should have let Valdez come inside at all those meetings of Gamblers Anonymous. He'd appointed himself my keeper after hearing all the warning signs, et cetera, et cetera. Of course I'd had a mortal sponsor as part of the program but Valdez had taken over after some unfortunate backsliding on my part. I'd finally gotten the message, along with maxed out credit cards, and quit cold turkey. I've been clean now for four years, six months and twenty-two days. And, believe me, Valdez is counting.

I looked inside the tent. I could smell the excitement. What would one game hurt? Texas Hold 'em. I could see a table with an opening—

Oof! I was flat on my back, staring at the sky overhead. A fifty pound dog sat on my chest.

"Get off, you mutt! You're not allowed to treat me this way." I shoved at Valdez. He didn't move an inch.

"Sorry, Blondie. Mr. Blade ordered me to take care of you. His orders trump your orders."

"Trump this, you mangy mongrel. No." Oof. "More." Oof. "Cheetos." Ugh. "For you." Damn it. I put everything I had into my next shove. Nothing. Valdez was something else and it sure wasn't just a Labradoodle.

"Now you're being mean. You know I love my Cheetos. But orders are orders." His paws pressed down on my shoulders when I tried one more buck. *"Give it up, Blondie. When I ramp up my strength, no vampire can beat me at arm wrestling."* He had the nerve to grin at me. *"One more buck and your left boob's going to pop free."*

How could such a spawn of Satan look so cute? If I didn't know better I'd think he was doing the whammy on me. I closed my eyes just in case and felt the swish of his wagging tail on my bare legs while I adjusted my bustier. At least only Tony Crappeta had witnessed this humiliation. If another vampire came out and saw me, flat on my back, with my dog sitting on my chest . . .

"Okay, okay, I give. I will *not* go into that tent." I opened my eyes and put my hands against Valdez's warm chest. If I got a good grip and yanked, I could take out a big hunk of fur. But I wouldn't. Because he was right. I didn't need to gamble. Ever. Again.

"You sure?" He was braced, like for pain in case I decided to let 'er rip.

"I'm sure. I'll even dance with Crapetta here if that will make you get off of me." I glanced at Tony. He was wide-eyed, but obviously still under the influence of the whammy I'd started before I'd been knocked on my ass.

"I'd pay money to see you dance with Crapetta." Blade strolled up. "Off the lady, Valdez. I can handle things from here."

"Of course. He called you, didn't he?" I sat up as soon as Valdez hopped off of me. So much for our pact that Blade would never know about the gambling.

"Valdez is obligated to me." Blade looked at the dog, then at me. "Don't blame him for reporting everything. He has no choice."

"Damn it, I'm sick of having absolutely no privacy." I reluctantly took Blade's outstretched hand and let him pull me to my feet. I brushed off the back of my skirt and discovered my forked tail was bent out of shape. Hey, *I* was bent out of shape. At least we'd had a dry autumn and I wasn't hip deep in mud.

Forget my dignity. That was long gone. I did my best to straighten my tail while Tony still stared. Time to cut him loose. I touched his arm.

"Crapetta, you can forget everything about this little scene. Go back in to the drink tent and get another double. Mr. Blade is here now."

Tony shook his head, then headed for the drink tent even though he'd barely sipped the drink in his hand. You had to love the whammy. I looked at Blade, then at Valdez. But you didn't have to love interfering, control freak vampires or their minions.

I picked up my purse, which had landed on the grass beside me, then turned on my heel and headed for the fence that lined the property. I needed darkness—to think, to straighten my skirt and to check my hair for leaves and grass clippings.

Valdez trotted beside me. *"Slow down, Blondie."*

"Gloriana, wait." Blade was right behind me. "Stay near the house. It's not safe in the dark."

"It's not that dark. Full moon tonight. Go away." I had a full head of steam and kept walking. "Both of you, just leave me alone." I was making pretty good time despite high heels and soft grass. I could still hear the music, but I'd put some distance between me and the tents where most of the crowd had gathered. Blade had fallen back a bit to give me space, but Valdez was right beside me.

"Gloriana, stop!" Blade ordered.

"Go to hell." I gasped and wobbled. A sharp pain. Hot, sliding through my arm.

"Hell? Isn't that where all blood-sucking vampires go anyway?"

Twenty-two

The voice was out of my worst nightmares. And the smell . . . I'd know it anywhere. Olive wood. Westwood. Where? I looked down at the arrow sticking out of my arm. It hurt like the devil himself was using his pitchfork on me. *Pull it out.* Arms wrapped around me, digging the arrow into my flesh.

"Ow! Shit! Let me go!" I did my best to break free from the two men who'd grabbed me. Then I felt the prick of a sharp point over my heart and froze. I'm brave but not stupid. I wasn't about to stake *myself* by making a wrong move.

Valdez was going nuts, attacking the men, his powerful jaws clamping down on one man's leg. But apparently they wore protective clothing because the guy kicked at the dog, but didn't release me or scream in pain.

"Valdez, go get help." At least I had the presence of mind to order him away. The goons had guns strapped at their waists and I doubted Valdez was bulletproof. Of course my pooch looked back at Blade first for permission, then raced away toward the house or the tents. Somewhere. I had a little thing like trying not to die to concentrate on.

Two muscle men held me at stake point. Good-bye, world. I looked at Blade and sent him a mental message to save himself. Blade made a vamp move toward me, but stopped when he realized that I could be finished off with one thrust.

I tried my own vamp move, but a day without Bloody Merry and arms of steel holding me kept *that* from happening.

"Give it up, Blade. That is your name, isn't it? I don't think a dog can save you or your woman." Westwood landed on the grass a few feet from Jerry. So he did climb fences, the sneaky bastard. I recognized him from his pictures and the shop. Joe Ordinary with tinted glasses and a bow and arrow pointed at Blade's chest.

My heart leaped into my throat. Which would have been a good thing if I really could have managed it. Someone tries to stake you, you just make your heart jump out of the way. Okay, so I was hysterical.

"Tell your men to let her go, Westwood. I think I have what you want." Blade's smile made my insides clench. He was showing his fangs. Which even in the moonlight obviously would make an impressive addition to any necklace.

I tried another vamp move, no go. So I ground my heel into the foot of the man on my right. Damn, steel toed boots?

"A fine trophy. I believe I have you both where I want you. Smile, pretty lady. Let me see what you've got." Westwood actually grinned, arrogant bastard.

"I'll show you—" The stake jabbed me, drawing blood. "Take him down, Jerry."

Blade was behind Westwood and had a knife to the man's throat before you could say "vamp whammy."

"Well, hell. I guess I underestimated you." Westwood decided I was a good consolation prize and aimed his arrow at my chest. "Cut my throat and my men will finish off your little friend. My final gift to you."

"And what would you have my final gift to you be?" Blade's voice was pure steel. As hard and sharp as the knife gleaming in his hand. As his "little friend," I had to admire Blade's control. I knew he wanted to rip into Westwood in the worst way.

"Let me go. Then my men will release your woman." Westwood got points for guts. His voice quavered slightly, but his arrow never wavered.

It was aimed at my heart. Wasn't that overkill? Hah, hah. I was having a major meltdown, but didn't dare give in to it. If Blade could hang tough, so could I. Even though there was an arrow sticking out of my arm that the guy on my right thought needed to be jerked around to keep me in line. I blinked back tears of pain, not daring to take my eyes off Westwood.

"Prove you mean what you say. Put down your bow and arrow, Westwood. That *is* your name, isn't it?" Blade stared at me for an endless moment, telling me to be brave. Somehow he would save me. Save me? When he could take out Westwood?

My throat closed and my eyes filled again. I couldn't ask him to abandon his revenge for Mac on my account. I struggled against the hands gripping me. If I could just fling them off . . . But Westwood obviously hired serious muscle and I was losing blood from my arm and now from my left boob. I froze when that damned stake pricked me again.

"Kill him, Jerry. No way is he going to let me go." I had to get Blade to save himself. "Look at what he's got around his neck. You have to make him pay." The infamous horrible, totally appalling fang necklace.

Blade jerked and Westwood finally dropped his bow as blood welled from a cut on his neck. Blade's pain-filled gaze met mine.

"You will let the woman go, Westwood. Now."

"Not while you've got a knife at my throat." Westwood actually had the nerve to grab Blade's arm. Not that it did any good. He was no match for a vamp in top form. And Blade, his plaid a sharp contrast to Westwood's camouflage, fairly vibrated with vamp power. More blood ran down West-wood's neck and you could see the fight go out of him.

"What do you want us to do, boss?"

I gasped when the stake pressed deeper into the swell of those breasts I'd been so determined to show off. If I got out of this alive, I was wearing a Kevlar turtleneck.

"Release her, Westwood." Blade's fangs were full out and I could feel the tension in Westwood's men but I couldn't read their minds. They had on the same damned glasses Ryan had worn. Westwood wore them too. But Westwood's hired guns had to be scared witless to be in the presence of real vampires.

Of course they didn't release me. I was their only leverage. I let my own fangs run out and snarled.

"See these? They're nothing compared to what's coming. Your boss can't save you. Our dog is going to bring back a hoard of hungry vampires. If you want to live, you'd better run right now."

"They take orders from me, vampire." Westwood still sounded calm. The guy had nerves of steel. "Let *me* go, Blade, and I'll order my men to release the woman."

"Don't do it, Jerry. We'd be fools to trust his promises."

"I give you my hunter's oath." Westwood's eyes gleamed behind his tinted lenses. "And the word of a Westwood."

"The word of a Westwood?" I managed a laugh. "Yeah, right. Where's my Bible? Swear on that and we might believe you." That got a reaction from Westwood. He stiffened and looked wild-eyed and up, like he expected lightning to strike or something.

I croaked out another laugh. "What? You don't think vamps read the Bible? How would you like me to quote scripture?"

Blade was giving me looks, like shut up and run if I got the chance. Hey, I was buying us time. The vamp reinforcements had to be here soon. I was terrified Jerry was going to do something heroic and get himself staked on my account.

"Just let me go." Westwood was pale but didn't fold, the tough big game hunter until the end. Me, I was shaking like a bikini model in a blizzard. "My men will release the woman, I promise."

"I feel better, don't you, Jerry? But before you let their boss go, I wonder if we should ask Frick and Frack here if they really want to let a vampire go." Their grips on my arms tightened. I didn't need to be a mind reader to know they weren't about to take that chance. I looked down at the wooden stake still drawing blood.

Okay, if I'd ever needed vamp power, this was it. I stared at the wood poking my breast. I was dimly aware of barking and shouts coming toward us as I focused my thoughts on one outcome. Please, please, please let this work. I narrowed my eyes, held my breath and practically wet my pants as I concentrated.

Heat. Heat. Come on, baby, light my fire. A wisp of smoke. A flash. Woo hoo! The men screamed when the stake burst into flames. I'd done it! Hot freakin' damn! I fell on my butt, suddenly free as they ran for their lives.

Good move. Glinda the Good Witch flew in at an angle, one of her gold heels catching Frick on the back of his head as he scrambled up and over the fence. Scarecrow and Lion were a blur of fur and straw as they took off after Frack.

"Gloriana." Blade was beside me.

I lay back on the grass, my head spinning. The smell of burning lace and, gulp, flesh, hit me right where I lived and everything went dark for a moment. Someone touched me. I focused enough to recognize Flo as she pulled the arrow from my arm and pressed her hands gently against the wound. I could feel vamp magic surging through me, healing, working a miracle.

I sighed as someone raised my head and pressed a glass to my lips. I drank thirstily. Transylvania's finest. Did they have a web site?

Everything was still hazy when strong arms lifted me and carried me toward the house. Blade again. I drank in his familiar scent. It beat the hell out of my own reek.

"Jerry, did you get Westwood? Tell me you took the bastard apart." I managed to focus on his face. He looked beyond grim. I took that as a no.

"When I saw you catch fire, Gloriana . . ." Blade swallowed. "I sliced his arm. He won't be drawing a bow any time soon. But forget that. Are you all right?"

"She's more than all right, Blade. Everyone saw. She made the stake catch fire. She was brilliant." Damian pushed a pillow under my head as Blade laid me on a sofa in the living room.

"Move, both of you." Flo pushed the men out of the way. "Let me see your breast, Glory. The stake hurt you. And the fire."

"Maybe she should get out of that tight top." Damian peered over Flo's shoulder.

"Idiot. No peep show for you. Turn your back. Jeremiah, hand me your knife." Flo smiled at me. "You are a little scorched, Glory, but I'm so proud of you. Setting a stake on fire! Damian's right about that. You were brilliant." Flo cut the laces on my bustier and my boobs sprang free, shouting hallelujah. I put my hands over my nipples.

"Thanks, Flo, I think I'll live now."

"Hush, let me heal you." She clucked and put her hand over the burn and laceration on my breast. "Look at you. This must hurt like the devil."

"Yeah, actually." I gasped when she pressed against it and then sighed as the pain vanished. "I love you, Flo. Will you marry me?"

"I think she's delirious. Someone bring her another drink of that Fangtastic." Flo tossed a pillow over my chest and studied my face. "How do you feel, Glory?"

I took inventory. Arm, check. Breast, check. No aches, no pain and I was bloody brilliant. I sat up and looked around the room. Way too many people stared at me like I was Damian's surprise of the night. I clutched the pillow with both hands.

"Show's over, folks. It's party time." I struggled to my feet, then wobbled and had to lean on Flo. Some people applauded and I bowed. I felt my cape slide over my shoulders. I pulled it around me and dropped the pillow.

"Thanks." I looked back to see who had done it. Blade. Still looking grim. "Hey, I'm okay."

"Sit down, Gloriana. You've had a shock." Blade put his arm around me when Flo stepped aside.

"We've both had a shock. What did you think of my pyrotechnics?" I patted his cheek. "Bet you didn't think I had it in me."

"Nothing you do surprises me, lass. I'm just sorry I failed to take out Westwood." Blade was obviously taking the blame for the whole fiasco.

"You kept him from killing me, Jerry. How can I ever thank you?" I reached up to kiss his cheek. I could think of a few gratitude moves that would please us both. Later. "You chose me over revenge. A hard choice."

"No choice at all, lass. I've seen one friend staked by the bastard, I'll not see another." Jerry faked a smile. "I'll get him another day."

Friend. I stepped back, not even close to faking a smile. "Of course you will. Westwood's days are numbered."

Blade started to say something when Damian stepped between us and handed me a glass of Fangtastic. I gulped it gratefully and felt instantly stronger.

"Where the hell was our security? No way should this have happened. On *my* grounds." Damian shook his head. "I'm so sorry, Gloriana."

I had the same question about the security because it beat the hell out of agonizing over being Blade's "friend." At least tonight we'd dodged the Westwood bullet, so to speak. I turned to Damian.

"Maybe you need to electrify that fence. But who would have suspected Westwood of having the guts to crash a vamp Halloween party?"

"Westwood's guts are ours. It's only a matter of time." Flo pushed her brother out of the way. "Does he really wear a fang necklace?"

"Tell you later." I glanced at Blade, but he'd turned away to stare out at the lawn through the open French doors. I could tell by the set of his shoulders that he was barely holding it together. I took yet another goblet of Fangtastic. This one from Hercules. The music started and I felt Valdez warm against my legs.

Glinda the Good Witch and her entourage hurried into the room, their frustration evident. Even Sheba's tail twitched as she made a beeline to Valdez and rubbed against his chest. I heard him growl and put my hand on his head.

"Any luck?"

Freddy shook his head. "He had one of those Hummers waiting for him on the side of the hill near the fence. It was armored, like a tank. There was no point in chasing him. He'll just park somewhere and wait for daylight." Freddy straightened his mane and looked me over. "You all right?"

"I'm fine except for the fact that I ruined a perfectly good bustier." I looked down at the scorched and mangled lace contraption that had fallen to the floor. I refrained from stomping it, barely. Good riddance to that torture device.

"Come with me, Glory. We'll raid Damian's closet." Flo herded me out of the room and up the stairs. Inside Damian's bedroom, we bypassed the coffin bed and Flo flung open the door to a room-sized closet.

"I think a silk shirt." Flo frowned. "Too much black. Here, this will do. Short sleeves. Knot it at the waist. But keep it open and sexy. The night's not over yet." She tugged off the cape and helped me slip on the shirt.

The burgundy silk felt good on my skin. I glanced down and saw the scar where I'd almost been staked. The mark

would be gone by morning, but I'd never forget the feeling.
I'd been an inch away from death. I shuddered and leaned
against the doorjamb.

"Yes, a near miss, Glory. You are still, as you say, shook
up." Flo smiled sadly.

"You should have seen it, Flo. That fang necklace. And
knowing Mac's . . ." I slid to the floor and put my head on
my knees. I felt Flo's hand on my back.

"And Blade let Westwood go?"

I looked up and took a shaky breath. "Yeah. For me. And
right now he's probably wondering what the hell he was
thinking."

"I'm sure Jeremiah would make the same choice again if
he had to. He loves you, Glory."

"He called me his friend." Not crying. Not crying. I
breathed through the urge.

"Do we not love our friends?" Flo put out her hand and
pulled me to my feet.

"Yes, we do." I gave her a quick hug. "Thanks again. For
healing me."

"Anytime. But not soon, okay?" Flo was suddenly all
business. "Let's head downstairs. Let everyone see our heroine, especially the handsome men. Jeremiah and Damian
will be worrying."

Flo took my arm and guided me past the bed and out the
door. I was getting my second wind, thanks to two glasses of
Fangtastic. Heroine? Had to love that. But then I saw Blade
standing at the foot of the stairs. He wasn't overjoyed. He'd
missed his chance at Westwood. Because of me.

Tony Crapetta hovered anxiously near the door to the porch.
"Get out your money, Jerry. Tony, I'm ready for that dance."

"Money?" I heard Damian ask. "I'll dance with you,
Gloriana, for free."

I looked Damian over. The sheets on the coffin bed had
been rumpled. Had he been a busy boy tonight? Not worth

thinking about. Of course I didn't really want to dance. But I *had* to get out of there.

I pulled Tony outside. At least he managed a credible two-step, though I could tell from reading his mind that he was pretty confused by all the weird shit going on around him. Flying vamps, flaming stakes and hot women asking him to dance. Too bad he wasn't allowed to tell anyone about Damian's parties.

Yes, I was hot, flaming as a matter of fact. But when the music ended, I was running down, big time. Adrenaline can take you only so far.

"Thanks for the dance, Tony." Valdez had stayed close, right on the edge of the dance floor. At least he'd been blessedly silent in front of Crapetta.

"Sure, Miss Gloriana. You look a little . . . tired. How about we go in here and see the show?"

"Sure." *Here* was the third tent. I collapsed on a chair facing the stage set at one end. The Wizard I'd seen earlier was doing some pretty amazing things with his magic wand. A frog hopped out of a shifter's low-cut bodice and I wondered if Froggie could be the same one who'd been Prince Charming in tent one. Probably. Queen Liz sat front and center, staring a hole in the wizard as she quietly shredded the pleated ruff she'd ripped off her own neck.

"Kenneth is here." Flo's voice whispered inside my head. *"Join us in the library if you feel up to it."*

Did I feel up to it? Not really. But I had to know if Kenneth had killed Margie. I murmured an excuse to Tony and got up, Valdez on my heels. I headed for the house and remembered the way to the library even though I'd never actually been there except in Damian's warped imagination. I stepped inside and shut the door behind me.

Kenneth stood in front of the fireplace. He'd gone for a Rhett Butler look tonight. His chin was up but he was looking anywhere but at the vamps confronting him.

Diana, Scarlett O'Hara in red taffeta to his Rhett, sat in a chair close by. Her face was pale and streaked with tears. Obviously she and Kenneth had something going. Since before Margie's death?

"How can you accuse him of hurting Marguerite? Where is your proof?" She wiped her wet cheeks with shaking hands.

"We don't need proof, Diana." Richard Mainwaring stood beside Flo. "All Kenneth need do is tell us he didn't do it and this will be forgotten."

"Tell them, Kenny." Diana jumped up and ran to his side. Or as close as she could get in a hoop skirt. "Tell them you didn't do it. You said you and Margie had an open relationship. That she didn't care if you and I had an affair." She stared up at him, obviously didn't like what she saw and stepped back. "Say you didn't kill her."

"I . . ." He held out his hand to Diana but she shook her head. "Diana, please."

"Not until you tell everyone here that you didn't kill Margie."

Kenneth dropped his hand and looked wildly around the room. "Damn it, Mainwaring, get out of my head. You too, Blade."

Hmm. I looked at Richard. He was definitely concentrating. Blade was on the other side of the room, obviously very intent on Kenneth too. I didn't bother. I'd had enough mental gymnastics for one night.

Kenneth pressed his hands to his eyes. "Florence, stop it! All of you! Just stop it!"

"We know the truth now, Kenneth, so don't bother to deny it. Why? Why did you kill Marguerite?" Flo stepped up and poked him in the chest.

"She wouldn't let me go!" Ken's eyes blazed and Diana gasped. "She treated me like her chattel. She *made* me so she owned me." He looked at Flo. "I'm a man. Oh, yes, she gave me permission to have affairs. Permission." He ran his hands through his short cropped hair. "And she took her own lovers. But I always had to belong to her. Body and soul."

"Liar. You wanted her money. You could have left her at any time. But with only the clothes on your back." Flo looked like a vengeful goddess in Kevlar, her bright yellow targets quivering with her rage.

"Marguerite didn't treat me fairly. I'd earned what I asked for. But she laughed at me." Kenneth looked around the room. If he was looking for sympathy, he was out of luck. For some reason his gaze fixed on me.

"You understand, Gloriana. You left Blade and look how hard it's been. You have to work, sell used clothes, for God's sake."

My well of sympathy for Kenny's plight had just run dry. "I make an honest living, Kenneth. I'll never be ashamed of that."

Kenneth realized he was done for. Diana had crossed the room to get away from him. Blade had his hand on his sword and Flo and Mainwaring looked ready to rip Kenneth apart. With a cry, Kenneth ran past me to the door. I started to make a grab for him and Valdez snarled.

"Let him go." Mainwaring looked at me then at each one in the room. "This is over and he knows it. I'll take care of it." He kissed Flo's cheek and silently left the room.

Diana slumped in a chair. Flo went to her side and pulled her to her feet. "Did I ever tell you about my lover in Budapest? He had a Spanish wife, but because he was tired of her, he didn't bother to tell me she existed." Flo pulled Diana out of the room, chattering away about lovers, gypsy curses and a Lipizzan stallion.

I locked eyes with Blade, aware that Valdez had left us alone together.

"Quite an evening." I know. Inane. But I was running on empty. Too much had happened. I'd almost died. And, while the vamp magic is cool, it takes a lot out of you.

"I can't believe he killed Marguerite." Blade was beside me and took my hand. "I know he loved her once."

"Once." I felt his rough hand cradling mine. He handled me carefully. Always. And gave me my freedom, though I know he'd hated to, control freak that he is. We *were* friends. Hopefully always would be. As for lovers—

"Jeremiah, there you are. I've looked everywhere." Mara stood in the doorway. Cleopatra. Complete with asp twined around her neck. The silk toga, which left one shoulder bare, could have been painted on her slim body. Her makeup gave her eyes an exotic slant that was positively mesmerizing.

Bitch. She was doing the whammy on me. To get me out of the way? I threw up a block, though it zapped the last of my waning strength.

"Nice costume, Mara." The asp moved. Okay. It was real. "Bet you win the contest."

"I don't care about that. Tell me what happened with Westwood. All the vampires are talking about how brave Jeremiah was. That he drew blood." She grabbed his arm. "How did Westwood get away? Surely you didn't let him go to save *her.*"

Her. Me. Glory, not glorious, with my bent tail, horns lost—God knows where—and Damian's silk shirt in lieu of the scorched lace on my bustier. I was obviously a nonstarter in Mara world.

"He escaped because I lost my concentration, Mara. I'm sorry." Blade was staring at me. He didn't blame me for his lost concentration, did he? He shook his head and touched my hand. "A whole bloody forest could catch fire and I should still be able to get the job done." He turned back to Mara. "We'll get him another night. I promise."

"Glory, *cara.* You need this." Damian appeared in the doorway and handed me yet another goblet of Fangtastic. By now I was positively swimming in the stuff, but I took a token sip.

"Thanks." I set the glass on a nearby table. "And thanks for the shirt. I'll have it cleaned and return it to you."

"Keep it." Damian took my arm. "I still haven't shown you my dungeon."

"Another night, Damian." I looked down at Valdez. "What say we go home, puppy? I think I've had all the excitement I can stand for one night."

"But we haven't had the surprise yet." Damian eased me out the door, ignoring Blade's ominous grumble and Valdez's growl. "Come outside. Look up."

I stepped out on the terrace. I had to admit the warm Fangtastic and now the cool night air helped clear my head. The band finished a song, then there was a drum roll.

"Ladies and gentlemen. Look to the skies. I give you nature at its finest." Damian made a terrific ringmaster of his own paranormal circus.

The strange and the exotic came out of the tents. Lacy appeared with her werewolf in tow. She looked me over, gave me a hug, then handed me my purse, which she'd found on the lawn.

Showtime. We all gasped as hundreds, thousands, tens of thousands of bats flew overhead in perfect formation. They soared and swooped, almost noiseless except for an occasional keening sound. More than one vamp suddenly morphed into bat form and joined them. CiCi snapped her magic wand in two when Tin Man threw off his cap and headed skyward.

"What do you think, Glory?" Damian had his arm around me, an inch away from copping a feel. Hello? Hadn't I been scorched there less than an hour ago?

He nodded toward the sky and the bats formed letters. *G.L.O.R.Y.* Aw, gee. Was that sweet or what? His fingers fondled my right boob. Oh, what a great guy. He'd been careful to grope my uninjured boob. I stopped him with a look.

"I think you throw a heck of a party and I think I'm flat partied out." I saw Mara clinging to Blade as they looked skyward. Tony Crapetta stood a few feet away, gaping at the bat spectacular. "Tony, you got a car here?"

"Sure, Miss Gloriana. Did you see that? They spelled your name."

"Mr. Sabatini's a swell host, isn't he? Now can I get you to take me and my dog home? Fifty percent off anything in the store. I just got in a new leisure suit."

Tony looked uncertainly at Damian.

"Very well. Another night, Gloriana. You must come back alone and we will . . . play." Damian brushed my hair back from my face and dropped a kiss on my lips. Then he nodded at Tony. "Take her home and see her safely inside her apartment if you value your life."

"Yes, sir, Mr. Sabatini." Tony held out his arm. "This way, Miss Gloriana. My car's out back."

I leaned on him a little, more drained than I wanted to admit. Valdez stayed mercifully silent, though I could tell he was on high alert as he scanned the parking area. Behind me, I heard Damian announce the winner of the costume contest. The Queen of the Damned, I mean Nile, of course. I looked back to see Mara beaming and brandishing her asp. Blade was watching me leave, but didn't make a move to come after me. And didn't that suck?

"You ever ride in a genuine vintage VW bus, Miss Gloriana?" Tony wrenched open the door of a pea green van and put his hand on my elbow. "Step up now. Careful."

Valdez jumped in beside me and I threw my arm around him. He did smell like a fruit salad. A tear escaped and ran down my cheek. Fortunately, Tony was too busy cranking the engine, which didn't seem inclined to start, to notice. Perfect, just perfect.

Twenty-three

🦇

Twenty-four hours later and I was comfortably settled in my living room surrounded by girlfriends. A day's healing, vamp sleep had me back to my old self. Sort of. Physically I was okay. Mentally? I was up one minute because I'd, yes, made a stake catch fire. And down the next because neither Blade nor Damian had rushed over tonight to check on me.

So I was taking a night off. Di had hooked me up with a student who was reliable and I'd left Lacy training her to run the shop. The fact that Lacy had been glowing after a night of hot sex with her wolf man hadn't helped my attitude any.

I'd decided a *Seinfeld* marathon might cure what ailed us. We needed to laugh and Flo got us going when she insisted Kramer had to be a shifter.

"Look at that hair, Glory. I'll bet he howls at the full moon. If I could just smell him . . ."

Flo had appropriated a case of Fangtastic from Damian as a get-well present and we were at the point where someone should propose a toast.

Diana and CiCi were trying, but still didn't share the festive mood. They held their goblets high anyway. It was up to me to come up with something brilliant.

"Here's to female vamp power. Can't beat it." I know, pretty lame, but true enough to satisfy the moment.

"I'll drink to that." Flo smiled and clinked her glass against mine. "This is nice. I like having girlfriends."

"A lot less complicated than boyfriends." I stared down at my glass. "Jerry lost his chance at Westwood because of me and Damian—"

"Damian is no one's boyfriend. Not for more than a nanosecond." Diana gulped her drink and reached for a bottle to refill her glass.

"She's right, Glory. You'd do well to concentrate on Jeremiah." Flo picked up the remote. "Ready for another episode?"

"Not yet." Jeremiah. Somehow I felt like things had changed between us. And not for the better. But I wasn't in the mood to dissect my love life.

"What's going on with Richard, Flo?" I'd expected him to be here, panting after Flo as usual.

Florence glanced at Diana. "He and I are taking a break. This holy crusader deal he's got going is more complicated than I thought. He's very . . . ruthless."

"Ruthless?" I cocked an eyebrow at her. "This from a woman who was ready to rip a little old lady's throat out because she stepped in front of her at a shoe sale?"

"*I'm* a little old lady and no one gets between me and my Ferragamos." Flo's smile was an evil promise of retribution in the event that ever happened again.

"So what's really wrong with Richard? He's kind of grown on me." I know, this was a real turn around. But I liked the way he'd handled Kenneth. I really hadn't wanted to be at the takedown. And it would have been horrific for Diana.

"You were there!" Flo put down her glass. "'I'll take care of it.' he says. He treats me like a helpless female."

CiCi shook her head. "They all do. The male dinosaur vampires anyway. We need younger men. Men who understand that women are more than their equal."

"Amen." Diana took a deep swallow of her drink then sighed. "But what Richard does is a noble undertaking. When vampires are betrayed, where else are we going to get justice?"

Time for a subject change. "CiCi, what happened to Tin Man last night?"

CiCi grimaced. "Apparently the bats have more appeal to him than I do. I hope he flies to Devil's Hole and straight down to hell." She clinked her glass against Flo's. "I say we give up men. Derek is teaching me to use the Internet. I've discovered a Web site devoted to a woman's pleasure and with the most amazing . . . toys. BigOdotcom."

"Glory, get out your laptop." Flo looked at Diana who'd snorted. "Come on, admit it, Di. You can please yourself better than ninety percent of male lovers can please you."

"Not arguing." Diana drained her glass again. "This stuff is good. While you've got the laptop out, Glory, let's order some more."

"In a minute." I put down my glass and walked to the kitchen. Valdez lay stretched across the threshold and I stepped over him to open the snack cabinet. I headed back out to the living room with a bag of Cheetos in my hand and a bowl.

"Now you're talking, Blondie. Let's celebrate. Westwood's gone to ground and I'm surrounded by beautiful powerful women." The dog sidled up to Flo and was rewarded with an ear rub.

"Some day, doggy, you and I are going to have a long talk. About who and what you really are, no?" She leaned down to rub her chin against his head.

"No, I mean, yes. I mean, who's going to eat those Cheetos anyway?" Valdez licked his chops.

"I am." I poured a sample into the bowl and picked up one fluffy piece. I smelled it and, idiot that I am, my fangs ran out, the vampire version of an erection.

"You're going to actually eat? What a concept. You can't imagine how hard it is to run a coffee bar where we bake muffins all day." Diana jumped up. "Any chocolate in the kitchen?"

"I think Lacy left a candy bar here last week when she decided to go on a diet. We're supposed to be holding it in case she weakens. Check the top of the fridge."

"Eating. What I wouldn't give for just a taste of something sweet." CiCi had a wistful look. "I vaguely remember the *mousse chocolat* my father's chef made for us. So rich and delicious. It was centuries ago."

"Found it." Diana came in waving a Hershey bar.

"Break it in half." CiCi looked at Flo. "Are you going to try to eat too?"

Flo shook her head. "No, thanks. Been there, done that." She picked up a Cheeto and dropped it into Valdez's mouth. "But you girls go ahead. If you need healing, I'm your woman."

"Healing?" Diana sniffed her half of the candy bar. "Is this stuff going to hurt us?"

"No pain, no gain." CiCi licked the chocolate and sighed. "I'm going for it. Flo, you're on standby."

"I'm going for it too." I leaned back and was about to drop the Cheeto into my mouth, when someone buzzed from downstairs.

I jumped up and hit the button for the intercom. "Who is it?"

Could Jerry have decided to stop by? I glanced back at the girls. CiCi and Diana each took a bite of chocolate and moaned with ecstacy.

"Delivery for Ms. Gloriana St. Clair. I can just leave it here by the door, ma'am."

"Fine. Do that." I threw open the apartment door, Valdez at my heels as we ran downstairs. I saw a delivery van pull away from the curb when I looked through the window beside the front door. A package. I opened the door and nudged it with my toe. Could Westwood have sent a bomb? A last act of revenge? But the large padded envelope wasn't ticking when I nudged it again. I leaned down and saw who'd sent it. *Hmm.*

"Okay, Glory. What's that?" Flo stood at the top of the stairs. "Bring it up. The chocolate's gone and Diana and CiCi have survived."

"Good." I hugged the package to my chest. A present from Jerry.

I dropped down on the couch and ripped open the large envelope. A Kevlar vest. I unfolded it. Oh, wow. Not just any old vest. Painted on the front was a familiar yellow shield.

"Wonder Woman." Diana laughed. "Who sent you that?" She made a grab for the note that had slid out with the vest, but I got it first. I read it out loud.

"Gloriana, you are brave and amazing. But wear this the next time you take on the bad guys. Blade."

Flo, Diana and CiCi sighed.

"Now *that's* romantic." Diana swiped at her brimming eyes.

"You think?" I stared down at the vest, then at the note. Yeah, for Blade the gesture was downright sappy. I grinned and picked up the Cheetos bag again.

"I don't know why I'm afraid to eat a Cheeto. I'm Wonder Woman. Right, girls?"

"Careful, Glory," Flo warned as I dropped the first bite into my mouth.

The crunch, the taste. I was in Cheeto heaven. I chewed, then braced myself and swallowed. Would it go down? Yes! I popped another one into my mouth. Then another. My stomach clenched, but I kept chewing. I've always liked to live on the edge, you know? And now I had the vest to prove it.

Read on for a special preview of
Gerry Bartlett's next novel

Real Vampires
Live Large

Available now from Berkley Books!

Whump, *whump, whump, whump.*

"Please remain calm. The fire is out. The fire is out. Firemen are on their way and are clearing the smoke out of the building."

I was wet, cold and lying on concrete. My baby dolls were tangled around my hips and Valdez was barking into my ear.

"Fire?" I took a breath. Smoke. Oh, shit.

"Yeah, fire. I dragged you up here." Valdez bumped me with his cold nose. *"But you're okay now, Blondie. Right?"*

"Fire!" I swallowed and sat up. A helicopter sporting the logo of a local TV station hovered overhead. Nice. My chubby thighs would be on the evening news.

"You dragged me up here? Flo! Diana!" I jumped up and looked around. I may sleep like the dead, but once the sun goes down, I'm operating on all cylinders. I saw the other resident vamps—Flo, Diana and a guy I knew lived on the third floor—laid out on the roof. They were all wet and all in various stages of stirring. The sun had obviously just slipped below the horizon.

"*Yep. I'd say our old buddy Brent Westwood decided to take a parting shot.*" Valdez growled and leaned against my leg. "*Somebody threw a firebomb into your shop and the fire spread from there. Whoever did it had a hell of a nerve pulling that in broad daylight. Of course it's Monday and the shop was closed. Mugs and Muffins was probably open though. I wonder—*"

"Shut up, Valdez. I . . . My God!" My legs folded and I sat hard on the concrete again. Just about anything, from a wooden skewer to a chopstick, could take a vamp out while she's sleeping. And a fire . . . No amount of healing sleep could bring a vamp back from being a crispy critter. I rubbed my dog's ears. He'd *saved* me.

"How do you know this was Westwood?" We'd been fighting off the big game hunter who thought vamps were the biggest game of all ever since I'd arrived in Austin. After a recent showdown, we all figured he'd move on to easier prey. Parting shot.

"*Who else? People love your shop. Only an asshole like Westwood—*"

Whump. Whump. Whump. Whump. "Medical assistance is on its way. Please wave if you're all right."

"Yeah, right. Smile for the camera, you mean." I picked up my sodden sheet and threw it over my head.

"How are the others?" I pushed to my feet again and wobbled over to Flo like Casper the not-so-friendly ghost, Valdez at my heels. Of course my roommate *would* sleep in the raw. Valdez had draped a wet sheet over her but the rotors were blowing everything on the roof all to hell. Flo sat up, giving the camera a nice shot of her boobs.

"We're on camera, Flo. You might want to wrap your sheet a little tighter."

"What's happened?" She pushed back her dark hair and looked around, then up. "They'd better not be taking my picture. I need my hair dryer, my makeup."

Hopefully, they didn't have audio. I could hear the lead-in now. "Fire victim runs for blow dryer as rescuers battle blaze."

I looked at Valdez. "My shop?" My voice cracked. I'd built Vintage Vamp's Emporium from nothing into a thriving business that actually supported me.

"I figure it's probably gutted." Valdez sat down and scratched his ear. *"Of course I was pretty busy. When the smoke alarms went off, I had to clear you guys out. And the stairwell was solid smoke."* He coughed, sneezed, then looked at me for sympathy.

"My hero!" I dropped to my knees and threw my arms around his neck. I sniffed wet fur, a mix of dog and smoke. Valdez coughed again and I looked at him, really looked at him. "Seriously. Are you all right?"

"Yeah, I'm okay." Cough, cough.

Okay, now he was faking it. I sat back. Maybe he deserved a little slack. "How did you manage to get all of us out?"

"It wasn't easy. It was still daylight, so I had to pile you guys up inside the stairwell with the door open for ventilation until the sun went down. I had a hell of a time keeping all of you from frying."

"Frying. Oh my God."

"We are alive, no?" Flo sat down and put her arm around me. Her Italian accent comes out when she's stressed. "And once again our puppy has saved the day." She patted the dog's head. "We are dead without you, *signor.*"

Valdez puffed out his chest and looked up. *"You think I'll be on the evening news? You know they're going to want an interview."*

"Sure. Right. Talking dog saves sleeping vampires. Sorry, but you'll have to settle for a bag of Cheetos."

"Now you're talking."

I gave him a final ear rub, then walked over to check on Diana. She ran the coffee shop downstairs. If my shop was toast, so was hers.

"Di, are you okay?"

She coughed and sat up. "What happened?" She wore cute red plaid flannel jammies and her sheet, wet of course, coordinated in navy blue.

"Fire. Someone firebombed my shop, probably yours too if Westwood did it." I reached out and pulled her to her feet.

"What?" She glanced up, then shot the finger at the helicopter. "Buzz off, vultures." She headed for the door to the stairs. "I've got to check on the shop." Mugs and Muffins. Like me, Diana has to support herself. If her shop had been hit too . . . Well, this was really, really bad. For both of us.

I grabbed her before she could open the door. "Wait. The firemen are working their way up here. The building's full of smoke."

"My shoes!" Flo was on her feet, her sheet wrapped into a strapless sheath.

I don't think the fire got that far. The building's security system went off as soon as I heard something crash through Blondie's shop window. The fire trucks got here pretty quick after that." Valdez spent my sleeping hours on hyper alert. Thank God.

"I say, how did we get wet?" The third floor vampire had joined us. He was a sight in an old fashioned nightshirt, but good looking in a college professor kind of way. His British accent was cute. We'd met him at some vamp meetings. Dennis, David, something like that.

"Sprinkler system in the halls. You got wet when I dragged you out of bed and up the stairs to the roof."

"But my door was locked. Double deadbolts." The prof stared at Valdez.

"So I did a little damage. I couldn't just let you guys fry."

Fry. I swallowed a lump the size of Valdez's food bowl.

"Brilliant! You don't even know me." The male vamp had obviously just found his new best friend.

"I saved all the vamps in the building." Valdez was visibly preening, and why not? *"It's my thing. You'd think some of those shifters would have been around, but no such luck. So I handled it."*

Shifters. Shape-shifters, that is, live in a couple of the apartments. A were-cat, my friend and employee, lives right across the hall. I took a shaky breath and felt sick again. This time I couldn't blame it on Cheetos or an evil mind meld. If Valdez hadn't been who or what he was . . .

The stair door slammed open and three firemen dressed in full bright-yellow gear ran onto the roof. The first one threw off his helmet and ran his hand through his short brown hair.

"Anybody hurt? You folks okay?"

We stayed huddled together, looking appropriately shocked and disoriented.

"The fire. It didn't spread to the apartments, did it?" If I had lost everything I owned . . . I've had to start over before, but it's hard, really hard.

"No, ma'am. Sprinkler and alarm systems saved the day." The fireman sounded pure Texan. "You got good response time too. The fire itself didn't have a chance to spread upstairs. Just the smoke."

"The sprinklers didn't go off in the apartments, did they?" Flo was suddenly right beside the fireman and grabbed his arm. "I have a most valuable collection that will be ruined if it gets wet."

Flo's collection of Ferragamos, Prada, Manolos, et al. The fireman looked down at her, obviously liked the way Flo's sheet was slipping and patted her hand.

"No, ma'am. Only the hallways have sprinklers. Fire's out now. Smoke's just about cleared. Do any of you folks need the paramedics?" The fireman whipped out his walkie talkie when Diana coughed.

"No! Really! I'm fine. Just the night air and wet clothes." Diana managed a smile. "Can we go in now? I'm freezing."

Actually we were lucky. For mid-November in Austin, it was fairly cool, but not even close to freezing. Maybe I was being too literal. A vamp doesn't feel heat and cold like a mortal does. So I faked a shiver.

"Yeah, let's move inside if that's all right."

"One minute." The fireman spoke into a walkie-talkie. "Let me get the all clear." Another fireman showed up in the doorway with a stack of blankets. We each took one gratefully.

Whump. Whump. Whump. Whump. Channel whatever was getting this all on tape. Flo decided to take advantage and planted a big wet one of thanks on the cute fireman's lips after he announced we were good to go. Then we all hustled into the stairwell and out of camera view.

"What started the fire?" I looked at Valdez.

"Arson." The fireman had a grim look as he stopped at the top of the stairs. "Someone broke the windows in the stores downstairs and tossed in incendiary devices." The fireman couldn't take his eyes off Flo. She was busy rearranging her sheet again, flashing the entire crew. Probably unintentional. She was really anxious to check out that shoe collection.

The fireman's walkie-talkie squawked again. "How'd you folks get up here? The smoke alarm wake you?"

"Sure. Who could sleep through that?" Professor Vamp patted Valdez. "This fellow barked too, though. Just to be sure we knew to take it seriously."

"No kidding." The fireman, Flo attached to his side, gave Valdez an admiring glance. "But why are the doors knocked down? And who the hell could do that? I mean, three apartments look like they were hit with a battering ram . . ." Flo looked up into the fireman's eyes and he was under the whammy.

As damage control, it was a Band-Aid. We'd have to whammy every fireman who'd seen the doors Valdez had obviously knocked down. I looked at Di and the professor and they went to work on the other firemen coming down the stairs behind us. Before we got to the bottom, the guys had no memory of anything other than knocking the doors down themselves because they were looking for victims.

We stepped outside and I got my first look at what used to be a pretty cute vintage clothing shop. Thank God for sprinkler systems. The windows were shattered, the area right in front of them totaled. It didn't look like the fire had penetrated the closed door into the back room, though. I felt wobbly as I picked my way around broken glass. Diana cried out and I saw that Mugs and Muffins had received the same treatment. If Westwood had done this . . .

"Folks, you've got to let the paramedics look you over. It's our policy." Cute Fireman led Flo over to an ambulance. You can bet she wasn't letting anyone put a stethoscope to her barely beating heart. And, sure enough, the men around her smiled and nodded and let her walk back to us without a checkup. The whammy at work again.

"They won't bother us now. Let's go upstairs." She sniffed. "The whole building smells like smoke. My shoes had better not be ruined."

Diana looked at her with red eyes. "Your shoes? Your *shoes*? Excuse me? Do you see my shop? Glory's shop? We're out of business!"

I grabbed Diana's arm. "We'll be fine. Damian's bound to have insurance." Hope. Pray. Damian Sabatini was Flo's brother, and he owned the building. "Upstairs. Get a shower and some dry clothes."

"Electricity will be off for a while, people." Another fireman, a captain according to his helmet. "Here are some flashlights. But please just gather what you need for the night and make plans to sleep elsewhere. Until the building inspector gives the go ahead to occupy the residences."

I realized we were lucky no one had asked why we all were ready for bed at what must be seven in the evening. We were a pretty strange looking group.

We heard a shout and I saw Diana grabbed by two of her employees. I caught some snatches. Slow time of day. No customers so both workers had been in the back area making up a batch of the muffins the place was famous for. At least neither of them had been hurt.

A car pulled up behind the fire engine and a man jumped out. Damian aka Casanova. He's a sexy vampire, but I'm now immune. He'd played some dirty tricks on me while trying to add another notch to his bedpost.

Did I mention he's our landlord? I was actually glad to see him and his look of concern. *Please let him have insurance.* I sure didn't. I know. I know. But the premiums! I looked back at the shop. Maybe I'd rethink my priorities if my business survived this.

"Florence, Gloriana, are you all right?" He grabbed Flo and looked her over. "Diana?"

"We're all fine, Damian." Flo hugged him before we all turned to head upstairs.

"Wait!" Someone grabbed my arm.

"Donna Mitchell, Channel Six News. The fireman said this is your shop?" A female reporter dressed in a blazer and running shoes thrust a microphone near my mouth. I started to brush her off, then glanced at the front of my shop again.

"Yes. This is . . . *was* my place. Vintage Vamp's Emporium, offering fine clothing and accessories from the past at bargain prices." Okay, so I had to plug it, even if I had no idea if I even had a shop any more. Tears filled my eyes and the camera zoomed in. Nothing like a tragedy to boost ratings.

"Any idea what happened, Ms. . . . ?"

"Gloriana St. Clair." I hitched my slipping blanket up on my shoulders. My wet hair dripped into my eyes. I was damn mad and looking pitiful worked for me right now. Valdez pressed himself against my legs and looked up at me soulfully. "We all work night shifts, so my dog here helped wake us up." I patted him on the head and he showed his teeth in a doggy grin. "Someone did this on purpose."

"Are you saying this was arson?" The reporter was all business now, gesturing at the cameraman so he could pan to the broken and blackened windows.

"Absolutely." I looked directly at the camera when it was aimed at me again. "And I want to put whoever did this on notice. I *will* re-open. I will *not* just disappear."

"Gee, you make this sound like a hate crime. Are you, um, a minority?"

Blonde, blue-eyed white girl a minority? I smiled and read the reporter's mind. *Hmm.* I could set her straight—ha, ha—but why bother?

"I'm a woman, trying to support myself. Some people"— maybe I was digging a hole here—"don't like independence or people who are different."

The reporter thrust the microphone at Flo, who had somehow managed to pull her hair back into a chic ponytail, her sheet now a toga that Julius Caesar himself had probably taught her how to wrap.

"Are you Ms. St. Clair's partner?"

Flo grinned, obviously reading the reporter's mind too.

"Glory and I haven't been together long," she linked her arm through mine, "and the business is all hers. Me, I'm into new. I have a wonderful shoe collection, spared from the fire, thank God. I just hope Glory's business survives this." Flo actually kissed my cheek and I swear I jumped a foot.

"We're not—"

"Hush, Glory. Let me tell Donna about my shoes." Flo began rattling off designer names until the reporter's eyes glazed over and she signaled the cameraman to cut.

"I think we have enough. Excuse me, I see an arson investigator has arrived. Good luck with your business, Ms. St. Clair. Here's my card, if you need to contact me for a follow up."

Follow up. I took one more long look at my shop, shook my head then went inside the apartment building. The halls were wet and the smell of smoke made my nose run and my eyes sting. I climbed the stairs, then stepped over the door

Valdez had knocked down to get me out. The frame was broken, the locks shattered. I felt him beside me.

"You really are a hero, Valdez." I dropped to my knees and buried my face in his damp fur. Oh, great. *Now* I cried. I held on to him and felt Flo patting my back. I know blood sucking vampires are supposed to be tough, but we're still human, sort of. We have *feelings*. I swear sometimes I think if I didn't have bad luck I'd have no luck at all.